1979

It is the winter of discontent, and reporter Allie Burns is chasing her first big scoop. There are few women in the newsroom, and she needs something explosive for the boys' club to take her seriously.

Soon Allie and fellow journalist Danny Sullivan are exposing the criminal underbelly of respectable Scotland. They risk making powerful enemies — and Allie won't stop there.

When she discovers a home-grown terrorist threat, Allie comes up with a plan to infiltrate the group and make her name. But she's a woman in a man's world . . . and putting a foot wrong could be fatal.

VAL McDERMID

1979

Complete and Unabridged

CHARNWOOD
Leicester

First published in Great Britain in 2021 by
Little, Brown
An imprint of Little, Brown Book Group
London

First Charnwood Edition
published 2022
by arrangement with
Little, Brown Book Group
An Hachette UK Company
London

A catalogue record for this book is available
from the British Library.

ISBN 978–1–4448–4819–9

Published by
Ulverscroft Limited
Anstey, Leicestershire

Printed and bound in Great Britain by
TJ Books Ltd., Padstow, Cornwall

This book is printed on acid-free paper

For all the friends who walked by my side
through lockdown.

And especially for Jo; to paraphrase
Robert Burns, 'we twa hae paiddled in the sea
and pu'd the ramsons fine; we'll tak a richt
guidwillie waught for auld lang syne.'

The best-laid schemes o' mice and men
Gang aft agley

To a Mouse
Robert Burns

Prologue

Fat flakes blew into his face, cold wet kisses on his cheeks and eyelids. Last time there had been a winter like this, he'd been a wee boy and all he remembered was the fun — sledging down the big hill, throwing snowballs in the playground, sliding across the frozen lake in the park. Now, it was a pain in the arse. Driving was a nightmare of slush and black ice. Walking was worse. He'd already wrecked his favourite pair of shoes and every time he took his socks off, his toes were wrinkled pink sultanas.

But there were advantages. No one would ever know he'd been here. His footprints would be erased within the hour. There was nobody else on the street. All the curtains were drawn tight to keep the night out and the heat in. The children were indoors now, their every outdoor garment drying on kitchen pulleys and steaming clothes horses after a day in the snow. Everybody else was huddled in front of the TV. There had been enough snow this January for the novelty to have worn off. Even the corporation bus he'd overtaken on the main drag had been empty, a ghost ship in the night. The only people he'd passed had been a couple of die-hards headed for the pub. There was an eerie stillness in this side street, though. The snow suffocated the engine noise from the few vehicles that had braved the blizzard. He felt like the last man standing.

Head bowed against the weather, he almost missed his destination. At the last moment, he realised his mistake and wheeled abruptly into the lobby of the tenement close. He took a deep breath, brushing the snow from his eyebrows.

He climbed the stairs, rehearsing what he'd been planning all day. He was standing on the edge of the road to nowhere. Maybe it was late in the day to start thinking about protecting his future, but better late than never. And he'd figured a way out. Maybe more than one.

It wouldn't be easy. It might not be straightforward. But he deserved better than this.

And tonight, there was going to be a reckoning.

1

It started badly and only got worse. Blizzards, strikes, unburied bodies, power cuts, terrorist threats and Showaddywaddy's *Greatest Hits* topping the album charts; 1979 was a cascade of catastrophe. Unless, like Allie Burns, you were a journalist. For her tribe, someone else's bad news was the unmistakable sound of opportunity knocking.

★ ★ ★

Allie Burns stared out of the train carriage window at white, broken only by a line of telegraph poles. They were miraculously still dark on one side, sheltered from the blustery wind whipping the snow in sudden flurries. The train sat motionless, trapped in mid-journey by drifts blocking the tracks. She glanced across at Danny Sullivan. 'How come winter always brings Scotland to a standstill?'

He chuckled. 'It's just like *Murder on the Orient Express*. Stuck on a train in a snowdrift.'

'Only without the murder,' Allie pointed out.

'OK, only without the murder.'

'And the luxury. And the cocktails. And Albert Finney in a hairnet.'

Danny pulled a face. 'Picky, picky, picky. Anybody would think you were on the subs' table, fiddling with my commas and misrelated participles.'

Allie laughed. 'I don't even know what a misrelated participle is. And I doubt you do.'

3

'I did once, if that counts?'

They subsided into silence again. They'd met unintentionally on the freezing platform of Haymarket station on the second day of the year, colleagues returning to work after spending Hogmanay with their families. There were plenty of her fellow hacks Allie would have hidden behind a platform pillar to avoid, but Danny was probably the least objectionable of them. If he was sexist, racist and sectarian to the core, he'd done a good job of hiding it. And there was no escaping the fact that after time spent with her parents, she was desperate for any conversation from her own world. The nearest she'd come was the first paper of the year, with its coverage of the International Year of the Child, an imminent lorry drivers' strike and cut-price blouses in Frasers' sale.

She'd met up with a couple of school friends for a drink in the village pub, but that had been no better. The chat started awkward and stilted, veered on to the comforting common ground of reminiscence, then backed into a cul-de-sac of gossip about people she didn't remember or had never met. The past few years seemed to have severed her from old acquaintance.

As the train had pulled out of Kirkcaldy on the first leg of the journey back to Glasgow, Allie had felt the lightness of reprieve. She'd waved dutifully to her parents, standing on the snowy platform. They'd driven her the eight miles to the station from the former mining village of East Wemyss where she'd grown up, and she wondered whether they shared her sense of relief.

They had nothing to say to each other. That was at the heart of the discomfort she felt whenever she returned home. She'd slowly come to the realisation

4

that they never had. Only, when she was growing up, that lack of connection had been masked by the daily routines of work and school, Girl Guides and bowling club, Women's Guild and hockey team.

Then Allie had gone to university in another country and been parachuted into life on Mars. Everything in Cambridge had been strange. The accents, the food, the expectations, the preoccupations. She'd quickly assimilated. She believed she'd found her tribe at last. Three years flew by, but then she was unceremoniously cast adrift.

And now, after two years in the North-East of England learning a trade, she was back in Scotland. It wasn't what she'd planned. She'd been aiming for Fleet Street and a national daily. But the news editor on her final training scheme post was an old drinking buddy of his opposite number on the *Daily Clarion* in Glasgow. And it was a national daily, if you counted Scotland as a nation. The strapline on the paper said, 'One adult in two in Scotland reads the *Clarion*'. The wags in the office added, 'The other one cannae read.' Strings had been pulled, an offer made. She couldn't refuse.

She'd had five years of a sufficient distance to keep her visits home to a minimum. But now it was impossible to avoid the significant dates. Birthdays. Family celebrations. And because it was Scotland, Hogmanay.

Which meant three evenings of endless Festive Specials and musicals — *Oliver!*, *My Fair Lady*, *Half a Sixpence*. She'd wanted to watch Jack Lemmon and Shirley MacLaine in *The Apartment*, but once her mother had read the brief summary in the newspaper listings, that had been firmly off the agenda. Allie didn't want to revisit the torture so she simply said, 'How was your New Year?'

Danny scoffed. 'Like every New Year I can remember. We've got the biggest flat, so everybody piles in to ours. My dad's got five sisters — Auntie Mary, Auntie Cathy, Aunty Theresa, Auntie Bernie and Auntie Senga.'

Allie giggled. 'You've got an Auntie Senga? For real? I thought Senga was just a joke name?'

'No. It's 'Agnes' backwards. She was baptised Agnes, but she goes by Senga. She says, anything to avoid being called Aggie.'

'I get that. So your five aunties come over?'

Danny nodded. 'Five aunties, four uncles and assorted cousins.'

'Only four uncles?'

'Yeah, Uncle Paul got killed at his work. He was crushed by a whisky barrel in the bonded warehouse down at Leith.' He pulled a face. 'My dad said it might have had something to do with a significant amount of the whisky being inside Uncle Paul at the time.'

'So you have a big family party?'

'Yep. Same every year. The aunties all do their specialities. Theresa borrows the big soup pot from the church and makes a vat of lentil soup. Mary does rolls on potted hough. Cathy bakes the best sausage rolls in Edinburgh, my mum makes meat loaf, Bernie brings black bun that nobody eats, plus shop-bought shortbread, and Senga produces three flavours of tablet.'

'Bloody hell, that's some feast.' He didn't look like someone who existed on that kind of traditional Scottish diet. Danny was slender as a greyhound, with the high cheekbones, narrow nose and sharp chin of a medieval ascetic. Only his tumble of collar-length

6

curls made him look of his time.

He grinned. 'No kidding. There's enough in the house to feed half of Gorgie. And enough drink to open our own pub.'

'So what do you do? Eat and drink and blether?'

'Well, we eat and drink and then everybody does their party piece. That keeps us going till it's time to turn on the telly for the bells. And then Dad puts the Corries on the record player and it just gets more raucous. A few of the neighbours come in to first-foot.'

'Sounds like a form of self-defence!'

Danny shrugged. 'It's a friendly close. What about you?'

Allie was spared from answering when the door at the end of the carriage clattered open and the conductor staggered through, loaded with a pile of blankets. As he approached, he distributed them among the handful of other passengers. 'We're going to be stuck here a while yet,' he announced, a gloomy relish in his voice. 'We've got to wait for the snowplough to get here from Falkirk and it's making slow progress, I'm told. And the heating's went off. Sorry about that, but at least we've got some blankets.'

He handed each of them a coarse grey blanket that felt more suitable for a horse than a human. Allie wrapped it around her, nose wrinkling at the smell of mothballs. 'Are you feeling the cold?' Danny asked.

'Not really. But now the heating's off, we'll lose our body heat pretty quickly.'

He eyed her across the narrow gap between their seats. 'If you came and sat next to me, we could share the blankets. And the body heat.' He gave her a wide-eyed smile. 'I'm not trying anything on. Just being selfish. Look at me, there's nothing of me. I really suffer with the cold.'

There was no denying that he was well wrapped up. Walking boots, corduroy trousers tucked into thick woollen socks, chunky polo-neck sweater peeping out of his heavy overcoat. Woolly gloves, and a knitted hat sticking out of a pocket. Allie didn't think she'd ever seen anyone better equipped for the cold. Not even her grandfather, a man addicted to being out in the fresh air whatever the weather. A lifetime of the coal face would do that to you. 'OK,' she said, pretending a reluctance she didn't feel. He was probably the only man in the newsroom who didn't give off a predatory vibe. Arguably, you had to have the instincts of a predator to be a good reporter. But equally, you should know when to turn them off.

Allie swapped seats. They fussed with the blankets till they'd constructed a double-thickness shroud around themselves. 'What shift are you on next?' she asked him.

'Day shift tomorrow. You?'

She pulled a face. 'I'm supposed to be on the night shift tonight. Unless that bloody snowplough gets a move on, I'm going to be in big trouble.'

'You've got time. It's barely gone three. And even if you don't make it in on time, you'll not be the only one. You working on anything or just the day-to-day?' He spoke with a casualness that begged the return question.

'Waiting for the next news story to drop. You know what it's like on the night shift. What about you?'

He smiled. 'I've been chasing a big one. An investigation. I've been on it for a few weeks, in between chasing ambulances. I got a whisper from somebody who didn't even know what he was telling me and I've

8

been trying to bottom it ever since. Mostly in my own time. Grunts like you and me, we're not supposed to do stories like this. We're supposed to pass it on to the news desk and let one of the glory boys lead the charge. We get to do the dirty work round the edges, but we don't get the bylines.'

It was no less than the truth. There was a cohort of reporters who had titles — crime correspondent, chief reporter, education correspondent, court reporter and half a dozen others. When the lower orders uncovered a big story, it would immediately be snapped up by one of the guys who could claim it for his fiefdom. 'So how did you hang on to it?'

'I haven't told anybody about it yet,' Danny said simply. 'I'm holding on to it till it's too far down the line for anybody to take it off me. But it's dynamite.'

Allie felt a pang of jealousy. But it wasn't directed at Danny. It was more a longing for a major story of her own. 'What's it about? When's it going to be ready?'

'Soon. All I need is the last piece of the jigsaw. Next long weekend, I've got to make a wee trip down south and find the final bits of sky.'

So, not long then. The *Clarion* staff worked four long shifts per week, a pattern that was so arranged that it gave them five consecutive days off every three weeks. Allie still hadn't entirely worked out how best to use the time, though until the winter had set in she'd been developing a taste for hillwalking. But she was working up to buying a flat and she could see an endless vista of decorating and home improvement in her future. 'Good for you. If you need a grunt — '

Again the door clattered open. This time, the guard was red-faced and agitated. 'Are any of youse a doctor?' He looked around, desperate. 'Or a nurse?'

9

Before anyone could respond, from behind him, a woman's scream split the air. 'I'm going to fucking kill you, ya bastard.'

2

Allie sprang to her feet, open-mouthed. Her eyes met Danny's and without a word spoken, they both raced for the door. Danny pushed past the guard, shouting, 'I'm a first-aider.' Allie used his momentum to carry her through at his back. A woman lay sprawled along one of the three-seater bench seats, trackie bottoms round her ankles, blood smeared down her thighs and soaking into the coarse velour upholstery. A man stood over her, lips drawn back in a rictus. Allie stopped in her tracks.

Her first thought was that the woman was the victim of a violent attack. Then she registered the pale dome of her belly. 'She's having a baby.' As redundant comments go, she knew it was right up there even as she spoke.

Danny kept going though, not breaking stride till he was at the woman's side. 'I'm a first-aider, OK, pal?' he said to the man, who took a couple of stumbling steps backwards, nodding like one of those novelty dogs that old men had on the parcel shelves of their cars.

The woman hadn't stopped roaring and yelling since they'd entered the carriage and it didn't sound like she was about to quit any time soon. Danny shifted so he could see what was going on between her legs then looked up at Allie. In spite of his air of confidence, she could see apprehension in his eyes. 'Hold her hand,' he said. 'Try and calm her down.'

Terrified at the responsibility, Allie edged forward

11

and grabbed one of the woman's flailing hands. Somehow it was simultaneously clammy with sweat and sticky with blood. She turned to the man, whose expression had turned piteous. 'What's her name?'

'J-J-Jenny,' he stammered. Then, more firmly. 'Jenny. She's not due for another fortnight.' He fished a battered packet of No. 6 out of his jeans, jittered a cigarette out of the packet and sparked up, dragging the smoke deep into his lungs.

'Baby's got a whole different schedule,' Danny muttered, shrugging out of his overcoat and pushing up his sleeves.

Allie gripped Jenny's hand and stretched out to push her thick dark hair back from her sweating face. 'It's going to be all right, Jenny.'

'Fuck you, fuck do you know?' Jenny yelled.

'My pal knows what he's doing.' Allie gave Danny a pleading glance.

'That's right, Jenny.' He gave a nervous laugh. 'I was brought up on *Emergency Ward 10*. You need to take some deep breaths, darling. I can see your baby's head, your wean's determined to get out into the world. But the bairn needs your help. Needs you to stop fighting it.' He leaned forward. Allie didn't want to think about what he was doing. Just the thought of slimy blood and whatever else was down there was making her stomach churn.

She turned back to face Jenny, whose eyes were rolling back in her head like a frightened horse in a Western. 'I know it's sore,' she said gently. 'But it'll soon be over, Jenny. And then you'll be holding your wee one in your arms. You'll be a proud mammy, and all this will just be like a bad dream, honest.'

12

Jenny convulsed suddenly, screaming again, crushing Allie's hand in her grip. 'That's good, Jenny,' Danny gasped. He was sweating as hard as Jenny now. 'Push again.' He waited. 'Now breathe. A deep breath for me. I can see a shoulder. Now push again, darling. You can do this.'

The next twenty minutes passed in a blur of blood and sweat, Jenny's moans, Allie's encouragement, Danny's anxious glances and a chain of cigarettes from the father-to-be. Allie kept repeating the same meaningless phrases. 'You're doing great,' and 'You're a star, Jenny,' and 'Nearly there.' She was aware that other people had formed an audience around them. Then all at once, Danny had a red and purple bundle in his arms and the thin wail of a newborn baby struck a counterpoint to Jenny's groans.

'Well done, you've done amazing,' Allie said.

'You've got a son.' Danny turned to grin at the man behind him, whose knees gave way as he collapsed on to a seat. Tears sprang from his eyes.

'I love you, Jenny,' he cried, his voice thick and hoarse.

'I still fucking hate you,' Jenny sighed. But the rage had gone from her voice.

One of the other passengers produced a towel. Allie kept her face turned towards Jenny, determined to avoid what was going on at the other end. She helped Jenny sit up, inching her along the seat so she could prop herself up against the window. Then Danny passed Jenny the baby, wrapped in the towel, his little face scrunched up against the assault of sights and sounds and sensations.

The father staggered to his feet and pushed through to Jenny's side. He kneeled down beside them and kissed his son, then the new mother. 'You're incredible, Jenny,' he said. 'I love you. Gonnae marry me?'

Jenny looked down at him, and in the moment, Allie saw a hint of steel behind her exhausted eyes. 'Fuck me, Stevie. If I'd known that was all it would take to get you to ask me, I'd have fell pregnant ages ago.'

Danny leaned over and muttered to Allie, 'Great quote, that's a strapline if ever I heard one.' He registered her surprised expression. 'It's a page lead at the very least, Allie. Maybe even the splash.'

'If it is, it's your story,' she said. 'You saved the day.'

He shook his head. 'It's a woman's story. You know that's what the desk will say.'

He had a point. She was growing accustomed to the twisted logic behind the allocation of stories. It had taken years for women reporters to gain a toehold in national tabloid newsrooms. Eventually it had dawned on the bosses that some stories benefited from what they called 'a woman's touch'. Allie understood perfectly the motivation behind her hiring. That didn't mean she had to collude in it, though. 'You delivered the bloody kid,' she protested.

He looked down ruefully at his bloodstained hands and the streaks on his jumper and trousers. 'Exactly. I've suffered enough. You know the kind of shit I'll get from the guys in the newsroom. It'll be, 'Ooh, Matron,' like I'm in a Carry On film every time I turn around. Plus they'll want a picture byline of the reporter on the spot and that could screw me up for doing any undercovers. Once I break this story I've got on the go, I'll get the chance to do the big investigative stories. Look, Allie, all you've got to do is say it was some mystery man who refused to give his name.'

'What? And get bawled out by the news desk for

coming back with half a story?'

Danny scanned the bystanders and saw the guard keeping a cautious distance from the group of well-wishers round the new family. He stepped across to him. 'I'm a reporter on the *Clarion*,' he began.

The guard took a step back. 'I never did anything wrong,' he said hastily.

'No, pal, nobody's even hinting at that. But it looks like we're hogging the limelight if we do a story about me birthing a baby on a train stuck in a snowdrift. But see if it was to be you in the story? You'd be the hero of the hour. And it's not like you didnae come for help, right?'

The guard looked confused. 'But all these folk saw what really happened.'

'They'll forget all that, they'll just tell all their pals about seeing a baby born on a train. My colleague here' — he pointed to Allie — 'she'll write the story. Jenny and Stevie, they don't care who gets the credit.' She had to admit, his smile was charming.

'I don't know . . . ' The guard was wavering.

'You might even get a commendation or a raise or something.' He turned back to Allie. 'Have you got a camera on you?'

She nodded. 'In my bag.' She always carried her compact Olympus Trip 35 around with her; her first news editor had instructed her not to leave home without it. 'There's never a bloody pic man around when you need one,' he'd said.

'Away and get it,' Danny told her. 'They'll want pix.'

3

Allie pulled the final story pad from her typewriter and carefully separated the top sheet and the copies, screwing up the messy black carbons and throwing them in the bin. Top copy for the news desk, second copy for the copy taster, third copy for the picture desk, and the faded pink sheet for her own desk drawer.

She added each of the pages to the bottom of its pile then did a last read-through.

Station staff in Glasgow got a surprise yesterday when a train arrived with an unexpected extra passenger.

Jenny Forsyth went into labour on the 2 p.m. Waverley to Queen Street train which had been stranded in a snowdrift.

But thanks to the quick wits of guard Thomas Mulrine, 47, Jenny arrived in Queen Street station as the new mother of a bouncing baby boy.

Jenny, 23, and her boyfriend Stephen Hamilton, 25, were returning to their home in White Street, Partick, when the drama unfolded.

Heavy snow had blocked the line between Falkirk High and Linlithgow, leaving the train stranded.

Before the snowplough could free the trapped carriages, baby Craig decided to put in an early appearance. Alerted by Jenny's screams of pain, Mr Mulrine took over and delivered her son to applause from her fellow passengers.

And if that wasn't drama enough, Stephen was so pleased by the safe arrival of his son that he got down on one knee and proposed to Jenny.

A delighted Jenny said, 'If I'd known that was all it would take to get him to ask me, I'd have fallen pregnant ages ago.'

The proud dad said, 'Craig wasn't due for another fortnight so we thought it would be fine to go through to Edinburgh to bring in the New Year with Jenny's mum and dad. I never thought in a million years she'd end up giving birth on the train.

'I don't know what would have happened if the guard hadn't stepped in. He was the hero of the hour.'

But Mr Mulrine denied he'd done anything heroic. 'It's my job to take care of the passengers. I've never had to deliver a baby before, though. And I hope I never have to do it again. Luckily my wife had one of our three children at home, so I did have some idea of what to do. But it was a big responsibility. I'm just glad it ended as well as it did.'

The train was finally freed half an hour later and completed its journey to Glasgow without any more surprises.
Mr Mulrine radioed ahead so there was an ambulance waiting to rush mother and baby to nearby Glasgow Royal Infirmary where they

were checked over by medical staff who pro-
nounced both to be fit and healthy.
A spokesman for British Rail said, 'We're
delighted that Craig arrived safely. We will
be giving this very special baby a free train
travel pass for life.'

Fourteen paragraphs. A touch on the lengthy side, but it was a slow news day and she might get away with it. She'd snapped half a dozen pics of the happy family, with and without the sheepish Thomas Mulrine, and handed the film over to the picture desk as soon as she'd arrived in the office. She'd already had to endure the heavy-handed banter of the picture editor and his minions. 'At least they've all got their eyes open,' he'd said grudgingly, after taking the piss out of the Christmas party photographs that took up the first half of the film.

Allie distributed her copy and was halfway back to her seat when Gavin, the night news editor, shouted her name. She made her way cautiously back to the U-shaped arrangement of desks where the news executives held court. Gavin Todd was a skinny whelp of a man whose suits hung on him as if his bony shoulders were a hanger. Everything about him was a work in progress, though not in the right direction — his hair was thinning and greying, his posture had grown even more hunched in the few months Allie had been there, and the proportion of whisky to tea in the Thermos he brought to work seemed to be rising steadily. Every night, he'd start on the flask within ten minutes of the day shift leaving. At nine on the dot, he'd be off to the pub for his break. She'd been there a few times and watched him sink five large measures of whisky — 'wee goldies', he called them — in just over an hour. Then he'd buy a quarter bottle to keep him going till he departed at some random point between one and two in the morning.

She eyed him warily as she approached. Early in the shift, Gavin resembled a normal, reasonable newsdesk jockey. Which was to say, dealing with him was a bit like juggling a grenade whose pin was on the point of clattering to the floor. But as the whisky took hold, his speech and his brain grew slurred and his frustration spilled over into querulous complaint. 'This copy,' he said.

'Yeah?' Better not to engage till you were sure which Gavin you'd be dealing with.

'You were there, right? You were on the spot?'

Allie nodded. 'Aye, I was.'

'So what's this?' He slapped the sheets of paper against the edge of the desk. 'How come it's not an 'I' piece? You should be milking it, Burns. The other papers'll have the story by now. The only thing making this exclusive is you being there.'

'But it's not my story, Gav. The drama, that's all about Jenny and the guard and the marriage proposal.' She felt a crushing sensation in her chest. Was she ever going to get the hang of this? Everybody else seemed to operate on instinct, an instinct she didn't possess.

Before Gavin could get into her ribs again, the night editor materialised at his elbow. Arnie Anderson was the opposite of Gavin in almost every respect. Corpulent and cheery, black-haired and bearded, he took his breaks in the office canteen rather than the pub, stuffing himself with the home-made soup and pies that were permanent fixtures on the menu. 'Nice wee

19

piece, Burns,' he boomed.

'Should have been an 'I' piece,' Gavin whined. 'The lassie was there. That's the exclusive.'

'Gavin, Gavin,' Arnie let out an exaggerated sigh of disappointment. He gave an expansive gesture at the picture desk with his beefy arm. 'The pics, that's the exclusive. That's the splash. Something cheerful instead of the endless bloody blizzard stories that everybody's sick of already. We'll go across five columns with the pic. But we'll have to give it a turn on to page two to get all the copy in. And that means we've got room for you to do a five-par sidebar about your dramatic train ride, Burns.' He dismissed her with a wiggle of his fingers. 'Are you still here?'

Allie retreated, leaving Arnie leaning over Gavin's shoulder, pawing through the stories in his basket. She inserted a fresh copy pad into her typewriter and stared at the blank page with a mixture of terror and hatred. 'I need it by nine,' Arnie shouted at her as he turned towards the back bench, where the decisions about layout and content were made.

'Fuck,' she muttered. Like all her fellow graduate trainees, she'd read her Tom Wolfe and her Joan Didion, her Nick Tomalin and her Truman Capote. She'd dreamed of swelling the ranks of the New Journalism. But working first on a local evening paper and now on a daily tabloid had been a rude awakening. Even the feature writers wrote in tabloidese, a weird jargon of clichés and shortcuts. Anyone with cancer was 'fighting bravely'; any woman over the age of fifty was a 'battling granny'; under fifty, chances were she'd be a 'blonde bombshell'. By the time the subs had finished with Allie's copy, she'd have bet a pound to a gold watch that Craig would be a 'miracle baby'. So where did her 'I' piece sit in that shallow puddle?

Allie considered the advice an older colleague had given her in her early days covering magistrates courts and council meetings in Newcastle. 'How would you tell it to your pals in the pub?' he'd asked. 'Ten times out of nine that gives you your intro.'

'I am NEVER going to have a baby,' was what sprang to mind. She didn't need a sub to tell her that wasn't the place to start a *Clarion* story. In spite of the anti-Catholic sentiment that still fuelled the paper's employment policy, mothers were madonnas in this news universe.

Allie rummaged in her bag for her cigarettes: Silk Cut, the smoke of choice for everyone pretending they were weaning themselves off tobacco by going for the mildest possible hit. She tried to stick to ten a day, and mostly she succeeded. Tonight, she might not make it, she conceded wryly, lighting up with a disposable lighter. Another element of pretence — she wasn't in this for the long haul that a Zippo would signal. She inhaled deeply, her fingers deliberately covering the pinprick holes that were designed to allow some of the toxic smoke to dissipate before it reached the smoker. Who was she trying to kid, she wondered.

In the pause for thought that the cigarette offered her, she managed to come up with something she might get away with. 'It was supposed to be a routine train journey. Instead, I witnessed a New Year miracle on the tracks between Edinburgh and Glasgow yesterday.' Already, she hated herself.

She knocked out another four paragraphs that began with a scream, continued through hand-holding and ended with what she thought was the only decent line in the piece. 'My New Year's resolution?

Take a First Aid course.'

As she typed the final sentence, Gavin slunk up behind her and looked over her shoulder. 'Are you nearly done? Lucky there's no news to speak of. Arnie's giving you a big chance here, the splash and a turnover.'

Allie yanked the copy pad from the typewriter. 'All done.'

Gavin snatched the story from her and bustled off, ready to take the credit for getting the words delivered in time for the first edition deadline. At the end of the line of desks he turned back to face her. 'Don't just sit there, Burns. Make yourself useful. Away and get one of the drivers to take you on a round of calls. Remember, you're only as good as your last splash.'

4

Allie was not the only *Clarion* reporter struggling with copy that night. On the other side of the river, in his first-floor tenement flat in Pollokshields, Danny Sullivan was trying to put together a rough draft of the investigative story that he was convinced would change his career from a down-table hack to someone to be taken seriously. Ever since he'd sat enthralled by *All the President's Men* one hot summer evening three years before, he'd dreamed of being a Scottish Woodward or Bernstein. He'd have preferred to have been the more glamorous, clean-cut Robert Redford character, but deep down he knew he was more like Dustin Hoffman, scuttling from location to location in badly fitting clothes, tirelessly grafting away at the tiniest lead till it gave up its secrets. But in one key element he knew he was like both Woodward and Bernstein — he recognised he had the makings of a great story. Giving it maximum impact on the page was the hard part. Especially since there were still a couple of yawning gaps.

The seed of the story had fallen into his lap by chance two months earlier. Sunday afternoons meant compulsory attendance at his parents' flat for dinner. It involved him in a perpetual swapping of shifts and favours so he could make it. Not that Danny minded. He loved his mother's cooking and he got on fine with his parents. The one bone of contention was his mother's discovery that since he'd moved away from the family home in Edinburgh he'd given up attending

Mass. Initially he'd made work the excuse, but eventually he'd admitted he simply didn't want to go any more. Marie Sullivan had reacted angrily at first, but his father had worked the Sullivan charm on her and now when the subject came up, she assumed an air of resigned martyrdom. She'd done her best, and if Danny had chosen the road to hell, well, he was a grown man and that was his decision.

Annoyingly, his older brother Joseph professed a continued commitment to the family faith. He still lived at home and dutifully went to Mass every Sunday with his parents. Danny was pretty sure it was only mouth music, just as he was certain that Joseph only stayed under his parents' roof because it was cheaper than having a place of his own. It amazed Danny how often Joseph's job in insurance supposedly took him away from home overnight. Danny couldn't for the life of him imagine what that involved unless it was an excuse for nights on the razz. His mother had told him it was because Joseph serviced the wealthiest clients who demanded a personal service. It was one of those explanations that explained nothing but sounded impressive. Joseph had always had a knack for those.

Danny couldn't remember a time when he'd trusted his brother. He thought the Scottish word 'sleekit' could have been coined for Joseph. Smooth, sly and non-stick as a Teflon frying pan, that was his brother. His parents were always inclined to give him the benefit of the doubt because he'd been adopted. They'd struggled for years to conceive, but as sometimes happens, no sooner had they taken on an adopted child than Marie had fallen pregnant with Danny. Their determination not to make Joseph feel the lesser child had often swung too far in the opposite direction, in Danny's opinion. Coupled with Joseph's cheeky charm, things always seemed to work out to his advantage.

So one Sunday in November they'd all been sitting round the steak pie, mashed potatoes and frozen peas, talking about the ending of the Ford strike. It made a change from his mother's usual rehashing of Father Martin's homily. The car workers had originally demanded a 20 per cent pay rise and a shorter working week. The company had tried to hide behind the government's pay policy and offered 5 per cent. After a crippling eight-week strike, Ford had caved in and settled at 17 per cent. 'I wish I could get a rise like that,' Eddie Sullivan had said, tipping a daud of tomato ketchup next to his potatoes. He was a van driver for a local biscuit factory where the owner had refused for years to allow trade union membership. 'The way things are going, you boys will be earning more than me soon.'

Danny suspected that milestone was long behind them but he had no intention of humiliating his father. 'The government's trying to keep inflation down,' he said.

Joseph chuckled. 'Some folks don't have to worry about inflation. The clients I work for, they're bulletproof.'

Marie frowned. 'How can that be? We all have to get our messages in the same shops and pay the same taxes. How can they be immune?'

Danny thought Joseph's smile was condescending. 'At Paragon, we have ways of getting round the rules.'

'It's always the same,' Eddie sighed. 'One law for the rich, another for the poor.'

25

'The law's the same for all of us,' Joseph said. 'But like I said, there are ways round it.'

'How?' Danny asked.

Joseph tapped the side of his nose. 'That's something you'll never need to know, wee brother.'

His words burned, but Danny didn't want to start a row at his mother's dinner table. Better to keep his powder dry, and find out exactly what schemes Joseph had going on under the table. If what his brother had hinted at was the truth, there might be a story there.

He'd started by paying a visit to the head office of Paragon Investment Insurance, an imposing Georgian building with a pillared portico at the heart of Edinburgh's small financial district in George Street. He'd pretended to be the personal assistant of a North Sea oil company director and he'd left with a sheaf of brochures and an earful of claims about PII's ability to preserve the wealth of their clients. No details, but a definite air of sunny promise.

The language of high finance wasn't one Danny was fluent in, but he ploughed through the brochures and drew up a list of questions. The *Clarion* had a financial correspondent, in spite of their readership seldom having more in the way of investment than a £5 Premium Bond an auntie had bought for them at birth. Peter McGovern was a neat little man with a series of neat little three-piece suits and nondescript ties. The only memorable thing about him was a pair of oversized thick-rimmed glasses like Brains in *Thunderbirds*. Danny had never understood why a grown man would base his style on a kids' TV puppet show, but it took all sorts. McGovern spent most of his afternoons in the office pub, imaginatively called the Printer's Pie. It was a low concrete box that squatted on the north bank of the Clyde with high horizontal window slits that looked more suited to a wartime pillbox than a place of pleasure. The clientele was an incongruous mix of well-heeled but badly dressed hacks, and down-and-outs from the nearby Model Lodging House. It was there that Danny had fronted up the office money expert.

He placed a large Famous Grouse in front of McGovern and sat down opposite him at his regular corner table. McGovern looked up from the pink pages of the *Financial Times* and frowned. 'What's this in aid of?' he asked, pleasant enough.

'I need a wee bit of guidance,' Danny said, taking out the notebook where he'd listed his questions.

'I'm not some kind of racing tipster,' McGovern said, a disdainful expression crossing his face as if a bad smell had drifted past. 'I didn't get where I am today by giving away the fruits of my contacts book.'

'Not that kind of guidance. I'm looking into something and I don't have the expertise to understand everything I've found out. I thought you might be able to explain?'

'Is it a story, son?' Now McGovern was all geniality.

'I don't honestly know yet. I need to have more of a sense of what this shite all means.' He tapped his notebook.

'You want my help, you cut me in on the story when you nail it.' He folded his paper, took out a slim tin of Henri Wintermans Café Crème cigarillos and ostentatiously lit one with a gold-and-tortoiseshell Dunhill lighter.

Danny thought about it for a moment. He'd be doing almost all of the work; he didn't want to share the credit. But without help, he didn't know what he should be looking for or where to begin looking. 'Additional reporting by,' he said.

McGovern shook his head. 'And, laddie. And.'

He sighed. 'OK. Sullivan and McGovern.'

McGovern gave him a stern look. 'Other way around. Alphabetical order.'

Danny grinned. 'Danny comes before Peter.'

This time McGovern cracked a matching smile. 'OK, son, let's see what you've got.'

★ ★ ★

Danny came away from the Printer's Pie wondering if that had been what students meant when they talked about tutorials. McGovern had listened to Danny's questions and swiftly read through the brochures he'd brought along, with the air of a man on familiar territory. Then he'd taken Danny through them, point by point. The bottom line was that McGovern thought PII were offering sophisticated tax avoidance advice.

'That's not illegal. Some of it sails pretty close to the wind, but they'll have run their schemes past some expensive Treasury counsel — ' Registering Danny's confused look, he relented. 'Lawyers specialising in tax law and how to get round it.'

'So it's not a story?'

McGovern drained his glass. 'On the face of it, no.'

'But there's something off-key here,' Danny persisted. 'Nothing I can put my finger on, but you know that feeling when you catch something out of the corner of your eye and you turn round and there's nobody there?'

McGovern nodded. 'Journalist's instinct. It's stood me in good stead over the years.'

'So maybe worth a wee bit of digging?'

'Why not? You've nothing to lose.'

'How do I go about that?'

'Go back to the source who sent you sniffing in the first place. And meanwhile, I'll ask around about PII.'

Taken aback, Danny said, 'I wasn't expecting that.'

'Neither was I, laddie. Neither was I.'

5

It had taken the best part of November for Danny to become convinced he really did have the kind of story he'd dreamed of. In his spare time, he'd poked around the newspaper cuttings library, searching for anything he could find on insurance fraud and tax evasion. The bottom line he kept butting up against was that nobody who'd made a pile wanted to pay the Labour government's high taxes. But he couldn't find anything dodgy in the cuttings that matched the PII prospectus. If he was going to get any further with this, he was going to have to do some sneaking around.

And so, on the second Sunday in December, when he knew Joseph would be at Mass with his parents, he plucked up the courage to use the door key he still owned and let himself in. He went straight to his brother's bedroom and opened the wardrobe where he knew he'd find Joseph's briefcase, a black leather box with brushed aluminium trim along the edges of the lid and the base. It was a badge of pride and Joseph carried it with the same reverence a paratrooper would afford his SLR rifle.

And it was unlocked. Why would it not be? His parents would never dream of invading the sanctity of Joseph's briefcase. Danny flicked through the contents. A couple of the familiar PII brochures. A car magazine. Then, more promising, a slim black address book. Danny wished he had a spy camera like James Bond in *On Her Majesty's Secret Service*. He'd come back to it if he had time, he decided, and try to copy some of the contact details. A couple of leaflets from banks about their investment services. He'd almost given up hope of finding anything useful when he came across a single sheet of paper in Joseph's handwriting.

Brian McGillivray – Jan – 100k
Wilson Brodie – Feb – 125k
Andrew Mutch – March – 130k

It meant nothing to him, but it was something out of the ordinary. Something that didn't fit with what he understood of the world of whole life and endowment policies. Danny copied the list into his notebook. Then he looked up the names in the address book. Each one had a listing, complete with addresses and numbers for phone and fax. He noted the details, then replaced everything as he had found it.

He hurried from the flat and headed for a café across from Haymarket Station, in the opposite direction to the chapel his family would shortly be leaving. He could kill the best part of an hour in there with a mug of tea and the Sunday papers. That way, he'd arrive at the usual time with nobody any the wiser.

★ ★ ★

At the start of his shift next morning, the newsdesk had sent Danny straight out on a job with a photographer. A run out to Falkirk to interview a family whose car had been swallowed by a twenty-foot sinkhole that had appeared overnight at the bottom of their driveway. 'Fucking wild,' the photographer had said. 'I'm not parking anywhere near their house.'

In the end, it had been by the numbers. Mystery

sinkhole, family wake to find their car floating in a wee lake of sewage, everybody bewildered, water board refusing to accept any responsibility. They were back to Glasgow in time to make it to the pub for a quick pie and a pint before anyone noticed they'd been away too long.

Danny seized the moment to buttonhole Peter McGovern who was, as usual, drinking alone behind the pink barrier of the *Financial Times*. 'Do these names mean anything to you?' he said without preamble. He rattled them off; McGovern's eyebrows rose progressively higher.

'Why do you ask?'

'I got sight of a piece of paper my source didn't want me to see. These are the names on it.'

'Interesting.' McGovern went through his routine with the Café Crème and the Dunhill. 'Brian McGillivray is the man behind WestBet. He owns somewhere in the order of forty betting shops and he's a presence on the racecourses too. Wilson Brodie has a chain of seaside amusement arcades on the Costa del Clyde. You know the sort of thing — bingo, slot machines, pinball. And those daft crane claw machines where you never manage to grab anything worth having. Andrew Mutch is a builder. He specialises in local council contracts — schools, old people's homes, offices. Do you see anything in common there?'

Danny frowned. 'McGillivray and Brodie, their businesses are all cash. So, they can lie about their incomings and cheat the taxman. But if Mutch is doing council work, that'll all be done with invoices and payments straight into the bank, no?'

'You're in the right area of the forest. Mutch could easily be laying his hands on large sums of cash. Say your project requires a hundred grand of materials. You buy them legitimately, you sell them for cash at a discount then you buy inferior materials with some of that cash. And hey presto, you've got a pot of untraceable ready money. And that's what these three guys have in common. High-profile, respectable busi-nessmen looking for a way to weasel out of their tax liabilities. Any notion of how they're doing it?'

Danny shook his head. 'But I think we're talking big money. Between a hundred and a hundred and thirty grand.'

McGovern paused with his cigarillo halfway to his mouth. 'That'll be some story if you can bottom it. So, can you?'

Danny sank the last of his pint of heavy. 'I wouldn't be here if I didn't think I could.' He wished he felt as confident as he sounded. The truth was, all he had was a very long shot.

★ ★ ★

After his conversation with McGovern, Danny had pondered his next move. It was possible that drink might loosen Joseph's tongue at the various family parties over the festive season, but Danny couldn't rely on that, and besides, he didn't want to set any alarm bells ringing. His brother had never been inclined to provide details of the life he led outside the four walls of his parents' flat; he much preferred the sort of oblique hints that made him sound intriguing and important. When pressed, he would never let himself be pinned down. Danny didn't even know if he had a girlfriend to show off in the passenger seat of his flashy red Triumph TR7.

33

If Danny was going to dig up anything solid, he was going to have to take a risk and go to the fountainhead. But he'd have to pick his moment to avoid stirring any suspicion in his brother. That year, Christmas Eve fell on a Sunday, which meant there would be an even longer Mass than usual in the morning for starters, with Midnight Mass to follow later.

Danny laid his plans carefully. He phoned his mother late on Saturday afternoon and explained he was having to work on Sunday morning to cover for a colleague whose daughter had been rushed to hospital. A wee tug on the heartstrings always did the trick where Marie Sullivan was concerned.

Early on the morning of Christmas Eve, he drove to Edinburgh, revelling in the empty roads, and parked down the street from his parents' flat. His Ford Escort was nondescript — he'd chosen it precisely because it would be unobtrusive on the stake-outs he dreamed of doing — and he slid down on the seat so he was barely visible. He waited for the best part of an hour, growing progressively colder, hoping the odd flurry of snow wouldn't obscure his view.

But finally the three Sullivans emerged, scarved and gloved, collars raised, and set off briskly towards the chapel. Danny gave it five minutes in case any of them had forgotten something crucial, then he let himself into the flat, revelling for a moment in the warmth before going through to Joseph's room. He went straight to the drawer in the bedside table, hoping that was still where his brother stashed his keys. There was the TR7's on its leather fob, next to the key to the outside door of the close and the pair that unlocked the flat itself. And underneath them, another bunch. Two Yales, a mortice and a pair of small keys that looked as if they'd fit a desk or a filing cabinet.

'Ya beauty,' Danny murmured, pocketing the keys.

* * *

Half an hour later, he was walking down the alley that ran alongside Paragon's building, trying to look nonchalant. When he'd been promoted to having his own office two years before, Joseph hadn't been able to resist showing off to his wee brother. 'I bet you'll never have an office like this,' he'd boasted, walking Danny up to the third floor and unlocking his door with a flourish.

In spite of himself, Danny had been impressed. OK, the room was pretty small and it looked out on the alley, but it had dark wood panelling to waist height and a big framed print of a sailboat on one wall. The desk was veneered fibreboard, like the one Danny sat at every day. But Joseph had a big wooden chair with a carved back and arms, whereas the *Clarion* reporters hunched over their typewriters in badly adjusted battered secretarial ones. There were two visitors' chairs upholstered in dark tweed and a filing cabinet in the corner behind the desk. Two telephones sat on the desk on either side of a leather blotter. He'd muttered something vaguely complimentary and made his escape as quickly as he could, knowing his parents had already had the tour of the office that Joseph would somehow have turned into a vehicle for them all pitying poor Danny.

Today, though, he was planning on turning the tables. If he found what he was looking for — even though he didn't know what he was looking for — it would be a Christmas present that would shift the balance between the brothers for ever.

Danny let himself in at the side door. There was no security guard. Why would there be? There was nothing worth stealing. No burglar worth his salt could be bothered with second-hand office equipment. Danny ran light-footed up to the third floor and let himself into Joseph's office. He locked the door behind him and started on the desk drawers. The top two were unlocked and contained nothing of interest — brochures, a pile of Joseph's business cards, stationery, and the usual muddle of paperclips, elastic bands and pens.

The bottom drawer was locked. Danny sorted through the keys. One of the small ones opened the drawer. The first thing he saw was a sheet of paper with a list of names. The same names he'd seen before, with the addition of one other. And what sounded like the runners in the 2.15 at Musselburgh.

Graeme Brown – Dec – 125k – Snagglecat 2
Brian McGillivray – Jan – 100k – Meridian Flyer
Wilson Brodie – Feb – 125k – ?Benbecula IV
Andrew Mutch – March – 130k – Lady Lydnia

Danny picked up the paper to photograph its contents with his Kodak Instamatic and noticed there was a scribbled note on the other side.

Maclays So'ton –Jespersen Nassau

He had even less idea what that might mean. But when it came to ferreting out information, he knew where to start looking. He glanced back into the drawer and realised there was a metal box under the sheet of paper. He lifted it out and sat in on the desk. It was secured with a small but serious lock which yielded to the second key on Joseph's ring.

Danny stared down at the contents, his stomach cramping in shock.

6

Danny had never seen anything like it. A box full of money. Thick bundles of used notes bound with fat rubber bands. Not pound notes, or fivers. That would have been astonishing enough. But most of these bricks of money were £100 notes, with a few £20 wads among them. It was awesome.

It was also terrifying. There was no innocent explanation for this. No interpretation that didn't involve danger. His mouth dried, his tongue seeming to fill his mouth.

He wanted to slam the box shut and run, to forget what he'd seen and never be troubled again by its implications. And then his ambition kicked in, his reporter's instinct trumping his misgivings.

The first thing he had to do was figure out how much money was in the box. Gingerly, as if it might disintegrate in his hands, he eased out a bundle of hundreds. He slipped the rubber band off and fanned them out. He'd never seen a £100 note before. If they hadn't shown signs of wear and tear, he'd have taken them for forgeries.

He picked up a handful and studied them. They were an assortment from the three Scottish banks that had the right to issue notes. The Royal Bank of Scotland, dark red, its watermark panel showing Adam Smith, a detailed line drawing of Balmoral on the back. The Bank of Scotland, red and brown lines that looked like they'd been made by the Spirograph set he'd had as a kid. Sir Walter Scott gazing out at him; the view of the bank's head office building from the Mound. And the Clydesdale, a scarlet drawing of Lord Kelvin on the front and an imposing university lecture theatre on the back. He held them to his nose and sniffed. They smelled like money, that unmistakable mixture left by hands and wallets, bodies and smoke.

Next he counted the notes. A total of one hundred, making each bundle £10,000. That was more than he'd paid for his flat. More than he'd earn in two years, before tax, including his expenses. There were another eight bundles of hundreds in the box. And five bundles of twenties, some English notes among them, St George slaying the dragon next to the queen's head. A hundred grand, laid out before him.

As he stared at the cash, his brain started working again. *Brian McGillivray — Jan — 100k — Meridian Flyer.* Was this McGillivray's January payment for a racehorse? Or something else? Either way he should take another pic.

There were no more answers in the drawer, nor in the filing cabinets, which contained nothing more exciting than what appeared to Danny to be perfectly normal client files of insurance policies covering property and life assurance. Time to tidy up and get out.

★ ★ ★

Getting through Christmas Day had been tough. Trying to act casual around Joseph was a struggle for Danny. It was a giant step from never quite trusting his brother to acknowledging he was actively dishonest. And the next step was how he would deal with that. Danny didn't think he could walk away from a

39

story that could make his career, a story he could be proud of breaking. But what would it do to his parents?

Danny forced himself to join in the Christmas rituals. The exchange of presents — a new Marks and Spencer jumper from his parents, a flashy silk tie from Joseph — then cans of beer for the men and a sweet sherry for his mother. Roast turkey dinner with enough leftovers to keep them going for a week. Clootie dumpling and cream, the old silver threepenny pieces his mother had hoarded wrapped in greaseproof paper stuffed into the pudding to endanger the teeth of the unwary. Then After Eight mints and the queen on the box. *Goldfinger*, with local hero Sean Connery playing James Bond. Followed by stupid game show Christmas specials that Marie laughed along to while the three men dozed in their chairs. Then the big film. *The Sting*, with Robert Redford and Paul Newman. The story of the complicated con trick made Danny uncomfortable, and he couldn't ignore the nagging reminder of Redford in *All the President's Men*. Bob Woodward would know exactly what he needed to do next.

As the titles rolled, he pushed himself out of the settee and groaned as he stretched. 'I'd better be getting back to Glasgow,' he sighed.

'I thought you were staying, son?' His mother looked hurt.

'I'd love to, Mum, but I'm on the day shift tomorrow, and the weather forecast isn't great.'

'Be a good excuse for skiving, if you got snowed in,' Joseph drawled.

'That's no way to think,' his father said, almost stern. 'Danny's got responsibilities to his shift mates.

If he's not there, somebody else has to pick up the slack, is that no' right, son?'

'Aye, Dad. And I'll be back for the New Year. No way am I missing that.'

It took another quarter hour for him to escape, his mother insisting on packing up a turkey leg and a massive wedge of dumpling to fortify him in the coming days. But at last he was on the road. He pushed his cassette of *Power in the Darkness* into the slot and turned up the volume, the punching beat of '2-4-6-8 Motorway' driving everything else from his mind.

★　★　★

Boxing Day was just like any other in the life of a daily newspaper. Next morning, Danny was due to start his shift at ten, but he arrived an hour early and headed straight for the library. The duty librarian looked up from his breakfast, so startled to see anyone in his domain at that time of day that he squeezed his bacon roll so hard the brown sauce oozed out and coated his fingers. 'Christ, Danny, you gave me a fright,' he exclaimed. 'Where's the fire?'

'Nothing to worry about, eat your roll. It's not cuttings I'm after, I just want to look something up off the reference shelves. No need for you to get off your backside.' Danny gave him a cheeky smile and carried on past the grey metal shelves with their impenetrable filing system that no reporter had ever been permitted to learn. There was no chance of the librarians being made redundant, not while they were the only ones who knew how to find whichever brown envelope was required.

The reference room was at the far end. Three walls

of books and a long table under the window with its unrivalled view of the car park and the brick wall beyond. The shelves contained a collection of reference books that encompassed an astonishing range of subjects. From *Jane's Fighting Ships to the Michelin Red Guide: Great Britain and Ireland via Crockford's Clerical Directory, Debrett's Peerage and Baronetage* and ten years' worth of *Whitaker's Almanack*. What Danny was looking for was on the bottom shelf — an unbroken line of fat spines in pastel shades. Blue and grey, pink and coral, ochre and green, they encompassed the current phone directories for the whole British Isles. He crawled along the floor till he found what he was looking for and pulled out the volume that included Southampton.

Danny sat cross-legged with the thick directory in his lap and looked up 'Maclay'. There were two entries in the residential section of the book. One was a James T. Maclay in Burgess Road. The other was a W. J. Maclay, Applewood House, Applewood Lane, Hythe. Not for the first time, Danny wished phone books were illustrated. It would be helpful to see the houses attached to the addresses, just to give forewarning of the kind of person you were dealing with. It was a mad idea, he knew that. The books would have to be impossibly cumbersome, and they'd take forever to compile.

He moved on to the business section at the back of the book and turned the pages impatiently. Maclays didn't just have a listing, they had a box advert across two columns. 'MACLAYS, the premier boat broker on Southampton Water. Luxury craft specialists.' Complete with a line drawing of a sleek two-masted yacht. And an address and two phone numbers.

42

What if the mysterious names on the paper weren't racehorses? What if they were boats? Otherwise, what did a boatyard have to do with insurance? More to the point, what did it have to do with his brother? He needed Peter McGovern.

★ ★ ★

It was another two nail-biting days before the financial correspondent came back to work. Danny tracked him down to the pub in the early afternoon and plonked a large whisky in front of him.

McGovern tipped his glass in a salute. 'A merry Christmas to you too. So, did you manage to make good use of the festive season?'

Danny hesitated. Was he giving too much to McGovern? Could he trust him not to double-cross him and punt the story as all his own work? It wouldn't be the first time Danny had had his fingers burned by a so-called colleague. On the other hand, McGovern had been giving him useful information, not keeping it to himself. And Danny was all at sea when it came to the financial stuff.

Reluctantly, he took out his notebook and opened it at the page where he'd made his notes. 'I found another list.' He showed the page to McGovern.

He frowned. 'Graeme Brown . . . ' He held up a finger to stop Danny interrupting. Then he gave a satisfied smirk. 'Launderettes. And some suggestion of drugs as well. You'd need to ask Wee Gordon Beattie about that. His cop contacts keep him current on the bottom feeders. So again, you're looking at somebody who potentially might be in a position to evade the taxman.'

'There was a name on the other side of the paper,' Danny said, mentally filing away the new information. 'I did a bit of digging and I discovered Maclays of Southampton are boat brokers. They specialise in luxury craft. That's maybe where these guys are spending their money?'

'Nice work,' McGovern said slowly. 'But it's not much use to them out on the ocean wave, is it?'

7

International Directory Inquiries had suggested where to look next in his quest to follow the money. The only Jespersen listed in Nassau was Jespersen Marine with an address on Frog Cay. Danny waited till late afternoon when the newsroom was a cauldron of clattering keys, cigarette smoke and desperate focus on getting stories to the newsdesk early enough to claim a spot in the first edition. Then he called the number, drumming his fingers on his notebook as the unfamiliar foreign ringtone sounded in his ear.

He was on the point of hanging up when the insistent bleep was interrupted by a bass voice with all the gravel of Louis Armstrong. 'Yeah, this is Jespersen's. Can I help you?'

He'd been rehearsing his approach, but in the moment, Danny lost his grasp on what he'd planned. 'You sell boats, right?'

'That's why we're called Jespersen Marine, sir. Buying and selling boats is what we do. You in the market?' The line was amazingly clear. Danny had never made a transatlantic call before and he'd been expecting something more akin to tuning in to Radio Luxembourg on medium wave on the transistor radio he'd listened to under the bedclothes in his teens.

'My name's David Black. I'm calling from Scotland. My boss is in the oil business and he's thinking about selling his boat.'

'O-K,' the man said, stretching the first vowel to three syllables. 'What kind of boat is it?'

Danny cleared his throat. 'I don't have the details. He just asked me to check out a couple of boatyards. It's a sailboat, a big one, sleeps half a dozen.'

A ripe chuckle came down the line. 'You're going to have to give me more information than that before I can tell you whether we'd be interested. You need to send us the boat's spec, its age, that kind of stuff. And some photographs. Then we can have a proper conversation.'

'I can arrange all that,' Danny said. 'What's your name? And your address?' He scribbled the details on his notepad. 'How do you deliver the sale proceeds back to your clients?'

'We can do a bank transfer anywhere in the world. Or we can help set up a local account here, if that's what they want. Makes it easier to reinvest in a new boat. Where is the boat right now?' Conrad Jespersen asked.

It wasn't one of the answers Danny had prepared. 'The Canary Isles,' he improvised. 'Lanzarote.' His armpits felt clammy.

'Hmm. Gonna take upwards of three weeks to sail her here, so you've got time to FedEx that info across to us here and we can call your guy and let him know whether we're interested. I'm taking a guess that he's not gonna be on the boat.' He chuckled again.

Danny made an attempt at a conspiratorial laugh. 'Not much chance of that, he's a bit of a fair-weather sailor.'

'Is he thinking of replacing his boat? Because we are the top dogs round here when it comes to luxury craft. New or classic.'

What to say? 'He was talking about maybe a catamaran.'

'We can help there. We're the best show in town, David. I'll look forward to getting a package from you. You have a good day, now.'

'Thanks. You too.'

Danny replaced the receiver and exhaled deeply. The man at the next desk raised his eyebrows and glanced across. 'Christ, Danny, you sound like a whale coming out the water.'

'Just a tricky wee call,' Danny muttered. A tricky wee call he'd negotiated well enough to have worked out how his brother's clients were getting their money ashore. Or should that be 'offshore'?

★ ★ ★

That had been his last newsgathering act of 1978. Now he was starting the working year by trying to get a rough draft of his story down on paper. Sure, there were holes in it. But for Danny, the best way to make sure he asked the right questions was to write what he thought of as 'the story so far' before the crucial interview. What he'd learned over the New Year break had made clear the path ahead. As he'd told Allie Burns on the train, his next long weekend would provide him with the perfect opportunity to plug those holes with hard facts.

But that night, he was struggling. The adrenaline buzz of his train journey had dissipated and finding the right way into the story wasn't easy. Danny had never worked a story as big as this, and he was surprised by his anxiety levels. He had his own tried-and-tested ways of dealing with stress, but tonight, he instinctively knew he needed a different solution. He needed to talk to someone who understood the game.

47

But not someone like McGovern who would try to steal his story out from under him. Or deliberately unsettle him out of jealousy.

Someone like Allie Burns.

She was on the night shift, he recalled. Writing up her dramatic 'baby on the train' story. He checked his watch. Just after nine. Gavin Todd would be on his break, leaning on the bar of the Printer's Pie, a large whisky clenched in his grasping wee fist. At his side would be Allie's shift partner, accompanying the boss because he was senior to her and therefore entitled to extend his break to match Todd's. Allie would have to settle for holding the fort till they returned.

Danny picked up the phone and rang the news reporters' line. As he could have predicted, Allie answered on the second ring. '*Daily Clarion* news-room, Alison Burns speaking.' Using her given name because that was the rule. He was Daniel Sullivan on his bylines, she was Alison. Except on the night when she'd annoyed one of the news subeditors, who'd marked up her copy as being by Alister Burns.

'Hi, Allie, it's Danny. Have you had your break yet?'

'Me? No, I'm minding the shop while the big boys fill their boots.'

'I was wondering if you fancied a curry?'

A pause. 'Tonight?'

'Yeah, I'm kind of wrestling with that story I was telling you about. I could do with a friendly ear to bounce it off.' Another pause. 'My treat,' he added.

'And there was me thinking it was my irresistible wit and charm that you were after.' She sounded amused rather than offended.

'Another time. Tonight it's your brains I want to pick.'

48

'You talked me into it. I'll have fish pakora, lamb bhuna and a paratha. I'll see you in the canteen at half past ten. They should be back by then.'

'Deal.'

'And bring a couple of cans of lager, Danny. It's thirsty work, listening.'

★ ★ ★

Allie put down the phone, wondering why Danny Sullivan had chosen her as his sounding board. He probably thought she owed him, since he'd handed her the miracle baby splash when he could have legitimately hogged it himself. She hardly dared let herself think it was because he liked her, or trusted her. Back in her local paper days, she'd been burned more than once by so-called mates.

She'd never forget the time she'd been sent on a training day at the local TV station. They'd been shown round the news operation, beginning in the copytaker's room. Looking over the shoulder of one of the typists, Allie had been stunned to recognise the sentences appearing before her. Word for word, they were the very ones she'd written the previous afternoon for the next edition of her own paper. 'That's my story,' she'd blurted out.

The copytaker didn't even pause, nodding towards the copy pad next to him on the desk. Allie picked it up and read the first three paragraphs of her story. But it wasn't her name at the top of the page. 'By Andy Barratt,' she read aloud. Her fellow trainee, a friendly guy who was always interested in her stories, just as she was in his.

'The thieving shitehawk,' she growled. Not only had

49

he sold her work out from under her, he'd exposed her to any blame that might accompany the leaking of the story ahead of their own paper using it. And because TV news stories didn't come with bylines attached, the finger would point straight at her if anyone from her newsroom spotted it.

That day had taught Allie an indelible lesson. Now, she guarded her work carefully and doled out her trust in very small doses. Maybe Danny Sullivan was someone she could depend on. Or maybe he was just trying to ingratiate himself, all the better to betray her down the line.

She was distracted from her fretting by the copy taster, who dropped a sheet of news agency copy in front of her. 'Can you check this out, see if there's any arrests in Scotland?' he asked.

Allie scanned the page. Six men had been arrested in Lancashire and were being held under the Prevention of Terrorism Act. The short piece said they'd travelled to the UK on a ferry. It didn't specify where from, but it was a code well understood by reporters. Suspects from Ireland, probably Republicans but possibly Unionists.

Allie put a call in to Strathclyde Police control room at Pitt Street in the city centre and asked for the Duty Officer. Five minutes later, she'd learned — not for publication — that the men were a cell of known foot soldiers in the IRA and that there was no indication that there were any others on their way to Scotland, either by sea or by road. She reported her findings to the copy taster, who promptly rammed the story on the spike, killing it. 'No use to us,' he muttered, turning back to his basket of incoming agency stories.

Just after ten, the first edition arrived, one of the

elderly 'copy boys' dropping a bundle on the news-desk and detouring to hand one directly to Allie. 'I see you got the splash,' he said with a grin that revealed the perfect smile of false teeth. 'Good for you, Allie.'

'Thanks, Sammy. I just happened to be in the right place at the right time.'

'That's a handy knack. Stay lucky, doll,' he added, moving on to his next drop.

She was skimming through the paper when Todd and her shift partner, Big Kenny Stone, returned from the pub, both flushed from drink and cold. 'It's fucking freezing out there,' Big Kenny complained. He shook his head to dislodge the melting snowflakes that had landed on his thick dark hair. 'Better wrap up if you're going to the pub.'

'I'm heading down to the canteen,' Allie said, grabbing her shoulder bag.

'The canteen? You'll not get anything down there this time of night. It's just the vending machines.'

'Danny Sullivan's bringing me a curry.'

'Ooh, get you.' He began to sing the opening bars of 'Love Is in the Air'. He even sketched a few dance steps, surprisingly agile for such a big man.

Allie shook her head in dismissal, a scornful smile on her face. 'You're just jealous because you're not getting a curry.'

He held his hands up in submission. 'And that's all I'm jealous about. You're welcome to a nice night in with Danny Boy.'

She pulled a face at him and marched off across the room to the stairs. But as she trotted down two floors to the canteen, her mind circled back round to Big Kenny's song. Did she fancy Danny Sullivan? He wasn't bad looking, if you preferred the waif to

51

the hunk. Definitely more David Bowie than Burt Reynolds. He was always clean and tidy, which was more than you could say for those of her colleagues who didn't have put-upon wives or girlfriends to iron their shirts and take their suits to the dry cleaners. He didn't join in the sexist banter of the newsroom, or wave the semi-naked pin-up Page Three girls under her nose like some of the men did, urging her to compare herself to them.

If she had to go out with someone from work, Danny Sullivan was definitely the best option. And where else was she going to meet a man these days?

Allie liked to think of herself as a feminist. Not a man-hater, obviously. But she'd decided she didn't need to define herself in terms of a relationship. Still, there were times when she thought wistfully that it might be fun. And maybe Danny Sullivan was someone she could have fun with?

8

But romance didn't seem to be on Danny's agenda that night. Not if his choice of venue was anything to go by. The large canteen was divided in two. One half had wipe-clean vinyl seating dedicated to the men who wore overalls and left stains from ink and oil on the seats. The other half, where Danny was sitting, had chairs covered in tobacco-brown fabric, carpet on the floor rather than tiles. Both halves smelled of fried food and stale cigarette smoke. It was, Allie thought, marginally better than the pub, which added the rancid note of spilt beer to the mix.

She spotted Danny at a table discreetly situated behind a wooden trellis with plastic ivy half-heartedly trained through its grid. Not exactly hidden, but clearly semaphoring the private nature of their conversation. His attention was on the plastic carrier bag in front of him. He was lifting out tinfoil cartons, too hot to handle comfortably, judging by the way he was juggling them on to the table. As if sensing her approach, he looked up and smiled. 'Grab some cutlery,' he greeted her.

Allie swerved towards the canteen counter and picked up spoons and forks then, as an afterthought, knives. Some people ate curry like it was meat and two veg, she'd learned since arriving in Glasgow. By the time she made it to the table, he was peeling off the cardboard lids and setting out the dishes beside two of the thick white plates the canteen food was served on.

'Dinner is served.' Danny flicked the lids off the dips for the pakora and pushed them towards her. The fragrant spices reminded her she hadn't eaten since she'd left Fife hours before.

'You spoil me.' She reached for her starter.

He shrugged. 'No such thing as a free dinner. The price is listening to me trying to make sense of this investigation I'm getting bogged down with.'

'If you deliver it as well as you did that baby this afternoon, you'll have no worries.'

'Honestly? I'd rather birth a wean on a train than try to get this straight.'

Allie wolfed down her food as Danny laid out the story so far. He spoke between mouthfuls, leaving space for her to absorb what he was saying and to ask for the occasional clarification. As he wound to the end of what he knew, she shovelled in the last of her lamb with a wad of paratha and chewed pensively. 'You know I know nothing about investigations?' she said at last.

'From what I've seen of you, you've got good instincts and you've been trained well. What do you think? Is this a story?'

'You know damn fine it's a story, Danny. You're not there yet but you're not far off. You said earlier you were going to nail it down on your next long weekend. What are you planning? Are you going to confront your brother and get him to spill the beans?'

His eyes widened and he leaned back in his seat. 'Are you kidding me? There's no way Joseph will admit to anything. If I front him up, he'll laugh in my face then get everybody involved to cover their tracks. No, I've got a different plan. That's what I wanted to run past you.'

54

'You said you're working with McGovern. Why not run it past him?'

Danny shook his head, doubt obvious on his face. 'He's not a hard news guy. He lives and dies by being on the inside with these guys. I don't think he'll betray me, but I don't think he'll stick his head above the parapet either. He'll not want to do anything that might screw up his precious contacts book.'

'So what's the plan?'

'I'm going to go to Southampton. I thought I'd play the same kind of game I did at Paragon — tell them I work for a top oilman in Aberdeen who's looking to take advantage of the Paragon plan. Tell them I've spoken with Joseph but my boss wants me to check out the set-up for myself. Because that's the kind of guy he is.'

Allie considered. 'It might work. Especially if you drop Joseph's name into the mix. But aren't you worried what will happen when the story comes out? Joseph's been involved in an illegal scam. He can't pretend he didn't know what was going on. He's going to be arrested, isn't he? And what will that do to your family?'

Danny's look of dismay said it all. People's capacity for denial never ceased to amaze Allie. It usually worked to her benefit, though; interviewees never thought they'd be the ones to come off worse in print. 'I thought I could keep his name out of it,' he said, a weak attempt to save himself.

'How are you going to do that? As soon as you mention his name to the ship brokers, you're putting him squarely in the frame. You can't produce a reliable contemporaneous note of the interview that leaves him out. This is going to end up in court, the brokers will say the reason they trusted you is that you gave the name of their contact at Paragon.' Allie tried to keep kindness in her voice, but it was a struggle.

'I know, but how else am I going to get them to trust me?'

They stared glumly at each other over the congealing remnants of their supper. Then Allie said slowly, 'Can't you use the name of one of the clients? Ideally, one who's already gone through their system. In a way, that would lend even more conviction to you being on the inside.'

He frowned. 'What if they phone up to confirm?'

Allie shrugged. 'Then you're screwed. But you'd be even more screwed if they phoned Joseph to confirm.'

He sighed. 'Good point. So I could use the December guy, Graeme Brown, to establish my credibility.'

'And then when you write the story, you could just leave Joseph out altogether. You'll have to name this Brown guy in your story anyway, and you'll have to front him up before the story gets in the paper. You'll never get it past the lawyers unless you give him a chance to put his side of the story.'

Danny groaned. 'Now that's something I'm not looking forward to: the bloody lawyers picking over every sentence with a fine-tooth comb.'

Allie felt for him. The previous year had seen a record-breaking libel case against another Scottish newspaper. At seventeen weeks, it had been the longest ever trial in the Court of Session, the damages demand of nearly half a million the largest ever in a Scottish court; judgement was due any day now, and nobody in the world of newspapers was optimistic about the outcome. And it had been an insurance company who had taken them on. The lawyers at the

Clarion would be twitchy as hell over anything controversial that involved the insurance business. 'So you need to nail it down at all four corners. You'll have to confront Joseph's boss at Paragon as well as the cheating bastards who have taken advantage of the scheme. And although they'll act the innocents, you'll have to push the boatyard for a quote too.'

Danny nodded. 'I know. But first I have to get Maclays to confirm how the scheme works.'

'That's where you're going at the weekend?'

'I managed to find out in a casual conversation with my mum that Joseph is going down south tomorrow. Just overnight, she said. He'll be back late on Thursday. He didn't say where he was going but he's flying from Edinburgh Airport. I checked and there's a direct flight to Southampton. My guess is he'll be going down there with a bag of money. I'll drive down on Thursday and go to Maclays on Friday.'

'You're taking a chance, walking in there on your own. A bunch of crooks with access to plenty of blunt instruments and a raft of boats that could sail you out into the middle of the English Channel and dump you overboard?'

Caught in mid swallow, Danny sprayed beer over the tinfoil containers. 'Jeez-o, Allie, you've been watching too many episodes of *The Professionals*. If it was a team of Glasgow gangsters, I'd be worried, but this is white-collar crime. If they're going to fight us, they'll do it with lawyers, not heavies.'

Allie wasn't sure she believed him. She recalled men she'd encountered at Cambridge who'd ended up in the City. They might not get their own knuckles bruised, but she was pretty sure some of them knew chaps who would handle that sort of thing for them.

57

And that wasn't the only risk Danny faced. 'What about the weather? There's more blizzards forecast for later in the week. Are you going to be able to get there if the roads are really bad? Will the airports be open for Joseph to get there?'

Danny's eyes betrayed him, showing the worry he was trying to hide. 'I'll manage,' he said, uncharacteristically abrupt.

'You could wait till next month. It's not like anybody else is chasing the story.'

He shook his head. 'You don't know that. It's not like Joseph's the only man in the world who knows what's going on. Any one of the tax dodgers could mention the scheme to one of their pals who turns out to be on the side of the righteous.'

She could see he was hungry for the story, hungry for what it would bring in its wake. Kudos, opportunity, reputation. She knew herself well enough to understand that she'd be the same. She didn't have the heart to argue against him any further. 'Is there anything I can do to help?'

Danny busied himself stacking the containers. He couldn't meet her eye and Allie didn't know why. He crushed the edges together and tipped the shiny sculpture back into the carrier bag. He gave her an unreadable look, up and under his eyebrows. 'I left school before I even sat my Highers,' he said, almost inaudibly. 'I'm great at nosing out stories and getting folk to talk to me. But I'm no writer.' He swallowed hard and raised his head. 'If I'm really going to make an impact with this story, it needs to read like the real thing. Would you take a look at my copy when I've got it down? Maybe give it a bit of a polish?'

Allie didn't hesitate. Not simply because she owed

58

him for handing her that night's splash. But because her instincts were still always to hold out a hand. 'I'm not sure how much help I'll be, Danny. But you can count on me.'

9

The next couple of days offered few opportunities for Allie to think about Danny and his investigation. When the night shift finished at four in the morning, she was always desperate for bed, crashing out for even longer than she slept during regular hours.

She'd realised after her first rota on nights that the curtains in the bedroom of her rented flat were woeful when it came to keeping out the daylight. And broken sleep was worse than a broken heart to Allie. Rona Dunsyre, one of the embattled trio who ran the women's pages, had overheard her complaint in the canteen queue and pointed her to a company who sold second-hand hotel furnishings. Allie had spent a morning in their warehouse, poking around among battered dining chairs and chipped bedheads before she'd unearthed a cache of dusty dark red velvet. She'd handed over a chunk of her second month's wage for a pair of thick floor-length drapes that had originally come from a hotel ballroom, and never regretted a penny of it. When she'd saved up enough to buy a place of her own, accommodating the curtains that made her room a dark cocoon would be a deal-breaker.

The day after her curry with Danny, she didn't surface till mid-afternoon, then lay in the bath reading a novel she'd picked up in the second-hand bookshop in Otago Lane on a freezing afternoon in December. She'd only gone in to get out of the cold for half an hour, but as always, she'd come out with half a dozen books. This one, *Laidlaw*, was set in a working-class Glasgow she recognised immediately. It was described as a detective novel but it was unlike any she'd ever read. The protagonist, Jack Laidlaw, was the strangest fictional cop she'd encountered. He kept Camus alongside the whisky in his desk drawer and moved out of his family home into a hotel for the duration of a murder investigation. There was no mystery either. The killer was fingered from the very beginning. But she was intrigued by the quality of the prose, which was an uncommon feature in the detective stories she'd previously read. And when characters spoke, they spoke in the recognisable rhythms of the street. Allie knew she needed to learn more about her adopted city, so she kept topping up the hot water, reluctant to break the mood of the book by getting out of the bath.

When she turned the final page, Allie was shocked to see it was already after six. She had less than an hour to get dressed, grab something to eat and get to work. She threw on her clothes and ran down the stairs and into the street, hailing a taxi on the busy main drag by the Botanic Gardens. She had just enough time to dive into the canteen and pick up a bacon roll before her shift began. Rona Dunsyre was on her way down as Allie ran upstairs. 'Hang on a minute,' Rona said. 'Are you on the night shift?'

'Yeah, and in two minutes I'll be late.'

'Do you fancy meeting up for lunch tomorrow? It's about time we got to know each other better. Solidarity, and all that?'

Allie didn't hesitate. 'Great idea. Where? And when?'

'There's a pure dead brilliant wee Italian restaurant

on Great Western Road at Kelvinbridge. La Parmigiana. Do you know it?'

Allie nodded. She'd passed it often and thought it looked worth trying, but so far she hadn't had anyone to eat there with.

'Can you make one o'clock?'

'I think I can manage to be awake by then.'

'I'll sort it. See you then. Away and keep the miserable gits on the newsdesk happy.'

Allie slipped her coat over her chair and settled into the desk where she had a single dedicated drawer. She had an ally — and maybe more — in Danny, and now she had the possibility of a friend in Rona. Although she managed her own company well enough, Allie was at heart a sociable creature. She missed the companionship she'd found on the training scheme in Newcastle even more than her student friends. Maybe now the tide was turning. The loneliness that had seeped into her since the move to Glasgow might finally be over.

★ ★ ★

Studying Rona Dunsyre from afar, Allie had already decided that she liked her. She guessed Rona was in her late twenties or early thirties. She dressed with a swagger, the only person in the office who wore bright colours, splashes of contrast in scarves and handbags. Her hair was the flyaway blond of Debbie Harry, though she avoided the flamboyant make-up of the rock star. Rona opted instead for an almost naked look, apart from lush dark eyelashes and well-shaped brows that defied the local tendency to the thin line and improbable arch. But it wasn't just her looks that intrigued Allie, it was her style. She was

62

loud and opinionated, but her delivery always had a teasing edge of humour that allowed her to get away with it in the testosterone pit of the *Clarion*. Watching Rona, Allie had realised that humour was the key to survival for a woman in that office. Taking the piss out of herself as much as others was the weapon she had to cultivate. Giving up a couple of hours' sleep to have lunch with Rona would be a sacrifice worth making.

The restaurant was busy and Allie paused on the threshold, trying to spot Rona in the bustle. First impressions of wood panelling, discreet prints and terracotta roof tiles on the walls, full tables and mouth-watering aromas. A waiter bounced up to her. '*Buongiorno, signorina*. Do you have a reservation?'

'I'm meeting a colleague.'

She'd barely got the words out when he beamed. 'You are with *Signorina* Rona?'

'How did you know?' Allie asked as she followed him through the tight press of tables towards the rear.

He glanced over his shoulder. 'She said you looked like a reporter. With the raincoat like Robert Mitchum.'

Allie flushed. She'd spent a slice of her first pay cheque on a classic Burberry mac because she thought it was what a reporter should wear. Another bum note to set alongside being female. Her Burberry was always the only one hanging up on the reporters' coat rack.

But before she could respond, he'd delivered her to the furthermost table from the door, a four-top that commanded a view of the whole room. Rona was already seated, cigarette lit, glass of red wine in front of her. 'Park yourself, Allie,' she greeted her. 'You like red or white?'

'It's breakfast time for me,' Allie protested.

'Right enough. Sandro, bring Allie a Bloody Mary.' Rona grinned. 'Breakfast of champions, so it is.'

Allie made an attempt at a protest but she was too late. 'Thanks,' she said. 'That'll make the afternoon go with a swing.'

'Well, you need something to do that.' Rona passed the menu over. 'I already know what I'm having, I always have the same thing. Spaghetti carbonara and garlic bread. Best I've ever tasted. Trust me, it's not Mother's Pride.'

'Just as well, given the bread shortages I was reporting last night.' Allie glanced at the menu, but she already knew she'd go with Rona's recommendation. She still didn't know much about Italian food; Indian or Chinese had been her habitual takeaways at university, and she'd not ventured much beyond them since. 'Same for me, then.'

The waiter arrived with Allie's drink, and Rona ordered the food with a wee joke about Allie falling under the spell of the menu. Then Rona turned the full beam of her attention on Allie. 'So, how's it going?'

'It's a bit different from where I was before. Because I was part of a training scheme, there were a lot more women in the newsroom, for a start.'

'That's the *Clarion* for you. Three women reporters, but you're never on the same shift, right? Because we all know what would happen then: you'd all just sit around swapping knitting patterns and gossip.'

Allie gave a wry smile. 'As opposed to the guys, who only sit around swapping gossip.'

'But they appreciate you being there because it saves them having to do the miracle baby stories, right?'

'You'd noticed.'

64

Rona laughed, a big, cheerful noise that turned heads at nearby tables. 'I'll tell you a beezer miracle baby story. There wasn't a woman on duty, so they sent Big Kenny Stone out. The story went, forty-five-year-old woman thought she had an ovarian cyst, only they discovered she was seven months pregnant. Big Kenny came back and wrote up the tale of how they'd been trying for years to have a wean, and they'd given up hope. He even managed to make it a bit of a tearjerker. So it goes in as the page 5 lead with a big photo. And what do you think happened next?'

'Enlighten me.' Allie took a swig of her Bloody Mary, which hit her straight between the eyes.

'A guy phones up and tells the newsdesk that he's the husband of the miracle mum. That she's only living with her fancy man and she's already got three kids from her marriage. Then the eldest grown-up daughter rings up and reads the riot act. Big Kenny has to eat shit and write a 'no' quite miraculous' retraction.' Rona laughed, and this time Allie joined in.

The lunch was the most fun Allie had had since she'd moved to Glasgow. Tales from behind the scenes at the women's page, delicious food and a second spicy Bloody Mary kept them going till just before three. Then over coffee, Rona said, 'But they do let you do some proper stories too. I've seen a couple of good ones with your byline.'

Allie pulled a face. 'Sometimes. Mostly on the night shift or the backshift when there's not many reporters to choose from.'

'You did the Pope dying rerun. That was pretty spectacular.'

It had been a night Allie would never forget. She'd been alone in the office on the night shift. Gavin Todd had been in the pub with Big Kenny and the other duty reporter was out on a job. The copy taster had delivered a Press Association snap saying the Pope had died. 'That was last month,' Allie had said.

'Naw, this is the new one that's kicked the bucket. We need a splash and a spread, and we need to be off stone in forty-five minutes.'

She'd felt her heart kick in her chest. She'd tried to summon Todd and Big Kenny from the pub, but they'd thought she was at the wind-up and Todd had slammed the phone down on her. So she'd called for cuttings from the library and persuaded one of the sports reporters to help. 'You call Archbishop Winning for a quote and I'll write the spread from the cuttings,' she'd instructed him. Somehow, they'd cobbled together a front page and the two middle pages with minutes to spare. She'd actually had the legendary experience of the deputy editor grabbing the copy pads from her typewriter one paragraph at a time to distribute to the subeditors' table.

When the first edition dropped, the news that was barely an hour old was on the streets. 'And when Gavin came back from the pub, did he thank me for saving his arse? Did he congratulate me on a job well done? No. He ripped me to shreds for not getting him back from the pub.'

Rona scoffed ruefully. 'Typical. I can see you've got what it takes, Allie. But you're going to have to carve out your own niche. They're not going to give you anything.'

'I know. That triple murder in Dundee — I'm not going to get a sniff of that, even though the victims were women. The real problem is I don't have the contacts I had in Newcastle. I'm competing with a room full of guys who have wee black books full of the

66

men who matter.'

'What you need is the women who matter. Stick with me, I'll make sure you get the chance to make a different set of connections. I'm always coming across women who have a tale to tell that doesn't fit the women's page.'

'Do you not want to follow them up yourself?'

Rona shook her head. 'I know what I'm good at and I love it. I totally admire what you do, dealing with people when their lives have fallen to bits, but I know I couldn't handle it.' She grinned. 'I mean, I'm interviewing Lauren Bacall next month. That's my idea of paradise. What you do? It scares me to death. I'll stick to the fluff, thank you very much.'

'It's not just fluff, what you do. I saw that piece about the domestic violence refuge they've opened up in Dundee.'

Rona patted her hand. 'That's kind of you, but we both know ninety per cent of what I get in the paper is pure candy floss. You can bring a different kind of story to the paper. Here's a wee tip for starters. The devolution referendum's not too far away now. The political boys will be all over it, backslapping with their pals, noses in the trough. But there are quite a few women in the mix now. One or two in Labour but quite a few in the SNP. They get as cheesed off as we do about being sidelined by the boys. You want my advice? Get in with the pro-Devo women and you'll pick up stories nobody else will get.'

'Thanks. That's a good idea. But why are you being so helpful?'

Rona grinned. 'Because I'm a feminist, Allie. And I can spot a sister.' She paused. 'Just don't for fuck's sake tell anybody.'

10

It had still been dark when Danny set off for Southampton. He'd considered setting off straight after work the previous evening, but when he'd checked the weather forecast and the road reports, he'd changed his mind. More snow was forecast and there were reports of the A74 being reduced to one lane in several places. The road improved dramatically once it reached Carlisle, across the border in England, but that was a hundred miles away. In weather like this, it could take as much as four hours to cover that distance.

It wasn't much better in the morning, but the lorry drivers' strike meant the traffic was noticeably lighter than usual. Danny felt his sympathy for their cause rising in response. The gritters and snowploughs had been out, however. Although there were high banks of dirty slush on both sides of the carriageway, getting out of Scotland was easier than Danny had feared.

He kept himself alert with his mix tapes of upbeat driving music, singing along with everything from Gloria Gaynor to Blondie, passing through David Bowie, Grace Jones and Elton John on the way. But even that couldn't make the miles pass more swiftly. He fell into the trap of checking the odometer at the end of every track, growing more dispirited as they didn't rack up fast enough. At this rate, he'd be driving well into the evening.

The weather eased a little as he travelled further south. Somewhere in the Midlands, he pulled into a grim transport café. He imagined it was normally packed with lorry drivers stoking up their grease levels for the next stage of their journeys. But today, the combination of the strike and the weather had left the parking area almost empty. Danny parked near the entrance and walked into a fug of cigarette smoke, condensation, chip fat and bacon. It was blissfully warm. He ordered sausages, bacon, beans and chips and wondered why he was doing this. The story wasn't going anywhere. Nobody else could be chasing it. Maybe he should have listened to Allie and waited for the worst of winter to pass.

But he already knew the answer. From the very start, journalism had been like a virus in his brain. He couldn't resist the pull of a story. And he couldn't ignore the prick of ambition that spurred him on. The combination was impossible to fight. Tomorrow was never soon enough when a story could be pursued today. He'd expected everyone in the newsroom to be the same. Discovering that wasn't the case had been a shock; for so many of them, it was the wages, the expenses, the approval of the drinking culture, the pure swagger of the job that kept them going.

The reason he'd warmed to Allie Burns was the recognition that she was like him. She was frustrated by the limitations of what she was being assigned. The difference was that she hadn't figured out where to find the stories that would let her carve out a niche, the way this story was going to do for him. But her talent for words could help him, and if that helped her in the long run, he had no problem with that.

When his food arrived, he shovelled it in like a boilerman stoking a fire, barely tasting it, conscious only of his desire to be back on the road, back with the vision of the story to pull him forward through the gloomy afternoon and the cold, dark evening. Music blaring, he covered the miles, driven onward by the thought of what the morning would bring.

* * *

Southampton looked dismal through the grimy bedroom window of the downtrodden hotel Danny had checked into fourteen hours after he'd left Glasgow. To be fair, he thought, pretty much anywhere would look dismal in the thin morning light, sleet falling on the dirty slush below. The bed had sagged, the pillows and the towels had been equally thin but he'd slept like the dead after the stress of his long drive.

He was the only resident in the stuffy breakfast room. He forced himself to eat the rubbery egg and the gristly sausages that appeared in front of him, washing it down with annoyingly dainty china cups of tea. Then it was back to the car, his body complaining as he folded himself behind the wheel.

He pulled in at a petrol station, where he had to queue to top up his tank behind anxious motorists desperate not to be caught out by the tanker drivers' strike. While he waited, he went inside and bought a street map of the city. He plotted a route that would first take him to Burgess Road and Applewood Lane, to scout out the possible homes of the boatyard owners. Then onwards to the brokerage itself.

Burgess Road comprised a wide mixture of properties. There were shops with flats above them, solid brick-built semis, undistinguished terraces and, opposite what looked like parkland, some bigger detached houses. James T Maclay's address was a brightly lit newsagent's shop with two storeys above street level.

Danny decided it didn't shout prosperity; not the Maclay he was looking for, he suspected.

Applewood House was a different proposition. It stood on a narrow tree-lined lane, made narrower by the remains of the snow that was gradually melting. As he drove slowly along, Danny caught occasional glimpses of the river between the grand detached houses that dotted the east side of the road. Applewood House was the last one he came to. It was a four-square Georgian house in grey stone with a pillared portico, three tall windows on either side. On the floor above, another six windows mirroring them and a large circular window above the porch. A sweep of gravel drive led to the modern addition of a three-car garage. The severity of the building's lines was emphasised by the garden; manicured lawns and groups of shrubs pruned to military neatness. There was no sign of life within. It was, he thought, the kind of house that confident money would buy. Clearly expensive but the opposite of ostentatious.

All the showiness was reserved for the boat brokerage. It was a short drive from the house on Applewood Lane but light years away in every other respect. Two buildings, modern brutalist cubes painted sky blue, flanked the entrance, over which a splashy sign proclaimed, MACLAYS – THE HIGH LIFE ON THE OCEAN WAVE. Danny drove in and found a parking space outside the building marked, RECEPTION AND SALES. Beyond the car park, he could see an array of yachts on hard standing, covered by blue tarpaulins with the company logo. Further on, he glimpsed a wharf with more, bigger boats.

Danny grabbed the neat black briefcase he used when he wanted to impress people with his seriousness

71

and picked his way across the slippery tarmac. The reception area was small but they'd spent money on making it look good. Decent carpet, comfortable chairs, dramatic photographs of yachts under sail. Nothing scuffed or tired-looking, not even the middle-aged receptionist. Danny gave her his best smile. 'Hello. I've come down from Aberdeen to talk to someone about the arrangement you have with Paragon Investment Insurance.'

She looked profoundly unimpressed. 'Have you got an appointment?'

'I'm sorry, it was all a bit last minute. When my boss gets an idea in his head, he just goes for it.' He tried for rueful and apologetic. 'He was talking to someone about the system over the New Year and he came back full of it.' Danny clapped his free hand to his chest. 'So here I am, dispatched through the cold and snow.'

The woman chuckled. 'Poor bloody infantry, eh?'

'Something like that. I don't suppose . . . ?'

'You want Billy. He handles all the Paragon business. You're in luck. He's in this morning. He was supposed to be meeting a client from London, but he's called off because of the weather. Take a seat. What's your name?'

'Charlie Wishart,' he said. He'd been at school with Charlie Wishart. A big lump of a lad who'd become a bus driver. 'I'm in the oil business.'

She perked up. 'I'll see what I can do.'

★ ★ ★

Bill Maclay was the perfect match for Danny's notion of what a yachtsman should look like. Weathered jeans,

72

a navy Guernsey and deck shoes. He was around six feet tall, broad in the shoulders and narrow in the hips, with a thatch of dark blond hair just starting to silver at the temples. When he smiled in greeting, his face became a map of wrinkles the wind and sun had scrawled there, blue eyes glittering beneath heavy brows. 'From Aberdeen, Penny said?' He held out a hand and Danny obediently shook it. Calloused and strong, it made Danny feel soft and insignificant.

They were meeting in Maclay's office on the first floor. It looked out over the brokerage yard to Southampton Water beyond, steel flecked with slashes of white. 'That's right,' Danny said. 'I'm sorry to turn up out of the blue. But my boss doesn't like to be kept waiting . . .'

Maclay shrugged. 'I don't envy you that drive in this weather. Penny said you wanted to talk to someone about the work we do with Paragon Investment Insurance?'

Danny nodded. 'My boss is an oilman. We work for a major American company. North Sea oil is going very well for us and he earns large bonuses. Large cash bonuses. He heard that Paragon had come up with a scheme to protect men like my boss from the taxman.' He smiled, almost apologetic. 'My boss never takes anything on trust. So he sent me to talk to you, to get it from the horse's mouth.'

Maclay gave him a long measured stare. 'Tell me what you know,' he said.

'I'm not sure I've got all the details right but what I've been told is that you sell yachts to Paragon customers. The yachts are sailed to Nassau, where they're sold on, and the proceeds are paid into a bank over there. Out of reach of the taxman.' The moment of

73

truth. Either Maclay would spill or Danny would be out on his ear.

Maclay cocked his head to one side. 'Sounds like you've wasted your time, Mr Wishart.'

Danny felt a cold weight in his stomach. How could he have ballsed this up? Did Maclay not trust him? 'What do you mean? That's what the Paragon people told us.'

'Who did you speak to at Paragon?'

He had one chance to recover this. In the moment, he realised the weakness of his plan. Naming one of the offenders would almost be an invitation to Maclay to call them up and confirm Danny's story. Besides, the man with the cash, the man who made the mysterious visits on clients' business, he must have been the man Maclay dealt with. And Joseph was travelling back to Edinburgh. He couldn't be on the end of a phone, not today. Danny took a deep breath. It wasn't like he was throwing his brother to the wolves. 'Some guy called Sullivan,' Danny said. 'He explained it all to me.'

11

In spite of her eagerness to hear how Danny's trip had gone, Allie hadn't wasted the days till they were both back in the office. On Sunday, she was back on the day shift, disorientated and short-changed on sleep as always happened on a one-day transition from nights to days. But at least Sunday was usually a quiet news day. Desmond, the deputy news editor, was in charge, a lumbering ox of a man who hid his insecurities behind bluff, bullish banter. His greatest sin was a lack of imagination. His idea of setting the news agenda on a Sunday morning was to focus all his attention on the *Sunday Thistle*, a publication that was read around the world by ex-pat Scots wallowing in nostalgia for a native land that had never existed outside its pages. It also boasted an ageing circulation among those who still lived in Scotland and who wanted to believe that nothing much had changed since the 1930s. For anyone of Allie's generation, it held no attraction.

Running the Sunday newsdesk, Desmond loved to scour the columns of the *Thistle*, tearing out stories he thought were worth following up and scattering them among the duty reporters. Which would have been fine, if the stories had offered any follow-up angles. What made it worse was the invariable imprecision of the stories. They tended to feature vague addresses, often in streets that ran for the best part of a mile. Sometimes they were a straight lift from an edition of the paper from twenty years before, as Allie had found to her cost on her second week on the *Clarion*.

She'd been sent out to Knightswood, a council estate in the west of the city. It had been built as a garden suburb between the First and Second World Wars, its neat streets comprising semi-detached houses and so-called cottage flats — blocks that resembled large semis but which were in fact four flats. It was the sort of place that gave council housing a good name.

The story seemed straightforward, potentially amusing. A Mrs Aggie Mackenzie faced eviction from her flat because of complaints to the council from the neighbours about her pet parrot. Not only was the parrot loud, it also possessed a rich and ribald vocabulary. According to the *Thistle* reporter, one neighbour had said, 'I've had to stop the minister coming to visit because of the terrible swearing that bird screams at everybody.'

The only address was Archerhill Road, the longest street on the estate. Allie tried the phone book first. There was a J. Mackenzie and a T. McKenzie. If she was in luck, it would be one of those. Nobody from the picture desk wanted to come with her. 'If it works out, we'll send somebody out to do pix,' was the most she could squeeze out of them. So she summoned an editorial driver and headed for Knightswood. Of course, neither of the Mackenzies in the phone book had heard of Aggie Mackenzie and her parrot. But it being Sunday, she headed for the church and waited till the service was over. She drew a blank with half a dozen members of the congregation, but her luck changed with the deaconess, who gave her precise directions.

Allie rang the bell of the downstairs flat and waited. She was poised to ring again when the door inched open to reveal a stooped woman with an ancient face

76

and thick glasses. Allie hesitated. 'Mrs Mackenzie?'

'Aye, hen. Who are you?'

'My name's Alison Burns, I'm a reporter with the *Clarion*.'

'The newspaper?' She seemed astonished. 'What's the newspaper got to do with me?'

'It's about your parrot.' Seeing the woman's look of confusion, Allie forged on desperately. 'About the complaints to the council about the noise nuisance.'

'My parrot? You're here about my parrot?'

'Yes. After the story in the *Sunday Thistle* today.'

'Today?'

Allie produced the cutting from her bag. 'There you go. That's you, isn't it? Mrs Aggie Mackenzie of Archerhill Road?'

Suddenly the old woman hooted with laughter, rocking back and forth. 'By jingo, they've got nae shame. Hen, that story was in the paper twenty year ago.'

'Twenty years ago? Are you sure?'

'Hen, I might be old but I'm not wandering in my wits yet. Twenty years old, yon story. My parrot's been dead seventeen years past.' She shook her head. 'Somebody's been playing a joke on you, hen.'

'I'm sorry,' Allie said, pink with embarrassment and anger.

'Don't you be sorry, I've not had a laugh like this for years.'

Back in the editorial car, she'd told the driver what had happened. He'd laughed too. 'Bloody Desmond on the desk,' he said. 'Stupid bastard never learns. Every Sunday, he sends one of you guys out on a *Thistle* story. It's either ancient history or totally made up in the first place.'

'How does a paper get away with that?' Allie was still raging.

'Different rules, Allie. It's not a paper, the *Thistle*. It's a comic.'

With that in mind, Allie showed her face in the news-room then slunk off to the library to avoid a *Thistle* assignment. She buried herself in cuttings about the SNP's recent history and the devolution debates for a couple of hours then returned upstairs to find Desmond had taken three of the other day shift reporters off to the Press Club to play snooker. His place at the newsdesk had been taken by a forty-something woman with blazing red hair and black-rimmed glasses. She looked up as Allie approached. 'I wondered where you were hiding. You must be Allie Burns,' she said in an accent Allie had learned to identify as 'posh Glasgow'.

'I am, and I wasn't hiding. I told Desmond I was away down to the library. If he'd needed me, he knew where to find me.'

The woman twisted her mouth into a wry smile. 'Typical bloody Desmond. Divide and conquer. I'm Fatima,' she said. 'Fatima McGeechan.'

Allie tried to hide her surprise at the name. She'd never seen anyone who looked less Arabic than the woman running the desk. 'Good to meet you.' It came out more of a question than she'd intended.

The woman sighed. 'Let me explain two things. I'm not a Muslim, I'm a good Catholic girl. Well, a good Catholic girl gone bad, if you want to be pedantic. And pedantic is one of the many attributes a good hack should cultivate. Here's how the story goes. My mother was desperate for a child that just wasn't com-ing until she went to the shrine to Our Lady of Fatima in Johnstone and prayed there. Hence the name. And anybody who tries to shorten it to Fats — the only thing they're going to shorten is their life expectancy. Clear?'

Bossy, then. 'Clear.' A pause. 'You said, two things?'

Another sigh. 'I'm here under protest. I'm an editor at the BBC up the road at Queen Margaret Drive. When your esteemed news editor has exhausted his list of Sunday casual desk execs, he bribes me with a double shift payment to come in and hold Desmond's hand.' A sardonic smile. Allie was beginning to like Fatima.

'I suspect you earn every penny.'

'And more besides. So what were you doing down in the library? Apart from dodging the *Sunday Thistle* bullet?'

Allie considered. A lie could be unravelled in a thirty-second conversation with the duty librarian, and she wouldn't put that past 'Don't call me ''Fats''. So she shrugged. 'I've only been back in Scotland for three and a bit months. Before that, I was in England for five years. With the devolution referendum coming up, I figured it would be helpful to get some background under my belt.'

Fatima nodded her approval. 'Smart. Sadly for your education, I've got a job for you. ID just in from a fatal car crash just north of Carlisle last night.' For a moment, Allie's chest contracted, remembering what Danny had been up to. But relief came with Fatima's next sentence. 'A van driver from Kilmarnock. The word is he was taking a delivery down to Preston. It was part of what should have been on a lorry load heading south, but because of the strike . . . well, you get the picture. Away and talk to the grieving widow and don't come back without a collect picture. Get an editorial car and — ' She raised her voice to attract the attention of the picture editor. 'Get a snapper, there might be something to tug the heartstrings if they've got photogenic kids.' She snorted. 'Who am I kidding? Take a snapper anyway.'

Nobody liked a death knock. But Allie knew she was good at it. It was definitely one situation where being a woman was an advantage. Nobody felt threatened by her except when she was trying very hard to be threatening. It was also a test. Her first assignment from Angus Carlyle, the ruthless, shameless and graceless *Clarion* news editor, had been a quadruple death knock — four teenagers killed in a late-night car crash on the Rest and be Thankful road. Nobody expected the new girl — Cambridge graduate, training scheme product — to manage that on her first day.

Allie came back with pictures of all four, plus quotes from devastated parents and siblings. It was a quiet Sunday and it earned her a splash with her debut story. 'You'll do,' Carlyle had said. Then spoilt the grudging compliment with a final two words. 'For now.'

And so she went off to do Fatima's bidding. Hunkered down in the passenger seat of the company Cortina, Allie went through the notes she'd made, committing the list of women's names to her memory along with their party affiliations. Now all she had to do was figure out how to transform them into useful sources.

12

Monday was dreary outside and inside the newsroom. The prime minister had flown back from a conference in the Caribbean, tanned and in denial about any crisis back home. He probably hadn't noticed the weather either, Allie thought as she struggled to cover the aftermath of the New Year blizzards. The big freeze followed by the thaw spelled misery for millions. Well, it was more like thousands, but the alliteration of 'millions' read better. Official statements claimed it had landed Scotland with a £10 million bill. Dozens of homes were uninhabitable because of burst pipes, and the temperatures were plummeting again. Although it was a guaranteed page lead, putting it together meant she had to endure deskbound tedium and endless phone calls. No chance to pursue anything of her own, and no Danny Sullivan till the next day.

Back home, she heated up some soup from the freezer and tried to distract herself with the TV. *Blake's 7*, and *Strangers*, Don Henderson playing the idiosyncratic Detective Sergeant Bulman with his gloves, his inhaler and his habit of taking the bus to crime scenes. Allie would be the first to agree she hadn't spent a huge amount of time with coppers, but she'd never come across one remotely like Bulman. Between him and Laidlaw, she was forcibly reminded of the gap between fiction and reality when it came to the investigation of crime. How much more interesting her professional life would be if it imitated art more closely, she thought.

In spite of the gas fire, the living room was growing chilly, so she headed for bed with *The Women's Room*, another second-hand find. Somehow, it lacked the grip that *Laidlaw* had exerted and it fell from her hand as sleep overtook her.

★ ★ ★

By the time she woke next morning, Danny Sullivan was already at his typewriter on the other side of the city, making a final fair copy of his notes from Southampton. Even after a solid nine hours' sleep he still felt drained, but he was determined to have his story straight for Peter McGovern. And even more importantly, for Allie. She'd be the one sprinkling it with stardust, after all. He couldn't explain why, but he wanted to impress her with his achievement, even if it needed her polish to make the best impression.

The past few days had been gruelling. The interview with Bill Maclay had demanded focus and concentration as well as the energy it took to maintain a false front. He hadn't realised how much it had taken out of him till somewhere south of Birmingham, he'd been overwhelmed with the urge to sleep. He'd ended up in an anonymous chain hotel in a Black Country town whose name he couldn't recall till he checked the receipt. Danny forced himself to drive the rest of the way back on Saturday, his aching body protesting at two nights in terrible beds and two days cramped in a car seat. The driving conditions were still atrocious, and he'd never been happier to make it home.

The ordeal hadn't finished there, though. He still had to get through the ritual Sunday family meal, knowing what he knew now about his brother. Danny had fidgeted throughout the train journey to Edinburgh, unable to settle, dreading the possibility that somehow his fishing expedition to Southampton had been uncovered. But his fretting had been in vain. It was just like any other Sunday. Joseph self-important, boasting that the weather hadn't prevented him travelling down south to service his wealthy client. Danny struggled to maintain his composure. But nobody noticed anything amiss, apart from his mother taking offence at his refusal of second helpings of apple sponge and custard. 'I was out for my tea last night,' Danny lied. 'Ate too much curry.'

He'd tried to make an early getaway, but his father had insisted they play cards. He loved Solo, and it was a game that required four players. The afternoon trickled away and by the time they'd finished, Danny was ninepence poorer and the snow had started again. His heart sank as he took in the thick flakes cascading past the window. The road outside was blanketed once more, the scarce traffic crawling and sliding along. A bus attempting to stop slithered sideways and came to a stop at an angle, blocking most of the road. 'You're not going out in that,' his mother proclaimed. 'Your bed's made up, you can stay over till morning.'

There were times when argument was futile and this was clearly one of them. Mrs Sullivan made a mound of sandwiches from the leftover roast lamb they'd had for lunch and they munched their way through them as they slumped in front of the TV. Joseph sprawled in his chair, working his way through a few cans of lager, never pausing for long between sardonic comments about plots, presenters and pundits. 'I can't believe you spend your life running after stupid wee stories about the likes of her,' he said, pointing at a Scottish actress. 'She couldn't act her way out of a puddle.'

'At least I'm not some rich man's lackey, running about at their beck and call in a blizzard,' Danny muttered.

Joseph scoffed. 'I'm nobody's lackey. What I do, it's a vital role in the lives of powerful men.'

'Aye, right.'

'Stop bickering like bairns,' his mother ordered. 'I'm watching this. You're not too old to be sent to your beds.'

Joseph and his father chuckled. And everyone settled down again till the next needle. Now Danny was confident he hadn't been rumbled — or, if he had, his brother didn't know yet — his anxiety levels had dropped, only to be replaced by a simmering outrage this his brother had the nerve to sit there, lording it over them all, when he was up to his neck in a criminal conspiracy. It took an effort of will to be civil. As soon as he could reasonably get out of the stifling family embrace, Danny announced he was heading for bed. 'Busy week ahead,' he said.

Joseph grinned. 'Really? Ambulances to chase, panic buying to report?'

'Your brother does an important job,' their father said. 'There's more worthwhile things in life than helping rich folk get richer, Joseph. Working people deserve to be told what's going on around them. Wrapping it up in daft wee stories is what Danny has to do to get folk's attention to the stuff that matters. Right, Danny?'

'That's about the size of it.' Grateful for his father's intervention, he'd escaped to the small, chilly bedroom where he'd grown up. The piles of Superman and Batman comics remained under the bed, arranged in date order, all in mint condition. They'd been Danny's escape from the humdrum as a boy; he still flicked through them when he spent a night in the family home. His mother had often threatened to give them away, but she'd eventually recognised how serious her son had been when he insisted that deciding their fate was his decision alone. Now, to calm himself and escape the tension that had been gripping him all day, he fished out a sheaf of Dennis O'Neil's issues from the early 1970s. The idea of Batman as an obsessive righter of wrongs, confronting killers who murdered without compunction was a potent reminder of the kind of journalist he wanted to be.

As he knocked his notes into shape, he was fired up again by his determination to make the world a fairer place. He sensed that same sense of purpose in Allie Burns and hoped he was right. Soon he'd know for sure.

* * *

Allie was already at her desk with a carton of coffee and her first cigarette of the day when Danny arrived. Deliberately casual — for she knew better than to offer ammunition to gossip or malice — she greeted him as he passed behind her on the way to his own place. 'Good weekend?' Casual, as if she didn't care one way or another.

'Not bad,' he replied, equally nonchalant.

They kept their distance till the morning news conference drew all the executives away from their seats round the H-shaped central desks, then Danny crossed behind Allie and leaned over, pointing to something with absolutely no relevance on the newspaper she had open in front of her. 'Library, in five,' he muttered.

She found him alone in the reference room. The librarians also knew the time of the news conference and invariably sneaked off to the canteen for a mid-morning snack. 'How did it go?' Allie demanded, perching on a table.

Danny leaned against the shelves, arms folded across his chest. 'Honestly? It's hard to see how it could have gone better. I got in to see the boss right away and he totally fell for my cover story. I made a wee change to my original plan — I dropped my brother's name, because I knew he'd be in transit and Maclay couldn't call him to check. I followed it up, dead casually, with the name of the December guy on Joseph's list and that was the Open Sesame.'

'He told you how it works?'

Danny nodded, losing the struggle to stay cool with a cheek-stretching grin. 'The whole thing. Just like I'd worked out. There's a minimum investment of a hundred grand. The so-called investors buy a yacht, cash on the nail. A crew sails it to Nassau, no questions asked. Jespersen's sell the boat and the payment goes into a brand-new numbered account in a Nassau bank that has no obligation to tell the UK taxman anything. Presumably Paragon takes a slice off the top. Then Maclays take a ten per cent commission. The investor pays the crew directly, in cash again. Jespersen's take another ten per cent when they sell it on. So instead of paying the taxman eighty-three per cent of those cash bonuses, they probably only lose around a quarter. And it's all completely illegal.'

'That's an amazing story, Danny. You've done a

brilliant job. What a bunch of greedy bastards.'

'I doubt that's how they see it. Clever bastards, that's how they'll think of themselves.'

'Not clever enough, it turns out.'

'Serves them right for trusting my crooked brother.' Danny looked away, his glee momentarily wiped away.

'You'll have to protect him when you write it, though?'

Danny groaned. 'I'm starting to think he doesn't deserve protection.'

'Is that why you dropped his name into the interview? Even though you said you wouldn't?'

'No, I told you. I realised if I relied on the name of a previous client alone, Maclay could blow me out with one phone call and that would alert all of them to cover their tracks somehow. I did it really casually. 'Some guy called Sullivan,' I said, and just motored straight on.'

Allie shook her head. 'I hope that's good enough. I can't help thinking of your family, Danny. You told me just last week how close you all are, how well you all get along. If Joseph is as much of a smoothie as you say, he'll find a way to make this all your fault. He won't be the outcast. You will.'

He made a fist and punched one hand into the palm of the other. 'I don't care for myself. But I don't want to hurt my mum and dad. Joseph's adopted, did I tell you that?'

Allie shook her head.

'They thought they couldn't have kids, so they adopted him. And then I came along.' He laughed without warmth. 'The original miracle baby. They've bent over backwards all his life to make him feel like he was the one they really wanted. It'd break their

87

hearts to see him disgraced. And yeah, you're right. I'd be the one to catch the blame.'

'So can you find a way to do it? To keep Joseph's name out of it?'

Danny scowled. 'I was thinking about it all the way back from Southampton. I can put Joseph's boss front and centre.'

'You think that'll work? What about the byline? Presumably he's Joseph Sullivan?'

Danny shrugged. 'Chances are, either his boss or someone else in Paragon will put two and two together when they see the byline.'

'And they're not going to believe him when he says it's just a coincidence.' Allie could see her arguments were making Danny uncomfortable, but she suspected things were going to get a lot more uncomfortable for him if he paid her no heed.

Now there was a stubborn cast to his jaw that she'd not seen before. 'He'll maybe get the bullet, but I know Joseph. He'll not carry the can inside the family. Or when he goes looking for another job. He'll find a way to argue his innocence. Make out that when he found out what was going on, he came to me. He'll find some lie to keep his nose clean.'

Allie reached out and put a hand on his shoulder. 'At least you can leave his name out, though. It's not like you're weakening the story. Just giving it a wee tweak.'

Before he could say more, they heard voices and one of the librarians walked into the reference room. 'Oh, lovebirds,' he teased.

Allie drew her hand back as if Danny was a sheet of flame. 'Is that the best you can do?' Her voice was a tease. 'I see why you're down here and not up on the editorial floor.'

That earned a genial laugh, at least. 'Conference is out,' the librarian said.

Danny pushed off from the shelves and made for the door. 'See youse,' he muttered on his way out. Allie followed, but slowly. It wouldn't do to return to the newsroom hot on Danny's heels. Bad enough that the librarian had teased her. She'd have to talk to Danny again about Joseph. Just not somewhere with prying eyes and flapping ears.

To fill a few minutes, she picked up a paper. The Scottish National Party had formed an unlikely alliance with maverick Labour MP Tam Dalyell to shout down demands by Scots living abroad, and others of Scots descent, to have a vote in the upcoming devolution referendum. They insisted that only 'full-blooded Scots' should be entitled to vote. 'Jeez,' Allie muttered. Five years away, and this was the country she'd come back to?

On the other hand, there might be something in it for her. Allie tucked it away in a corner of her mind to follow up when she had the chance. Those politically connected women Rona had talked about might have something to say about 'full-blooded Scots'.

13

His conversation with Allie had crystallised Danny's own fears about the effect his story might have on his life. He loved his parents. He'd been keeping aspects of his life under wraps since he'd first become a journalist. The secrets he kept would only lead to arguments and disapproval. The truth was, if Danny had explained the reality of what he had to do in the service of the news and beyond, his parents would be horrified. As it was, they'd be appalled at the revelations about Paragon Investment Insurance. Adding Joseph to the mix would break their hearts.

He was sent out on a job within minutes of his return to the newsroom but he had no recollection of what the story was. He sat hunched in the back seat of the editorial car, ignoring the lively football conversation going on between the photographer and the driver. What had he been thinking, putting his own ambition ahead of his family?

It wasn't too late to pull back from the exposé altogether. He wasn't like some of his colleagues, who would shout from the rooftops about a lead even when it was nothing more than the barest whisper of a possible story. But Danny's habit of caution suited him; it meant he didn't have the newsdesk forever on his shoulder demanding an update on his progress. And that in turn meant he could still walk away from it. He could tell Peter McGovern that it hadn't panned out, that there was a perfectly innocent explanation he hadn't grasped because he was a babe in arms when it came to financial arrangements. It'd be no skin off McGovern's nose.

And Allie would understand. Wouldn't she? She wouldn't think any less of him if he killed the investigation, would she?

Danny knew the answer to that, and it wasn't the one he wanted. He didn't know Allie well, but what he did know was that she was no coward. She didn't get into fights with the newsdesk execs for the sake of making a feminist point, but she had a way of putting things that gave them pause. Take that triple murder in Dundee a few weeks ago. The crime corr had been all for insinuating the three women had been bringing men back to the 'death flat' for drink-fuelled orgies, even though two of them were residents of a home for single elderly women and the third had been their cleaner, only two weeks married. Allie had listened to the discussion then suggested they could generate more impact on readers if they made the victims out to be three ordinary women who'd been terrorised and killed by violent robbers. 'I thought we wanted our readers to care about our stories?' she'd asked, wide-eyed. 'Feel the fear those women felt?'

Angus Carlyle had paused and given her a shrewd look. 'The lassie's got a point. Writing it that way, it gives every woman in Dundee the shivers. I like it. See, I told you, boys. Having a woman's perspective has its uses.'

Danny had caught her eye as Allie returned to her chair, and she'd winked at him. 'Nicely done earlier,' he'd said in the canteen queue later.

She'd shrugged. 'There was nothing in the report that even hinted at the angle they were thinking of running. I was trying to make them see salaciousness

91

about sex isn't the only way to sell papers.' Then she'd been served ahead of him and headed out, her bacon roll in a brown paper bag.

So Allie wouldn't be impressed if he took the coward's way out. And yet, she'd been the one to point out that he'd have to protect his crooked big brother. It wasn't like he hadn't already been thinking that very thing himself. The idea of pinning the whole thing on Joseph's boss had been the only alternative he'd come up with on that long drive north. But the more he thought about it, the more it seemed fraught with risk. What if the boss then tried to pin it on Joseph when he was confronted with what Danny had discovered? What if he made the connection between Danny and Joseph and made out it was a conspiracy between the brothers? And even if Danny did walk away from it, Allie already knew enough to piece it together herself. She wouldn't do it for the glory, he thought. But she might do it because it was the right thing.

There were so many ways this could end badly.

The car came to a halt. 'Wake up in the back there,' the photographer called cheerily, turning in his seat and smacking Danny on the leg with a rolled-up copy of that morning's *Clarion*. 'Time to meet the Osmonds' nut.'

Now Danny remembered. A teenager who'd dressed as a waitress and hidden all night in the restaurant of the hotel where the singing sensations were staying. Too naïve to realise stars like them didn't take breakfast in the dining room like everyone else. The happy ending had been that the story made its way up to the Osmonds' suite and they'd sent down autographed copies of their latest album.

Danny trudged up the path, clichés already forming

in his head. Nonsense like this was the reason he couldn't let the tax fraud story go. How could he slam the escape hatch shut on his fingers?

★ ★ ★

Allie was halfway down the stairs at the end of her shift when she heard running footsteps clattering behind her. At the half-landing, she swung round, making Danny swerve into the bannisters to avoid hitting her. He clutched his side, exclaiming in pain. 'Sorry,' Allie said, 'I thought it was somebody in a hurry to get past.'

'No,' Danny croaked. 'Just somebody trying to catch up with you.' He straightened up, wincing, and reached into the inside pocket of his jacket. He pulled out a folded wedge of paper. 'This is everything I've got so far. I know it's a lot to ask but . . . '

'I'll knock it into shape. But not tonight, I've got something on.' His crestfallen expression nearly softened her but she held firm. Much as she wanted to be part of this story, she wasn't going to be anybody's pushover. 'I'll work on it tomorrow night, OK? Then I'm on my days off, so you can bring a curry round to mine on Thursday night and we can go through the copy then.'

The offer seemed to perk him up. 'Great. I really appreciate it.'

'Have you made your mind up to leave Joseph out of it?'

Danny nodded. 'If you can find a way to do it. It pisses me off that he'll walk away with clean hands, but I can't do that to my mum and dad.'

Allie frowned. 'I'll have to figure out a way to finesse

how you saw the money.'

"An anonymous source' is the usual line.' His mouth twisted in scorn.

She made a non-committal noise. They were going to have to come up with something a bit better than that if they were going to get it past the paper's lawyers. 'I'll leave you a note of my address in your pigeonhole tomorrow.'

'OK. Enjoy your evening.'

She couldn't help laughing. 'Trust me, you wouldn't be saying that if you knew where I was going. I'll see you tomorrow.' Allie sketched a wave and, aware of his eyes following her, trotted down the stairs and out into the freezing night.

★ ★ ★

An hour later, Allie paused outside one of the many pubs on Byres Road. The shops had been closed for hours and even the temptation of a warm pub and a cold pint wasn't enough to draw many people out. Sleet was blowing through again, and it was that as much as her goal for the evening that overcame Allie's nerves and drove her inside. She'd gone home to change out of her smart black trousers and dark red fine wool jumper. She'd gone for jeans and a collarless grandad shirt under a tank top, swapping her Burberry for a chain-store tweed blouson that she'd convinced herself was the epitome of smart casual. It was a judgement she'd been forced to revise when her mother had commented approvingly on it. But at least it wouldn't frighten the horses at an SNP meeting, and that was the main thing.

The meeting was in an upstairs room. A couple of

dozen people were already there, dotted around in tight little groups. Seven or eight middle-aged men in badly fitting suits with pints in their hands; a trio of thirty-something women, heads together in close colloquy; half a dozen obvious students, four girls and two nerdy guys who she suspected might be there because it was their only chance of being in female company; a scattering of earnest-looking young men studying folders whose covers displayed party branding; and two slab-faced men in their twenties who looked like they'd come straight from a building site, if any building sites were operating in weather like this. A few people glanced up as Allie entered, but nobody paid her much attention.

She made a quick decision and sat down by the students. She wasn't so much older than them and she'd dressed to avoid intimidation. A girl immediately introduced herself and the others but before they could say more, one of the women detached herself from her friends and came over. 'Hiya, I'm Muriel. I'm the membership secretary for the branch. We've not seen you here before?'

Allie smiled. 'I'm interested in devolution. I thought I'd come along and see what the SNP has to say. Do I have to be a member?'

Muriel smiled. 'You're supposed to be, but in this branch, we don't mind letting folk try before they buy.' She pulled a bundle of papers from her bag and handed one to Allie. 'There you go, an application form, if you want to take things further.' She returned to her friends.

'They're desperate for people to join,' one of the students said. 'But they can't even agree among themselves what they want. The hardliners want nothing

95

short of independence and they think devolution's a sell-out. The rest are gradualists. Devo now, jam tomorrow.'

'Maybe so,' one of the lads chipped in. 'But they're all we've got.'

Any further discussion was cut short by one of the suited men calling the meeting to order. The next hour was fundamentally the same as every other political meeting Allie had ever attended, either as a student or a reporter. Minutes, matters arising, droning through the agenda. About as inspiring as cold rice pudding until they got to AOB.

One of the students jumped to her feet and said, 'I've got some other business. We need to lobby the Scottish Secretary about student votes in the referendum.'

'Students get a vote,' the chairman interrupted. 'If you register to vote at your university address, you can vote there or at the address where you normally live.'

'That's the point I'm trying to make,' she persisted. 'We're registered twice but we can only vote once. And since the government changed the rules and said we'd only get devolution if forty per cent of the registered electorate voted for it, we're caught in a trap. A student's 'yes' vote is cancelled out by the other vote they can't cast. And a student who votes 'no'? Their vote is doubled up because the vote they didn't cast also counts as somebody else who didn't vote yes. You see what I'm saying?'

Allie scented a story. There was a moment of stunned silence as the student's words sank in. 'That cannae be right,' one of Muriel's pals said.

'It's right enough,' the shorter of the two builders

96

said. 'It's all part of the same conspiracy to stamp on us. We need to stamp back.'

'Enough of that,' the chair said. 'We'll not have talk of violence here.'

'It's the only language they'll understand,' the other builder chimed in. 'We'll have to take to the streets before this is over, you wait and see.'

A hubbub of conversation broke out. As far as Allie could tell, nobody was taking either the students or the builders seriously. The young woman slumped to her seat. 'Told you it'd be a waste of time,' the lad on her left muttered.

Sensing a story, Allie leaned in. 'You should take it up with the NUS. That's what the students' union's for. Speaking up for your rights. Talk to your local president.'

'That's not a bad idea,' another said. 'These dinosaurs here don't even get the point we're making. We could do that in the morning. Get a protest moving.'

Satisfied she'd started something, Allie made her excuses and left. She had the quote and a name to attach it to. In the morning, she'd talk to the union officials. By conference, she'd have a story for the newsdesk. It turned out she owed Rona Dunsyre a drink rather sooner than she'd expected.

★ ★ ★

While Allie was in a pub in the West End, Danny was in a very different pub in the city centre. The kind of stories he would hear in the course of the evening were not the kind of stories that would ever find a home in the *Clarion*. But they were stories that spoke to him. He sat at the bar nursing a Bacardi and Coke, wondering whether he was pursuing this tax fraud investigation because he was drawn to trouble like a rabbit in the headlights. Or if it was simply that he found those bright shiny lights irresistible.

14

Allie stared at Angus Carlyle. 'Is this some kind of a joke? I bring in a perfectly good news story, and you give me this?'

Carlyle undid the top button of his shirt and loosened his tie. The unbuttoning usually didn't happen till after the conference, but something was clearly bugging him today. Allie suspected it had something to do with her bringing in a devo story that the political team had missed. And instead of bollocking them for missing it, and letting her nail the story down and write it herself, he was giving it away to someone else and handing her this nonsense. 'It's a page lead if you handle it right,' he grunted. 'You're good at the light-touch stuff.'

'If you'd let me do the other stuff, you'd see I was good at that too.' Chin up, shoulders back, she stalked off. She knew when she was beaten.

'*Nil illegitimi carborundum,*' Big Kenny Stone said with a grin as she dropped into her chair next to him. She always felt like a wee lassie beside him; Big Kenny was built like a rugby prop forward, all shoulders and thighs, and ears that looked like they'd been modelled by a child whose natural bent did not lie with Play-Doh. His shirt seams always looked on the point of bursting. Coupled with his shock of dark hair, the comparison with the Incredible Hulk was irresistible.

'I've survived bigger bastards than Carlyle trying to grind me down,' she muttered, reminding herself that she was Big Kenny's equal, not his junior. 'Have you

99

seen this pile of shite?' She tossed the flimsy sheet of paper in front of him.

He read it and laughed out loud. 'A nude beach promised for Ayrshire. That's some story to run in the middle of the coldest January for fifteen years.'

Allie snatched it back and read it again. In a survey of every local authority in the UK by a naturist organisation, the only council who had responded were in Ayrshire, and they'd indicated they were open to discussion. 'I brought in a perfectly good story and Carlyle gave it away.'

'So if you can't join them, beat them.'

She gave him a sharp look. 'How?'

And he told her.

★ ★ ★

Two hours later, Allie and her favourite photographer, Bobby Gibson, were walking through the dunes above the beach in question. There was a scrappy dusting of snow on the sand and every step broke a thin crust of ice. The narrow blades of the marram grass that maintained the dunes' integrity were silvered with frost but still sharp enough to cut any naked flesh that might brush against them. That wasn't an issue for Allie or Bobby, wrapped up like polar explorers.

But it might yet prove to be for Sandie McAllister. The Page Three *Clarion* model wore only a pair of wellies and a thin satin robe as she picked her way down to the beach. The tide was high and there was only a narrow strip of sand between the dunes and the battleship grey sea. A northerly wind whipped streaks of white foam along the tops of the waves. There wasn't another creature with a pulse in sight.

'Fucking hell, are you paying me danger money for this? If I get pneumonia, I'm going to fucking sue you, Bobby G.' Sandie shivered and tucked her hands under her armpits, doing a little dance on the spot in a bid to generate some body heat.

Bobby quickly prepped his cameras. 'Sooner you do it, the sooner you'll have done it,' he said cheerily. 'OK. Allie, grab the wellies, I don't want them in shot. Sandie, as soon as Allie gets out the road, I want you to chuck your robe on the sand and run into the water.'

'You bastard,' the model said through chattering teeth.

'And once you're in to your waist, I want you to turn round and wave your arms in the air with a big grin.'

'Fuck's sake,' Sandie muttered. 'At least you'll not need the ice cubes for my nips today.' She took a deep breath and stepped forward. The motor drive on Bobby's camera started whirring and clicking and with professional aplomb, Sandie shrugged out of her wrap and started running, shouting 'Fuck! Fuck! Fuck!' with every step. She barely paused at the water's edge and plunged onwards, leaping the wavelets then pushing against the incoming swell.

'I hope we're paying her well for this,' Allie said.

'She knows she'll get a good show in the paper,' Bobby replied cheerily, snapping away as Sandie turned to face them, breasts pert, nipples stiff as wine corks, hair flying in the wind, a practised grin on her face. She threw up her arms in the top half of a star jump, then folded them over her chest and stumbled back to shore. Allie ran down the beach to meet her with the fluffy bath sheet she'd bought on expenses

101

on the way there.

Sandie practically fell into her arms, her skin changing from white to scarlet as the blood rushed to the surface. Allie rubbed her vigorously, steering her up the beach and through the dunes. Back at the deserted car park, she helped the model dress. 'I can't feel my fucking fingers or my fucking feet,' Sandie swore. Bobby poured a cup of coffee from a Thermos, and Sandie clutched it like a lifeline. Two swallows in, Bobby added a slug of whisky from his hip flask. Sandie swigged, shuddered and smiled. 'I might live.'

They drove up the coast to a hotel Bobby knew. 'Swear to God they do the best fish pie in the west,' he promised. Allie found no reason to quibble. While the photographer and the model sat with their whiskies by the spluttering log fire in the bar, Allie settled at a quiet table in a far corner to write her copy. *Clarion* style demanded a story like this be larded with obvious humour; no pun could be too heavy-handed. She lit a cigarette and scribbled down some possibilities.

Allie stared unseeing at the bar, letting her ideas churn. At last, she stubbed out her cigarette and began to write.

Today the Clarion exclusively reveals the naked truth. Following a nationwide survey, only one council in the UK is willing to strip for action and provide a nudist beach.

Some might have the bare-faced cheek to say Ayrshire is too cold to keep abreast of fashion.

But model Sandie McAllister has proved them wrong. There might have been snow on the ground but it didn't stop her streaking down the beach and into the scudding waves of the chilly sea.

Afterwards, she said, 'Once I got over the shock, I felt amazing! It was so liberating to feel the waves against my

102

skin. I hope the plan goes ahead — it will be fantastic on a summer's day!'

The council's Leisure Services committee agreed in principle yesterday to provide Scotland's first public nude bathing beach.

They've not yet chosen where people will be able to strip off, but committee chairman Adam McGurk said, 'There's no shortage of secluded beaches on the wonderful Ayrshire coast. They have fine sands and beautiful views. And Ayrshire is an area that already provides many facilities for visitors.'

The survey was conducted by the UK Naturism Association. Their chairman, Colette Hannigan, said, 'This is a very happy outcome for us. We wrote to every council in the UK and this has been the only positive response. If this goes ahead, our members will flock to Scotland.'

The only remaining question is what will the councillors wear for the opening ceremony. Steady the Buffs!

She returned to Bobby and Sandie and checked she was OK with the quote, then persuaded the hotel receptionist to let her make a phone call from the office. 'I'll get them to call straight back,' she promised before ringing the *Clarion* copytakers. She identified herself, read out the hotel's number and replaced the handset. Within a couple of minutes, she was dictating the story down the line. At the end, the copytaker transferred her to the newsdesk.

'I've filed my copy,' she told the assistant news editor. 'Bobby G has pix. We're heading back now, but we've got to drop off the model in Paisley on the way.'

'Aye, right. Anything to make sure you get back too late to be sent out on another story,' came the grumble in return.

'I didn't make the weather,' Allie said.

'Check back in half an hour, there might be queries.' The line went dead. It was hard to imagine what those might be. She had quotes from all the relevant people. She might even have exceeded her daily pun quotient. But she did as she was told, and as expected, there were no queries.

There was no sign of Danny when she got back to the office. She was handed a bundle of copy — Press Association, a couple of freelances and one of the Edinburgh office staffers — about the picketing of salt depots and the resulting threats to road users and bus services. 'Eight pars, keep it tight, Burns,' the assistant news editor said, already distracted by the next item on his schedule.

★ ★ ★

The flat was freezing when Allie got home. She drew the heavy curtains and turned on the gas fire in the living room and closed the door behind her when she went through to the kitchen. There were the remains of a pot of chilli on the stove and while it heated, she made a couple of slices of cheese on toast to serve with it. She poured a glass of Sicilian red wine and sat at the table in what had once been a bed recess, poring over Danny's notes as she ate. There was no getting away from it. In spite of Danny's dull and, frankly, clumsy prose, this was a cracking story. There was nothing the *Clarion*'s readers liked more than seeing white-collar crooks get their comeuppance. Allie supposed it gave them hope that the world might one day be a fairer place.

The reactions of the perpetrators of the tax fraud were obviously still missing, but there was enough here to produce a draft that would make the newsdesk sit up and pay attention. That was all she'd promised Danny, but looking at the material in front of her, she knew it wasn't going to be easy to convey the complexity of the story. Still, she'd made that promise and she had to stick to it.

She finished her dinner and washed up, her mind on the words she needed to find. By the time she returned to the living room, the temperature was bearable. She sat down at the big table in the bay window and stared at a blank sheet of paper. The intro was always the key. You knew you'd cracked it because, once that was right, the rest fell into place almost without thinking. But to get the intro right, you had to be in command of your material and she wasn't confident of that yet.

Allie read through Danny's notes once more, closed her eyes and breathed deeply. Then she began. Her fourth attempt was almost there. Next time, she thought she'd cracked it.

An illegal scheme to rob the taxman is making a group of wealthy Scottish businessmen even richer.

It was a start. She knew it would flow from there.

15

The working day seemed to last forever. Danny spent most of it talking to an assortment of retail managers about the staggering news that prices in the shops had literally doubled in the past five years of the Labour government. But at last his copy was written and the newsdesk gave the nod to the early day shift reporters. Before he left the office, Danny phoned through his takeaway order for an extravagant selection of Indian food. Anything to get to Allie's flat a few minutes sooner, not to mention impressing her with his generosity. When she opened the door, he brandished the two bulging carrier bags that were filling the close with the rich aroma of curry spices. 'Ta-da!' he greeted her with a grin.

'Did you invite the whole day shift?' Allie giggled, ushering him in.

She looked pleased to see him, he thought. She hadn't dressed up like someone who was going out for the evening, but he thought she'd taken a bit of trouble with her hair, and the polo-neck jumper she was wearing made the most of her in a way her office clothes never quite managed. 'You can stick what's left in the fridge and heat it up tomorrow.'

She led the way through. 'Are you trying to win me over with garlic naans? Stick the bags down on the table next to the plates and get your coat off.'

Danny did as he was told. 'It's good to see you, Allie. I've been looking forward to this all day.' His lean face crinkled in a smile that reached his eyes, making them sparkle in the bright kitchen lights.

She took his coat, shaking the melting snow off the heavy sheepskin that seemed obligatory wear among male reporters in the winter months. 'There's beer in the fridge. Get a couple out while I hang up the dead baby lambs.'

When she returned, Allie went straight to the cutlery drawer and grabbed a handful of spoons and a pair of forks. 'Food first, then we'll get down to business.' Seeing his expression, she added, 'Don't look at me like that. If we start on the copy, we'll be so caught up in it the food'll be stone cold before we get to it. And I hate to see a good curry go to waste.'

Danny groaned. 'You're a hard woman, Burns.'

'Always keep them waiting, that's my motto,' she said archly, flashing him a quick glance before she set about opening up the tinfoil containers. She inhaled the smell and breathed a sigh of satisfaction. 'Bloody hell, Danny, this is a feast.'

'So get stuck in. The sooner you've filled your boots, the sooner I get to hear what you've made of the story.'

Neither had much to say while they made impressive inroads into their lavish dinner. Finally, Allie gave her plate a final wipe with a scrap of naan and pushed it away. Danny, who'd been first to finish, drained his beer. 'You can't put it off any longer.'

Allie looked anxious for the first time since he'd arrived. 'I'm kind of nervous about what you'll think.'

'It'll be better than anything I could have managed. The way you write, it's like you've got an instinct for how to tell a story. I've watched you. You knock out great copy in half the time anybody else in the newsroom manages.'

'Flattery,' she muttered. 'Come through to the living room.'

Armed with a fresh can of beer, he followed her through, liking what he saw. A ferociously fashionable three-piece suite of brown corduroy and tubular steel was arranged round the gas fire, a low glass and chrome coffee table between them. In the bay window, an elderly gate-leg table held a portable typewriter and a stack of fresh paper. Bookshelves ran along most of the back wall, and an alcove by the fireplace contained a music centre surrounded by an extensive collection of vinyl and tapes. 'You like your music,' Danny said, stepping over to examine her stash. 'I haven't heard of half of these.' He pulled out a couple at random. 'Andy Roberts. Silly Sisters . . . oh, Pink Floyd, that's more my thing. *Wish You Were Here*, that's pure genius.'

'I thought you were desperate to see my deathless prose?' Allie teased, picking up a few sheets of paper from one of the shelves.

Danny stepped away from the music and held out his hand. 'Maybe I'm kind of nervous too.'

She handed him her work and waved him to a seat, settling in the chair opposite with the carbon copy of what she'd given him. A quick glance took in the tight line of her mouth and the faint furrow between her brows before he focused on the words. 'I hope you don't think I've fucked it up,' she muttered.

Within the first couple of sentences, Danny knew she had no cause for nerves.

By Daniel Sullivan
    Additional reporting by Peter McGovern and Alison Burns

An illegal scheme to rob the taxman is making a group of wealthy Scottish businessmen even richer.

The money laundering scam involves luxury yachts and secret accounts in private banks in the Caribbean. Hundreds of thousands of pounds are laundered every month for their clients by a small cabal of crooks.

Today the *Clarion* can exclusively lift the lid on the dodgy deals organised by a top Edinburgh insurance and investment company.

Our investigation reveals a world where shoeboxes filled with undeclared cash are swapped for expensive oceangoing craft which in turn are sold on in countries where the taxman can't get his hands on the proceeds.

The fraud is the brainchild of Edinburgh company Paragon Investment Insurance whose HQ on the city's prestigious George Street hides a shabby secret. Clients bring their untraceable cash to Paragon's offices.

Our *Clarion* investigative reporter personally witnessed wads of cash that were destined for a yacht brokerage on the south coast of England.

Among the businessmen who have invested in Paragon's scheme are Graeme Brown, whose Spin 'n' Top launderette chain has branches throughout Scotland, and bookie Brian McGillivray, whose WestBet betting shops are a common sight on Scottish high streets.

According to documents seen by our reporter, Graeme Brown paid £125,000 for a boat called *Snagglecat 2* in December last

year. And only this month, Brian McGillivray handed over £100,000, the minimum amount
allowed by the scheme, for a yacht called
Meridian Flyer.

We tracked the money to Maclays, a boatyard
in Hythe, on Southampton Water whose slogan
is 'The high life on the ocean wave'.

Boatyard boss Bill Maclay claimed his role
in the enterprise was solely to sell boats to
clients who chose to pay in cash. 'There's
nothing wrong in what we're doing,' he told
our reporter. 'It's my job to buy and sell
boats. Our clients are successful businessmen, not criminals. We check their bona fides
with Paragon Investment Insurance.'

We asked why all the boats bought by Paragon clients end up in the Caribbean – in the
well-known tax haven of Nassau in the Bahamas. Maclay said, 'Where would you rather
sail? In the wind and rain of the English
Channel or in the warm waters of the Caribbean? Our customers are the kind of men who
can afford to fly out for a week or two on
their boats somewhere the sun shines and the
winds are gentle.'

Maclay admitted he recruited the crews who
sail the boats across the Atlantic. 'Like I
said, our clients don't want to be sailing
rough seas in gale-force winds. So taking the
boats to where they do want to sail is part
of the service.' The clients pay the wages
of the crew, and Maclays take a 10 per cent
slice of the purchase price as their commission.

'What our customers do with their boats once they get to the Caribbean is up to them.'

But once the sleek sailboats arrive in Nassau, they're not berthed in any of the luxury marinas or private moorings on the island. Instead, the brand-new craft are delivered to Jespersen Marine on Frog Cay.

Boss Conrad Jespersen told us, 'Buying and selling boats is what we do.' And that's exactly what they do with the expensive yachts that have been delivered from Southampton. The owners never see their boats, never mind sail them.

When Jespersen Marine buys boats, like Maclays they take a 10 per cent commission.

We asked how the proceeds from sales in Nassau are returned to the boat's owner. He said, 'We can do a bank transfer anywhere in the world. Or we can help set up a local account here if that's what they want.'

TO COME: Face to face showdowns with Gregor Menstrie, chief exec PII, Graeme Brown and Brian McGillivray.

Phone showdowns with Bill Maclay and Conrad Jespersen.

Quotes from Inland Revenue

Quotes from Lothian Police

SIDEBAR: Paragon's chief executive, Gregor Menstrie, 39, is the son of a banker. He grew up in North Berwick and was privately educated at the exclusive Glenisla School

which charges boarders ?x-a-year. He claims
to have a degree from the London School of
Economics but the LSE was unable to confirm
that.

After ten years working for a variety of
investment companies, he set up
PII five years ago. He lives in a five-
bedroomed house in Cramond with his wife
Venetia and their two young sons.

Danny came to the end and let out a low whistle
of approval. 'Fucking nailed it, Burns. Where did you
get that stuff on Menstrie?'

'Most of it from the office library. But I rang the
LSE and checked whether he actually did have a
degree from there.' Allie's expression turned mischie-
vous. 'They were very forthcoming when I explained
I was from the Lothian and Borders Fraud Squad.'

Danny shook his head, admiring her nerve. 'That
took some brass neck.'

'I'm from Fife, Danny. Gallus is my middle name.'

'I'll bear that in mind. I'll need to change the byline,
though. It'll need to be 'By Daniel Sullivan and Peter
McGovern, with additional reporting by Alison Burns'.'

'How? McGovern hardly contributed anything,
according to you.'

Danny shrugged. 'It was the deal.' He flicked
through the pages again. 'There's one wee thing bothering me, if I'm honest.'

"Our *Clarion* investigative reporter personally witnessed wads of cash," Allie interrupted.

'Yeah, it points the finger straight at Joseph, doesn't
it?'

Allie sighed. 'It's the only piece of solid evidence we

have, Danny. Without that, it's hanging on a shoogly peg, unless one of the clients rolls over and spills the lot. If Joseph was the only person who touched the cash, then yes, it would point straight at him. Surely it must have come from somebody else?'

'How?'

Allie leaned forward in her chair, eager. She seemed to be energised by the very process of being questioned, of having to find a justification for what was in her text. It was the opposite of how these interrogations made Danny feel. 'Well, somebody has to have passed the cash to Joseph. Or it could have been a secretary who saw something she wasn't supposed to. Or it could have been one of the clients boasting to his pals. For all Menstrie knows, we could have had somebody undercover in his office.'

'But that's not what happened.' Danny felt a cold current of worry in his stomach.

'Danny, from everything you've told me about your brother, he's capable of coming up with an explanation himself. More than capable.' She frowned, then said, 'Obviously, you can't do the showdown with Menstrie.'

'But it's my story,' he protested.

'The showdowns will have to be simultaneous,' she said. 'Otherwise they'll be on the phone to each other as soon as we front them up and we'll never get another word out of any of them. It would make sense to get McGovern to front up Menstrie. It keeps you at a distance. Keeps your name out of Menstrie's eyeline. Besides, it means McGovern actually has to do a bit of heavy lifting for his byline. Meanwhile you do the launderette king or the bookie.'

Danny stared at the copy without seeing it. 'I suppose,' he said, aware he was sounding like a sulky wee

113

boy. He sighed heavily, took a swig of his beer then said, 'At least he'll know the right questions to ask. The lawyers will take him more seriously than they'll take me. OK, we'll keep 'the wads of cash' in.' He met her eyes. 'But I want you to do the third showdown.'

Allie looked startled, and he couldn't work out why. She had a stake in the story too now. 'They'll never go for it,' she said. 'There's no miracle babies in it.' Her smile was wry.

'Tough,' he said. 'It comes as a package.' He drained his beer then folded up the copy. 'It's the only way I can thank you for this.' He shifted forward in his chair, on the verge of standing up.

'Are you off?' Allie sounded both surprised and disappointed.

He glanced at his watch. 'I've got to type this up on office copy pads.' *And I have someone to meet.* He gave her his most apologetic smile. 'I need to be ready to hit Angus with this first thing.' He stood up.

'Oh. OK.' Allie tossed her copy of the story on to the coffee table and made for the hall. By the time Danny had caught up with her, she had his coat off the peg, holding it open for him to thrust his arms into the sleeves. 'Thanks for the curry, it'll keep me going for the whole of my long weekend.'

Unsure how to respond, Danny struggled into his coat. 'I really appreciate what you did.'

'Sure, any time. Call me when Angus has finished slapping you on the back,' Allie said, stepping back.

Danny turned to face her and awkwardly shuffled forward. He put his hands on her shoulders and moved in on her, carefully planting a dry-lipped kiss

114

on her cheek. 'I'll call you tomorrow.' He made for the door, turning at the last minute and giving her the full hundred-watt smile. 'Promise.'

16

There was only enough milk for one mug of coffee. Allie made it last as long as she could; she didn't dare leave the flat to go to the nearby shops in case she missed Danny's call. However hard she tried to convince herself this was no big deal, she struggled to concentrate on the P.D. James novel she'd started the day before. Her eyes were drawn to her watch every few minutes. Eventually, she gave up and pulled *Pictures on a Page* from where it was waiting on the shelf. Since she'd started her traineeship, she'd been fascinated by the books that the great newspaperman Harold Evans had written about the craft of journalism. She'd not had time to devote much attention to his newly published tome about the power and practice of photojournalism. Even if she couldn't focus on the words, at least she could appreciate the images.

When the call came, it wasn't from Danny. When Allie snatched up the receiver, she heard the familiar nasal tones of the newsdesk secretary. "Z'at you, Allie? He wants you in right now. I've sent a taxi to your flat on the account.'

It clearly wasn't a request. 'I'll see you soon.' As she spoke, the blast of a car horn sounded from the street below. She dropped the handset on its rest and made for the door, grabbing her bag and coat on the way. Jeans and an unflattering Aran jumper would have to do. It was her day off, after all.

'Where's the fire?' the cabbie demanded as she got in. 'I was told this was double urgent.'

'You know what they're like,' Allie said. 'Always a matter of life and death, and then it's tomorrow's chip paper.'

* * *

Allie found Angus Carlyle in his office, sprawled in his executive leather chair, Danny's story spread across the desk in front of him. 'The third musketeer,' he announced with the kind of flourish that created the impression of an invisible cavalier hat. Danny was hunched in a visitor's chair in one corner with the air of a cowed child waiting for the next blow to fall. There was a sheen of sweat on his forehead. In contrast, Peter McGovern looked relaxed, one ankle on the opposite knee, a cigarillo burning between his fingers. Today's shirt was as pink as the *Financial Times*, a fine white stripe running through it. The only touch of elegance in the room, she thought.

'This is some tale,' Carlyle boomed. 'So, additional reporter Alison Burns, tell me what your part in all of this is?'

She flicked a sideways glance at Danny, who was no help. 'I did the background on Gregor Menstrie,' she said. 'I spoke to the London School of Economics. They said they had no record of him ever studying there. And I helped Danny knock the story into shape.'

Carlyle smiled. It reminded her of a lion baring its teeth. 'Ah, that explains why it reads like something a journalist might write. You might not be top of the pops when it comes to bringing the stories in but you've definitely got a knack for stringing a few pars together. Maybe you're wasted as a reporter. Maybe you'd be better placed doing rewrites on the subs

117

table.' It was a typically back-handed compliment and it stung, as she knew it was meant to. Carlyle liked to keep his infantry on the back foot. Only the specialists like McGovern received the benefit of his good graces. They were the ones who might be tempted to jump ship and join the opposition, after all.

Allie said nothing. There was no possible response that wouldn't hand him more ammunition.

Carlyle suddenly sat upright in his chair and steepled his fingers. 'It's a great story. I want to run it big across two days. Obviously we'll have to do the showdowns that the Boy Wonder here has outlined at the end. There's only one problem, and it's a three-hundred-and-twenty-seven-thousand-pound problem. Anybody here know what I'm talking about?'

'The *Sunday Mail* judgement last week,' McGovern said. 'But that was different.'

'How?' Carlyle demanded, leaning across the desk, his big head looming like a predator sizing up dinner. 'It looks pretty bloody similar to me.'

McGovern drew in a mouthful of smoke and breathed it out as he responded. 'The *Mail* said the insurance company were obtaining money by false pretences. That they were promising returns on investment that they knew couldn't materialise. That turned out to be very hard to prove because the prospectus was carefully worded. The insurers were able to hide behind the excuse that they were hard-working but incompetent rather than criminal. This is entirely different, Angus. We're accusing Paragon of knowingly conniving at defrauding the taxman.'

'And we can take the readers through every simple step,' Danny chipped in.

Carlyle ignored him and harrumphed. 'It makes

me nervous,' he said. 'Very bloody nervous. And if it makes me nervous, you can bet it'll have the editor shitting his breeks.'

McGovern chuckled. Allie couldn't quite believe her ears. She turned to see his face; his expression was equally amused. 'Calm down, Angus. That's what the night lawyer is for.'

'The *Mail* has lawyers and they still ended up in the shit.' Carlyle slumped back in his seat again. 'OK. I'll talk to the lawyer when he comes in. If he gives us the green light, we'll do the showdowns next week.' He gazed up at the ceiling, clearly thinking. 'Wednesday, so we can run it Thursday and Friday. Class dismissed.' He waggled his fingers, waving them off. 'Don't go far, Danny. I'm confident the lawyer will have some questions for you.'

On the far side of the door, McGovern patted Danny on the shoulder. 'It'll be fine.'

Danny took a step away. 'He just put me through the wringer.'

'That's what he's paid for,' McGovern said. 'If you can't stand up to Angus, how can the paper expect you to stand up to a lawyer if it ever comes to court?' He strode off towards the bank of lifts, insouciant as a flâneur on a Paris boulevard.

'He's got a point,' Allie said. 'You shouldn't let him bully you. It's a great story. You can stand it up, even if nobody caves in the showdowns.'

'Thanks,' Danny said. 'You'd better get back to your day off. Sorry about you getting dragged in. I'll let you know how I get on with the lawyer.' He turned away and slouched back to his desk, apparently discouraged.

Allie watched him, wondering. In his shoes, with a

story like this under her belt, she'd be irrepressible. She really liked Danny. *Really* liked him. But he was going to have to dig deep and find some assertiveness if it was going to go any further than that. It was a fine line to walk, she knew that. Simon, who she'd gone out with for most of her second year at Cambridge, had let her walk all over him in his desire to please. The affair had died of boredom. But Matthew, a brief fling in her final year, had been determined to be in charge of every aspect of their relationship, even its end. After she'd dumped him, he'd gone round every one of her friends he'd ever met telling them what a bitch she was. She hadn't chosen well in the past, it was apparent.

This time, she really hoped it could be different.

* * *

It was so cold her cheekbones hurt. But for the first time in days the low grey Glasgow skies had lifted, giving way to the kind of bright blue day Allie had grown up with on the east coast. It was a clear light she missed, and seeing it lifted her spirits. She decided to walk home. Up past the motorway that slashed a wound through the city, then down the fag end of Sauchiehall Street towards Kelvingrove. There were still piles of frozen gritty slush by the roadsides but pedestrians had worn a path along the pavements; walking no longer felt like a life-threatening activity.

The sunshine brought out the rich red sandstone of the Kelvingrove Gallery and the Kelvin Hall opposite, its garish circus posters shouting their promises across the street. Beyond them, the grim charcoal outlines of the Western Infirmary and the Gothic spire of the university reminded her that this was a city of contrasts; beauty and ugliness, extreme poverty and extreme wealth, drugged depression and savage humour.

Allie turned up Byres Road towards home. Her savings had been growing significantly every month; after years of making every penny count, first as a student then as a trainee, her *Clarion* salary felt like riches beyond dreams of avarice. Her expenses alone were only slightly less than her previous wage. She reckoned she was close to having enough for the deposit on a flat. The only drawback was that the mortgage company would demand six months of payslips. But she'd cross that line next month; it was time to start checking out the market.

Byres Road was where the estate agents had pitched their tents and Allie spent the rest of the morning browsing their windows. She knew exactly what she wanted — a tenement flat with two or three bedrooms, a short walk from the shops and the bus routes into town. A quiet street, ideally. Thankfully, there appeared to be several options, and a few of them were within her price range. She didn't care if they needed work; her father loved DIY and she knew he'd happily spend his weekends helping her knock it into shape. The grinding discomfort of conversations about nothing would be worth it.

By the time she got home, it was mid-afternoon. Her answering machine was clear of messages. She wasn't sure how to interpret that. Had the lawyer given the story the kiss of death? Or was he telling Danny what needed to be in place before they could consider running it? Were they working out how to conduct the showdowns? Or had it simply been put on the back burner, subsumed by the live news stories of the day? Whatever it was, why hadn't Danny called her? Had she become irrelevant now that she'd given him what he needed? Surely he wasn't that kind of man? Had she misjudged him so badly?

Allie sighed. She missed not having a close friend in Glasgow. She hoped Rona Dunsyre might fill that slot, but there was still a long way to go there. She needed a distraction. Then she spotted the leaflet she'd dumped next to the phone. She'd picked it up at the SNP meeting. One of the men in suits had been about to toss it in the bin but she'd rescued it. NO TO DEVO, YES TO INDY, it was headlined. She scanned it swiftly, noticing it announced a meeting scheduled for that evening.

Friday evening TV held no appeal for her. She hadn't given up on life yet, Allie told herself. OK, some might not agree with that judgement, since she was seriously considering a political fringe meeting as an appealing alternative.

What the hell, Allie thought. Stories lurked everywhere. So did potential friends.

17

The meeting room was tucked away in an obscure passageway off the East Quad of the university. Allie arrived in good time and asked for directions at the main gate. She found it at the second attempt then, because she didn't want to be first to arrive, she prowled around the double quadrangle at the heart of the university. Five years before, she'd have been over-awed by the elaborate outsized Gothic architecture, its turrets and pinnacles blackened sinister by years of industrial pollution. But she'd spent three years in Cambridge surrounded by the real thing rather than its Victorian reincarnation. There was nothing here that could intimidate her now.

Allie arrived seven minutes after the advertised starting time, which probably meant she'd have missed nothing. More importantly, she could slip in at the back without attracting too much attention. Better to stay under the radar to start with till she sussed out the lie of the land.

The room was untidily arranged as if for a seminar. More than half of the chairs were occupied, and some had clearly been moved to allow people to sit closer to their friends. A couple of heads turned as Allie slipped in and found an empty seat near the door. Nobody seemed very interested in a new arrival.

She studied the room. Fifteen men, nine women. About half of them looked somewhere between her age and their mid-thirties, though it was hard to tell when people were dressed for the weather outside and the room wasn't much warmer. The others were older and a couple of them had that air of dishevelled entitlement Allie had come to associate with academics. There was a low murmur of conversation from a trio of young men over to her left. She thought she recognised a few faces from the SNP meeting earlier in the week.

One of the women disengaged herself from her two companions, shrugged out of a duffel coat and moved to the front of the room, perching casually on the edge of the desk. She wore a figure-hugging dark blue jumper over jeans tucked into knee-length low-heeled boots that looked as if they hadn't seen polish since they'd left the shop. Allie clocked that detail automatically and read it as a marker of middle-class affluence. People like her had grown up with the habit of making things last. They knew that boots and shoes lasted longer if they were given care and attention. You could only indulge in deliberate shabbiness if you were sure new shoes would be forthcoming when you needed them.

'I'm Maggie McNab,' she said, tucking her long dark hair behind one ear. She smiled, lighting up a strong-boned face with deep-set dark blue eyes. 'Thanks for coming tonight. Before I go any further, I need to say that we're not affiliated with the SNP or associated with them in any way, shape or form. We regard the SNP as collaborators in colonialism and we believe their slavish support of the devolution offered by their Westminster masters is nothing short of a betrayal of the interests of Scotland and her people. We believe nothing less than full independence is what our country needs and deserves. If you're uncomfortable with that, then we're not the crew for you.' She spoke with the confidence and the accent that came from a Scottish private school education.

There was a moment's silence, then one of the trio of young men said, 'Well said, Maggie,' and his friends clapped in a half-hearted way.

Allie sat back and listened while Maggie gave a fifteen-minute lecture on the economic and social reasons why Scotland would be stronger as an independent nation. She outlined the promised land that lay in wait for the country once it had shaken off the shackles of Westminster with a zeal Allie found unsettling. She hadn't previously given independence or even devolution a great deal of thought. It looked like that was going to have to change.

Maggie ceded the floor to one of the older men. Professor Alexander Jameson held a chair in Modern History, which had always seemed like an oxymoron to Allie. He held forth about the existing divisions between Scotland and England — the legal systems, the educational syllabi, the practice of Christianity, the cultural landmarks. Here, Allie could see some substance to the ideas. Her years in England had driven home to her differences that were far from obvious.

Maggie took the floor again. 'We have to take advantage of the devolution conversation to change the agenda,' she began.

'How are we going to manage that?' The question came from the same man who had shouted his support earlier.

'We need to hijack the conversation, Deke. We need to remind people at every opportunity that it's time to stop going cap in hand to anybody else.'

'Practical terms, though, Maggie. How do we hammer home the point in practical terms? How do we

125

make them pay attention the way they've been forced to do in Northern Ireland?'

There was a moment's silence. Everyone in the room knew very well the tactics that the IRA had used in the province. But it hadn't brought the UK government to its knees. It hadn't even brought them to the negotiating table. 'We go to every single meeting, Deke. Friends and foes, we don't differentiate. We make our points in the guise of asking questions. There are six different official campaign groups, and we need to hit them all. Yesses and Noes, equally. Deirdre's brought a box of leaflets too, you should all grab a handful and take them with you. And don't forget the commercial radio stations. They do phone-ins as part of their schedule. Check them out whenever you can, get on air whenever you can. If we're going to win hearts and minds, we need to work at it.' There was more in the same key from a couple of other speakers.

Deke and his pals seemed unimpressed. One was grumbling in a low voice. Deke muttered something that sounded like, 'the same old song'.

But another spoke more sharply. 'Keep it buttoned. You'll get your say later. Jeez!' Obediently, they settled down.

His words intrigued Allie. What did he mean by them? There were signs that the meeting was close to breaking up. Allie slipped out and laid in wait in one of the dark corners of the quad with the aim of unobtrusively picking up their trail. At last they emerged in a tight knot. Now she could see their faces, she thought they looked a bit too old to be undergraduates. Perhaps they were doing postgrad degrees, or maybe they were on the first rungs of their careers. They had the bounce and energy of young men who

126

were still buoyed up with possibility.

They walked swiftly off the campus without a glance to either side. She followed them down the hill to the Spaghetti Factory on Gibson Street. Allie had been there a couple of times. There was a line of booths up one side; if the men chose one of them, she might be able to get close enough to eavesdrop. She didn't think they'd paid enough attention to her earlier to recognise her.

Allie hung back, pretending to study the menu while she watched where the men ended up. It could scarcely have been better. They'd gone for the booth farthest from the door. Although the restaurant was fairly busy, there was a half-booth beyond them that was vacant. She'd be sitting with her back to them, hidden by the high seat backs, but probably close enough to hear what they were saying. She hurried to the table, face averted from them and shrugged out of her coat.

The men ordered three pints of lager and, when the waitress returned with their beers, three pizzas with the speed of familiarity. Allie discovered that if she leaned right back in her chair, she could hear most of the conversation.

'Honest to Christ, what a bloody talking shop.' She recognised Deke's voice.

'If they'd had that much hot air on the *Titanic*, that iceberg would have stood no chance.'

The other two hooted with laughter. 'Nice one, Ding-dong,' Deke said.

'It's true, though. I mean, *leaflets*. Most folk throw them straight on the fire. We need to put on our thinking caps and come up with something with a bit more oomph.'

127

'But what? You're always saying that, Gary, but we never get any further.' The third voice was quieter, but all the more insistent for it.

'I know, Roddy. We need a plan. Look, let's put some serious thought into this. We'll go to the next round of meetings — all the bloody meetings — and we'll reconvene in the pub. And we'll each come up with a concrete idea, OK?' It was Gary, aka Ding-dong in the driving seat now.

'What? You're giving us homework?' Deke, incredulous.

'What's the alternative? We keep going to meetings just so's we can bitch about them afterwards?'

Deke guffawed. 'You got a point there, Ding-dong. OK. Next week it is. Now, what are the chances of the weather letting us get to the football tomorrow? Will we get some games or will we be stuck with the bloody pools panel?'

And they were off on one of those arcane sports conversations that might as well be in Swahili for all Allie understood or cared. Somehow it kept them going through their pizzas and another couple of rounds of drinks. Allie ate as slowly as she could, but in the end, she gave up on the hope that they might say something more interesting. She settled her bill and slipped out into the night.

All the way home, Deke's words at the meeting swirled round her head like a murmuration of starlings. *How do we make them pay attention the way they've been forced to do in Northern Ireland?*

18

Allie's long weekend ended at ten on Tuesday morning when she clocked on for the late day shift. She'd heard nothing from Danny since the meeting in Angus's office. She didn't want to admit it, but she was disappointed. She'd thought there was the start of something between them, but maybe that had been wishful thinking.

She'd barely got her coat off, however, when Danny appeared at her elbow with a couple of grease-stained paper bags. 'Bacon or Lorne?' he said.

Allie hadn't grown up on the square sliced sausage so beloved in the West of Scotland. Quite why something so chewy and fatty had attained its heroic status escaped her. 'Bacon,' she said without a moment's hesitation.

Danny shrugged. 'Win some, lose some. I had you down as a gourmet.' He passed her one of the bags and pulled out his own well-fired morning roll, brown sauce oozing over the edges of the Lorne sausage.

'What have I done to deserve this?' Allie bit into the roll, savouring the crispy bacon fat that burst into flavour on her tongue.

'We've got a meeting with the lawyer in half an hour. I thought you might need building up.'

She studied him as she ate. She wasn't the one who needed building up, she thought. There were dark smudges under his eyes and his fingernails were shorter than nail clippers could manage. 'Have you had much to do with the lawyer before?' she asked.

Danny shook his head. 'A couple of queries, that's all. Just clarifications. You?'

'I've never spoken to the guy. I presume it's a guy?'

'It's four different guys. They take it in turns.'

'Are you nervous?'

He looked incredulous. 'Why would I not be? This is the biggest deal of my career.'

Allie smiled, hoping she looked more reassuring than she felt. 'But the story's copper-bottomed. You've stood it up. You shouldn't be nervous, you should be walking in there like you're the king of the world and he's the footman.'

Danny shook his head, wondering. 'You've got more balls than me, Allie. No, let me rephrase that. You've got more balls than the entire day shift.'

'I've had more practice, that's all. I'm a woman in a Neanderthal's world. Every single day I have to face down somebody, just to prove I've got the right to be here.' She grinned, to take the edge off. 'You're already one step ahead of me. And your story's solid.'

He grunted. 'It's solid because you wrote it solid.'

'So, we're a team. It'll be fine, Danny.' Allie said it like she believed it.

★ ★ ★

Five minutes with the lawyer and she wasn't so sure. They met in Angus Carlyle's office — McGovern, Danny, Allie and Carlyle. The lawyer was a compact man somewhere around forty. Everything about him was neat and designed to put everyone else in their place — the parting in his perfectly barbered hair; the well-trimmed moustache; the smoothly ironed shirt; the knot in a tie that signified some affiliation that

130

those who mattered would recognise; the advocate's striped trousers and black waistcoat, bottom button undone; the French cuffs with the heavy gold links. He could have been the second lead in a fifties Hollywood movie — Cary Grant's best friend, James Stewart's sidekick, Katharine Hepburn's about-to-be-dumped fiancé. He greeted McGovern cordially. 'Peter, good to see you.' Then he turned to the others. 'We've not met. I'm Fraser Drummond. Fraser the Razor to my opponents. Because I'm so sharp.' A neat little triangular smile.

Carlyle stirred. 'Let's see how you do against Rock and Paper here.'

Drummond was flummoxed. 'Sorry?'

The news editor sighed. 'Rock, paper, scissors. Or in your case, razor.'

Drummond looked momentarily murderous. 'Quite. Now, to business. I've read the copy and I have some questions for you. This will take a while, so make yourselves comfortable.' He sat at the desk, pulled a pad towards him and uncapped a heavy gold pen.

The three reporters sat. Allie eyed the lawyer warily. She'd met men like him at Cambridge and time hadn't mellowed her feelings.

'How did you come across this story in the first place?' Drummond asked.

Danny looked at Carlyle, who nodded. He took a deep breath. 'My brother works at PII. Paragon Investment Insurance. We have a family dinner every Sunday and we were talking about how hard inflation is on most families. And my brother started boasting about how Paragon's clients didn't have to worry about inflation. That they had ways round it. So I went to Paragon and picked up a brochure and showed it

131

to Peter, who explained it to me. But it still didn't add up. So the next chance I got, I took a look in my brother's bedroom and I found a piece of paper with a list of names on it, a note of a large sum of money against each one and what sounded like the name of a racehorse.' Danny managed a tight smile. 'I know now they're the names of boats. There were a couple of other names too, which I later tracked down to boatyards. One in Southampton and one in Nassau in the Bahamas.'

Allie realised that the version Danny was giving the lawyer wasn't exactly how it happened. For a moment she wondered if that was accidental and whether she should correct him, but she chose to bide her time. And moments later, she was grateful she'd done it. Drummond's next question was, 'How did you start to make sense of all these fragments of information?'

'I spoke to Peter. And he pointed out that the men on the list are successful businessmen who all run companies that deal in large amounts of cash. We thought this might be a money laundering scheme.' Danny's voice cracked and he coughed. 'Sorry. Dry throat.'

Drummond studied him. Allie could feel her pulse racing; it wasn't hard to imagine how much worse it was for Danny. 'The copy mentions wads of cash. Did you actually see these 'wads of cash'?' His tone placed quotation marks round his words.

Danny took a deep breath. 'Yes. It was in used notes of mixed denominations. I have a pic.'

'And where did you see it?'

'In my brother's room. On a subsequent occasion. The day before he made one of his regular trips out of town. A trip I now know was to a boatyard in Southampton, where the yard owner confirmed that he knew my brother.'

This was a bigger lie. Allie understood why Danny was misleading the lawyer. If he confessed to secretly entering Paragon's offices, it would undermine the whole story. The dubious legality of how he'd obtained his evidence would be used by Paragon's lawyers to throw dust in everyone's eyes. Carlyle's eyes narrowed as Danny's words sank in. He knew the truth was being massaged.

But Carlyle was sitting out of Drummond's eyeline and the lawyer continued, oblivious. 'How do you know that money came from Paragon? How do you know it had ever been in their offices?'

'Where else would my brother get his hands on a hundred thousand pounds? My dad's a delivery driver, we grew up in a rented tenement in Gorgie. I've never seen a thousand pounds in notes, never mind a hundred thousand. It was in Joseph's briefcase. It goes to the office with him every morning and comes home with him every evening. The boat broker, he confirmed he deals with Paragon. That his arrangement is with them. My brother's just the messenger.'

Drummond sighed. 'It's not exactly proof, though, is it?'

'The note of the names and the details? It was on Paragon headed paper.'

Drummond tapped the end of his pen on his pad then turned to Carlyle. 'Who's doing the Paragon showdown?'

'Peter. Danny needs to keep his distance, we're trying to keep his brother out of it as far as we can.'

'Well, that's something to be grateful for. But Paragon might not be so considerate. What if they were to suggest that this scheme was nothing to do with them? That it was all the brainchild of your brother?'

Allie could almost feel the tension vibrating off Danny. Instinctively, she spoke. 'How would a junior clerk manage to run a scheme like this? Even if he'd worked it out, how would he get clients to come on board? Businessmen like these, they deal with the organ grinder, not the monkey. And how would he explain his monthly absences for his trips to Southampton? It would be a pretty feeble attempt at getting off the hook.'

Drummond raised one eyebrow. She wondered how long he'd practised that in the mirror. 'Good points, all of them. Peter, bear all Miss Burns' points in mind when you meet with Gregor Menstrie.' He turned to Carlyle. 'I presume Danny and Miss Burns will be doing the showdowns with the two most recent contributors to the scheme?'

Carlyle grunted his assent.

'And Southampton?'

'Gil Patterson from the London office.'

Drummond made a note. 'Good. Always reliable, young Gilbert. Now, I hate to tell you how to do your job, Angus, but I think it would be a good idea to send Miss Burns and Danny along to one of the men earmarked for a future transaction.'

After a long moment's silence, Allie asked, 'I don't understand. What's the point of that?'

Carlyle rolled his eyes and leaned forward. 'Sometimes I forget how new you are here. It's possible you and Danny will get nothing out of Brown or McGillivray except flat denials and the names of their lawyers. I'm hopeful that Gil will be able to persuade Maclays that it's in their best interests to confirm the scam for us and pretend they didn't really know what was going on, but if that doesn't work, our best chance is to go for the ones who haven't committed their crimes yet. You explain to them that we're about to run the story, and we've been told that they were among the businessmen who were approached, but we understand they decided not to touch it with a bargepole. And we'd like to show people that there are honest businessmen around, blah, blah, bloody blah. And so we get our confirmation that way. Do you see?'

Allie nodded, feeling stupid. 'I get it.'

Carlyle's answering smile was surprisingly warm. 'Lucky for you the lassie was here to ask the question, eh, Danny? Right away youse go and make your arrangements. Simultaneous showdowns, please.'

In the corridor, Danny leaned against the wall, faint patches of colour reappearing in his cheeks. Peter strolled past, one hand in his jacket pocket, already taking out the Café Crème tin. 'I'm away to the pub, I'll see you later. Shall we say ten for the showdowns?' He didn't wait for a reply.

'Let's go down to the canteen,' Allie suggested. 'We'll get more peace there than in the newsroom.'

They huddled in a corner, hunched over milky coffee. 'Pushy bastard, Fraser the Razor,' Danny said.

'If it ever came to a court case, the other side's lawyers would be a lot more pushy.'

'I suppose.' He let out a puff of breath. 'At least they didn't kick it into touch.'

'And you got away with avoiding the whole truth and nothing but the truth.' Her smile was wry.

Danny glanced up momentarily. 'I could hardly tell him nothing but the truth. I'd have been pulling the rug out from under my own feet.'

'But you had keys. It's not like you broke in. And

135

you didn't steal anything.'

Danny shrugged. 'I had no right to be there, though. It makes us look like the bad guys.'

Allie wasn't comfortable with the deception, but accepted it wasn't her decision. 'How are we going to set up the showdowns? I've never done anything like this before.'

Danny smiled. 'I've got a wee idea about how we do that.'

19

Wednesday morning at quarter to ten found Allie walking past the sandstone facade of the County Buildings in Ayr, plastered with sleet by a vicious east wind. When she'd called to make her appointment with Brian McGillivray, the receptionist at WestBet had told her, 'It's just past the county offices on the opposite side of Wellington Street, you can't miss it.' If Allie had realised how long the County Buildings were, she wouldn't have parked so close to the seafront. By the time she spotted the handsome double-fronted stuccoed building with its garish WestBet sign, she felt nothing like a tough investigative reporter ready to confront a criminal.

A heavy wooden front door stood open, leading to a small vestibule and a half-glazed door beyond, its brass fittings buffed and polished. Allie tried the handle, but it was locked. She pressed a bell push on the jamb and heard a distant peal. Through the glass, she saw approaching a compact middle-aged woman with a tight perm, a tweed skirt and a pale pink twin-set. The woman peered at her, then opened the door. 'You'll be Alison Burns,' she said. 'Come away in, you must be perishing.'

Allie followed her inside, conscious of melted sleet dripping from her short dark hair. 'I look like a drowned rat,' she said, apologetic.

The woman glanced at her wristwatch. 'You've got ten minutes before His Nibs is expecting you.' She pointed down the hall. 'There's a ladies lavatory down

137

there, away and give your hair a rub with a towel.'

Seven minutes later, Allie returned, hair still damp but less like an orphan of the storm. 'Thank you.'

'Nae bother. You don't want to make a bad first impression. Follow me.'

Allie obeyed and they climbed a flight of stairs, the bannisters and treads gleaming with polish. The woman showed Allie into the middle room facing the street, its walls decorated with photographs of horse races, jockeys' silks garish. 'Mr M, it's the lady from the paper,' she said, closing the door behind her and leaving Allie facing a dapper middle-aged man sitting behind a massive mahogany desk. His suit was the height of fashion with wide lapels and shoulder pads, but the shade of blue was too startling, and he'd have looked better in the next size up. His mousy hair curled over his collar and was carefully arranged to disguise how far it was receding from his temples. 'So,' he said. 'Alison. Take a seat.'

There were two visitors' chairs, both lower than McGillivray's. It was a pathetic ploy, she thought. It made her feel less bad about employing Danny's suggestion for how to persuade him to agree to an interview. 'Thanks for agreeing to talk to me,' she said, her smile stopping a fraction short of a simper.

'I'm very flattered that you're here on a day when there's such important news.'

Allie panicked momentarily. What had she missed? 'Important news?'

'The Abba divorce. Goodnight, Vienna for Agnetha and Bjorn.' He looked smug.

'Oh.' *Eejit*. 'I don't cover showbiz, so it's not a burden on my shoulders.'

'That's a pity, I was hoping for some inside gossip.

138

I'll just have to settle for feeling proud that you consider me one of Scotland's leading entrepreneurs.' He delivered the word with a flourish.

'Well, you can hardly walk down a High Street without seeing a WestBet shopfront. And we're eager to hear what business leaders think of the upcoming referendum.' Allie rummaged in her bag and took out the little Sony Pressman she'd treated herself to when she'd got the *Clarion* job. 'Do you mind if I record this? I'd hate to misquote you.' She waved it at him.

'That's a neat wee thing,' he said. 'Sure, be my guest.' An expansive gesture. 'Better safe than sorry.'

Allie pressed 'record' as he opened a wooden cigarette box on his desk and offered it to her. 'No thanks.'

'Sensible lassie,' he said, lighting his own. 'Makes your breath smell. Nobody wants to kiss a lassie who smells like an ashtray.'

Or a *man*, she thought. 'Mr McGillivray — '

'Brian,' he interrupted. 'We're all friends here, Alison.'

Another smile. 'Brian. Can I ask which way you'll be voting in the referendum?'

He took a deep drag of his cigarette. 'I make no secret of that, Alison. It's a big thumbs-down from me.' He delivered his verdict as if it were unassailable.

'Why is that?'

'It's pretty obvious if you're a businessman like me. MPs' salaries and expenses, new buildings, secretaries and security men. And how's that going to be paid for? The likes of you and me, Alison. We're the ones that are going to be paying for somebody else to do the job the British government are already doing.' He waved the hand holding his cigarette so the smoke swirled around his head.

'You don't think Scotland deserves a bigger say in its own affairs?'

McGillivray snorted. 'Have you ever actually met any of our MPs? I wouldnae trust them to back the winner in a one-horse race. Noses in the trough, the lot of them. And the state of the country? Unions holding us to ransom, fish and fruit rotting at the docks, supermarket shelves empty? No, we've got enough government in this country as it is.' He was warming to his theme. 'The Labour Party couldnae run a raffle, and none of the others are any better. Give us a parliament with one hand and take more taxes with the other. As if they don't rob us enough now.'

He was almost making this too easy. 'It sounds like you don't agree with this government's tax regime?'

'Are you kidding me? Do you have any idea how much tax we pay in this country? We've got a top rate of 83 per cent. Every pound I earn above a certain amount, I get to keep 17p. Big fat hairy deal. It's like they're saying to guys like me, 'Don't get above yourself." He shook his head. 'So, no. I don't want to spend more money on politicians.'

'Do your accountants not help you to save money?'

He scoffed. 'Pennies. It's daylight robbery, I tell you.'

Allie took a deep breath. 'Is that why you sought advice from Paragon Investment Insurance?'

McGillvray's face closed tight as if a shutter had been pulled down. He crushed out his cigarette savagely. 'Sorry?'

'Is that why you decided to take part in Paragon's money laundering scheme? The one that helps you evade your tax responsibilities?'

He sat still as a statue, his eyes glittering as they

watched her.

Allie persisted. 'We know you paid a hundred thousand pounds in cash to a boatyard on Southampton Water. Maclays boatyard. That money bought a boat called *Meridian Flyer*. It was sailed across the Atlantic to a boat brokerage in Nassau, where it was bought for cash. Nassau has a famously secretive banking regime. No tax either, on funds like that.'

He inhaled sharply then gave a tight bark of laughter. 'I thought you were a journalist, not a fairy story writer.'

'We're running the story tomorrow. This is your chance to put your side of it. '

'This is a steaming pile of shite. You'll get the arse sued off you if you print a word of this.'

'It might be hard for you to manage that from a prison cell,' she said, sounding infinitely more calm than she felt. 'What you've participated in, it's fraud. It's tax evasion. Al Capone was the biggest gangster in America, but they never got him for masterminding murder or robbery or gun-running. He went to jail for fiddling his taxes. And knowing what we know, I'd say that's where you're headed.' She wasn't quite sure where her nerve was coming from but it wasn't deserting her.

'You've got no evidence. You've got no evidence because this is a pack of lies.'

'We know you're a client of Paragon. We know Paragon brokers the deals and we know they handed over a hundred grand of your money to Maclays just the other week. I don't know if your boat's in Nassau yet, but you'd better hope it is before the Royal Navy seize it on the high seas and confiscate it.'

'Get out,' he said, his voice low and dark. 'Get the

fuck out of my office, you lying little bitch.'

Allie refused to back down in spite of a shiver of apprehension. 'If I was you, I'd seriously consider talking to me. Maybe you didn't know what Paragon were up to. Maybe you're the kind of innocent who trusts an investment firm even when the deal they're offering sounds too good to be true. Me, I'd rather people thought I was stupid than crooked.'

McGillivray's face had turned dark red. 'You've got nothing on me. This is just a daft wee lassie's fishing trip.'

Allie grinned. 'Stupid *and* crooked. I hadn't considered that possibility. In that case, there's probably nothing I can do for you, Brian.' She got to her feet. 'Enjoy tomorrow's *Clarion*.' She stood up and turned for the door.

'You've no idea who you're dealing with here, do you?' His voice was thick and angry. She suspected he'd forgotten about the tape recorder. 'I know people that'll make you wish you'd never been born.'

Allie looked over her shoulder and what she saw sent a frisson of real fear through her. He was on his feet, the veneer of affable civility wiped away. She saw the street fighter beneath, the man who had clawed his way to the top of a cut-throat business. 'Thanks for your time,' she said, getting out while the going was good. She hurried down the stairs and out the front door. Then she broke into a run and didn't stop until she was safely behind the wheel of her car with the door locked.

Then Allie let the fear in, her hands trembling and her teeth chattering, her legs too weak to drive. She felt the opposite of heroic. There had been genuine menace in McGillivray. For the first time since she'd started in journalism, Allie understood the power of a threat. Nobody had ever raised a hand to her in anger. Her vulnerability had always been in her imagination; footsteps behind her on a dark street, the unexplained noises of an old building late at night, the drunken leering of an idiot at a party. This, though — this was different. This felt real.

She turned off her tape recorder and wondered how Danny was faring. Part of her hoped he was celebrating forcing an admission from Graeme Brown; but the part of her she was ashamed of hoped he was sitting in his car shaking as hard as she was.

20

They met in a half-empty pub in Dunoon that smelled of wet dog, cigarette smoke and sour beer. Danny was frowning into a half-empty pint glass of flat lager when Allie arrived. 'How did it go?' she greeted him, collapsing on to the ancient chair opposite.

He raised his eyes and shrugged. 'Water off a duck's back. He basically said nothing at all. Referred me to his lawyer and showed me the door. Did you do any better?'

'He got angry. And then he threatened me.' She took out her tape recorder and waved it in front of Danny. 'I've got it all on tape. He denied it, but he lost the heid and said the kind of things you don't say if you're whiter than white.'

Danny brightened. 'That's a start. Here, let me get you a drink. What'll you have?'

'Vodka and tomato juice. That's the only kind of lunch I'm going to be able to keep down after that ferry crossing.'

Danny grinned. 'A bit rough for you, was it?'

'Not so much rough as wallowing like a big fat hippo in a muddy pond. And the state of the toilets?' Allie pulled a face and made a retching sound. She watched him cross to the bar, thinking again that there was something about him she really liked. It wasn't only that he was probably the most attractive man in the newsroom. It was more to do with his refusal to play the macho game; he wasn't ashamed to let her see his nerves come close to getting the better of him.

And he was willing to ask for help when he needed it. Even help from a woman.

Danny came back with her drink. 'I wonder how Peter got on?'

'I asked when I phoned the newsdesk to bring the boss up to speed. But he'd not been in touch. Let's hope he managed to get Menstrie to cave in. I get the feeling he knows the right buttons to press when it comes to dealing with bent businessmen like him.' She took a swig of her drink and checked her watch. 'Did you say two o'clock to Brodie?'

'Yeah. I checked out his address. The office is above his amusement arcade on Argyll Street. About three minutes' walk.'

They took their time finishing their drinks and going through their strategy one more time then set off through the gloomy afternoon. The door to Wilson Brodie's office was tucked away unobtrusively between a hardware store and the garish lights of the amusement arcade with its neon promises. There was no brass plate, just the number on the door. 'You sure this is right?' Allie asked, finger poised over the bell.

'This is the address he gave me.'

Allie rang the bell, wincing as a drip fell from the gutter above and slithered down the side of her neck. 'I hate winter,' she muttered.

The door was opened by a skinny youth in flared jeans and a grubby Aran jumper. 'Youse here for Wilson?' he demanded.

'That's right. Mr Brodie's expecting us.'

'Right. You're the reporters, right? How come there's two of you? And not a photographer?'

Another drip assaulted Allie. 'We're like the polis. We go around in pairs. Now, can we come inside or will we just keep Mr Brodie waiting a bit longer?'

The lad stepped aside and waved them in as elaborately as a bewigged flunkey. 'Up youse go.' His tone was nippier than his gesture.

'We'll get a photographer along another day.' Danny's tone was diplomatic as he followed Allie upstairs.

As they rounded the final flight, they came face to face with a baby-faced man in his mid-thirties. His halo of permed hair wouldn't have looked out of place on a celebrity footballer. Dark tailored slacks, open-necked pink shirt under a mauve V-necked sweater in fine wool. 'I'm Wilson Brodie. Sorry about wee Ednie,' he said. 'I'm trying to train him up, but honest to God, I sometimes think a monkey would be easier.'

The young man growled behind Allie's back.

'Away down the stairs and make sure Big Sandra's not cheating me on the bingo.' Brodie turned into the only open door on the landing. The desk sat over in one corner. Filing cabinets lined one side wall and a garish 1950s pinball machine dominated the room with its primary colours and flashing lights. They followed him in and he pointed to a couple of folding chairs propped in the corner. 'Grab a seat.' He dropped into his own luxurious leather chair and lounged casually in its embrace.

They did as they were told and perched on the narrow wooden seats. 'Thanks for seeing us,' Allie said, taking out her recorder. 'Do you mind if I record this? In the interests of accuracy?'

'You're worried you might misquote me on the referendum? That's not a hanging offence, darling.' His sardonic smile turned his cherubic looks sinister.

'I like to think of it as an archive of my interviews,' she said. 'In case I decide to write a memoir one day.'

146

Brodie guffawed. 'I like you. You're smart.'

'Nice of you to say so.' Allie made a show of hesitating. 'Look, I need to level with you, Mr Brodie. We're here under false pretences.'

He tilted his head to one side. 'What? You're Jehovah's Witnesses, here to tell me about Jesus? That's some length to go to.'

Danny took over. 'We're here because we're about to run a story about a money laundering scheme.'

At his words, Brodie straightened up, his face stripped of all bonhomie. 'You've come to the wrong place. It breaks my heart, but I bend over like a good girl and let the taxman screw me over.'

Allie smiled and found her most reassuring tone. 'We know, Mr Brodie. That's why we want to talk to you. Our sources tell us that you were one of the leading businessmen approached by Paragon Investment Insurance and invited to join their tax evasion scheme. But you said no.'

A long silence. Nobody moved. Nobody even blinked. Then Brodie waved his hand dismissively. 'I think you've got the wrong guy.' He cleared his throat, his eyes flicking back and forth between the pair of them.

Danny sighed and shook his head. 'Your name's on a list. Alongside a six-figure sum. Round about the same amount Celtic paid Kilmarnock for Davie Provan last year, in fact.'

Brodie seemed to hunch into himself.

Danny continued. 'Only you're not in the football transfer market, Wilson. You were headed for a different kind of transfer market. One where your money turned into a luxury yacht and then magically turned back into a pile of money in a bank in the Bahamas.'

'I never did anything wrong,' Brodie bleated.

'No, but you were going to,' Allie said, keeping her tone conversational. 'In legal terms, that's what's called a conspiracy. Not many people know this but when it comes to jail time, you can actually get more for a conspiracy than for the offence you were conspiring to commit. That would be a killer, wouldn't it? Gregor Menstrie gets five years and you go down for ten.'

Brodie's forehead gleamed under a sheen of sweat. His dark blond curls seemed to wilt before their eyes. 'You're trying to scare me,' he said, lips tight against his teeth.

Allie scoffed. 'You've got us all wrong. We're here to help you. We know you're in this up to your oxters, but right now, you're still in the clear. You haven't handed over the money yet. You can come out of this ahead, Wilson. You tell us everything, and we paint you as the good guy. The one who did the right thing.'

He snorted. 'Aye, right. And what's going to happen to me then? Just say I had any beans to spill and I spilled them, how's that going to go down? I like being able to walk, darling.'

Danny pulled his chair forward, the legs scraping the floor tiles. He found a hard edge in his voice. 'This is an insurance company, not the Mafia. Trust me, these guys are going down. We have the evidence. Your choice right now is whether you come out of this smelling of roses or chin deep in shite.' He shrugged. 'Up to you, pal.'

'And by the way,' Allie chipped in. 'I might be here to save your sorry arse, but I'm not your darling. So what's it to be, Wilson?'

21

Allie didn't get as far as hanging up her coat. As she approached the newsdesk, Carlyle's secretary caught her eye and said, 'They're all in the conference room. Typewriters set up and everything.'

They were all there — Danny, worried frown; McGovern, leaning back in his chair, cigarillo on the go, filling the room with blue smoke; Carlyle, feet on the desk, deep in some copy; and Frazer the Razor in the corner, issuing instructions down the phone to remind everyone how important he was. Four pairs of eyes turned to her and Carlyle waved the thin sheaf of paper at her.

'Gil did a fine job down in Southampton. He persuaded the Maclay lad if he spilled the lot, he'd get off more lightly.'

'Works so often,' McGovern said. 'You'd think folk would have learned by now what a load of bollocks that line is.'

Carlyle's grin was evil. 'Lucky for us they're so gullible. Anyway, he told Gil how he met Gregor Menstrie at the Southampton Boat Show back in 1977, how they went on the piss together and Menstrie talked him into his little scheme. They've pulled it off a dozen times now. Maclay even showed Gil the list of names. It's like a Who's Who of dodgy Scottish businessmen. Who knew there was that much cash swilling round our poor benighted country?'

'It's the oil, isn't it?' McGovern said. 'Half the names on that list are connected with the oil business one way or another. God, this country could be rich if we were cut loose from those bastards down south, always going on strike at the drop of a hat.'

'Maybe so, but we'll leave the politics out of this,' Carlyle ruled. 'This story's strong enough on its own. Danny did the groundwork and now Gil's nailed it down. He's putting in a call to Conrad Jespersen in' — he consulted his watch — 'about an hour. It doesn't matter if he blows us out, we've got more than enough to run with.' He stood up and hoisted his trousers somewhere in the region of where his waist might once have been. 'Danny, Peter — type up your interviews. Burns, bring yourself up to speed with Gil's copy.' He thrust the pages at her. 'Soon as you've pulled all the interviews together, get writing. Two parts. First part, the scam and the set-up. Second part, we name the dirty dodgers. Then I'll have my fight with the lawyers. We'll hold back on running it till Friday and Saturday so we've got time to get the rewrites done so we give it a good show in Friday's paper.' He made for the door then paused, swinging round to turn the full beam of his most serious stare on Allie. 'This is your big chance, Burns. Don't let me down.'

The news editor marched out, head thrust forward at a determined angle. Danny sat down behind one of the typewriters and rolled a copy pad on to the platen. McGovern pulled a sheaf of paper from his inside pocket. 'I knocked my copy out on my portable as soon as I'd done the interview. They keep it behind the bar at the Printer's Pie for me.' He laid it down beside a vacant typewriter and gestured towards Allie.

Her mouth was dry with apprehension at the scale of the task before her. She cleared her throat and tried to look as if this was just another routine story. 'Danny, can you write up our interview with Wilson Brodie first?' Allie asked, moving to the other typewriter. 'I think we need that for today's piece. We can put him front and centre as the main source for the way the system works. Points the finger away from Paragon a bit?'

Danny nodded. 'Sure.'

'And has anybody got the original copy? From memory, I think we can stick with the opening pars.'

The lawyer stirred. 'I've got a set here.' He picked up a sheaf of papers and proffered them, making no move to bring them to her. Before Allie could cross the room to him, Danny was on his feet, snatching the pages from the lawyer and taking them to her.

What was it about guys and their games? Always jockeying for position, always establishing the pecking order. It must be exhausting, Allie thought. But as she inserted a fresh pad into the typewriter, it occurred to her that women did exactly the same thing. Only the style was different. She laid the first page of her draft next to her and began typing.

'Not so fast, young lady.' It was McGovern.

She looked up, puzzled.

'The byline. You've got it wrong. It should read 'By Daniel Sullivan and Peter McGovern, with additional reporting by Gilbert Patterson and Alison Burns.''

This was too much. For once, she wasn't going to defer to a senior reporter. 'Are you kidding me? Whatever Danny offered you at the start, you only did one interview. I've done two interviews *and* I'm writing the copy.'

McGovern shrugged. 'Danny and I had an agreement. Without my advice, he'd never have put the story together. Just because Angus is giving you a chance to see whether you're up to playing with the first team doesn't mean you get the star billing.' McGovern would probably have described his smile as 'avuncular'. Allie's word would have been, 'condescending'.

'Children, can you save this for the pub?' Fraser Drummond butted in. 'I need all the time I can get to go through this with a fine-tooth comb. The last thing we want is for us all to end up in the witness box because I had to rush to judgement. So can we just get the bloody story written?'

McGovern headed for the door. 'If you need me, I'll be in the bar.'

Allie let out a long sigh. She re-read her original story and decided the first six paragraphs were as good as they were going to get. Then she began hammering the keys.

One of the men who turned down the approach of Paragon boss Gregor Menstrie has revealed the workings of the scheme to *Clarion* reporters.

Menstrie offered amusement arcade king Wilson Brodie membership of an exclusive scheme to beat the taxman over dinner at Glasgow's prestigious Ubiquitous Chip restaurant. The two men met at the exclusive Ashton Lane eatery last summer.

Brodie said, 'I thought we were meeting to talk about investment opportunities. I run a very successful business and I was looking for ways to make my money grow. I wasn't expecting him to try to draw me into a conspiracy to defraud the taxman.

'Some people might think the business I'm in isn't as respectable as running a bank or a chain of shops. But I'm an honest man and I run a chain of honest businesses. I was shocked that a man like Gregor Menstrie would be running a crooked game like this. And even more shocked that he'd think I was the kind of man who would want to be part of it.'

We asked Mr Brodie why he thought Menstrie might have invited him aboard. 'I honestly don't know,' he said. 'The only thing I can think of is that ours is a cash business. I declare my turnover and my profits to the taxman but if I was a crook, I could easily syphon off some of that cash and keep it for myself.

'To be honest, I was insulted by his offer. I wish I'd walked out as soon as he started hinting at it, but I was curious. So I let him explain how the scheme works. He was adamant that it was foolproof. According to him, I could launder massive amounts of cash and end up with a big nest egg that the taxman couldn't touch.'

She was over the first fence and away. The words flowed, a flying carpet carrying Allie along, oblivious to everything except the bundles of other people's copy that were the threads she had to draw together. And the flow would continue all the way to the presses the following night, ink pouring on to newsprint, guillotines slicing the rolls into pages and binders folding those pages into the next day's *Clarion*. Then, breaking into bundles like waves breaking against rocks, into liveried vans and trucks, train wagons and island ferries, carrying Allie's words to millions of eyes, the *Clarion* went about its daily business.

22

By the time they made it to the Printer's Pie late on Thursday, the first edition had landed and every journalist still at the bar knew Danny was the hero of the night, with Allie a surprising second. Their glasses had no chance to empty; for once, all the shades of the newsroom from mild disdain to contempt were set in abeyance and they were the toast of the place. Allie grinned at Danny, both flushed with delight.

When last orders were called, a handful of the hardcore hacks were all for taking the celebration on to the Press Club. Allie shook her head. 'I don't want a sore head in the morning. There's going to be fallout from this. And the editor's still got to sign off on part two.' She could see the bonhomie start to drain away; any minute, she'd be back to being a killjoy woman.

Danny came to her rescue. 'She's right, boys,' he said, spreading his hands in a gesture of regret. 'There'll be plenty chance to celebrate when the polis start hauling folk out of their big houses and into the cells.' He drained his pint and shepherded Allie to the door, accompanied by wolf whistles from a couple of the drinkers and a V-sign from Danny.

The cold hit them like a slap. Danny moved to the kerb, scanning the Clydeside for a passing taxi. They didn't have long to wait. Danny opened the door for her and made to close it. 'You not coming?' Allie asked.

'We're going in opposite directions,' he said, putting the door between them with a heavy thud.

It was the truth. But Allie, still fizzing with the exhilaration of the night's work, had let herself hope for a different ending. She scolded herself in the back of the cab for not being satisfied with her part in a job well done, and pulled out her copy of the paper to remind herself. She didn't have the splash byline — that had been reserved to Danny and Peter, on the grounds of space. But there she was on the two-page spread on pages four and five — 'Additional reporting by Gilbert Patterson and Alison Burns'. It was less than she deserved, she thought. But she'd set down a marker in the newsroom today. It would be hard to dismiss her and relegate her to miracle babies after this, surely?

* * *

There was a residual buzz in the newsroom on Friday morning. It was always the same when an exclusive hit the streets. Everybody knew the opposition would be playing catch-up, trying to find their own angle on the story that had made the morning bulletins on the commercial radio stations as well as the BBC's Good Morning, Scotland. And the other reporters would be scrambling through their contacts books in a bid to find something that would help them reclaim their place in the perceived hierarchy.

Allie barely had the chance to acknowledge a couple of grudging congratulations before she was summoned back to the meeting room where she'd hammered out the story. Danny was there already, eyes faintly pink, face peaky. Fraser the Razor was sitting on the deep windowsill, smugly holding forth. Danny kept slumping down in his chair, then collecting himself with a start, legs and arms struggling to find a comfortable position.

'Ah, Miss Burns,' the Razor greeted her. 'Nice of you to join us. I've been through your copy for part two, and there are one or two revisions you need to make. It's important we don't stray into potentially expensive speculation.' He stood up and thrust a bundle of copy at her. 'I'm off to hold Angus's hand. The police are apparently on their way for a full and frank conversation with him. I suggest you get your copy sorted out asap. Angus may want to spirit you away out of the reach of the long arm of the law till we get part two out on the streets.' He gave her a wolfish grin. 'Get to it, Miss Burns.'

Danny watched him leave with a jaundiced eye. 'What an arse,' he muttered.

'You look like shit,' Allie observed mildly, rolling a fresh copy pad into the typewriter. 'I thought you were heading straight home last night?'

He looked shifty. 'Changed my mind.'

'Don't tell me you went to the Press Club with the professional drinkers?' She typed the bylines as she spoke.

Danny screwed up his face in disgust. 'I'm not that stupid. I hooked up with a couple of pals in a wee club I know up the town. I made the mistake of telling them I was celebrating . . .' He groaned.

Allie chuckled. 'Serves you right.' She read through the notes the Razor had scribbled on her copy. 'Bastard's taken out some of my best lines.' Sighing, she started reworking the story. It wasn't a quiet business. The keys clattered, the type bars hammered the paper, the bell rang at the end of each line and the carriage return ratcheted its noisy way back to the beginning.

'Fuck's sake,' Danny muttered. 'You'd think, given how many hangovers journalists have to put up with that somebody would have invented a silent typewriter by now.'

'Electric ones are a lot quieter,' Allie said absently.

Danny scoffed. 'I don't see the management springing for them any time soon. Plus, can you imagine the likes of Big Kenny Stone with an electric typewriter? He'd have it battered to death in a matter of days.'

'Do something useful, then. Go and get me a coffee.'

Danny looked momentarily disconcerted then managed a wry smile. 'Fair enough,' he said, hauling himself up like a bag of golf clubs straightening itself.

Left to herself, Allie drilled down and focused on the lawyer's demands. By the time Danny returned, she was on the home straight. He began to speak, but she cut across him. 'Gimme a minute, I need to get the ending just right.' She clattered her way to the end of the paragraph, pulled out the copy pad and gave a shuddering sigh. 'That's it,' she said. 'I managed to do all that the Razor wanted and still keep it buzzing along.' She tossed the pads across to Danny. 'Take a look, tell me if you see any problems.'

Danny picked up the copy and read it with meticulous attention while Allie lit a cigarette and leaned back in her chair. She didn't really want the coffee she'd sent Danny for, but she made a show of drinking from the thick white mug. She felt curiously deflated. The work was done; there would be repercussions, but they'd probably not be hers to handle. It had been a great ride, but now the horses were back in the stable and she'd have to find her next mount.

He looked up from the last page. 'Great job, Allie. I

couldn't have given it the spin like you do.' He began to split the pads into their individual copies.

She knew it was nothing less than the truth. 'We're a good team.'

Danny opened the door and shouted, 'Copy.' He turned back to her. 'Now we just need another belter to make sure nobody forgets we're the top dogs.'

'I might have a wee notion about that.'

He raised his eyebrows in a question, but before he could say more, one of the elderly copy boys stuck his head round the door. Danny handed him the copies. 'Take them round, Sammy.' Before he could ask Allie what she had in mind, the phone on the table rang, startling them both.

She was closest. Before she could speak, the news-desk secretary said, 'Call for Danny, I'm putting it through.' Allie held the handset out to him.

'It's for you.'

Danny's smile had a whiff of anxiety about it. 'Daniel Sullivan,' he said, making it a question. Whatever the response was, it was clearly unwelcome. He flushed dark red from the neck up, then almost immediately paled again. Allie could hear a raised male voice but the words were indistinct.

'I can't discuss this now,' Danny stammered. 'Can we talk about this — '

Whoever was on the line wasn't in the mood to wait. And they had plenty to say. Danny kept trying to interject but his caller continued to overwhelm him. At last, he ran out of steam. 'If you're that worried, you should get your side of the story in first.' Danny gabbled, eyes wide and panicked, sweat greasing his forehead. 'I've done my best to keep you out of it — ' Again the caller took off on a rant. But this time Danny was more insistent. 'Play the innocent. You were just the messenger,' he shouted. 'For once, don't act the big man.' And he slammed down the phone.

The silence that followed had an almost physical presence. Danny screwed his eyes tight shut and sank into a chair. 'I'm guessing that was Joseph?' Allie said, her voice soft.

He nodded. 'He's raging. Well, what he actually is is shit scared, but he always hides it behind his temper. Always has.'

'Surely he must realise you've done all you can to protect him?'

Danny scoffed, shaking his head. 'Not my brother. All he sees is his house of cards collapsing round his ears because of me. And what makes it worse, according to him, is that I didn't give him any warning.' He threw his hands up in a gesture of despair. 'I mean, what difference would that have made?'

'None. His best defence is looking as stunned as everybody else. Unless he's a better actor than Robert De Niro, he'd never have been able to pull it off if you'd marked his card. Did he say what's happening at Paragon?'

'Gregor Menstrie's a no-show at the office. Everybody's running around like headless chickens. Apparently almost nobody knew about the scheme, so they're all freaking out.' He groaned, head in hands. 'What have I done, Allie?'

'The right thing. And you've done your best to protect Joseph. Which, incidentally, I don't think he deserves. But he's your brother, and you needed to do what you could for him. And you're still doing that, by the way. What you told him just now? That's the best advice you could have given him.'

'I don't think he's listening to me right now.'

Before Allie could say more, the door opened a crack and the newsdesk secretary slipped in. 'Message from Angus,' she said. 'He's in with the polis and they're not very happy. He doesn't want you to talk to them till tomorrow's paper hits the street, so you've to go out the editor's stairs right now. You've not to go home. I've booked you a couple of rooms at the Ivanhoe up at the top of Buchanan Street for tonight and Angus says you've to get anything you need on expenses. Zat clear?'

Allie was taken aback. She'd never imagined this would be the outcome of an investigation. It felt over-dramatic, as if they were all playing preset roles in a script. 'We're on the run?'

The secretary rolled her eyes. 'Who do you think you are? Princess Leia? You just need to stay out the road till the story lands. And one of you needs to be on the end of a phone at all times.'

Danny nodded. 'Could you not have booked us in somewhere a wee bit classier?'

'It's not a jolly. Besides, nobody's going to look for youse in a dive like that.'

23

The secretary hadn't been joking about the Ivanhoe. Its grand entrance was broadly in keeping with the vast House of Fraser department store at the bottom of Buchanan Street. The unloved interior owed more to the dingier end of Sauchiehall Street, where Danny had found himself not long after they'd checked in. 'I need a walk to clear my head,' he'd told Allie. 'Can you hold the fort for an hour?'

Head down, he wove through the crowds braving the icy pavements and the shelves stripped bare by a combination of panic buying and the weather breaking the links in the supply chain. His brother's words echoed in his head, refusing to grant him peace. 'Selfish fucking bastard,' Joseph had said. 'I knew you were jealous of me, but I never thought you'd go this far. How could you do this? I could go to the jail over this.'

Even if he could have elbowed a word in sideways, Danny had understood the futility of reminding his brother that he was the one who'd chosen the path of criminality. 'You've destroyed me,' Joseph had continued. 'Not just me either. You should have seen our mother's face when Dad showed her the paper this morning. I thought she was going to collapse. You snivelling wee ... shite.' The last condemnation delivered at top volume.

As always, Joseph knew how to cause the most damage. As if Danny hadn't spent days and nights fretting about what his revelations would do to the family. He knew his mother would be distraught. In his head, he ran through the rationale he longed to give his parents. His story would bring down a group of greedy men who weren't just criminal but also completely immoral. Nobody wanted to pay massive taxes. But if you lived in a society, you paid the price of keeping the show on the road. If you didn't like the price, you used the ballot box or you went and lived in some other country that didn't believe in the rich holding out a hand to the poor. He needed his mother to hear this from him, to counter whatever lies and deceptions Joseph had practised on her.

He feared it would be a waste of breath.

His internal argument had taken him almost to the red sandstone tenements of Charing Cross and the motorway that sliced through Sauchiehall Street. He made his mind up and turned abruptly, almost cannoning into a couple of young women cocooned in fun fur and leg warmers. They shouted their outrage as he pushed past. On any other day, he'd have paused and apologised.

Not today. He had more pressing matters to attend to.

★ ★ ★

Allie paced her cramped bedroom. The floral air freshener caught the back of her throat but it didn't dispel the underlying odours of other people's lives. She was going to go mad cooped up here all day with nothing to do, nothing to read. She'd thought she'd at least have Danny for company, but he'd abandoned her within minutes of them checking in. Frustrated, she'd shoved a note under his door asking him to call her as soon as he returned so she could run up to John Smith's bookshop on St Vincent Street to buy a book. Maybe even swing by Marks and Spencer to get clean underwear?

She threw herself on the shiny nylon bedspread, nearly sliding off as she shifted position. It was hard not to feel deflated after the excitement of the past few days. Was there any way she could sneak out and get to the meeting of the radical independence group that evening? The trio of turbulent young men would presumably be talking up the ideas they'd had over the week. It infuriated her that she wouldn't be able to find out what they were up to. If they were up to anything, she consoled herself. They wouldn't be the first young men on the fringes of events who talked a great game and produced nothing.

When the phone rang, she almost ended up in a heap on the floor. 'Hello,' she gasped once she'd grabbed the handset.

'Is that you, Allie?'

It wasn't Danny. It was better than Danny. 'Rona?'

'The same.'

'How did you know I was here?'

She chuckled. 'Secretaries know everything and they love showing off that they know everything. Is the Ivanhoe still possessed of all the charm of a rugby player's jockstrap?'

'That would be an improvement.'

'Doesn't seem fair. You've cracked the biggest story of the year so far and they've put you in that dump.'

'Angus thinks the polis won't come looking for us here.'

Rona groaned. 'The depressing thing is, he's probably right. Listen, I know you're under the cosh today, but we should celebrate your rise to the stars.'

Allie snorted. 'It'll be forgotten by Monday.'

'All the more reason to make the most of it. Lunch tomorrow work for you?'

Allie didn't hesitate. 'Perfect.'

'And afterwards, I'm going to take you shopping. Honest to God, Allie, your wardrobe needs some serious attention.'

'What do you mean?'

'Don't get all huffy on me. You're not making the most of yourself, doll. I don't mean you should dress like one of the secretaries, all tight skirts and peerie heels. But you've got the looks, you should make the most of them. I'll show you what I mean tomorrow. If you hate the idea, we'll just have a very long lunch instead.'

Intrigued in spite of herself, Allie gave a hesitant, 'OK. Just so long as we can swing by a record shop and pick up Elvis Costello's new album.'

'I think we can probably manage that. So, meet me at Rogano's tomorrow at one and we'll have fun.' And she was gone. Allie couldn't help grinning. She barely knew Rona but she knew enough to realise that when she promised fun, she meant it.

★ ★ ★

Danny's determination had survived his return march to the hotel. He picked up Allie's note when he got back to his room, but he laid it to one side. He had something more important to do first. He snatched the phone from its cradle, connected to an outside line and rang his family home.

He'd almost given up by the time the receiver was

165

picked up. His mother recited the familiar number, her voice hollow and tight. 'Mum? It's me. Danny.'

A pause. 'You've got some nerve, phoning here. After what you've done to your brother.'

'Mum, I couldn't ignore — '

'After all his hard work, he's done so well for himself. And you do this to him.'

Danny felt his chest tighten. 'I've done nothing to him. I've kept his name out — '

'But he was the one delivering the money. Even though he had no idea what he was carrying or what it was for. You've made him look like a criminal.'

'You really believe he had no idea?'

'He never questioned what his boss told him to do. He never did anything wrong. He was just doing his job.'

'So was I, Mum. It's my job to report when people are breaking the law, and that's what Paragon have been doing.' He heard his voice rising, as whiny as when he was a boy. It was a replay of childhood scenes — Danny being accused of Joseph's crimes, his denial not being believed.

'Maybe so, but Joseph was doing no wrong.'

'Just obeying orders, is that it?' He scoffed. 'You really think that lets him off the hook? Mum, you sit in church every Sunday listening to the priest talking about our Christian duty. Can you not see I'm the one doing the right thing here? Paragon are stealing off all of us. People who hide their money from the taxman, they're not stealing from the government, they're stealing from you and me, from everybody.'

'Joseph's no thief. He's a decent hard-working boy who's going to be out of a job because of you. He was sitting here in tears this morning. He's tried so hard to make something of himself. All he wanted was to make us proud of him. You should be ashamed of yourself, Daniel Sullivan.' Not a crack in that adamantine defence.

'If he loses his job, you should be glad he's not working for a bunch of crooks any more. Because who knows what they would have asked him to do next?'

'Are you stupid, Danny? If he loses this job, he'll not get another one. Because he'll be tarred with your brush. They're not stupid, the folk who run these companies. They'll see your name and his name and whatever the truth, they'll believe it was Joseph who gave the game away to a reporter. Nobody will ever trust him with anything confidential ever again.'

Driven mad with the unfairness of her reaction, Danny lashed out. 'Neither they should, Mum. Whatever he's got you believing, Joseph was in this up to his eyes. He knew exactly what he was doing.' He stopped abruptly, shocked at the words that had spilled out.

He heard his mother catch her breath in a stifled sob. Then she said, 'I never knew you could be so hard-hearted, Danny. It's not how we brought you up. You'd better not come through on Sunday. Your father's as disgusted with you as I am. You've broken our hearts, Danny. Nobody in this house is going to want to see your face here any time soon.'

The line went dead. Danny stood rigid, gripping the handset with white knuckles, hurt gripping his heart with a physical pain. Why would he expect history not to repeat itself? If he'd ever doubted his place in the family hierarchy, now he knew. Catholic guilt would always trump love. Poor Joseph's start in life would always, always put Danny on the back foot.

A shudder of grief passed through him and he

gently replaced the phone. At least now he'd confirmed where he stood. The choices he'd had to make, all of them, had put him outside the walls of family life.

So be it. He'd live with it.

Danny went into the bathroom and doused his face with cold water. He stared at himself in the mirror, drips running down his cheeks, eyebrows glinting in the light. 'Fuck it,' he sighed, and rubbed his face with the towel till his skin felt raw.

24

Allie answered the knock at the door, glad it was Danny at last. But as she took him in, she saw something clenched in the way he held himself. His eyes were febrile, his jaw tight. 'What's wrong?' She gestured to him to enter.

'Is it that obvious?' His voice was bitter but he came inside and crossed to the worn armchair by the window.

'You look . . . I don't know. Upset?'

He rubbed his fingertips along his cheekbone, as if trying to rub himself out. He swallowed hard. 'I rang my mum. I — ' He took a breath. 'I thought I'd better get it over with. Put my side of the story.' He shook his head.

Allie crouched beside him, covering his free hand with hers. 'I'm guessing it didn't go well.'

Danny cleared his throat, visibly gathering himself. 'Hard to see how it could have gone worse. Like a fucking soap opera. *Never darken our doors again. Poor Joseph, the innocent dragged through the mud by his evil wee brother.*'

'I'm sorry, Danny. That's so unfair.'

'I shouldn't be surprised, Allie. That's how it's always been. Poor wee lamb, he had such a terrible start in life, we have to make it up to him. Not like Danny, a wanted child, born into a loving home. I never get to forget how lucky I am compared with Joseph. He's always got away with everything. Lying, cheating, stealing, and always laying the blame on me.

'Danny started it. It wisnae me, it was Danny.' All my life, that's what I've heard. So why would I think this time would be any different?'

'But you know you're right, Danny. You were right to follow your instincts and do the story.'

'I might have been right, Allie.' He looked straight at her, his eyes moist. 'But I'm not so sure it was worth it.'

Allie stood up and perched on the end of the bed. 'They'll come round, Danny. From everything you've said about your family, there's a lot of love there. It'll be tough going for a while, but they're not going to cut you out forever.'

He gave a harsh bark of laughter. 'You don't know my mum. Remember I told you about my aunties? Well, there's one I never mentioned. Auntie Beattie. Her and my mum fell out years ago. Must be getting on for fifteen years now. I have no idea what the row was about. You ask anybody in the family, they just blank you and change the subject.' A wry smile. 'I reckon half of them have forgotten what it was all about. But not my mum. She's not spoken to Beattie since. Hell, Beattie's not crossed our door since. I wouldn't know her if I passed her in the street. I could have been at school with my cousins and I wouldn't have known. My mum will go to her grave not speaking to Auntie Beattie.'

'But that's different. You're her son. She loves you. And your dad, he'll not go along with that, surely?'

Danny shook his head. 'My dad does what he's told. And if she says I've broken the fifth commandment, she'll get the priest on her side and then it'll be no contest for my dad.' He stood up. 'I knew she'd be upset. I didn't realise how upset. I just need to accept it, Allie. I'm an outcast till she says otherwise.' He straightened his shoulders and turned to face her, a smile of fake brightness at the ready. 'Has the office been on? Any problems?'

'The Razor called with a couple of little queries but nothing I couldn't handle. I asked about the police. He said Angus had stalled them. Said he had no idea where we were. But you'll have to meet them tomorrow morning once we've named the guilty men.' Allie exaggerated the last two words, giving them the full TV cop show dramatic weight. Danny's pain was obvious to her and she was determined to do what she could to ease it. 'Danny — I don't mean to trivialise the situation, but maybe it would help things if you could make your mum understand the importance of the work you're doing?'

He frowned. 'Is that not obvious already? I'm exposing criminals here.'

'Yeah, but it's complicated by Joseph's involvement in the story. The good stuff? She's blind to that because all she's thinking about is the risk to her boy. She can't see the wood for the trees.'

Danny looked doubtful, but there was a trace of hope in his expression. 'You think? So how do I fix that? I can't force her to see past Joseph.'

Allie smiled. 'We give her something else to look at.'

'I don't understand.' A faint smile. 'You Cambridge types, you're too smart for the likes of me.'

'Remember I said I might have a notion of what we could chase next? Well, if that works out the way I think it might, we'd have a story that nobody could argue wasn't on the side of the angels.' In spite of the seriousness of her words, she couldn't help bouncing on the edge of the terrible mattress.

'Where's this big idea come from? You didn't have two thoughts to rub together a couple of weeks ago.' He sounded unconvinced, as if he suspected Allie of trying to cajole him out of his pain.

So she told him about following Rona's suggestion of chasing the women's stories and how it had led her to the radical nationalists. 'There were these three young men. Early twenties, trying to outdo each other in the big man stakes. I followed them to the Spaghetti Factory after the meeting and managed to eavesdrop on their conversation.' She paused for dramatic effect.

Caught up in her enthusiasm, Danny grinned. 'The Spaghetti Factory conspiracy!'

'Laugh all you like. They were talking about taking action that would make everyone take independence seriously. Direct action like the Irish Republicans have been taking.'

The smile disappeared from his face. 'Bombs?'

She couldn't decide whether he was incredulous or horrified. Either way, she'd drawn his attention from his issues with his mother for the moment. 'They didn't say. They agreed to go away and think about it for a week then see what they came up with.' Another dramatic pause. 'That week's up tonight. They'll be at the meeting, for sure. And I think we should infiltrate them.'

Danny threw himself down into the chair again. 'No way.' He shook his head. 'That'll never work.'

'Why not? We can make all the right noises.'

He gave her a pitying look. 'You've been away too long, Allie. The bit of it that'll never work is 'we'.'

'What do you mean?' But before the words were out, she already knew the answer.

'You're a woman. They'll never trust you, never take you seriously. There's an outside chance I can get close to them, but you'll never get so much as a foot in the door. I'm sorry, Allie. If they're as gung-ho as you say, they'd never accept you as one of the team.'

He was right and she hated it. The same old story of life in the newsroom — stick to the miracle babies, let the men carry the weight. It didn't matter how good she was, she'd always be dismissed because of her gender. Would this ever change? The only positive was that making his point had joined Danny to the project. Instead of coming up with a dozen objections to the basic idea, he'd moved straight to the logistics of how they would get inside the fledgling conspiracy. Allie sighed. 'You're right. It pisses me off, but you're right. We'll make sure we arrive separately and don't show any signs of knowing each other.'

'Tonight? We're doing this tonight?' His eyebrows rose.

'Well, that's when it's going to happen, so, yes, we'll be doing it tonight.' She spread her hands. 'It's not like we're doing anything else. It's got to be more interesting than sitting around in a dump like this.'

'But we need to be on the end of a phone. In case there's any last-minute queries. Or problems with the copy.'

He had a point. But Allie was convinced she had a story in her sights and she wasn't going to let go. 'They've had all day to pick over every word. The Razor has been through every little niggle. We'll be fine, Danny. Angus goes home at seven. We'll check in with the desk just before then. And I'll ring in every half hour, to be on the safe side. There's a phone box near the meeting room, I spotted it last week.'

'And what if there is a problem? What if they need to talk to me? We'll have to break cover then. And it'll be all over.'

Allie was nonplussed for a moment. But only for a moment. 'Simple,' she said sweetly. 'I'll set off the fire alarm.'

25

Danny insisted on splashing out on a cab to the university. 'It's raining, Allie. I'm not sitting in a meeting with wet feet.'

'OK, but let me out at the top of Kelvin Way. We don't want to be spotted arriving together.' Allie had to hide a growing anxiety about Danny's state of mind. He'd swung from the pit of despair over his mother's rejection to a fervid excitement about the task ahead. His cheeks were flushed, his eyes bright, and he'd made her run through her descriptions of their targets three times. 'Are you sure you're up for this?' she asked.

'If we don't do it tonight, we might miss the boat. We put down a marker with the Paragon story — this one could get us a seat at the top table. Maybe even a slot in Fleet Street.'

'Is that what you want?'

Danny took a deep breath. 'If you'd asked me that a week ago, I'd have swithered about it. Any reporter with an ounce of ambition wants to work for one of the big boys. I mean, don't you?'

'Honestly? Of course I do. The *Clarion*'s just a stepping stone. At least I hope that's what it is.'

'I get that. But what would have held me back was the thought of leaving my family. My friends too, but definitely my family. They've always been my anchor.' A bitter laugh. 'Now they've cut me adrift. So I need to take my chances where I can now.'

Allie felt a niggle of concern that she was exploiting his emotional state. But she reminded herself that she'd given him something to stop him brooding. Now she had to keep him focused. 'We need to go shopping,' she said firmly. 'Neither of us can turn up in our work suits. You need to get yourself a jumper or something, maybe even a pair of jeans. And I need to sort out a more casual look. Not to mention some clean underwear.' She caught his startled look. 'Don't worry, I'm not going to drag you round the ladies' lingerie department. We can't go out together in case the office rings, remember?'

Since Danny had already been outside, he insisted Allie go first. It was a relief to be free of the bedroom and she savoured the wintry air as she walked down Buchanan Street. The bookshop first; and the surprise of a Ruth Rendell paperback she'd not read before. *A Judgement in Stone* sounded suitably ominous for her mood and the first sentence was provocative enough to drive her to the till. 'Eunice Parchman killed the Coverdale family because she could not read or write,' was irresistible, she thought.

She cut across the grey expanse of George Square and down to Marks and Spencer. Because she knew her size in the store's styles, it was a whistlestop shop. A pack of three pairs of pants; flared trousers in wine-coloured needlecord and a simple dark grey crew-neck jumper. At least they were items she could happily add to her wardrobe afterwards.

After she'd released Danny from his hotel room, she changed into her new outfit and found the residents' lounge. It was a retirement home for shabby armchairs and faded prints of Highland scenery, but it was marginally less grim than her room. She left a message for Danny and settled down with her book.

In spite of its gripping qualities, she couldn't help

176

noticing the passage of time. How long did it take to buy a pair of jeans and a sweater? What was taking him so long? He eventually appeared almost two hours after he'd left, dressed in flatteringly cut flared jeans and a fitted tank top over a black shirt. Allie raised her eyebrows. 'You look like you're all set for a night out, not a political meeting.'

'Oh, I'm not wearing these tonight,' he said. 'I've got a boring pair of Levis and a very dull lambswool pullover for that. But I couldn't resist these. I thought I deserved a treat.'

'You look good,' she said.

'Thank you, that was the general idea.' His smile was infectious. 'Look, do you mind holding the fort for a bit longer? We don't have to make a move for a couple of hours yet and this place is driving me mad. I'm not like you, I can't lose myself in a book. I need to get out.'

Allie hid her disappointment. She'd hoped they could talk; learn more about each other, grow closer. 'OK, but you owe me. What are you going to do?'

He shrugged. 'Mooch round the shops? Gee myself up for tonight? Back here at seven?'

'Don't be late. I hate being kept waiting. And Danny?' She caught his eye and winked. 'Don't take any sweeties from strangers.'

* * *

They'd agreed Allie would give Danny a ten-minute start to get settled in to the meeting. He hurried from the taxi to the shelter of the quadrangles, his heart thudding. Apprehension growled in his stomach. Everything depended on his performance now. There was even more at stake here than when he'd reeled in Bill Maclay in Southampton. It wasn't just his future as a journalist that was on the line. It was his future as a member of his own family.

He owed Allie too. She'd helped to make his story have impact. And now it was his turn to help her land a story with her name first in the credits. Somehow, he had to worm his way into the confidence of a potentially dangerous trio of strangers and win them over. He'd had plenty of experience of risking the trust of strangers, but this time, it wasn't all about him, and that made the pressure all the worse. All he had for an in was Allie's recollection that the one called Deke supported Partick Thistle FC. Not much of a start, but better than nothing.

He walked in, scanning the room as fast as he could take it in. He thought he'd spotted Allie's targets, except there were only two of them. There was nothing special about them, nothing that would stand out in a crowd. But that would be an advantage if you were planning direct action of the loud and explosive kind. And nobody else came close to the descriptions. Maybe the third man had been held up. Or maybe he'd found something better to do.

Danny crossed the room, injecting a bit of swagger into his walk. He pulled up a chair next to the two men and dropped his chin in acknowledgement. 'Good evening,' he began, voice full of confidence.

'Aye,' one of them said cautiously. The other just nodded.

'Am I in the right place?'

'Depends what you're looking for.'

Danny gave him a calculating look. 'I was told this was the place to find men who were really serious.'

'I don't know about that, I like a laugh as much as the next man.' He smirked.

'Serious about this country's future. Serious enough to do something about it,' Danny said. 'If I got a bum steer — ' He held up his hands, palms out. 'I'll be out of your way. No hard feelings, no harm done.'

'And what if this was the place?' The other man chipped in.

Danny gave a broad smile, all the sincerity he could muster. 'Then I'm among friends. And I am a good friend to have in these matters.' He extended a hand. 'Paul Reilly.' No qualms about using his dead uncle's name, not in a good cause.

The first man took the handshake. 'Derek Malloch. Deke to my friends and fellow travellers.'

Danny did a low-level double-take. He pointed a finger at Deke. 'I've met you before. In a bar on Maryhill Road, after a Jags game. A couple of my pals are big Partick *Thistle* boys, they dragged me along to a game a couple of seasons back. We all got talking over a few beers.'

Malloch looked blank. Danny continued with a wee shrug. 'You'll probably not remember me. I'm a Jambo, so I try to keep a low profile in other folk's pubs.' He grinned. 'You know how it is.'

Deke fell for the lingua franca of football. 'Just as well, we don't love the Hearts at Firhill.'

Danny laughed. 'At least we don't let the rugby players wreck our pitch. So who's your pal, Deke?' He extended his hand.

More slowly, the other man took it. 'Gary Bell,' he said.

'Ding-dong to his mates,' Malloch said.

'Who sent you our way?' Bell asked.

Danny smiled and shook his head. 'I always protect my people. Start bandying names round and the next thing you know is the wrong people hear them.'

'How do we know you're not the wrong people?' Bell's chin jutted aggressively. One of these days, Danny thought, somebody was going to accept that invitation.

'You don't. But even Jambos can have their hearts in the right place. Glasgow doesn't have dibs on serious players. You can judge me by what I say and what I do. If you don't like it, just tell me to fuck off, and off I will duly fuck. Now, where's the third musketeer? I was told there were three of you.'

Bell gave Malloch a twitchy look that landed on stony ground. 'He's joining us later,' Malloch said, jovial and apparently relaxed.

Danny was spared further conversation by Maggie McNab taking the floor and giving them the pep talk. The meeting rumbled on, and Danny took every chance to interject. He was playing a finely judged game of a man passionate about independence, yet backing away from making any specific threats. He met Malloch's eyes more than once and earned an approving nod. It was working; they were starting to relax. But he couldn't afford to.

At last it was over. Out of the corner of his eye, he saw Allie slip out of the room. He leaned forward so the other two had to draw close. 'So much for the talking shop. How do we make this happen, boys? What's next?'

Bell sat back. 'Next we go and get something to eat and hook up with our pal Roddy. Then you can maybe tell us what you think should happen next.' His smile held no sincerity.

Danny rubbed his hands together in a mimicry of glee. 'Now that's what I call a plan. My treat, boys. Just to show we're all on the same side. Lead the way, gentlemen.'

Their destination was no surprise. They walked down the hill, Malloch passing easy judgement on the failure of everyone else at the meeting to grasp the bull by the horns. 'Or should I say, by the balls,' he laughed. 'They've got no idea how to wake up the sleeping giant that is Scotland.'

'I agree,' Danny said. 'I'm interested to hear your ideas about how we do that.'

'We need something spectacular,' Malloch said. 'Something nobody can ignore.'

'But it has to be something that doesn't put people's lives at risk,' Bell cut in. 'We want people to be impressed, not horrified.'

'Naturally,' Malloch said, breezy as a summer evening on Loch Lomond.

They walked quickly, keen to get out of the sleet. The Spaghetti Factory was their destination again. As they entered, an arm waved at them from the farthest booth. 'That's Roddy. Roddy Farquhar,' Malloch said, waving away the waitress who was heading towards them. 'We're sorted, darling.'

Drawing closer, Danny realised with a sudden constriction of his heart that Roddy Farquhar was no stranger.

26

For the second week running, Allie slipped unnoticed into the back table at the Spaghetti Factory. The place was half-empty; there were some advantages to the wintry blasts keeping people huddled round their own firesides. She'd followed Danny and the other two at a discreet distance and she was relieved to see they'd hooked up in the booth with the third member of the original trio. Already Malloch, Bell (aka Dingdong) and Farquhar were talking to Danny as if they'd been pals for ever.

Danny was facing the door, but he completely ignored her arrival. Not even a momentary flick of the eyes to give away an interest in her. He was in the thick of an animated exchange about football with Ding-dong. One of the many advantages of working for a paper like the *Clarion* was that you inevitably picked up a gallimaufry of information on all sorts of things in which you had no interest whatsoever. Even Allie now knew enough about Scottish football to fall back on Scotland's disastrous World Cup campaign in Argentina the previous summer. That was guaranteed to impose a gloomy silence in any company.

Once the quartet had placed their order, they settled on what they had come there to discuss. 'So we set each other a wee challenge last week,' Malloch said. 'Mibbes you can join in, Paul.'

'I'm always up for a challenge, Deke.' Danny sounded more expansive than she'd ever heard him in the office. Playing a part seemed to suit him. 'Lay it on me, man.'

'We don't want devo, Paul. We want full-fat indy. And we want to make people pay attention to how much better that would be for Scotland. The politicians are useless. They go with their begging bowls. 'Please, Mr Prime Minister, give us a wee bit of fake power so we can pretend we run our own affairs,'' Malloch said.

'So how do you do that?' Danny asked.

Farquhar said, 'We agreed to spend this week going to meetings and talking to folk and seeing whether we could come up with any ideas.'

'Interesting. So did you?'

'We might have,' Ding-dong said. 'What about you, Paul? You're the fresh blood round the table, what do you think?'

He wasn't the only one interested in the answer. Allie wondered what on earth Danny would come up with. She didn't have long to wait. 'A two-pronged attack,' he said. 'All these strikes that have been grabbing the headlines? Why are they news?' A pause. 'Because they inconvenience people. So you need to organise actions that grab attention because they put folk out. Blockade the bus station. Stage a sit down on the rails at Queen Street station.'

'That's not a bad idea,' Farquhar said. 'I bet we could get Maggie McNab and her crowd on board with that.'

'You just have fantasies about getting on board with Maggie McNab,' Ding-dong said, and they guffawed.

'Fuck off,' Farquhar whined. 'She's got a lot of support.'

'She needs it, with those tits. So, Paul, what's the second prong?' Malloch made the word sound ridiculous.

'Get celebrities on board to endorse what you're doing. Guys like Billy Connolly. Actors from *Garnock Way*. Magnus Magnusson. Sean Connery. When the big names get behind you, you get attention in the papers and on the telly.' Danny made it sound easy.

'And pop stars. The Bay City Rollers,' Farquhar said.

'Don't be daft. Twelve-year-olds dinnae vote,' Ding-dong scoffed. Farquhar yelped and Allie assumed one of them had landed him a friendly punch.

'What do you say, Ding-dong?' Malloch said. 'Any of those guys in your address book? Because they're not in mine. Nice idea, Paul, but I say we go back to what I was talking about last week. I say we learn the lesson from Northern Ireland. How did they get the politicians to take them seriously? Not with the ballot box. They blew the bloody doors off!'

Farquhar looked at Deke, apprehension obvious. 'They kill people. They're terrorists. That's not how you get support. I'm having nothing to do with murder.'

Ding-dong laughed. 'Get a grip, Roddy. Nobody's talking about killing folk. But Deke's right. A big bang's the way to get attention. You just have to pick your targets. Set your timer for when there's nobody there. And bingo. You get the message across and nobody gets hurt.'

'That's quite the ambition, boys,' Danny weighed in. 'And I'm not saying it's not a good idea. Because it is. It's a brilliant idea. There's just one small problem that I can see. Because none of youse looks like you're in charge of a quarry or a pit.'

It was a killer point, Allie thought as the silence drew out among them.

Then Ding-dong spoke. His voice was lowered but it still carried. 'I know a man.'

'What do you mean, you know a man?' There was a derisive note in Malloch's response.

Ding-dong elaborated. 'You said, this is the time for direct action. I know a man who has access to what we need.'

'And what exactly is that, Gary?' Malloch's sarcasm was unmistakable.

'An arsenal.'

The shock of his words hit Allie so hard the sounds of the restaurant seemed to disappear.

'Are you serious?' Farquhar exclaimed, his voice a mixture of awe and delight.

'Never more so, my man.'

'Who is this guy?' Malloch demanded.

'And how come you know a man with an arsenal?' Danny chipped in.

'I never said he had an arsenal. I said he had access to one. There's a difference.' Ding-dong on the defensive now.

'Like I said, who the fuck is he?' Malloch hit back.

'Terry. That's all you need to know. He's from Belfast. He's in an IRA Active Service Unit.'

'Get tae *fuck*,' Malloch scoffed. 'And we're only hearing about this guy now?'

'He's having you on,' Danny said calmly. 'If he was really in an IRA unit, he'd be sworn to secrecy. He wouldn't be mouthing off to somebody in the pub.'

Ding-dong wasn't giving ground. 'That's not how it went. I've known Terry since we were twelve. He came over that summer with his Boys' Brigade football team to play a tournament and he got put up with us.'

'Well, that's shite for a start,' Farquhar said. 'The Boys' Brigade, that's a Protestant thing. You don't get Catholics in the Boys' Brigade, and you don't get Protestants in the IRA.'

'You know all about it, do you?' Ding-dong challenged.

'My dad's in the Orange Lodge. I know what's what.'

'You're wrong.' Allie could hear Ding-dong's frustration. 'You know nothing. Terry grew up a Protestant in a Unionist part of town, that's how he was in the BB. He came back here with his team three years on the trot. My mum and dad felt sorry for him, with the Troubles and all that. So they invited him to come over and go on holiday with us to the caravan at Maidens a couple of times. Terry and me, we've stayed pally all these years since. Then he got engaged two years ago to a Catholic lassie that he met at his work, and he got the crap beaten out of him by the guys in his own neighbourhood. He had to move out of the street where he'd lived all his days. But the Catholic community, they welcomed him in. He told me it made him realise it was his community, the Unionists, that were the problem. So he joined the IRA.'

'So like I said, how come this is the first we're hearing about this Terry?' Malloch sounded both indignant and suspicious.

'Never came up. Christ, Deke, you're not my keeper. I don't know half the guys you work beside or the ones you play golf with.'

'Fair enough. So you think your man Terry could get us, what? Guns? Bombs?'

'Only one way to find out,' Ding-dong seemed nonchalant.

186

'How?' Danny said quietly.

'Aye, away across to Belfast and ask him.' Malloch ladled out the sarcasm again.

'I could do just that.' Ding-dong responded with defiance. 'What? You think I couldn't?'

It was one of those cliff-edge moments. 'We'd need money,' Farquhar said, giving Ding-dong a chance to save face.

'Well, we're fucked then,' Malloch said. 'Youse all know I'm permanently skint.'

Ding-dong pulled a face. 'I've got a couple of hundred put by.'

Farquhar scoffed. 'That's not going to get us far. What about you, Danny? You were quick enough to throw your hat in the ring. You gonnae put your money where your mouth is? Show you're really on our team?'

'I might be able to help,' Danny said, appropriately hesitant. There was a pause. Allie could imagine their open-mouthed stares. What was Danny playing at? 'I had a bit of luck on the Premium Bonds a while back. I've been waiting for the right thing to spend it on.'

Allie closed her eyes. This was too far, too soon. How was it that apparently ordinary men could wind each other to this pitch over a couple of beers on a Friday night? Apart from anything else, they'd only just met Danny. How could they not suspect they were being set up? They were like children. *Do you want to be in my gang? Do you speak fitba'?*

'So what are we waiting for?' Malloch gave a throaty chuckle. 'Are we going to be the kind of wankers who talk a great game then get stuck into making excuses? Or are we going to do something?'

'Only you know the answer to that,' Danny said. 'I'm in if you are.'

27

The four men stopped making plans when their pizzas arrived and as soon as they'd wolfed them, Malloch insisted that they go back to his flat with a carry-out to continue their planning in private.

All Allie could do was finish off her own calzone and head back to the horrible hotel. Before she'd even taken off her coat, she picked up the phone and dialled Danny's room number. When the answering machine kicked in, she spoke tersely. 'Call me as soon as you get in. I don't care how late it is.' She still couldn't decide whether to applaud him for seizing the moment or berate him for his recklessness. An 'I'll show you all' moment provoked, she was sure, by his anguish at what had passed between him and his mother.

She poured herself a drink and got ready for bed. She picked up her book, but only managed a few pages before sleep overtook her and it slid from her hand.

It was well after midnight when a noise woke Allie. It took her a dazed moment to realise it wasn't the phone but a knocking on her door. She clambered out of bed, pulling on jeans and sweater, and headed for the door. 'Who is it?' she demanded. She might be groggy with sleep but that didn't mean she had to be stupid too.

'It's me, Danny. Open up!'

Allie let him in. He looked frozen, his face pink and pinched with cold. 'Could you put the kettle on? It's Baltic out there.' She followed him in and plugged in the tiny kettle. 'Jeez, those guys,' he continued. 'Talk about 'light the blue touch paper and stand well clear.''

'I heard most of it. A contact in the IRA? And that Ding-dong? He just came out with it in front of you? When they'd only known you five minutes?'

Danny shrugged. 'I guess I was convincing. Or they're so desperate to be the heroes of the revolution that they couldn't resist the offer of a fighting fund.' He grinned and sat down at the table, his hands under his armpits.

'Oh yeah. And where did that come from? I don't remember us talking about funding a terrorist cell?' She stared him down. 'Jeez, Danny.'

He had the grace to look shamefaced. 'I know. It just felt like too good an opportunity to resist. Allie, this is a great story for us. The inside track on the Scottish Republican Army.'

'Is that what they're calling themselves? For God's sake, Danny.' Exasperated, she dumped the last remaining teabag in the single mug.

'They're not calling themselves anything. Yet. And they seem clear enough about choosing bricks and mortar targets. Avoiding innocent victims.'

Allie poured the boiling water and stirred. 'All the same. This is a helluva tightrope, Danny. Are we reporters or *agents provocateurs*? We need to keep our noses clean here.'

'I know, I know. But we can do that, we can control it.'

She had her doubts. But this wasn't the time to convince Danny. He was high on the excitement of the story. And probably a few beers too. 'So what happened when you went back to Deke's flat?'

Danny pulled a face. 'God, what a tip. It's a room and kitchen off Woodlands Road. Sink full of dishes, bin spilling over with lager cans and takeaway cartons. The clothes hanging on the pulley were the only thing that looked like they'd been cleaned since we got bumped out of the World Cup. You know that thing where your shoes stick to the carpet?'

'Yuck. I have to say, Danny, you don't get lassies living like that.'

'Hey, we're not all like that. That's not how I live, you'll see that when you come over to mine.'

It was the first time he'd even hinted at inviting her to his flat. Allie tucked it away to savour later. 'Never mind the décor. What about the conversation? Last I heard before you all started stuffing your faces was Deke coming back from the phone and saying his cousin was taking the dog for a walk. Was that code, or what?'

Danny laughed. 'No, his cousin was actually going to take the dog for a walk down to the pierhead to find out what time the ferry goes in the morning. He rang back at Deke's flat with the details.'

'They're going to Belfast? This morning?' She finished making the tea and plonked it down.

Danny wrapped his long fingers round the mug and smiled. 'Not all of them. Just Gary. Ding-dong to you. He was adamant he had to go by himself. And I get that. If his pal Terry really is in an IRA Active Service Unit, unlike our three musketeers he's not going to say word one to a complete stranger. Even if his old pal Gary vouches for him. So Gary's going across on the morning ferry to see about buying some ordnance from the IRA.' Danny shook his head, bemused. 'These guys are absolute bams, Allie.'

'How are we going to stop them?' She gave Danny a hard stare. 'We are going to stop them, Danny, aren't we?'

'Sure,' he said casually. 'We can work out the details later. We'll let the cops raid them either when they pick up the explosives or when they're about to plant them. Obviously we'll have to tell Angus what's going on once we've got the wheels properly in motion.'

'Obviously,' Allie said drily. 'So when's Ding-dong debriefing the rest of you?'

'Sunday morning. There's a café at St George's Cross. Apparently does the best fry-up this side of the river. Eleven o'clock, sharp.'

'I'll get there early.'

Danny gave her a sidelong glance. 'I don't think you should be there. You'll stand out too much.'

'That's not fair. This is my story, I dropped it in your lap. You can't cut me out of it now.'

'I'm not cutting you out, no way. I just don't want to take any risks at this point. They're all going to be a bit twitchy. All it takes is one of them to recognise you from the meeting or the Spaghetti Factory and the ball's on the slates.'

'They've never seen me. I've sat behind them, both times. And they didn't even glance at me in the Spaghetti Factory.'

'You underestimate yourself. You're a good-looking woman, and I bet Deke checked you out on his way back from the phone. He's that kind of guy. He was going on and on about the waitress all the way back to his flat. He'll have given you the once-over. It's you I'm thinking of.'

'Me and the story,' she grumbled, reaching for her cigarettes and lighting up. 'OK, have it your way.'

He gave her a smile of relief. 'Can I get a loan of your tape recorder? I can stick it in my coat pocket, they'll never notice.'

'If they do, you're in big trouble, Danny.'

'I'll be careful. But I think they're pretty harmless.'

'They're planning a bloody bombing campaign, Danny. They might be ineffectual but they're not harmless. And if the Irishman is with Gary, do not attempt to record him.'

'How dumb do you think I am?' He grinned. 'No, don't answer that. Do you want to meet up afterwards?' She gave him a look that would have withered a patch of brambles. 'OK, OK, sorry. I'll call you when I'm done, we can meet up.'

'I'll maybe take you up on your offer to inspect your flat,' Allie said, keeping it light.

'Not a problem. The cleaner comes on Thursdays so it's still pretty much pristine.'

'You've got a cleaner?'

He nodded. 'It's the best way to keep my mum off my back.' He spoke without thinking; his words stripped all the comfort from his face again. 'Not that that matters now.'

'She'll come round, Danny. She'll understand the importance of what you're doing.' Allie reached out and covered his hand with hers.

He nodded, unconvinced. He cleared his throat. 'I better get moving. What time is Angus throwing us to the polis?'

'We've to be in the office at ten.' She looked at her watch and groaned. 'Less than eight hours away.' Allie yawned. 'Thanks for coming by.'

He gave a bashful smile. 'Least I could do. It's your story, Allie. Honest, I haven't forgotten that.'

28

How had he got himself in this deep? Only hours before, the Gary Bell who had hooked up in the Spaghetti Factory with his two best mates and their new pal had been an ordinary bloke with a poor man's Rod Stewart haircut and a desire to see Scotland break free from the English yoke.

Now the Gary Bell driving down the A77 was a member of an insurgent group committed to the armed struggle.

Why did he always let himself be trapped by the urge to get everyone thinking he was the big man? Deke Malloch had been holding forth about the need to rise up for freedom, if only they had the means. Without a pause for breath or thought, he'd leaned forward across the table and uttered the fateful words. 'I know a man.'

The idle boast had somehow turned into a gauntlet thrown before young men too afraid to back down before friends. Their new pal Paul had offered to fund their expenses. So Deke Malloch had jumped up and headed for the payphone in the corner to ring his cousin in Stranraer to find out ferry times, And Gary Bell was tremulously facing his new role as quartermaster.

* * *

The Boy's Brigade team was long behind Terry Robinson. But Gary Bell knew that his old friend still turned out every Saturday in goal for a pub team in Andersonstown. He'd never been to Belfast before and the idea of going now made his stomach hurt. All he knew of the city was what he'd seen on the news; armoured vehicles and British soldiers on the streets, rioters throwing bricks and petrol bombs, roadblocks and official buildings nested in razor wire. But if he didn't at least make an approach to Terry, any credibility he had with the others would be lost.

He'd considered lying. Saying he'd made the attempt but Terry had blown him out. But Deke Malloch had scuppered that. 'I'll buddy you up as far as Stranraer,' he'd announced when Bell had announced his 'plan' to go across to Belfast on the ferry that Saturday. 'I can go and watch Stranraer with my cousin. It'll be a laugh, they're that close to the bottom of Division Two, they're bound to get gubbed whoever they're up against. Then we can go to the pub and you can pick me up on your way back.'

'I might not be back till Sunday.'

'Then I'll just have to make a night of it.' Malloch clapped him on the back. 'I want to hear the good news soon as.'

And so he'd had no choice. On the long drive down the Ayrshire coast to Stranraer, tucked into the armpit of the bottom left-hand corner of Scotland, Malloch alternated between criticising Bell's choice of cassettes and delivering a lecture on his own lurid version of Scotland's history, with the occasional foray into complaining about the inability of women to appreciate his charms. None of it helped Bell's nerves, already jangling like wind chimes. It was almost a relief to drive aboard the ferry. The prospect of four hours yawing and rolling across the grey swell of the

Irish Sea was more appealing than another minute of Malloch's opinions. Apart from anything else, Malloch's diatribes were making Bell wonder why they were even pals in the first place.

He bought crisps, Irn Bru and a pack of savoury cheese sandwiches from the grim cafeteria and found a quiet corner away from the lorry drivers, the clusters of squaddies returning from leave and the scattering of families making the crossing. Why anyone would want to go to Belfast in the dead of winter was beyond Bell. But then again, why on earth was he doing this? There was no question about his commitment to the cause. But he wasn't a man of violence, he was a bookkeeper in a Govan shipyard. He'd managed to reach the age of twenty-five without even having had a proper fight. And would a few explosions really make a difference? There had been dozens — no, hundreds of bombs in Northern Ireland, but it was still shackled to Great Britain. All they'd achieved was to make the IRA loathed throughout the land.

But maybe there was another way. A way to make a Scottish Republican Army have a positive impact. What had made the IRA pariahs was the blood on their hands. What if Bell and his mates genuinely managed to take a different route? What if they did what they'd sort of agreed and only blew up the symbols of the occupiers' power? Completely avoided bloodshed? There were plenty of those symbols dotted around the Scottish landscape.

They could start with the old Royal High School building at the foot of Calton Hill in Edinburgh, earmarked for the seat of the devolved administration that was probably not going to happen if Westminster kept moving the goalposts. Edinburgh city council had bought the building for the best part of two million, and another small fortune had been spent on tarting it up so it would be fit for the politicians. Blowing it up would send the message that Scotland wasn't waiting to be told what to do by the London government.

The Scottish Office in Edinburgh, that outpost of Westminster, was another target that would make the politicians sit up and take notice. The Scottish Secretary, Bruce Millan, was a balloon. Everybody knew he was a puppet of his bosses down south. Bell believed the Labour government's support for devolution was a pretence, nothing more than mouth music to pacify the Scots. Devolution was like giving sweeties to a toddler. It shut them up, but it rotted their teeth in their head. With a little help from their Irish friends, maybe Bell and his mates could show they weren't toothless yet.

The thoughts rumbling round his head kept him occupied till he drove off the ferry into the bleak grey early afternoon. An army checkpoint scrutinised every vehicle rolling off the ship, pulling over an apparently random selection for further checks. A soldier toting what Bell thought was some sort of semi-automatic rifle stood at the shoulder of the fresh-faced private who demanded to see Bell's driving licence. 'What's your business here today?' he demanded, his Yorkshire accent defiantly broad.

'I'm visiting an old friend. He's just got engaged, I promised him a drink.'

'Is he from here?'

'He is.'

The soldier frowned. 'How do you know him?'

Bell explained the football history and the family

196

holidays in the sort of tedious detail that he hoped would defuse any suspicion. But still he had to get out and open the boot to demonstrate he had nothing more threatening than a set of jump leads. Finally, he was waved through. He stopped at the first newsagent he saw and bought a map of the city.

Back in the car, he unfolded the map and drew out his route in blue ink. It looked pretty straightforward. He reckoned he'd be there by half-time so long as he didn't run into too many checkpoints.

He concentrated all his attention on not getting lost. The city passed in a blur of grim brick terraces leavened by the occasional vivid gable-end mural and kerbstones painted either Union Jack red, white and blue or the orange and green of the Republican colours. Constant glimpses of soldiers in camouflage, on patrol or manning checkpoints on side streets that radiated off the main drag. And then the disconcerting contrast of people going about their daily business, almost as if he was driving through one of the less prosperous areas of Glasgow. Women in headscarves against the cold, heavy shopping bags angling them to one side. Kids kicking battered footballs on waste ground. Men in donkey jackets smoking on street corners, drifting in and out of pubs and betting shops. Gaggles of teenagers, heads together, deep in whatever it was teenagers found to talk about. And the occasional pair of punks, driftwood left behind by a receding tide.

The park where Terry's team played wasn't much bigger than the two football pitches it contained. A dilapidated children's playground sat between the car park and the forty-four men chasing balls. Two small girls wrapped up in winter coats that doubled their size clambered over a witches' hat that creaked like a horror film soundtrack as it ground unevenly round. On a bench at one side, an old man in a tweed overcoat and a matching flat cap smoked a pipe and divided his attention between his newspaper and the girls.

Bell skirted the playground and scouted out the two matches. Terry was definitely not in either goal on the near pitch, so he walked the touchline till he could see the other game. At the far end, bouncing on his toes to keep warm, his torso swathed in a thick green sweater, Terry kept goal, his attention focused on the events unfolding on the pitch. Bell made his way down the touchline, passing a dozen or so spectators hunched into coats and hats and scarves, keeping themselves warm with invective directed indiscriminately at players and officials.

He approached Robinson's goal from behind but some presentiment of danger made the goalie swing his head round, away from the game and towards Bell. His face lit up in astonishment. 'Ding-dong! What the fuck are you doing here?'

'I came to see you.' Bell drew a flat half-bottle of Johnnie Walker from his coat pocket. 'I thought it was about time we celebrated your engagement.'

'You took your time. Mind, it's grand to see you.' He kept glancing over his shoulder at the game, but the players were involved in an ugly scramble at the far end. 'How's your ma and your da?'

'Good, they're good. Are you free after the match? For a wee drink?'

Robinson gave him a long hard stare. 'What are you after, Ding-dong? You're up to something, I can tell.'

It was the quickest leap to a conclusion Bell had

ever seen. 'Can a man not look up an old pal without having an ulterior motive?'

Robinson turned away, hands on hips. 'Not when it involves turning up in the middle of a war zone. Did you drive here?'

'Yeah, my car's over in the car park.'

'I'll meet you there at four o'clock. Now fuck off and take a walk. You're attracting way too much attention.'

Bell did as he was told, walking on to the far corner flag, then down the touchline without once turning back to look at his friend. What must it be like to spend your days in a permanent ferment of anxiety about being watched? He stopped behind the far goal for a few minutes, pretending an interest in the game that he didn't feel. He moved away, walking out of the park via a different gate from the one he'd entered by. He made a circuit of the park that brought him back to his car with ten minutes to spare. He climbed back into the driver's seat, grateful to be out of the cutting edge of the wind.

The light was leaching out of the sky by the time Robinson appeared, carrying a canvas holdall. He threw it into the footwell ahead of himself and settled into the seat, bringing a strong smell of sweat and stale tobacco with him. 'So let's have this drink, then,' he said, holding out his hand. Bell passed the bottle and his friend took a swig, wincing as the spirit hit his throat. 'Good stuff,' he said, tucking the bottle into his jacket pocket. 'You'll not be wanting any, with you driving, like?'

Bell grinned. 'I brought it for you.'

Robinson gave him a shrewd look. 'Is that supposed to be some kind of a down payment, Gary? You're not here because of my bonnie blue eyes, are ye?'

'Christ, when it comes to suspicious minds, you've got Elvis on the ropes.'

He sparked up a cigarette, squinting at Bell through the smoke. 'If you lived my life, you'd be the very same. So what's this all about, Gary?'

And so Bell told him. Robinson listened in a grim silence that made Bell ever more garrulous. 'We're on the same side here. We get independence, it's the break-up of the UK. Like what the Americans said about communism in Vietnam, it's the domino effect. We get out, you'll have a united Ireland in no time flat. Or if you went first, we'd fall in behind you if we managed to build enough support. To do that, we need to kick things off in a spectacular way, Terry.' Finally he ground to a halt.

'You've got nerve, I'll give you that. Coming to the lion's den and sticking your head right in its mouth.' Robinson sucked the last quarter-inch of his cigarette and ground it out in the car's ashtray. 'Before I even pass this up the line, you need to answer me two things.'

'Anything.'

'Are youse secure? Can you vouch for your cell?'

Bell nodded. 'I've known them six years or thereabouts. They're sound, man. Sound.' It wasn't quite the whole truth and nothing but the truth. But Bell trusted his instincts, and they told him that Paul Reilly was solid.

'And how exactly are you going to fund this?'

29

In the end, the encounter with the police turned out to be far less frightening than Allie had expected. She'd thought they'd be angry to have been kept in the dark about law-breaking and grumpy at being made to feel foolish by a bunch of journalists doing their job for them. But the two detectives who quizzed her were almost affable. They explained that they specialised in white-collar crime, so they were quick to grasp the principles at stake. She'd thought ahead and made a copy of her taped interviews, which seemed to surprise them. 'I could do with one of those wee machines,' the younger officer muttered.

Danny, who had been interviewed first, had waited for her and they walked back to the car park together. 'Did it go OK?' he asked anxiously.

'I think so. They didn't ask me anything I couldn't answer. How about you?'

'Well, there were a couple of things I had to skate around. Like the money. And I had to come clean about Joseph, obviously. They said they were planning on talking to him on Monday.'

'Maybe you should warn him? Tell him again to get his version in first?'

Danny sighed. 'I'll try. But I think whoever answers the phone will put it down on me.'

'Do you want me to make the call? Nobody's going to recognise my voice.'

He considered it for a moment, then shook his head. 'I don't want you dragged into the middle of this. I reckon I can get Auntie Senga on my side, she's always had a soft spot for me. She goes to the same chapel. She can collar Joseph after Mass tomorrow and get into his ribs. Tell him he needs to call the polis and play the innocent.'

'That's a better idea. He's more likely to listen to her than me.' Allie stopped by her car. 'I'll see you tomorrow. Good luck with the bams.'

'You don't fancy a bite to eat?'

Typical, Allie thought. The one time she actually had an arrangement, he asks her for a meal. 'Sorry, I've got plans. I'm meeting up with Rona Dunsyre. We're going to Rogano's, then round the shops.'

He looked surprised, but only said, 'Have fun. I'll call you as soon as I can tomorrow.'

'Thanks, but I'm on the back shift. I'll be leaving the house around half past noon. You'll have to reach me at the office after that.'

A worried frown. 'You can't really talk there, though.'

'If you can't call me before I leave for work, meet me in the canteen. I'll take my break around five.' He nodded, and she put a hand on his arm. 'Be careful, Danny. I know you think they're just a bunch of bams, but even bams can be dangerous.'

★ ★ ★

Rona was on sparkling form, which was exactly what Allie needed after the stresses and tensions of the previous few days. They started with Bloody Marys, and Allie insisted lunch was on her. 'That suggestion you gave me about making contacts — it's already paid off,' she explained. 'I brought in a good wee story

202

about student votes in the referendum. Of course, Angus promptly gave it to one of the political guys.'

'Surely that was before you hit the big time this week? You must be flavour of the month now.' Rona clinked glasses and winked. 'I knew you'd go far, doll.'

'I think they'll maybe take me a bit more seriously now. And I'm working on another story with Danny. One that I picked up at another indy meeting. I can't say much about it right now, but if it works out, it'll be a cracker.'

'Good for you.'

A pause while they ordered. Rona went for oysters but Allie was too scared of something that looked so much like snot and settled for smoked salmon instead. Then Rona insisted they both have the legendary fish soup. 'And we'll have a bottle of Muscadet,' she added. 'You need fortifying if we're going shopping.'

'About the shopping — '

'Don't argue with me, and don't take this the wrong way, Allie, but you need to step up a gear when it comes to your wardrobe. You need to dress for success, darling.'

'I'm not flamboyant like you,' Allie butted in.

Rona roared with laughter. 'Nobody in the *Clarion*'s flamboyant like me. Hell, there's not a hack in the city with a fraction of my flamboyance. I'm not suggesting you take a leaf out of my book. It wouldn't work for you. But you need to do yourself justice. Right now, you look more like a plain-clothes polis that buys her suits in the C&A sale than a hotshot reporter setting the news agenda.'

Allie flushed. 'I was a student for three years, then a trainee journalist earning buttons for two years. All I could afford was the C&A sale.'

Rona patted her hand. 'I get that. But that's history. You're on good wages now and you should be spending some of that cash on looking the business. I'm not saying, 'go mental'. But a swatch of style would go a long way to making them take you seriously. A tailored jacket, a flash of silk, a skirt with a bit of swagger — '

'No skirts.' This was the bridge Allie would die on.

'No skirts?'

'You come into the office in the morning with a pretty good idea of what you'll be doing that day. It's not like that for me. I could be scrambling down a motorway embankment to cover a five-car pile-up. I could be in a scummy East End tenement flat sticking to the settee. Or I could be freezing my arse off on a train station in the middle of nowhere waiting for a minor royal to arrive to do some charity gig. And sometimes I'm in situations where a skirt is a provocation. So, no skirts.'

Rona nodded. 'I take your point. Plus, skirts means heels and I can see how you might not want to go too far down that road either. But there are plenty of well-cut trousers out there, Allie, and I am on a mission to introduce you to them. You've got slim hips and long legs, you'll look bloody great. Not like me. There's a reason I go for skirts! Now drink up. Here come our starters and it's time to get stuck into that wine.'

As well as the wine, their lunch was accompanied by large helpings of gossip from the office and beyond. Allie didn't know who half the people in the stories were, but she tucked away the stories of indiscretions, humiliations and inappropriate entanglements for future use. They were, she knew, a kind of social currency in her professional life. There was little malice in the anecdotage, but occasionally her tone shifted

204

and Allie could tell Rona had reason for clear dislike. Which was, Allie thought, fair enough.

They moved on to what Rona was now calling 'the big makeover'. She gave her a critical look. 'I can only do so much with the shopping,' Rona said. 'You need to sort out your hair.'

'What's wrong with my hair?' Allie was genuinely curious. Her hair was thick and straight and cut in an easy-to-manage bob.

'You have fantastic hair. It's so dark and dense. But that haircut has about as much life as my grannie's musquash coat. It needs to be shorter, with loads of texture and a bit of attitude. You need a stylist who can really cut, and then we'll actually be able to see your face. I'll have a think and a look in my contacts book and give you a couple of names. Honest to God, Allie, you'll look like a new woman.'

'That's what worries me.'

Rona laughed. 'Trust me, I'm paid to know about this stuff. I get that you don't want glamour or flash, but there's no reason why you can't look in the mirror and feel good about yourself.'

After Irish coffees, Rona swept her up and they spent the afternoon in a whirlwind of fabrics and colours. Small boutiques, a couple of department stores, and finally, a cab to the West End to an actual dressmaker. 'Don't call her that,' Rona instructed her. 'Tailoress, that's what she likes to be called. She'll love you. You've got great shoulders and a good through line to those narrow hips. Tailoring will make you look the business without scaring off the punters.'

Allie gave a scornful laugh. 'A few more lunches like that one and my slim hips will be history.' But she submitted to being assessed, measured, moved into the light and matched against fabrics. By the end, she'd committed to three pairs of trousers, two jackets and a waistcoat. 'You'll look amazing,' Rona promised.

'I've spent a month's wages this afternoon,' Allie pointed out, toting half a dozen carrier bags.

'I know, you get value for money when you shop with me. See the discounts you got in those boutiques? Top whack.'

Allie laughed. 'Fair enough. They love you, don't they?'

Rona smirked. 'Don't they just? Now you're all set to knock the socks off those arseholes in the newsroom. They're not going to consign you to the miracle babies any longer. Though . . . ' She paused. 'I do have a nice wee story I could pass your way. I was going to hold on to it for a picture spread next week, but it might be more your style.' There was a tease in her voice as she linked arms with Allie and steered her into the Grosvenor Hotel at the top of Byres Road. 'Cocktail hour,' she announced as they swept towards the bar.

Rona wouldn't be drawn on the story till they were settled at the bar with a pair of Negronis. Allie had never tasted one before, but her first mouthful convinced her that someone had invented a way to make red Cinzano worth drinking. 'So what's this story, then? Are you trying to get me drunk so I'll fall for it?'

Rona gave her an arch look. 'Aye, right. It's actually a fun story, I'm just not sure it's right for the women's page. What would you say to Scotland's first pregnant football referee?'

On first hearing, the combination of words made no sense. 'I don't get it.'

206

'I have a pal who's the headmistress of a primary school in darkest Lanarkshire. They've got no male teachers, and the kids love fitba'. So she persuaded a couple of her colleagues to join her in sitting the exams so they can referee their school matches. They're some of the first ever women to get the qualifications. And now one of them has fallen pregnant. So she's Scotland's first pregnant referee.'

Allie burst out laughing. 'That's a great story. I love it. Woman in a man's world, right enough. If you don't want it, I'll have it in a heartbeat.'

Rona gave her a hug. 'That's my girl. It's all yours. I'll leave a note in your pigeonhole on Monday. When you've nailed your big exclusive, you can have a bit of fun with it. And meanwhile . . . what's the score with you and Danny? How come you've hooked up with him?'

It was an odd question, Allie thought. 'I wouldn't say 'hooked up'. I mean, I've always got on with him, he's not as much of a dinosaur as the rest of them. But then he approached me with this investigation. He had the bare bones of the story but he was struggling with writing it.' She gave Rona a considering look. 'There's a surprising number of reporters on the *Clarion* who basically can't write for toffee. Angus has had me doing rewrites for a few of them.'

'That's a sub's job, surely?' Rona seemed genuinely interested. How could she not know that, Allie wondered.

'Angus doesn't like the subs to think the news reporters write so poorly. At least, that's what I think is going on. So, Danny knew I was the spit-and-polish lassie and he came to me with his story and asked for help. And we worked pretty well together.' She shrugged with one shoulder and took a swig of her drink. 'That's all there is to it.'

'Yet you're working with him again? He must have something going for him? Something more than not being a dinosaur?'

Why was Rona so interested in Danny? Was there something more to it? After all, she was probably only a couple of years older than him. 'I got a lead on a great story. But it needs somebody on the inside. And it's got to be a guy. I can't say more than that, not yet. So I thought Danny could return the favour, that's all.' She toyed with her glass. 'Why are you so bothered about Danny? Are you *interested* in him?'

For a moment, Rona was nonplussed. Then she tipped her head back and roared with laughter. 'Me? And Danny Sullivan?' More laughter. 'Oh, Allie, you've still got so much to learn.'

Allie felt strangely affronted. She didn't know what to say. But Rona recovered herself and hugged her with one arm. 'I'm sorry,' she said. 'Danny could not be further from my type. I'm just pure dead nosy, Allie. How else do you think I got to be the fount of all wisdom? Never mistake journalistic curiosity for desire. It'll get you into all sorts of trouble.' Then she giggled. 'Me and Danny. The only thing less likely is Angus editing the women's page.' She knocked back her drink. 'And now I'm going to love you and leave you. It's been the best fun, Allie. But I've got a heavy date tonight and I need to go home and get tarted up.' She slipped off her stool, not in the least unsteady, and gave Allie a kiss on the cheek. 'We need to do this again. Soon.'

And she was gone. Allie stared at the empty glass and wondered what that last exchange had really all been about.

30

They hadn't even left the pub car park in Stranraer when Malloch cut to the chase. 'So what did you tell him?' he demanded when Bell reached Robinson's crucial question.

'The truth. That Paul's gran bought him five Premium Bonds when he was born, and one of them came up last month. And Paul's more than happy to spend a grand on the struggle.'

Malloch gave a delighted laugh. 'What did he say to that?'

'"Sure, isn't it the Irish that are supposed to have the luck?" Bell's impression of an Irish accent was excruciating, but neither of them cared. 'Then he burst out laughing and said it was very fucking ironic that a state lottery should fund the overthrow of its own power. I hadn't thought about it like that, but I guess he's right. I mean, a state lottery? That's exactly what the Premium Bonds are.'

'So are we on?' Malloch's left knee was bouncing up and down, his fingers drumming on the dashboard.

'I don't know. It's too soon to say. Terry's just one member of the cell, so he's got to pass it up to the next in command, and he'll pass it to a brigade commander. He said it might probably go all the way up to the Army Council.'

'How long's that going to take? It's not like we've got forever. It's only a matter of weeks till the referendum. We need to shake the place to its foundations before then, Ding-dong.'

Bell started the engine and manoeuvred his way through the piles of frozen slush to the road. 'I don't know,' he said mutinously. 'There's nothing I can do to make it happen faster. I told Terry it was urgent.'

Malloch's laughter had a curdled quality to it. 'Who knew the revolution was just as fucking bureaucratic as the government we've already got? I tell you, it'll be a different story in an independent Scotland.'

★ ★ ★

The Clock Café at the bottom of Maryhill Road was a generic Formica, plywood and vinyl interior with a thin coating of grease on every surface, including the framed photos of past Partick Thistle teams. Danny deliberately arrived a few minutes early for the Sunday morning rendezvous. He wanted to look eager, but not suspiciously so. Ding-dong Bell had beaten him to it, and was already halfway through a bacon roll. 'I woke up starving,' he admitted. 'All that excitement yesterday, I must've worked up an appetite.'

Before Danny could ask for details, Roddy Farquhar and Deke Malloch arrived together. They were, he thought, the least likely bunch of conspirators he could have imagined. Business was postponed while all four ordered a full Scottish breakfast, 'None of your tomatoes, for God's sake, we're no' jessies,' and mugs of tea.

'The suspense is killing me,' Danny said as the waitress shuffled off. 'How did it go?'

They all leaned forward, heads close together, and sat rapt while Bell retold his tale. When he reached the end of what he'd already revealed to Malloch in the car, his partner in crime exultantly exclaimed, 'How

210

great is that? Now we've just got to wait and keep our fingers crossed.'

Bell shook his head, a faint smile twitching the corners of his mouth. 'You're behind the times, Deke. Stop the presses, there's more news.'

'More news than last night? How?'

It was a question Danny wanted answered too. 'Did your pal phone you?'

Bell scoffed. 'Don't be daft. They're way too sharp for that. They know the Special Branch and the RUC are all over them. They don't take chances. No, I got a note through my door. Somebody must have delivered it during the night, it was just sitting on my doormat when I got up.'

'How did they get a note to you?' Farquhar asked. It was, thought Danny, the least interesting thing he could have asked.

'They'll have active units over here,' Malloch said loftily, as if the IRA's organisational structure were an open book to him. 'They'll have systems in place for passing messages. But what did the message say? Are we on, or what?'

Bell scrabbled in the pocket of his leather biker's jacket and pulled out a crumpled envelope. He was about to remove its contents when the waitress arrived and plonked four thick white pottery mugs on the table. 'Four teas, boys,' she said, her tone funereal.

They helped themselves, waiting till she was out of earshot again. 'C'mon, Ding-dong, don't keep us waiting,' Malloch muttered.

Bell unfolded the paper and waved it at them. Black capital letters on cheap lined writing paper. Before Danny could make out the words, Bell read them out. "Phone this number from a phone box. Sunday

211

morning at ten."

'That's it?' Farquhar, incredulous.

'And did you?' Danny, to the point.

'I did.' Bell, smug.

'And what happened?' Malloch, loud enough to turn heads.

'Keep it down.' Danny, urgent.

'I got a message. 'Outside the Butcher's Dog at half past nine tomorrow. You and the lucky boy and his winnings. You'll be met.'' Again, Bell's atrocious approximation of a Belfast accent.

'What does that mean, then?' Farquhar, again with the least interesting question.

Malloch let out a sharp noise of exasperation. 'It means we're in business. The fucking IRA want to do business with us, Roddy, you bell-end.'

Now the waitress was back with two loaded plates. She deposited them in front of Danny and Farquhar with what looked like the first smile of the day, judging by the effort it took. The other two plates followed immediately. Danny couldn't remember ever seeing a more heavily loaded breakfast feast — a link sausage, a square of Lorne sausage, three rashers of Ayrshire middle, two tattie scones, a slice each of black pudding, haggis and fruit dumpling, a spoonful of baked beans, two perfectly fried eggs and two pieces of buttered toast. It made the office canteen's offering seem scant, and nobody had ever said that in Danny's hearing. 'I think this might kill me,' he said.

'Quick, take it off him,' Malloch said. 'We need you tomorrow night. With a pocketful of readies, my man.'

Dear God, it was really happening, Danny thought. He was getting away with it. That moment of horrified recognition in the Spaghetti Factory had come to nothing. They'd genuinely taken him at face value. Allie was going to be over the moon about this. Two cracking exposés in a matter of weeks — they were the kings of the hill. Stories like this opened doors. He'd put money on him and Allie being in Fleet Street before the dust of the devolution referendum had settled.

He looked round the table and grinned. 'No bother. I'll sort the money out first thing in the morning. You can count on me.'

Malloch clapped him on the back. 'You'll be the first hero of the New Republic.'

Bell laughed. 'Aye, you'll look good on the stamps and the money.'

Farquhar appraised him, head cocked. 'Right enough, you've got the profile for it.'

Danny dipped a corner of his tattie scone into an egg yolk and bit it off. 'I'm not counting my chickens, boys. We've got a long way to go yet. This is just the first step.'

'Mibbes,' Bell said, suddenly serious. 'But it's one helluva first step.' He raised his mug. 'Here's to shaking off the shackles. Here's to the New Republic.'

31

Sunday morning barely dawned. A low grim sky hung over Glasgow, matching Allie's mood. Even the energy of Elvis Costello's *Armed Forces* wasn't enough to lift her spirits. The cheerfulness of Rona Dunsyre that had rubbed off on her the day before had worn thin with the contemplation of what she and Danny had embarked on. There was no word from him before she had to leave for work, and she tried not to make that grounds for anxiety.

She failed, of course. As she knew she would. Sunday backshift was never going to take her mind off what was going on. Anything of interest in the overnights had already been dealt out to the day shift; the backshift reporter's principal task was to mind the shop while everybody who wasn't out on a story went to the Press Club to play snooker. They'd roll back at some point between three and four, grumbling about having to do some work. Meanwhile, Allie sat at the newsdesk, answering occasional phone calls, swapping gossip with Fatima McGeechan, and working her way through a stack of local weeklies in the usually vain hope of finding a story worth pursuing.

When the rest of the team straggled back, Fatima told her to do the weather story. So Allie headed back to her own desk and started the round of calls. Police, coastguard, local Met Office and the AA. The usual Highland roads were closed, there were warnings of freezing fog and black ice, and the main road between Montrose and Arbroath was closed because of a collision between a jack-knifed lorry and a bread van. No injuries, just a diversion via Friockheim. She dropped off her copy and headed down to the canteen, hoping Danny would be there. Ideally in one piece.

He was in the same corner where they'd met for their first curry, looking no more relaxed than he had that night. He showed no signs of the buzz she'd felt from her involvement with stories that felt substantial. But then, she hadn't blown a hole below the waterline of the key relationships in her life. She picked up a can of Irn Bru and joined him. He greeted her with a wan smile. 'Well, I'm still alive. Cover still intact,' he began.

'How was it?' She ripped off the ring-pull and took a swig, loving the sensation of sugar and caffeine and a bite of ginger hitting her.

'A weird mix. It's exhilarating to penetrate a group like this without rousing any suspicions. Fuck, *I'd* be suspicious of me, turning up out of the blue like a fairy godmother. But on the other hand, it's terrifying that a bunch of eejits can get so far down the road to mayhem so easily. It's like none of it is real to them. They're like a bunch of wee boys playing cowboys and Indians.' He sighed and shook his head. 'They wind each other up, like it's a dare to see who'll bottle out first.'

'So what actually happened? Did Bell meet up with his IRA contact?'

Danny gave a mirthless laugh. 'Aye, he did. His pal Terry Robinson turns out to be as well-connected as Bell promised. He said he'd be in touch.' He outlined what he'd heard in the Clock Café earlier and Allie felt her jaw drop as he explained the plans for a meeting.

'Jesus, Danny,' she breathed. 'So what are you going to do?'

He chewed the corner of his thumb. 'I've got to go through with it, don't I? Otherwise we've got no story and they've got a direct line into a source of explosives. And they're mad enough to find the money somewhere else.' Another dry laugh. 'Nice respectable lads like them? They'll probably get a bank loan.'

'We can't hand over the cash, just like that! We're funding terrorism.' Allie shook her head in dismay. 'I said you should never have offered the money.'

'Well, it's done now.'

A long moment of awkward silence. Allie's mind was racing, trying to find a way forward that would work. 'A grand, yes? That's what we're talking about?' Danny nodded. 'Well, that's simple enough. Your bank won't hand over a thousand pounds in cash without a couple of days' notice. Why don't you turn up with a couple of hundred? Explain that was all you could get without letting them know in advance, but you'll have the balance to hand over when they hand over the explosives?'

Danny frowned. 'What if they think we're pissing them around?'

'They might put the fear of God into you, but they're not going to hurt you. Not with the prospect of another eight hundred quid to come.' Allie tried to sound more confident than she felt. 'Plus it gives us a chance to get our ducks in a row for the story. We need to do complete backgrounders on your wee pals. Addresses, employers, family, education, friends. And that means it's time to talk to Angus.'

Danny groaned. 'He's going to go mental.'

'He'll not go mental for long. He'll see what a brilliant story it is. We need him onside, Danny. And not simply because we need a full team digging into your new Republican Army. We need to protect ourselves. Right now, when it's you and me two-handed in the thick of this, it'd be very bloody easy to paint us as part of the conspiracy. Even to make it look like we've incited the whole thing just to get a story. But once we get the newsdesk on board, we cover our own backs. We go back to being the crusading journalists.'

Danny picked at the rim of his Styrofoam cup of lentil soup, scattering tiny white spheres over the table like dandruff. 'Except we did sort of kickstart it. Before I put the money in the mix, they were just a bunch of bams talking each other up. I made it so they couldn't back down.'

Exasperated, Allie said, 'Gonnae no' with the Catholic guilt. These guys were primed for trouble. Deke Malloch, in a public meeting, talking about the attention-grabbing tactics of the IRA. Gary Bell, jumping straight in with the offer of his IRA Active Service Unit contact. All we did was speed them along a road they were already driving down. That doesn't make it our fault. What we're doing is making sure they don't get to their destination. We need to talk to Angus. He's not just our boss, he's our insurance policy. Look at the way he got the Razor on board to cover our backs on your story.'

Danny looked ready to burst into tears. 'I understand what you're saying. It's the right thing. But not yet, Allie. Please, not yet.'

'Why not? We've come this far, we know what the story is. 'A ruthless gang of radical insurgents hell-bent on bringing terrorism to the Scottish referendum were closed down last night thanks to the *Clarion*.''

His mouth twisted in a wry smile. 'No question,

you're the lassie with the magic words. But here's the thing. We bring Angus on board now and tomorrow night will turn into a three-ring circus. We'll have snappers galore staking out the street outside the pub and all they'll end up with is blurry over-exposed shots nobody could ever pick out of a line-up. The glory boys will be all over it, trying to steal our story out from under our noses, dying for car chases and high drama. If anybody gets me into bother with the IRA, it'll be my own side with their grandstanding.'

'You're exaggerating.'

'You think? You saw how quick Peter McGovern was to snatch top billing on my story. They'll all be at it. You're still new at this. The guys are nice to you because you're a lassie and they don't see you as any kind of threat. You do them a favour, with the miracle babies and the women's stories. You've no idea how cut-throat those bastards are. Let me get through tomorrow night and then we'll confess to Angus.'

Allie bought a few moments by lighting up. She sighed out a long plume of smoke and stared unseeing across the canteen. 'I can't be there for you at half past nine tomorrow night,' she said. 'I'm still on the backshift. I'm not lowsed till ten. And you know there's no chance of an early cut when the night shift are still in the pub. You'll be out there on your own, Danny. And I'm not comfortable with that.'

'I'll be fine, Allie. I'm the boy with the money, remember? The goose that lays the golden eggs. I'll be wrapped in cotton wool. If anybody's going to get a smack, it'll be Gary Bell, for making promises he couldn't keep.'

Allie scoffed. 'Is that supposed to fill me with confidence? Because it disnae.'

'Give me tomorrow night. Then we'll tell Angus everything.'

'Then he can let the dogs out to dig through the mountains of uncollected rubbish in Deke and Ding-Dong and Roddy's back courts and find all their skeletons.' Allie's grin was more rueful than enthusiastic. She almost missed the glimmer of anxiety that crossed Danny's face. 'It's not what I'd choose, but you know the way things work better than I do.' She dipped her hand into her bag and came out with her miniature tape recorder. She pushed it across the table to him.

'I'm right, trust me.' This time, his smile reached his eyes, reminding her of how attractive he was when he relaxed. He picked up the recorder and tucked it into his inside pocket.

Allie stood up, knocking back the last mouthful of her drink. 'I need to get back upstairs.' She turned to go, then caught herself. 'By the way, any word from Auntie Senga?'

The brightness stayed in his eyes. 'She rang me earlier. She passed on the message and Joseph told her he'd already been in touch with the police. He said he'd told them the truth. That he was nothing more than the delivery boy, that he had no idea what he was carrying, that he's just a lowly clerk. A lowly clerk that drives a six-grand sports car.' She wasn't deaf to the irony in his voice. 'He's settled on his line, with the family as well as the cops. He's the victim, I'm the traitor. And it looks like he's conned the polis as well, since they let him go home after they interviewed him. Like I told you, he's good at the injured innocent routine.'

'And they've got bigger fish to fry. Why bother with

an expensive trial for a bit player like him?'

Danny shrugged. 'I suppose I should be glad. I don't want my mum and dad to go through that. But if everybody thinks he's the victim, where does that leave me? Even Auntie Senga thinks I need to keep my distance.'

'That'll pass, Danny. Like you said, when they see the good work you're doing, they'll understand that the last thing you wanted to do was hurt your family.'

He turned away. 'So we need to make this story work. Thanks for cutting me some slack. I promise. After tomorrow, we'll go to Angus. No more crawling out on a limb.'

32

Bell and Danny emerged from the pub at half past nine on the dot, as arranged. They weren't sorry to leave; the Butcher's Dog was a dingy dive for serious drinkers with nowhere else to be. They walked down deserted streets from the heart of the Calton district towards the wide sweep of Glasgow Green.

A few minutes later, Bell said, 'I hear footsteps. I think we've got company.' His voice was tentative.

'Good,' Danny said firmly. 'We're supposed to have company, right?'

They walked on, turning as directed into a narrow lane whose streetlights appeared to have been turned down several notches. 'It only feels darker, right?' Bell asked.

Before Danny could reply, a small hell broke loose. Two burly men cannoned into them from behind as a black taxi drew up alongside. Caught unawares, the two were easily huckled into the back of the cab, sacks that smelled of some sort of grain pulled over their heads and shoulders. They were hurled to the floor, each pinned down by heavy feet planted in their chests.

'Shut the fuck up and you'll be fine.' A Northern Irish voice, unmistakable.

Danny did as he was told. It never occurred to him to do otherwise. What mattered now was not to let fear overcome him. There had been an arrangement, he reminded himself. It had been short on details, but he had to believe this was part of it. The cab hurtled through the streets of Glasgow, cornering sharply at times, slowing at others, presumably for traffic lights. It was beyond Danny to form any idea of where they were going.

Time passed. Impossible to know how much. Inside the sacks, his breathing grew tighter as dust clogged his lungs and fear built in his chest. Then, without warning, the cab shuddered to a halt, engine still running. The quality of sound changed when the door opened. Danny was shoved out of the cab and yanked to his feet, the sacks hauled down to trap his arms at his sides. The sounds of effort around him led him to believe Bell was having the same experience.

A door creaked open, they were pushed through, stumbling against each other. Down a hallway, the door slamming behind them, cutting outside noises dead. Another door, and warmth hit suddenly. The sacks were dragged off and they stood, blinking and bemused, in somebody's living room.

The man sitting on the well-worn brown sofa was a familiar type. Hard muscles, tight little beer belly, jeans taut over heavy thighs. Celtic football shirt and sentimental tattoos on his forearms. What was less familiar but not unexpected was that his head and face were covered with a black balaclava. His eyes never left the two visitors. He looked them up and down and one corner of his mouth twitched in what might have been scorn.

'So, youse are the boys,' he said mildly.

Danny glanced around. Three other masked men; the two who had presumably abducted them and a third sitting on a dining chair, a sawn-off shotgun in his lap. 'And you must be the man,' he replied.

Sofa man chuckled. 'Call me Declan. It's not my

name, you understand, but it'll do.'

'Pleased to meet you, Declan. I assume you know why we're here?'

Not-Declan nodded. 'You'd like to make a purchase.'

Now Bell chipped in. 'We're like you. We're fighting for a cause. But we don't have an organisation as well-established as yours. We don't have support from across the Atlantic so we thought it made sense to look closer to home.'

'Across the Irish Sea,' Danny added.

'And why should we accept your custom?' Not-Declan asked, leaning back in his seat and lighting a cigarette.

'Because our goal is the same as yours,' Bell said, hitting his stride. 'Independence from the English state. We're tired of talking. It's time to take action. Just like your lot, our politicians are soft as shite. The SNP can't even decide if they want independence or if they'll settle for a devolved parliament.'

'One thing they are clear about,' Not-Declan said. 'Catholics not welcome here.'

Grown bold now, Danny shrugged. 'Show me a Scottish institution that doesn't have sectarianism somewhere in its bones. That's one of the things that's going to change in an independent Scotland. Look, we know we need to change, and when we get where we want to be, we'll remember who our friends are, make no mistake about that.'

Not-Declan said nothing.

'We're not asking for a handout here,' Bell said. 'We're willing to pay. We just need some help.'

'How do we know you're not trying to trap us? For all we know, youse could be working for the RUC or the Special Branch or MI5.' Not-Declan's voice had discovered a hard edge.

Bell shrugged. 'I'm spoken for by one of your own.'

Danny joined in. 'But you're right. You don't know. That's why you brought us here the way you did. We couldn't describe you and we don't have any idea where we are. We couldn't expose you even if we wanted to.'

'Look, all we want is to do a deal.' It was almost a plea from Bell.

Not-Declan's face covering expanded sideways as he grinned. 'Fair enough. What are youse after?'

Bell took a deep breath. 'Enough Semtex for four decent-sized explosions. Detonators and fuses.'

'Not much, then.' The sarcasm obvious. 'No guns?'

Bell shook his head. 'No guns. Just four bombs.'

'We don't deliver. You'd have to pick them up your-selves.'

The two Scots exchanged looks. 'We can do that. Just tell us when and where,' Danny said.

The Irishman nodded. 'And money up front. You were told, a grand in cash, used notes, I believe?'

Danny pulled a fat envelope out of his waistband and passed it to Not-Declan. In turn, he tossed it to one of the abductors, who began to count the bundle of notes. 'There's only two hundred there,' Danny said hastily. 'We only got confirmation yesterday morning and my bank won't let me withdraw more than that in a day unless I give advance notice. I can have the rest of it on Thursday.'

Not-Declan guffawed. 'Did youse ever hear the like of this, lads? They keep their money in the bank, so they do. You can tell they don't live in a police state like we do. Sonny, you don't keep your fighting fund in the bank, where the peelers can track its move-ments. You ever heard of a safe? Or even a cashbox under the floorboards.' He shook his head. 'Fuckin' amateur city.' Disgust and contempt mingled. 'No wonder youse had to come to the professionals.'

'Two hundred, boss,' the cash counter confirmed.

'Nothing happens now till we get the balance. In cash. We'll be in touch about the arrangements,' Not-Declan said.

'How can we be sure?' Danny couldn't help him-self.

There was no mirth in Not-Declan's laugh. 'Ye can't, sonny. That's just the way it goes. Now be good lads and put the sacks on again. And next time — don't fuck about with us.'

The abduction was played out in reverse. The two men were rolled out of the back of the cab on the south side of the river, at the edge of one of the empty blocks where the slum tenements of the Gorbals had once stood. They struggled out of their sacks and looked around at the scrubby grass littered with empty bottles and cans, chip papers and dog shit, trying to work out where they were. At the same moment, they both caught sight of the unmistakable frontage of the Citizens' Theatre, its banner advertising all seats 50p and a poster for Cocteau's *Orpheus*, Shakespeare's *Macbeth* and Goldoni's *Country Life*. That was enough to orientate them and they hurried off into the night. Danny was gripped with anxiety and uncertainty, and he suspected Bell felt the same. So much could yet go wrong, even if the Irish came good.

It didn't bear thinking about.

33

Angus Carlyle looked Danny and Allie up and down, perplexed. Neither was dressed for work; neither was scheduled to be in the office that morning. His eyes slid across to the shift rota to double-check. 'What's going on?' he demanded, belligerence his default.

'We need to talk to you,' Allie said.

'I kind of assumed that was why you were standing there on your day off, Burns. What's the matter?'

'Can we do this in your office?' Danny said.

'If you're looking for a raise after the Paragon story, you're out of luck. The kitty's empty. The bosses have raided the piggy bank to keep the printers from striking like every other bugger that feels hard done by.' He turned back to the copy in his fist, well aware that the attention of the entire newsroom was on him.

Frustrated, Allie said, 'I've got more sense than to give up my day off for something that pointless. We need to talk to you because we've got something you can do something about, boss.'

He gave her a comedy frown. 'That doesn't narrow it down much, Burns. I hope you're not leading this boy astray, I've barely got him trained up.' He grimaced for the gallery.

Allie rolled her eyes. 'We need to talk to you confidentially about another story.'

Carlyle sighed theatrically and gestured at his desk. 'Will this not wait till after conference? Can you not see I've got today's schedule to worry about? You're not the only ones with a story.'

Allie and Danny exchanged looks. 'We thought you'd like to get moving on this as soon as possible,' Danny said.

'Oh, for fuck's sake.' He looked at the clock. 'You can have fifteen minutes. My office, now.'

They trailed behind him. Carlyle held the door open ostentatiously and welcomed them in with a flourish. So much for keeping under the radar, Allie thought.

The news editor threw himself into his chair and loosened his tie. 'I'm listening.'

'I've been building up my contacts,' Allie began.

'Give the girl a gold star,' Carlyle interrupted. 'That's what you're paid for.'

'I've been going to political meetings,' Allie battled on, 'because the kind of people who go to them often have stories to tell. I was at a fringe meeting supporting independence the other week and I overheard three young men talking radical, insurrectionary tactics. They were invoking the IRA, saying that's what was needed to make the Scots rise up against Westminster.'

Carlyle snorted. 'The usual big talk. Scotland isn't going to rise up any time soon, not unless the revolution comes with a promise of free whisky and fish suppers.' He shifted his bulk, ready to rise.

'There's more,' Danny said. 'Allie brought me on board because she knew that they'd never let a woman in on their plans. I managed to get alongside them. Cutting a long story short, I'm slap bang in the middle of buying explosives from the IRA to blow up targets in Scotland.'

Shock froze Carlyle's face. But he recovered quickly. 'When you say, 'slap bang in the middle', what exactly do you mean?' He enunciated each word carefully, as if they might themselves explode.

Danny gave Allie a quick look. 'I went to a meeting with an IRA Active Service Unit cell and handed over a down payment for enough Semtex and detonators for four bombs.'

'You personally handed over cash? For bomb-making equipment?' Carlyle's look of horror finally brought home to Allie the recklessness of what they'd done. Yes, she'd argued to Danny that it would be possible for others to paint them as members of the terrorist group. But she'd only been using that as leverage to get him to come inside the tent with her. The reaction of her boss stripped away all the self-justification she'd been hiding behind.

'Christ,' Carlyle muttered. 'Who knows about this?'

'Just us,' Danny said. 'The other men, they've got no clue I'm a journalist. They trust me.'

Carlyle gave a bitter laugh. 'They trust you because you're funding their attempt at bringing terrorism to Scotland.' His hands curled into fists on the desk. He looked at Danny as if he'd cheerfully make him their target. 'You are so far over the fucking line here.'

'I couldn't think of another way to stop them except by standing the story up,' Allie said, defiant. 'And I couldn't think of another way to stand the story up except by going undercover. And Danny's already proved he can handle that.'

Carlyle squeezed his eyes shut in a frown. He shook his massive head like a tormented bull, then his eyes snapped open. He glared at Allie. 'You didn't think to bring it to me? To establish right at the start that this was an investigation? Not a bloody provocation?'

Allie stared at the floor. 'I thought you wouldn't take me seriously. Or, if you did, that you'd take it off me and give it to somebody else.' She looked up and met his gaze. 'I wanted to keep what was mine, Angus.'

A long, hard look. Then he almost smiled. 'Fair point.' But a change in the weather followed immediately. 'It doesn't mean you're not a pair of fucking idiots.' He stood up. 'I need to talk to the editor. We need to figure out how we nail this down without the pair of you ending up behind bars. Don't fucking move.' He left the room, muttering under his breath.

Allie gave a weak laugh. 'Well, that went well.'

'He didn't give us the sack. And he didn't throw the typewriter out of the window.'

'What are you talking about?'

'When Raymond Blackwood admitted screwing a gangster's wife to get the inside track, Angus was so enraged he threw Raymond's typewriter out of the window. Missed a pensioner's dog by inches.'

Allie giggled. 'That's not funny, Danny.'

'I know. The old woman fainted. The paper had to buy her off to stop her going to the *Daily Record* with the story. So right now, we're ahead.'

Neither of them could think of anything to say. Time crawled by. The longer they waited, the more convinced Allie became that she was sitting in the waiting room of the end of her career. Eventually, she caved and lit up a cigarette. Danny took that as a signal to jump up and start pacing.

Almost half an hour passed before the door burst open and Carlyle returned. He closed it carefully behind him and returned to his seat. 'First things first. You're both still employed. Which was not a given when I walked out of here, let me tell you. However, the editor, being a Unionist by breeding and by disposition, is delighted at the idea of a big story that puts the SNP's gas at a peep.'

'It's not the SNP — ' Allie attempted.

Carlyle held up a meaty hand. 'I know that. But the editor thinks anything that paints nationalism in a bad light knocks the SNP by association. So he's got a hard-on for this. And he's already sounding the trumpet for our bold journalism. You're in the good books for now, but you've got to deliver. So here's the game plan. You're coming off the shift rota, both of you. You're going to sit down and write full memos. I want every cough, spit and fart so far. Who, where, when and what. And meanwhile, we're going to work up full backgrounders on your guys. With total discretion, of course. Obviously Wee Gordon Beattie has the police contacts, but even better, he's got a Special Branch guy in his back pocket. If these guys have been caught so much as peeing up a wall after closing time, we'll know all about it. Unofficially. That goes without saying. We'll not bring the police in till your boys have got their hands on the kit. Now, when's the next step in this glorious crusade?'

'Danny's supposed to meet the IRA contacts with the balance of the money on Thursday night.'

Carlyle sucked in his breath through his teeth. 'That's tight, but we'll have to manage. I need a full outline of the arrangements, so we can work out how to cover it and still protect you. And we'll need to arrange for snatch pics of both sets of villains, the Irish and the Scots. Now, did you actually use your own money to make the deposit on these explosives?'

Danny nodded, and Carlyle threw a pen across the desk in exasperation. 'See the pair of you, you shouldn't be allowed out without a fucking nanny and toddler reins. OK, so here's what you have to do, Danny Boy. Make out an expenses claim for the money you donated to the IRA. And backdate it to the day before the handover. I will sign it and stick it in the bundle of this week's expenses. So it looks like this whole carry-on has been an authorised adventure.' He stood up and pointed to the desk. 'Bring another typewriter in here and the pair of you get to work. I want everything you've got before the end of the morning.'

He paused on his way out, his hand on the doorknob. He turned his head and glared at Allie. 'You're going to give me a heart attack, Burns, but you've got what it takes.' Then he was gone, the door banging shut behind him.

'So what am I? Chopped liver?' Danny muttered. 'I'm the one who brought in the Paragon story.'

'He knows that. But you've been here long enough to be part of the team. He's just making sure I know I belong too.' Allie got to her feet. 'I'm going to get another typewriter.'

Danny jumped up. 'I'll go.'

Allie tutted. 'I'm not made of china, I've been lugging typewriters around for years. Sit down and get to work.'

By the time she staggered back in with one of the heavy Remingtons, Danny was hammering the keys with his two-fingers-and-a-thumb approach. They exchanged a grin and Allie rolled a fresh copy pad on to the platen. For half an hour, the only sounds were the tap and click and ding of words forming on paper. Then Danny sat back and linked his hands behind his head. 'I need a break. I'm going down to get a cup of tea. Do you want anything?'

'Coffee,' Allie muttered without looking up from the page. She carried on writing her memo. She'd finished the outline of events and moved on to descriptions of the three men and what she remembered of their conversation.

When Danny returned, his eyes were wide and his hands were shaking, tea and coffee spilling over the rims of the mugs. He closed the door behind him, leaning against it as if to prevent anyone entering. His eyebrows were gathered in a tight frown. 'What's wrong?' Allie said, unnerved by his appearance.

'I saw somebody I didn't expect to see in here,' he stammered.

'Who?'

'I don't know his name. I — I can't explain. Look, I need you to go out there and find out who it is that's sitting with Wee Gordon Beattie.'

'Why? I don't understand —'

'Please, Allie. Just do it.' Insistent and unnerved. It was a combination she couldn't resist.

She slipped out of the door and looked across to the corner of the reporters' area where Wee Gordon Beattie, the crime correspondent of the *Clarion* perched. He was a wizened little man of indeterminate years, invariably dressed in a tweed jacket over a black polo-neck sweater and narrow black trousers like the ones the Beatles used to wear when they first became successful. Allie thought he looked more like a retired jockey than a journalist, but he sounded more like a crook himself, talking out of the side of his mouth in a broad Glasgow accent. On the occasions when she'd been deputed to write up his copy, she'd struggled to penetrate what he'd been saying. But there was no denying he had the most remarkable contacts on every side of the law — criminals, cops, fiscals and sheriffs all seemed to confide in Wee Gordon Beattie.

The man sitting next to him appeared to be in his late twenties. His dark blond hair was neatly barbered and he had the kind of unremarkable appearance that would blur into commonplace within an hour of meeting him. At first sight, Allie had no idea why he'd provoked such a powerful reaction in Danny.

She crossed to her own desk and raked around in her drawer. She glanced at the man with Beattie and frowned. Turning to Big Kenny Stone, she said, 'Who's that with Wee Gordon? I know him from somewhere but I can't think where.'

Kenny looked round. 'I don't know his name. All I know is he's Gordie's Special Branch guy. I've seen them together a few times.'

Allie shrugged. 'I must be confusing him with somebody else.' She fished an old notebook out of her drawer, as if that had been what she was looking for.

'What are you and Danny up to?' Kenny asked, almost as an afterthought.

'Just following up from the Paragon story,' she lied comfortably. 'A couple of loose ends.' Before he could say more, she moved away.

Back in Carlyle's office, Danny was hunched up in his chair, like a child who's been slapped. 'Who is it?' he demanded before she'd even shut the door.

'I didn't get a name, but he's Gordie's Special Branch source.'

What little colour remained in Danny's face drained away. 'Oh fuck,' he breathed.

'What is it? What the hell's wrong, Danny?'

His eyes flicked around the room, searching out invisible predators. 'I can't tell you here, Allie. Let's get this finished and deal with Angus and the editor. Then you can come back to mine and I'll tell you everything. Promise.'

34

Allie parked her car as instructed on a piece of waste ground between a pair of blackened sandstone tenements. No sooner had she stepped out of her car than a strange lumpy figure loomed up out of the darkness. Her hand closed in a fist round her keys, their points standing proud of her fingers in a vicious knuckle-duster. The figure came closer and she could see he was a man dressed in an apparently random collection of garments, from a woolly pompom hat to a distressed army surplus jacket whose original colour she suspected would still be questionable in bright sunlight. 'A' right?' he demanded with a gust of stale tobacco and rancid cider that could have stripped the flesh from a dead creature.

'Aye,' Allie said, trying to sidestep him.

'I'm Jimmy,' he announced. 'I'm the parking attendant.'

'This is a car park?' Danny hadn't warned her about this.

He spread his arms to encompass the waste ground with its broken bricks, clumps of half-hearted vegetation and crumpled beer tins. And half a dozen cars dotted around. 'That thing you just got out of? Is that a car, or am I seeing things again?'

'It's a car.'

'And is the engine running?'

She smiled. He was playing the familiar Glasgow game of genial sarcasm. 'Yes, OK, it's parked.'

'Now, I am responsible for the maintenance and

upkeep of this facility. So that'll be fifty pence, madam. If you want your wheels still to be on it when you get back.'

Allie dug into the jacket pocket where she always kept a handful of loose change for phone calls and parking meters. She picked her way through the coins, assembling the right amount.

While she was fiddling with the money, Jimmy said, 'You visiting somebody?'

She handed over the money. 'Why else would I be here? It's not like the area's teeming with attractions.'

'True. Who are you here to see, then? I might know if they're in. Save you a disappointing climb up to the third floor.' He winked. 'No extra charge, like.'

No harm in it, she supposed. It might even grant her an extra level of protection. 'I work with Danny Sullivan.'

Jimmy nodded. 'The Jimmy Olsen of the South Side. Aye, he's in all right. Got back about ten minutes ago.'

'Thanks, Jimmy.'

He stepped to one side and escorted her to the pavement. 'You have a nice evening, now, hen.'

Danny's flat was on the first floor of the tenement. The street door opened on to what Allie had learned to call a wally close — a hallway and staircase decorated chest-high with ceramic tiles, a marker of the more prosperous streets. In this case, the tiles were plain buttery yellow with a border of dark green, but they were spotless and in good condition. Danny was clearly doing well for himself.

He opened the door so swiftly she wondered whether he'd been hovering behind it, anxious for her arrival. 'Come on in,' he said, stepping back to let her pass.

The interior was not what she expected. The original features — cornices, dado rails, panelled doors — had all disappeared, replaced by clean, straight lines. The floorboards had been painted a dark glossy oxblood, and the walls were all white. It looked like it had been transplanted from a modern block. Before she could react, Danny said quickly, 'I bought it off an artist. He was moving to New York, he'd been trying to sell it for ages but people looking for tenement flats, they want the traditional look. So I got it cheap.'

'It's amazing. The rooms look enormous.' She followed him into the living room. He'd chosen furniture with the same clean lines. A white table in the bay window sporting a heavy black onyx ashtray and a trio of matching candlesticks, a pair of firm-looking black leather sofas, a big TV set and a black stereo. A black-and-white cowskin rug covered the floor between the sofas. On the walls were a series of framed black-and-white photographs of Hollywood icons. Danny waved Allie to a seat and she found herself staring at Marlene Dietrich in a top hat. There was something quite disconcerting about the star's gaze.

'Thanks for coming over.' Danny sat opposite her on the edge of his seat, hands clenched between his knees.

They were past the point of small talk. Allie was there for a reason, and it wasn't to discuss Danny's décor. 'I need you to tell me why you freaked out when you saw who Gordon Beattie was talking to.'

'I recognised him.'

'Obviously. But where from?'

Danny frowned and sighed. 'It's complicated. And when you told me who he is . . . it just got more complicated. I don't even know where to start.'

237

'At the risk of sounding flippant, why not start at the beginning?'

He blinked hard and gave her a piteous look. 'I'm like you, Allie.'

Baffled, she said, 'What do you mean, you're like me?'

He stared at the floor. 'I'm gay.'

It was so far from what she'd expected that all she could do was stare at him.

He looked up. 'We're two of a kind, stuck in the *Clarion* closet.'

'What on earth makes you say that? I'm not gay, Danny. I don't have a problem with you being gay, but I'm not a lesbian. Why would you think that?'

Dismayed, he flushed a deep scarlet. 'Because you and Rona Dunsyre. You hang about together.'

'That doesn't make us lesbians.'

Danny shook his head, puzzled. 'But Rona is.'

The surprises were coming at her like arrows. 'She is?'

'Did you not know? Really?'

'It never crossed my mind. How the hell do you know?'

'I've seen her out and about. There's a couple of gay bars in town . . . ' He buried his face in his hands. 'I've made such an arse of myself. I thought you would understand, I thought you were one of us.'

'Danny, I'm still your friend. This doesn't make any difference.'

He shook his head.

'At the risk of sounding like a cliché . . . My best friend from the training scheme, Marcus? He's a gay man. We swap letters most weeks. I won't pretend it didn't freak me out a bit when he told me. I'd never

238

really known anybody gay before. But now? I hardly think about it.' Allie jumped to her feet and crossed to sit beside him. She put a hand on his shoulder. 'I'm not going to judge you, Danny. I don't care who you sleep with. Tell me what's wrong. Until you tell me, there's nothing I can do to help.'

He reached up and grasped her fingers. 'I've never told anybody before. I mean, obviously the men I meet in bars, they know. But I've never said anything to my friends.' He scoffed. 'Or my family. And certainly not anybody at work. There's too much to lose. It's still against the fucking law for two men to have sex in this primitive bloody country.'

'You can trust me, Danny.'

He took a deep breath. 'I should have told you this before, but I was scared. When I walked into the Spaghetti Factory on Friday night and I saw Roddy Farquhar, I just about shat myself.'

'You recognised him?'

'Oh yeah, I recognised him.' Danny got up and opened a white cabinet set against the wall. 'I need a drink, Allie.' He slopped a large whisky into a glass and took a swallow. 'What about you?'

'Got any vodka?'

He waved a bottle of Smirnoff at her. 'You take Coke in it, right?' She nodded. 'Give me a minute.' He reappeared with a can and topped up her glass. He flopped back on to the sofa and clinked her glass with an ironic smile.

'I've seen Roddy a few times in town.' He gave a dry little laugh. 'Obviously I'm not his type because he didn't show any signs of recognising me. I thought I'd got away with it. No comebacks. Just a moment of panic.' He ground to a halt and drank more whisky.

'So what changed? What's any of it got to do with the Special Branch guy?'

'I've seen him before too, Allie. The last time I saw Wee Gordon Beattie's SB informer, he had his tongue halfway down Roddy Farquhar's throat.'

35

It was an explosive revelation. Allie could barely begin to grasp the implications. For a long moment, she struggled to find words. She clutched her glass as if it were a lifebelt in a turbulent sea. Danny swallowed his whisky and got up to pour another. When he had his back to her, she said, 'You mean . . . Beattie's source is Farquhar's, what — boyfriend?'

Danny sat on the far sofa, where Allie had started. 'I don't know whether it's that kind of relationship. Maybe more casual?'

'So is it just a sex thing? Or do you think he's chasing the same thing we are? That he's targeting Farquhar because the SB have got a sniff of their plans?'

Danny shook his head. 'I've no idea. But now Beattie's brought him into the picture, now he's using him as a confidential source . . . if he didn't know before that he was having sex with a potential terrorist, he certainly knows now.'

'I can't believe he was on an assignment,' Allie said slowly. 'The Branch would never knowingly employ a gay man.'

'They might. If they were running an undercover honeytrap.'

'If they were doing that, surely they'd be much more likely to set a female officer on the other two? Besides, they wouldn't need a honeytrap against Farquhar. If they'd had any suspicions of your guys and they knew he was homosexual, they'd just pull him in and use that for leverage. Like you said, it's against the law.

241

He could end up in court, he'd lose his job. From what I've seen of Farquhar, I think he'd cave.' Allie tilted her head back and frowned in concentration. 'So what does this mean for us? What's the set-up between him and Beattie anyway? Is he some sort of official liaison?'

Danny spluttered with laughter. 'Of course not. He'll have an arrangement with Wee Gordon. He tips Gordon off on stories and payments make their way into somebody else's bank account. His mum or his best pal. And if Gordon wants something copper-bottomed, he'll ask Mr SB to do some digging for him. It's not like he's the only polis that Wee Gordon has on his payroll. It's the main reason he's in the masons — most of the senior officers in Strathclyde Police are in the same lodge. How do you think Wee Gordon gets all his exclusives?'

Embarrassed at her naivety, Allie said, 'Will Beattie's guy recognise you?'

Danny spread his hands. 'I don't know. If he fancies Farquhar, I'm definitely not his type.'

'Are you serious? Gay men have a 'type'?' Allie hastily caught herself. 'I'm sorry, I've never had this kind of conversation with Marcus. Is it that simple? You only go for one kind of look?'

'Some men do. A lot of men do. You remember the Village People video for 'YMCA'? I've no idea what straight people made of it, but for gay men, it was a playful take on the kind of role-playing dress-up that some guys go for. That's not my scene, by the way. But you see them out and about in the bars. The leather men. The uniform queens. The glitter guys.'

Allie was bemused. It had never occurred to her that she might have a type. Since her mid-teens she'd had a few boyfriends. A couple of them had almost been serious, but she'd cut loose because she didn't think she loved them. Not deep down, not like the love songs said she should feel. The sex was fine, but it had never left her thinking, 'I want to wake up with you every morning.' She'd found them all attractive enough, but it had been their personalities — their intelligence, their sense of humour, their taste in music — that had drawn her to them. There was no template to their looks. The idea of choosing a potential partner based on their appearance seemed bizarre to her. She had no idea how to navigate Danny's world. 'So you think you won't have registered on his radar?'

'Probably not. But if he does recognise me . . . '

'He's not going to say anything, because if he does, he'll expose himself. He'll be just as nervous of you exposing him as you are of him exposing you.'

Danny drained his glass then wrapped his arms round himself. 'I thought this week couldn't get worse. This story was supposed to be the way to show my mum that the work I'm doing is valuable. To get me back into my family again. But if this comes out . . . ' His voice tailed off and his eyes brightened with unshed tears.

'It's not going to come out, Danny. There's no reason why it should. Farquhar hasn't recognised you and he's the only one who needs a bargaining chip. You and Beattie's source, that's kind of mutually assured destruction. Besides, we'll find out soon enough what the score is with him. Beattie's going to be asking him for background searches on all three of them. If Mr SB doesn't mention Farquhar's sexuality, I think it's safe to say you're going to be OK.'

'You really think so?' His pinched expression began

to relax a little as hope crept in.

'I do. We just have to wait and see and hope he's as eager to stay in the closet as you are.'

Danny winced. 'I don't want to be in the closet. It's not that I'm ashamed. I listen to Tom Robinson singing 'Glad to be Gay' and I despise myself for hiding who I really am. But I love my family; even though I think I've already lost them, I know if I told them the truth about myself, I'd have no chance of ever being part of it again. I love my work too. Being a reporter, it's what I always wanted. But can you imagine the dog's life I'd have in the *Clarion* if they knew?' He shook his head, his mouth a bitter line.

'I can't argue with that,' Allie said. 'It's hard enough being a woman in there. It'd be a hundred times worse for you.' Light dawned. 'Is that the real reason you don't want a picture byline? You're afraid somebody you've been with will expose you?'

He ran a hand through his hair. 'It crossed my mind early on. God knows, I'm so careful. I know guys who are completely wild. Totally reckless about who they have sex with. I'm not like that. But you can never be sure.'

Allie felt for him. She could barely imagine living a life that required hiding so much of herself from the people closest to her. 'Do you have anybody you can talk to?'

He looked away. 'I have . . . an arrangement. It's not ideal but I trust him.' He flashed her a quick look. 'Don't pity me, Allie. The world's changing. There's places I could move to and have a much more open life. London, Manchester. Maybe this story's the springboard for me to be out and proud.' He scoffed. 'I mean, there's got to be an upside to being the family

244

black sheep, right?' He straightened up and squared his shoulders.

Allie couldn't help admiring his refusal to give in. Or feeling rueful that she'd wasted her emotional energy considering him as a romantic prospect. 'Definitely.' She put her glass down on the floor. 'I guess I should be going. I thought Angus might have got back to us, but he'll have gone home by now.'

'Do you want to stick around? We could pick up a carry-out. There's a pretty good Chinese on the main drag. If you've not had enough of me whining like a slapped puppy?'

She laughed. 'You smooth-talking bastard. I love a good Chinese.'

★ ★ ★

They were finishing off the last of the sweet and sour pork balls and the chicken fried rice when Danny's phone rang. Their moment of escape was over. Danny hurried back to the living room and snatched up the handset. 'Hello?'

Allie, hot on his heels, put her head next to his. She heard the voice on the other end say, 'Paul? Is that you?' and felt the momentary hesitation as Danny slipped into character.

'Ding-dong, my man. What's going on?'

'Can you phone me back on this number? From a phone box?'

'There's no need for that if you're already in a phone box. I'm a nobody. I'm not on anybody's list, my phone's not tapped. Just tell me what's happening.' Allie encouraged him with a thumbs-up.

'I suppose.' A sigh. 'Well, same as last time, I got a

note through the door at teatime. So here I am in the phone box. I called at the set time and the guy said, same drill as last time, Thursday night. Only, make sure we've got the balance or there'll be displeasure. That's the word he used: 'Displeasure'.'

'Scary bastards.'

'No kidding. So, are you still OK for the readies?'

'Aye, it's all arranged. So I'll see you in the pub, same as before? Thursday night at nine?'

'I'm going to tell Roddy and Deke to meet us there. Wave us off, like. And we'll all hook up later back at Deke's flat.'

Danny and Allie exchanged a look. She shook her head, dubious. 'Is that wise?' Danny said. 'I don't mean meeting up later. I'm talking about the pub. They've told us to come by ourselves. If they're watching us and they see us with somebody else, I wouldn't put it past them to call the whole thing off. And give us a doing for good measure.'

'You think?' Bell sounded panicky.

'These boys? Definitely in their box of tricks, I'd say. We need to do exactly what they tell us, Gary. They're not messing, they're for real. Compared to them, we're amateur city.'

It was, she thought, a sharp reminder to them both that the territory she'd led them into was dark and dangerous.

Bell made an indeterminate noise. 'Mibbes.' A sigh. 'Aye, you're probably right. I was just looking for a wee bit of moral support.'

The last thing they needed was for Danny to walk into the lion's den with a shoogly sidekick. Allie stepped away and mouthed 'dinner' in a low voice. Danny nodded. 'We could meet up for a curry ahead of the pub?'

'No, Deke doesn't like spicy food. We should meet up at the Spaghetti Factory, where this all started. And it's handy for Deke and Roddy.'

'OK. Spaghetti Factory at half past seven? Then you and me can get a cab down to the Calton.'

'See you then, Paul.' He inhaled sharply. 'Fuck, we're really doing this. Can you believe it?'

Danny chuckled. 'It needs to be done, Ding-dong. And we are the boys to do it. We can be heroes, and not just for one day.'

Before Bell could speak, the pips went, indicating his money had run out. 'See you Thurs — ' he managed before the line went dead.

Danny laughed, the buzz of adrenaline lifting him. 'It's not exactly James Bond, is it? You never saw Sean Connery running out of change in a phone box.'

The two of them slumped on to the nearest sofa, leaning against each other as the excitement leaked out. 'I better phone Angus,' Allie said after a few minutes. 'He's going to want a head start on this.'

She struggled to her feet and fetched her bag, taking out the small cardboard booklet that contained the news team's home phone numbers. She perched on the arm of the sofa and dialled Carlyle. 'Hi boss, it's Burns,' she greeted him. She gave him a full rundown on Danny's phone conversation with Bell. 'So it looks like we're on for Thursday night.'

'This Thursday?'

'Afraid so, yeah.'

He swore fluently and extensively. 'I wish we had more time to prep this.' He blew out air through his lips like a horse. 'My office. Nine tomorrow.' As he replaced the phone, Allie distinctly heard, 'Fuck's sake . . . They're gonnae get somebody killed.'

247

36

Allie was halfway into her coat when the phone rang again. 'Angus,' Danny groaned. 'Probably wants us in at seven o'clock. Just hang on, see what he wants.'

But it wasn't the *Clarion* news editor. It was the last person Danny wanted to hear from. 'Joseph,' he said weakly when he heard his brother's savage tone.

'Aye, that's right, little brother.' He managed to make the word sound like an insult.

Everything Danny could think of saying felt ridiculous. *How are things? What have you been up to? Have the police charged you?*

'What? Nothing to say? No cheery greeting for your big brother?'

No point in avoiding the subject. 'Did you talk to the police?'

'I did. I spent Sunday afternoon and Sunday evening talking to the police. Oh, and a bit of Monday morning too. That's a long time to be shut in an interview room with shite coffee and somebody else's BO. Thanks to you.'

Danny's shoulders slumped. 'It wasn't really thanks to me, though, was it? If you hadn't got involved in your crooked scheme with your crooked boss, none of that would have happened.'

'Really? But Danny, I'm innocent here. I got caught up in something I didn't understand. I was just doing my job. Making a delivery for my boss. It wasn't my place to question what he was doing.' Joseph's voice was silky but there was still a hard edge close to the surface.

'The polis might have fallen for that, but you and me, we know different. I covered your back for Mum's sake. But I know you knew exactly what was going on. I saw the money in your desk drawer. I saw — '

'You were in my desk? In the office? How the hell did you manage that?' There was genuine shock in his tone.

'I borrowed your keys when you were at Mass. Not so smart after all, are you?'

'And you call me the criminal? You broke into my office, to find evidence to send me to jail?'

Now Danny's blood was up. 'I did the opposite of trying to send you to jail. It's me you've got to thank for the fact that the polis even entertained the notion that you were a mug, doing what you were told. I kept your name out of the paper. I could have shamed you in front of everybody — the family, your pals, your neighbours, everybody at the church. But I never. That's how you're still walking around without any charges.' He paused as an awful thought occurred to him. 'They haven't charged you, right?'

'I was always better at telling stories than you. It worked for the polis, at least. Shame it didn't do the same for Paragon.' Now his voice was a snarl.

'What do you mean? I know Gregor Menstrie's out the door, but if you're not facing any charges — '

'You've destroyed my life, you little shit.' Even from a few feet away, Allie could hear the venom. 'Paragon don't give a monkey's fuck what you wrote in the paper. They fired me, little brother. They fucking fired me. They said that even if what I said was true — which they did not believe, not a word of it — even if that was true, nobody would ever trust

Gregor Menstrie's puppet. It was me or the clients, and that was no fucking contest. So thank you very much, you horrible little creep. I'll never get a job like this again because you getting a story on the front page was worth fucking up your entire family.' Joseph was making no attempt to disguise his fury.

'No!' Danny despised himself for the rage and despair he could hear in his own howl. 'It was never about you, you selfish bastard. Oh, sorry, that's the forbidden word when it comes to you, isn't it? No, Joseph, it was never about you. It was about morality and honesty and working people like our parents who pay their taxes and believe that's the price of belonging in the kind of country we live in. Not the greedy arseholes who think they're entitled to get one over on the rest of just because they've got money.'

'Listen to yourself, Mr High-and-Mighty. You only cared about this story because you thought Mum and Dad would throw me out on my ear and make you the favourite son.' His laugh was the mocking yowl of a hyena. 'You couldn't have got it more wrong. They're furious with you. They believe I really am the innocent victim here and they hate you for what you've done to me. You're the outcast, Danny. You're the Judas Iscariot. So why don't you take your thirty pieces of silver and do what Judas did. Find a tree and swing from it.' The crash of the phone descending echoed in the white room forty miles away.

Danny fell back on the sofa, pulses pounding in his ears. He dropped the phone and made no attempt to wipe away the tears trickling down his face. 'I knew he hated me,' he said, his voice a broken rasp. 'I just didn't know how much.'

Allie crouched down at his side, gripping his hand.

'You didn't deserve that. He's lashing out because he's been caught out.'

Danny shook his head, his chest tight with a sorrow he'd never felt before. 'No, it's more than that. He feels betrayed. And he's right. Part of me was jumping for joy because I finally got the chance to paint him in his true colours in my mother's eyes. I'm ashamed of that.' He drew in a long sharp breath. 'And I'm going to pay for it.'

'So it's all the more important that you carry on doing work you can stand behind. Work like this story,' Allie said.

'This story? And what good is this story going to do? We've paved the way for a bunch of bampots to completely undermine the campaign for a Scottish parliament, never mind independence.'

Allie stood up. He could see the frustration in her face. 'They were well on the road to doing just that,' she said. 'We didn't set the ball rolling. Gary Bell was already polishing up his IRA contact to show off to the boys. And Deke Malloch is desperate to prove there's substance under his swagger. You're not making these things happen. You didn't force Joseph to break the law. You didn't talk those bell-ends into buying explosives from the IRA. Danny, what we're doing is *stopping* the bad things from happening.'

'I understand that. It's the collateral damage that keeps me awake at night.' He rubbed the tears from his face in a brusque backward swipe. 'Away home, Allie. I'll be fine in the morning. I just need to sit here quietly and get drunk.'

'I don't think that's a good idea. We both need to be sharp in the morning. You won't be doing either of us any favours if you turn up with a hangover.'

'So what do you suggest?' he asked wearily. He didn't rate her chances of coming up with something that would take his mind off his woes.

She glanced at her watch. 'It's too late to go to the pictures. What about a board game? Have you got Monopoly?'

'I didn't have you down as a capitalist running dog. I do have Travel Scrabble. I bought it to take on holiday last year but nobody wanted to play. They said I had too much of an advantage, what with me working with words.'

Allie snorted. 'Had they ever read the *Clarion*? Get the Scrabble out and put the kettle on, Danny. Best of three. Winner buys dinner.'

He pulled a face. 'Anywhere but the Spaghetti Factory.'

37

Allie's tailor-mades weren't ready yet, but she did have a couple of what Rona had called 'statement items' from their shopping trip. And since she wanted to impress, there was no better time to wheel them out. High-waisted trousers the flecked brown and gold of cigarette tobacco, and a russet tweed jacket over a simple cream cotton shirt, low-heeled brown ankle boots to complete the picture. She stared in the mirror and even without the haircut, she saw a stranger reflected back at her. But this stranger was a woman whose wardrobe looked like an active choice. A woman who meant business. It had taken Allie a while — and Rona's understanding of fashion — to work out how to dress the part of someone who should be taken seriously, but today she felt as if she was getting there.

She'd never needed that more. It wouldn't have hurt to have pulled it out of the bag on the Paragon story, but she hadn't been the lead on that so it mattered less. Today was different. It was her story, even if Danny was doing the undercover. Even more importantly, for the first time other journalists were assisting her, rather than the other way round. She needed gravitas today; she needed their respect.

At a quarter to nine, the office still had the air of the morning after the night before. A sports reporter stood at his desk, mug in hand, flicking through the back pages of the morning's papers. The features desk and the women's page office were empty. A lone sub leaned back in his chair, feet on the wastepaper bin, cigarette between his lips, magazine in his lap. There were a few more bodies round the news and picture desks, Angus Carlyle among them. He looked up as she approached. His eyebrows rose. 'Who knew you scrubbed up so well, Burns?' He hauled himself to his feet. 'My office.' He led the way, pausing to shout, 'Copy!' over his shoulder.

The copy boy arrived on their heels. Carlyle ordered a jug of milky coffee and half a dozen bacon rolls. 'And don't stint on the brown sauce,' he added. 'And when Danny Sullivan shows his face, send him in here.' He waved Allie to a seat and picked up the memos she and Danny had slaved over the day before. 'Good start,' he said. 'Danny Boy was right to bring you on board for the Paragon job, though. The boy can't write.' He shook his head, more in sorrow than in anger. 'The women's page used to have a fashion writer, Mary Begg. She could barely string a sentence together. But Andy Budge subs the women's page, and he writes like a dream. So Mary's cuttings file was impressive. So impressive she landed a job on the *Daily Mail* down in London.' He chuckled. 'They must have been fucking livid the first time her copy dropped. Anyway. Here's the point of this tale. At Mary's leaving do, Andy Budge turned up wearing a T-shirt that read, I WAS MARY BEGG.'

'Harsh,' Allie said. 'But funny. Don't worry, I'm not heading to the T-shirt printers any time soon.'

As she spoke, there was a perfunctory tap at the door and Danny stuck his head round. 'Sammy said I was to come through.'

'Amazing. Both of you, early. Park yourself, Danny and we'll see where we're up to.'

Alarmed at the seriousness of his expression, Allie

lit up a cigarette as Carlyle continued. 'I've got a small handpicked team working up the backgrounders on your three musketeers. Allie, when we're done here, I want you to track down this Maggie McNab and pretend to interview her about her group and their desire for an independent Scotland. Get her talking about the members, steer her to the three we're interested in and screw as much out of her as you can. I've got Wee Gordon coming in at half past nine to reveal what his contacts have to say. And then the four of us are going to sit down with Tony from the picture desk to work out our strategy for tomorrow night. Think you can manage that?'

'Allie's going off to interview the McNab woman, I get that. But what am I going to be doing?'

'You are going home to sit by your phone in case one of your co-conspirators needs to have his hand held. I don't want you anywhere near the background digging, just in case. All you have to do between now and tomorrow night is to avoid arousing any suspicion.'

A tap at the door and Sammy appeared with a laden tray. The aroma had the same effect as a mild electric shock. Everyone became more alert, more focused. 'Just a minute, Sammy. Allie, get pouring the coffees,' Carlyle said, taking a notebook-sized pad of forms from a drawer. He scribbled something on it, scrawled his sprawling signature across the bottom and handed it to the copy boy. 'Take that up to accounts, wait for it, and bring it back down to me.'

Sammy scuttled off and Allie served the coffees, her mouth clamped in a resentful line. 'That's the money summoned,' Carlyle said. 'First piece on the board.' He grabbed two bacon rolls and a coffee and made for the door. 'See you in the conference room at half past. I need to check that no mad bastard's written anything stupid on the schedule.'

'Well, he's taking it seriously,' Danny said. 'Springing for bacon rolls and coffee.'

'Not to mention eight hundred quid from accounts.' She checked him out with a quick glance. She knew him well enough now to see that he was as terrified as she was at the scale of what they'd unleashed. At the very least, they could both end up without a job. But the worst could be very bad indeed.

★ ★ ★

Of course Wee Gordon Beattie was late. He was the crime correspondent; in his eyes, that conferred a certain status that mere mortals had to be reminded of at every opportunity. Keeping everyone else waiting was only one of his strategies for making his point. Carlyle, familiar with his tricks, didn't bother to turn up in the conference room till he'd actually seen the crime correspondent arrive with his Special Branch source in tow.

So it was that only Allie and Danny were present when Beattie and his contact arrived. Allie had Danny in her eyeline; she was relieved to see he didn't even flinch. Wee Gordon headed straight for the plate of chocolate biscuits. Almost as an afterthought, he said, 'Tommy, these are a couple of our reporters. Danny Sullivan and Alison Burns. This is Thomas Torrance of the Special Branch. You'll forget ever having met him, if you have any sense.'

Torrance nodded acknowledgement to Allie, but paused at Danny, head cocked. 'Have we met before?'

Danny shook his head. 'I think I would have remembered. I'm pretty good with faces.'

Torrance shrugged. 'My mistake, you must have a double.'

Allie wasn't convinced by his response to Danny's denial. There was a watchful cast to his expression that she thought was more than simply a man accustomed to working on the shady side of the street. 'They say we all have one of those,' she said, aiming for inconsequential and scoring a bullseye.

She was spared from any further diversionary tactics by the arrival of Carlyle and Tony Visocchi, the *Clarion*'s veteran picture editor. About once a month, Visocchi threatened to retire, which provoked a resigned flurry of flattery from the editor's office. Feathers smoothed, Visocchi would magnanimously agree to stay, 'just till you find someone who can manage the complexities of a major picture desk'. He was a tubby little man with a magnificent mane of silver hair, styled into a dramatic flourish. Allie reckoned he must use more hair product in a week than she'd got through in a lifetime.

'Let's get down to business,' Carlyle said, making for the chair at the head of the table seconds ahead of Visocchi, who scowled and pretended he'd been targeting the one with the best view all along. 'Mr Torrance, thank you for your assistance. I don't know what we'd do without you at times like these.'

Torrance dipped his head with a cat-like smile. 'Happy to oblige, Mr Carlyle. We're all on the same side, after all.'

Allie wasn't sure how comfortable that made her feel. Torrance continued. 'But in this particular instance, you're ahead of the game. None of these three men has any criminal record. We pride ourselves on having our finger on the pulse of dangerous radicals, and they've attracted no attention whatsoever either from the Branch or from Strathclyde Police. Congratulations, Mr Sullivan.'

'It was me that spotted them,' Allie said.

Torrance raised his eyebrows. 'I do apologise, I was led to believe Mr Sullivan had infiltrated the gang.'

'I did,' Danny said. 'But only after Allie had sussed them out.'

Torrance spread his hands out. 'Whoever's responsible, well done. And I know from working with Gordon in the past that the *Clarion* will do the right thing once you've got your story.'

'We will,' Carlyle said. 'But I need a guarantee that you won't move on this till I give you the say-so.'

Torrance's expression was blander than a government minister denying a crisis. 'So long as they don't do anything to attract our attention. And so long as you make damned sure they don't get the chance to use the materiel they're acquiring. I'd hate to have to arrest Mr Sullivan and Miss Burns for conspiring to cause explosions.'

The silence was awkward. Carlyle leaned forward, his beefy forearms planted on the desk. 'I'll concentrate on my job and you concentrate on yours. That's what we pay you for, after all.' There was no mistaking who was the big beast in the room.

Torrance stood up. 'Keep me informed,' he said. 'Gordon knows where to find me.'

'As soon as the paper hits the street, you'll have everything you need,' Carlyle said.

'All I need is their whereabouts. And where the explosives are. Otherwise all bets are off and this will be the last favour I do the *Clarion*.' He gathered his coat around him and stood up. He pointed two fingers at Danny, like a pistol. 'Walk me out, Mr Sullivan, and take me through it one more time.'

Wee Gordon Beattie looked as if he'd been slapped. And Allie wondered whether Thomas Torrance's memory had inconveniently returned.

38

'That was a bit high-handed,' Visocchi said. 'You need to keep your boy on a tighter leash, Gordon. Remind him who's boss.'

'They like to make out they are,' Beattie said. 'He'll be fine.' He turned to Carlyle. 'So, Angus, what's the plan?'

'I've got a team beavering away on background. Burns too,' he acknowledged with a tip of his head. 'The Razor's coming in later to legal what we've got and what we're planning to do with it. Soon as Danny comes back, we'll run the strategy for tomorrow night. See how many holes we can pick in it. Are your boys ready to go out and get snatch pics of the three bombers?'

Visocchi waved an expansive hand. 'My boys were born ready. Soon as you've got addresses, we'll stake out the wee bastards.'

Beattie took an ostentatious look at his watch. 'I hope that sleekit wee boy Sullivan isn't trying to steal my contact.'

Allie wanted to remind him it had been the Special Branch man who had asked Danny to walk him out, but she thought better of it. No need to point up a possible connection between them.

'How did you get on to this in the first place, Burns?' Visocchi asked. 'Was one of them chatting you up?' A sly smile.

'Yeah, because that's what terrorists do. 'Do you fancy coming for a curry so I can tell you all about my

260

plans for the revolution?'' Allie rolled her eyes. 'I got it by putting myself in the right place and keeping my eyes and ears open.'

Carlyle smiled approval. Before anyone could say more, Danny reappeared, a little pink around the cheekbones. 'Sorry,' he muttered. He caught Allie's eye and drew his brows together in a slight frown.

'Tomorrow night, then. Danny, you're supposed to meet the other three at the Spaghetti Factory at half past seven, right?' Carlyle raised his eyebrows and Danny nodded. The news editor pulled a pad of paper towards him. 'So, one team in the restaurant. A pic man and a reporter to follow Malloch and Farquhar when they leave.' He noted it down. 'We know where Danny and Bell are going, so no need to be on their tail at that point. What about in the pub?'

'I'm wary about that,' Danny said. 'It's pretty much a dive. We drew some funny looks last time. I got the feeling they don't get a lot of passing trade. Anybody we put in will stick out like a sore thumb.'

'Plus,' Allie weighed in, 'it's not beyond the bounds of possibility that the IRA guys will also be staking out the pub. They'll want to make sure Danny and Bell haven't brought back-up with them. If they spot a possible tail, it could end really badly.'

'The lassie's got a point,' Visocchi said. 'I know some of our lads are on the scruffy side, but they're not going to pass for one of the coffin-dodgers from the Calton. Better to stay on the street, Angus.'

Carlyle frowned. 'That's the sensible option. But I hate to send any of my reporters into the lion's den without anybody at their back.'

'I'll be careful,' Danny said. He gave a half-laugh. 'I mean, I've been there before, I'm practically a regular myself.'

Allie couldn't help admiring his attempt at bravado. 'They'll be pouring your pint as you come through the door.'

'The serious business starts when you and Bell walk out the pub,' Carlyle continued. 'We're doing this mob-handed. But in the shadows. We know the route the pair of you took last time, and where you got picked up. We've no way of knowing if they'll follow the same pattern, but it's a start. So I want one man walking down on the other side of the street so he's passing the pub just after the half hour.' He tore off the top sheet and began to draw a rudimentary map. 'So he's coming down the hill a wee bit behind the pair of you. Further up the street, I want a car with two guys in it to follow your route from a distance. Behind that, another car with one guy in it. When you get to the first turning, that second car will pick up the man on foot. At the next turning, the first car peels off, cuts round the block and drops off its passenger.'

He held up the sheet of paper and pointed out what he meant. 'He emerges further down the street you and Bell are on, walking slowly so you pass him. The second car will drive past you and take a slightly different route to the far end of the lane where you got picked up. Make sense so far?' Everyone nodded.

'Tony, that lad of yours — Willie, is it? Runs about on a motorbike?'

Visocchi chuckled. 'Willie Suttie. Fancies himself one of they paparazzi.'

'I want him for the third follower. There's a wee vennel almost opposite that lane, and that's where Suttie's going to be waiting.'

'How do you know a detail like that, boss?' Allie was startled into asking.

Carlyle gave her a measured look. 'I could say, 'I know everything, Burns.' Truth is, I grew up in the Calton. I know these streets better than I know my own wife.' He saw her surprise and gave a wolfish grin. 'Surprised? I might have started off a rough diamond, but I've polished up since then.'

'I didn't mean — '

'So, Suttie's in the vennel. When the black taxi turns into the lane, he's going to come in behind it, overtake it when it stops to pick up Bell and Danny. When he emerges from the lane, that's the signal for the second car to get ready to follow. The first car follows the second car. Not right on its tail but close enough not to lose it. Suttie tucks in after the first car, and behind them all is a third car. The four are the long tail. Is that clear?'

'You're taking this seriously.' It was hard to tell whether Beattie was impressed or resentful.

'It's a serious business, bombing.' Carlyle glowered. 'I'm taking no chances. Danny's safety is our number one priority.'

'I thought preventing these clowns setting bombs was our number one priority?' Beattie pursed his lips primly.

Carlyle paused, fixing him with a level stare. 'Don't be a cunt, Gordon.' He turned back to Danny. 'Danny, you said it was your impression that you took quite a few turns on your journeys in the cab?'

'We got thrown around a lot, the way you do when you're going round corners in a black cab,' he said. 'It was hard to keep track, but I reckon it was seven or eight times.'

Carlyle nodded. 'So here's the plan. Every second turn, the lead vehicle does not make the turn and the tail closes up. Then the lead goes back to the end of the tail. We stay as far back as we can, but if the driver is keeping an eye on his rear-view mirror, he'll see a series of different vehicles behind him. It'll be too dark to make out any details, so we need to go for cars that look noticeably different. I'm thinking a Cortina, a Mini, a Land Rover, something like that.'

'Dave Thornton's got a Land Rover,' Visocchi offered.

'I've got a Morris Minor,' Allie said.

Beattie scoffed. 'Perfect. Nobody would ever suspect an old banger like that of being involved in a car chase.'

'And we'll use one of the office Cortinas,' Carlyle said. 'We do this right, we find out where the IRA house is.'

'What about afterwards? Do we wait and pick them up again?' Allie asked.

'I think that could be pretty risky. We don't have any idea what the layout might be. All we know is that it's a house or a ground-floor flat. It could be a quiet residential street where any strangers are immediately obvious. Or it could even be somewhere on the outskirts where there's no cover,' Carlyle said. 'Danny, your memo said they told you you'd have to pick up the explosives yourselves?'

Danny nodded.

'That sounds to me like they're not going to take you there. It's my best guess that they'll dump you somewhere with instructions on where and how to get the bomb-making equipment. I think we have to chance it. We'll know where the IRA suppliers are living and we'll know where the pick-up is. I say, let's be

264

guided by Danny. As soon as you can get to a phone without causing suspicion, fill us in.'

Allie raised a finger to catch his attention. 'Just a thought, boss. When you all meet up earlier, howsabout if Danny pushes for them to get together at Malloch's flat after they've been dropped off by the Irish guys? He can sell it by saying they're all in this together, they should be together when they pick up the explosives. And we'll have time to stake out Malloch's flat after we've tailed Danny to the IRA safe house.'

Carlyle beamed at her. 'That's a great idea, Burns. You think you can pull that off, Danny?'

He shrugged. 'I don't see why not. They'll be gagging to get back into the thick of things. I doubt they'll take much persuasion to hook up.'

'Good. That's that sorted. We'll iron out all the details and brief the teams tomorrow afternoon.' He beamed at Danny. 'This is a helluva story, coming on top of your Paragon exposé. I've been thinking about setting up a specialist investigation team for a wee while now. Play your cards right, and it could be your baby, Danny Boy.'

Beattie gasped. 'You said — '

'I changed my mind, Gordon. Obviously you'd have a role to play, but if we're going to be taken seriously, we need somebody running the show who can't be accused of being in the pocket of the polis. You can see the sense of that.'

Beattie flushed dark red. 'He's only been in the door five minutes.'

'Three years,' Danny said quietly.

Carlyle stood up. 'Jeez, my bairns fight less than you lot. Danny, away home and stake out your phone.

265

Burns, get on to Maggie McNab. When you've done with her, get back here and we'll look at what the diggers have turned up on our bombers. Gentlemen, thank you for your time.' He made for the door, Visocchi and Beattie in his wake. Beattie gave them a last poisonous glance as he left.

'You dropped lucky with this one,' he said. 'But don't forget who has the real sources round here.'

Danny watched him go. 'He can't help himself. He hates it when he thinks anybody's treading on his toes.'

Allie laughed. 'Male insecurity. He's probably got a willie the size of a chipolata.' Serious again, she said, 'What did Torrance want?'

Danny groaned. 'To tell me to keep my fucking mouth shut. He knew the second he saw me where he recognised me from. He pointed out I had more to lose than him if I tried to drop him in the shit. And that he has the power. 'I can always find an excuse for being somewhere the perverts hang out,' he said. Bastard.'

'Is he going to be a problem?'

Danny shook his head. 'Not if we keep our side of the bargain and hand him Scottish and Irish terrorists on a plate. And there's no reason why we won't be able to do that, is there?'

39

By the time Allie made it to Danny's flat, it was early evening and she was exhausted. She eased herself out of the car, back stiff and shoulders tight, wondering if this was what it would feel like when she grew old. Out of the darkness, a figure materialised at her elbow. 'You look pure dead knackered,' Jimmy said cheerfully.

'You do know that's not how you impress a woman?' Allie fished in her bag for coins.

He clicked his fingers. 'That's where I've been going wrong all these years. You've missed your pal, though,' he added as she dropped a 50p piece into his dirt-ingrained palm. 'He said to tell you he was just away to the shop for a pint of milk.'

'Thanks, Jimmy.' When she'd phoned Danny to say she was on her way over, he'd told her he needed to pop out and that there was a key on a string attached to the inside of his letter box. 'I'll wait for him inside. Much as I'd like to have a wee blether with you, it's too bloody cold.' She scuffed a lump of snow frozen to ice with the toe of her boot.

'Layers. That's the secret in the cold,' he said, falling into step as she crossed the uneven ground. 'See me? Under all this, I'm actually half the size I look. I keep myself insulated with layers. A semmit, two T-shirts, a shirt, a sweatshirt and a jumper underneath my coat. And then there's my long johns . . .'

This was more information than Allie needed. She didn't want to think about the state of Jimmy's layers.

The miasma was bad enough. 'Spare me the details.' They'd reached the pavement. 'Thanks for taking care of the motor.' She sketched a wave and walked into the close.

The key was where Danny had said and she was inside in the warm in a matter of moments. By the time Danny returned a few minutes later, she was curled up on a sofa, boots kicked off, a sheaf of copy in her hand. He stuck his head round the door, greeting her with, 'Tea or coffee?'

'Tea, this time of night. Any word from Ding-dong or the others?'

'Silent as the grave. You hungry? I made a big pot of corned beef stovies last night, there's plenty left.'

'Thanks. I've not eaten since this morning. I could eat a scabby dug if it was warmed through.'

'Yuck,' Danny said as she followed him through to the kitchen. 'I heard things were a bit different in Fife but I never knew it had got that bad.'

She chuckled and playfully punched his upper arm. 'Your stovies better be up to scratch, Edinburgh boy. If that smell doesn't go round my heart like a hairy worm, you're in big trouble.'

While Danny brewed a pot of tea and heated up the pan of food, Allie brought him up to speed. 'I was careful with Maggie McNab. She's very dismissive of their views — she says they're not representative of the group. Which, let's face it, we knew already. The rest of them are a bunch of hand-wavy academics and politics geeks. But I've got some quotes that'll sit nicely in the background piece.'

'That's handy. I wouldn't like to be in her shoes up at the university when the story breaks, mind you.'

Allie shrugged. 'She should be more careful about

the people she encourages to join her group. Meanwhile, back at the ranch, the rest of the guys are playing a blinder on the background stuff. I swear, I wouldn't have known where to start to get the detail they've picked up.'

'It's harder for women. You walk into a pub or a corner shop and bring up some guy's name, right away you've got everybody's attention for all the wrong reasons. Whereas I can go, 'Does Deke Malloch still drink in here?' and nobody bats an eyelid. No alarm bells ringing. What have we got?'

Allie spread the pages out. 'Addresses. Workplaces. Can you believe Roddy Farquhar is a maths teacher in Bishopbriggs?'

'All the more reason for him to stay deep in the closet,' Danny said. 'Even a whisper and he'd be out the door and on the dole before you could say 'Tom Robinson'.'

'That's ridiculous. Surely people know that being gay isn't the same as being a paedophile?'

'Your faith in humankind is touching,' he said bitterly, 'but it couldn't be more misplaced. Don't let the poofs near the weans, that's the mantra. What else have the guys dug up?'

'We've got family details, where they grew up and where they went to school. Oh, and an ex of Deke Malloch's revealing that he spoke to her about how the Scots needed to rise up against their oppressors.' She hunted through the papers and pulled one out. 'Here we go: 'I chucked him in the end because he bored me stupid with all his talk about how they'd set free the whole British Empire to be their own bosses, all except Scotland. Like we were prisoners that needed to break out the jail. He's got a bee in his bonnet the size of the Loch Ness Monster.' Great quote.'

'I'd have to agree with her. I've not spent much time with Malloch, but he is very fucking tedious. Have we got any other decent quotes?'

'Some stuff from workmates, pals from the pub. All a bit innocuous taken by itself, but it's fuel to the flames all the same.'

Danny returned to the cooker and stirred the pot. The rich aroma that filled the kitchen forced Allie to concede it was worth looking forward to. 'I managed to pin Angus down to the nuts and bolts of how we're going to do this,' she said.

'Let's eat first. When I dish this up, you're not going to be able to concentrate on nuts and bolts.'

It turned out he was right. Danny had learned his stovies from his mother, clearly one of those working-class women who could bring alchemy to bear on a trio of simple ingredients. Onions, potatoes and corned beef was an unpromising list but, in the right hands, it became far more than the sum of its parts. Danny ladled it out into a pair of wide-rimmed shallow soup plates with a small sigh. 'My mother might have excommunicated me, but at least I've got her best recipes.'

Neither had much to say apart from Allie's appreciative mumbles and Danny's occasional sigh of pleasure. He produced a couple of rolls to wipe their plates clean, and said, 'To quote your namesake, 'Then auld Guidman, maist like to rive, Bethankit hums.''

Allie groaned. 'All my life I've had Burns quoted at me.'

'Well, it is Burns Night tomorrow,' he pointed out. 'And we'll not be at a Burns Supper.'

'Danny, if I was to be at a Burns Supper tomorrow,

the chances are my only participation would be to dress up as Poosie Nansie and carry the haggis in. It's still an excuse for a boys' night out more often than not. Frankly, I'd rather be chasing round the back streets of the East End in my wee car.'

He pulled a face. 'I take your point. So, nuts and bolts?'

'Just a minute.' She returned with her bag and rummaged around before producing a Kodak Instamatic camera and a pack of three Magicube flashes. 'Nothing significant's changed since we ran through the basic plan this morning. Except Angus thinks it would be a great idea for you to get some pix of the explosives.'

'What? Has he lost his mind? I'll never geet away with that, they'll freak out.'

'Not if you play it right. Go with what an important historic moment this is, how there should be a record of this. The first night of the revolution!' He looked sceptical, so she pressed on. 'You take a pic of the three of them with the explosives, then get one of them to take a pic of you with the other two. That way it looks like you're as implicated as they are. It's a clinching piece of evidence.'

'I'm not happy about this.' He scowled.

'The IRA do it all the time, take pics of themselves with Armalites and all sorts.'

'Yeah, with balaclavas covering their faces. Even their own mothers wouldn't recognise them.' He folded his arms across his chest, his expression defiant.

'You can do it, Danny. They love you. You've made their dreams come true. You can persuade them. Imagine the impact of the three of them across the splash with the bomb-making gear.'

He couldn't help a smile twitching the corners of his mouth. 'Maybe. I'll talk to Angus tomorrow.'

'Good. We're presuming they'll tell you where to go to pick up the explosives. Angus is adamant that you have to stay with the other three till the pick-up happens and make sure you're with them when they decide where they're going to store them till it's time to act.'

He nodded. 'I'll make sure of that, don't worry. I can always play the 'I paid for them, I've got a right to know what's going on with them' card. But I don't think it'll come to that. When you get right down to it, they're soft as shite. I almost feel sorry for them.' He turned down the corners of his mouth. 'Stupid wee laddies.'

Allie grinned. 'Don't be feeling too sorry for them. So, once you've got the stuff stashed and you go your separate ways, you come back to the office and we get cracking on writing the story.'

Anxious again, Danny said, 'What if they want to celebrate? Get a carry-out and get pished?'

It was something that unaccountably hadn't come up in the discussions in the office. Allie puzzled for a moment then her face cleared. 'It's going to be getting on for midnight. There's no place open to get a carry-out at that time of night. You'll have to fall back on whatever's in the house already.'

Danny relaxed. 'And knowing this lot, that'll not be more than a couple of cans, if we're lucky. So I get back to the office, we write up the story, but not for Friday's paper, right? Because there's no way we can get it into the early editions?'

'Right. We write, the lawyers go through every dot and comma. That's when it gets tricky.'

'Because of the Contempt of Court Act,' Danny said, rolling his eyes. 'We can't publish anything that might prejudice a fair trial. It's always the issue for investigative journalism in Scotland. Another good reason for moving to Fleet Street.'

Allie shrugged. 'Thankfully, I'm not paid to work out how to get round the legal pitfalls. But Angus is and he reckons he can do a deal. He'll sit down with the Chief Constable and the Fiscal and tell them what we have. He'll argue that without our investigation, they wouldn't know a crime had even taken place, and our intervention has prevented even worse crimes. He'll tell them approximately where the arrests need to be made but he won't give them the exact addresses till the presses are rolling. That way, they can make the arrests before your three pals and the IRA cell know what's happening, but we get our story out there without the bastards' lawyers claiming they can't get a fair trial.'

'Skating on thin ice.'

'We knew that from the start, Danny. But Angus loves this story. He can already see the press awards lining up on his window ledge. He says even if we do get charged with contempt of court, the paper will pay the fine. It's worth it for the circulation, for the reputation as a campaigning newspaper.'

Danny got up and fetched a bottle of Famous Grouse and two tumblers from a cupboard. He set them down on the table and poured two large measures, pushing one glass towards Allie. 'You know who Gordon Airs is?'

'I've seen his byline. He's the chief reporter on the *Daily Record*, right?'

'Right. A few years ago, he covered a story a bit like

273

this. He had a meeting at gunpoint with a bunch of nutters calling themselves the Army of the Provisional Government of Scotland. They couldn't organise an explosion in a fireworks factory and they ended up in court. Gordon was called to give evidence against them and he refused to identify them as the sources of his stories.'

'That's what we're supposed to do, isn't it? Protect our sources? But we're not protecting our sources, we're hanging them out to dry.'

Danny looked faintly exasperated. 'That's not the point I'm getting at. The issue's contempt. The judge decided Gordon was in contempt of court. He got fined £500. But that's not all. He was sent to jail. Do you think Angus will go to jail for us, Allie?'

Allie picked up her glass and took a sip. She didn't really like whisky but she knew enough to understand liking wasn't always relevant. 'I don't need Angus to go to jail for me.' As the words came out of her mouth, Allie was surprised to realise that she meant them. 'People remember Gordon Airs ending up in jail for having integrity. I'd take that. I want people to remember my name, Danny. For the right reasons, and for a long time.'

40

All over Scotland — all over the world, Allie knew — people were celebrating her namesake. From Moscow to Minneapolis, gallons of whisky were being drunk, tons of haggis were being eaten and vast volumes of verse were being recited. When she'd been a teenager, force-fed the poetry of Robert Burns in her English class, she'd fantasised that she was descended from the national bard and that ancestry would give her a head start when it came to being a journalist. She'd been wrong on both counts, in spite of there being hundreds of direct descendants of the poet.

Now all she hoped was that this would be a different sort of Burns Night. That its events would make hers a name recognised and respected among her fellow hacks. It depended on so many others playing their parts, but at its heart, it was still her story. Carlyle had assured her that this time, hers would be the first name on the byline. She hoped he'd keep his word.

The team had assembled in the office at six. All six of the reporters who'd been assembling the background information on Bell, Farquhar and Malloch had handed over their notes and Carlyle had passed a copy of each over to Allie. Given the tight deadline she'd be working to, she needed as much of a head start as she could get. She read through the material rapidly then caught Carlyle's attention. 'Can I do a separate background piece on each of them? A sort of mini-dossier? Will that scrape in under the contempt rules?'

Carlyle drew in his breath. 'Not my decision, Burns. That's up to the Razor and his sleekit wee pals. But do it anyway and we'll fight them for it. And by the way — the editor had a meeting with the chief constable and the fiscal. They're not happy with our stated intentions, but they're both realists. We just have to keep a tight lid on this till the presses start rolling tomorrow night. If anybody slips through the net, we'll be the ones under the microscope. Maybe even under arrest,' he said grimly. 'I've told everybody the same thing. Anybody leaks and they will literally never work in this town again.'

Allie found a quiet corner and started drawing together the threads of the trio's lives. Meanwhile, by seven, two journalists were in place inside the Spaghetti Factory. The rest of the team were eating curry a few doors down, making the most of the time they had before they were due to be in position in the East End.

Just after eight thirty, Allie pulled the last sheet out of the typewriter and stuffed it into a large brown envelope to join the rest of the background material. The notes she and Danny had made previously for Carlyle were already locked in her desk drawer, and she added the envelope to her haul. She shrugged on her coat, pulled a woollen tammy on her head and made for the car, her stomach eating itself with nerves. Annoyingly, Rod Stewart's 'Tonight's the Night' was an earworm in her head. By the time she left the car park and headed along the Clydeside, she was humming it under her breath. She hoped it was prophetic, that nobody was going to stop them now.

★　★　★

Danny was every inch as anxious as Allie. The difference was that he couldn't show it. There was an unspoken convention among the young men that nonchalance was a sign of manliness. He had a shrewd suspicion that Gary Bell was freaking out at least as much as Danny himself, but he chose to hide it behind a macho performance, reliving the high points of his days on the football field. As if that was an advance validation of his suitability for that evening's activities. As if, Danny thought.

Malloch was ebullient, bouncy as a Super Ball, his conversation pinballing from one subject to another, his throwaway lines never quite as funny as he thought. He smoked incessantly. Even when his food arrived, he simply set his cigarette in the ashtray while he shovelled a few forkfuls of pasta into his mouth and swallowed, then went back to it. As soon as he stubbed out one, he lit another. Danny was starting to feel faintly sick. He wasn't sure if it was fear or second-hand smoke. He could at least do something about one of those. 'Gonnae no' do that?' he complained to Malloch.

'How?'

'The fags. Gonnae no', just while I'm at my dinner?'

Malloch tightened his mouth, his face suddenly hostile. Then he thought better of it and crushed out the current cigarette. 'Ya fanny. I thought you were harder than that,' he said, pretending mockery to hide his anger.

'I like to taste my food, not your cheap fags. I mean, Number Six?' Danny laughed. 'Could you not run to a bit of class like Dunhills?'

'Aye, well, some of us dinnae have a stash of Premium Bonds to fall back on.' Malloch couldn't hide the sourness.

Danny swallowed a mouthful of farfalle with salmon and cream sauce. 'It doesn't matter where it came from, it's what you do with it that counts. And here's the thing, Deke. I know that if it had been you and not me, you'd have spent it on Semtex, not fancy fags.' He gave Malloch a friendly tap on the shoulder and watched him relax.

The only one of them not betraying a sign of nerves was Roddy Farquhar, who'd barely said a word since they'd arrived. Now he cut in. 'Remind me again. How's it going to go?'

Bell rolled his eyes. 'Me and Paul have the meeting and hand over the cash. They tell us where to pick up the goods. We don't know for sure what happens next but it's my guess they'll dump us some anonymous place like last time. And we'll find a phone box and call you.'

'And we'll either come back to Deke's to hook up with youse or we'll meet where the pick-up point is. Whichever makes more sense. Where are we going to stash the gear?' Danny asked, trying to make it sound like an afterthought.

The others exchanged looks. 'The fewer that know, the better.' Farquhar studied his plate, scraping the last of the meat sauce on to his fork.

His words made Danny's guts churn. Surely they didn't think they could cut him out at this stage. 'I'm not planning on putting an advert in the paper,' he said, nonchalance gone. 'I'm into this for a grand, you don't get to shut me out.'

'Nobody's shutting you out,' Bell said. 'Roddy, you're well out of order. Paul's one of us now. We need to put it in a place we can get access to twenty-four

278

hours a day, some place nobody else can come on it by accident. When we talked about this before we met you, we decided the best place was the left luggage lockers at Central Station.'

Danny nodded. 'So who keeps the key?'

'Ding-dong,' Malloch said. 'He's the least likely to lose it.' He grinned and Bell shrugged.

'Sounds good.' Danny pushed his plate away and checked his watch. Quarter to nine. The nearer the meeting came, the worse he felt. 'We should make a move. We don't want to leave it to the last minute.' He stood up. 'I need a quick pish.' He hurried to the toilets, barely making it in time before he threw up. He stood over the toilet bowl panting, trying to flush away the evidence. He heard the door swing closed behind him.

'Paul? You OK?' Bell, full of concern. 'You turned pure green back there.'

'Dodgy fish,' Danny gasped, wiping his mouth and flushing again. He opened the cubicle door and gave a weak smile.

'It'd be weird if you weren't a bag of nerves. These Paddies, they're fucking terrifying. I didn't sleep a wink last night, if that makes you feel any better.' He turned to the sink and splashed cold water on his face. He turned back to Danny, drops of water landing on his jumper. 'Let's get it done, eh?'

Danny nodded. 'Aye. All for one and one for all, right?'

Bell grinned. 'You said it, pal.' He offered his hand and Danny shook it. 'Blood brothers, Paul. Blood brothers.'

★ ★ ★

Allie drove through the city centre five miles an hour below the speed limit, stopping on amber at the traffic lights, indicating far ahead of the junctions. How embarrassing would it be to be late for the stake-out because she'd been stopped by the polis? But her drive was uneventful, and she took up her position up the hill from the pub with a clear view of the street. She slid down, grateful for the Morris Minor's sit-up-and-beg seats that made it possible for her to hunker down out of sight.

The minutes trickled by. She watched a taxi draw up at ten past nine; Danny and Bell emerged and ducked into the pub. The drizzle that had made the air thick and damp earlier in the evening had turned into proper rain, splashy drops spattering her windscreen and making it harder to see clearly. She couldn't turn on her wipers; nothing would be more obvious than a parked car with a clear windscreen.

One of the other tail cars drifted slowly into sight, taking up station further down the hill. Allie checked her watch again. Almost half past. In her wing mirror, she saw a man approaching. The hood of his dark snorkel parka hid his face but she knew who it was supposed to be, and the slightly rolling gait was what she'd expected to see. Frank Heggie, another member of the newsroom rota. He had trouble with his knees from playing too much football as a young man, he'd once told her.

Before he drew level with her, a slab of light fell onto the pavement from the pub doorway. Danny led the way, with Bell at his heels. They paused momentarily, turning their coat collars up. Danny pulled a rolled-up baker boy cap out of his pocket and rammed it on his head as he turned downhill. Moments later, two figures emerged from the pub and fell into step behind Danny and Bell. One burly, one skinny as a whippet. Allie resisted the urge to follow them, holding her position until the dark red Cortina from the office fleet slipped past her. She hung back for what felt like forever, then released the handbrake.

The Cortina turned left and Allie picked up speed on the empty street, braking sharply before the turn to let Todd jump in. He muttered a greeting that she ignored as she swung round the corner. She could just see the Cortina's tail lights, then abruptly they disappeared as it turned right.

The chase was well and truly on.

41

Being bundled into the back of a black taxi with a bag over his head was no easier for Danny the second time around. Nor was there any reassurance in the knowledge that Allie and the others had his back. It would only take one mistake by any of the team tailing him for the evening to end very badly indeed. He didn't want to contemplate how the Irishmen might respond if they sensed betrayal. But he'd heard too many stories of what happened to informers to be able to put them from the front of his mind. He rolled around on the floor of the cab, smelling his own fear. Not even the anticipated roar of Willie Suttie's motorbike overtaking the cab eased his terror.

The format was identical. The cab ride, the indoor stumble, the wrenching revelation of somebody else's living room. Not-Declan sitting in state on the sofa in his balaclava, this time wearing a 1967 European Cup Winners replica Celtic shirt. 'Good to see youse again, boys,' he greeted them. 'Have youse the rest of the money?'

Danny took a tight roll of notes from his coat pocket and tossed it to Not-Declan. The Irishman stripped off the rubber band holding it together and let the notes fan out. With a grunt of effort, he leaned forward and summoned one of his sidekicks. 'Check it,' he said, then leaned back, his eyes sizing them up again. He lazily scratched his groin. 'Got your targets worked out?'

'We've got a shortlist,' Bell said. 'We've not made our final decision.'

'Don't fuck it up. I don't want my colleagues ripping the piss out of me for associating with wankers.'

'You've no worries on that score,' Danny said, wondering what Not-Declan would have to deal with when it all went arse over tit for him and his Active Service Unit.

'It's all there, boss,' the cash-counter confirmed. 'Used notes, non-consecutive.'

'Well done. We'll make freedom fighters of you yet.' The Irishman shifted in his seat, forcing his hand into the front pocket of his ridiculously tight jeans. His fingers squirmed visibly, then closed around something. He wrenched his hand free and threw the object at Bell's face. He fumbled it but Danny caught it on the rebound. It was a small key with a serial number stamped on it.

'So where does it fit?' he asked.

Not-Declan showed his teeth. It might have been a grin or a snarl. 'Central station left luggage lockers. Locker number 129. In case you can't remember, that's the number of goals Jinky Johnstone scored for the finest football club in the world. Now fuck off and don't let me hear from you again. You've had your free shot at goal.'

'Quite the price for a free shot,' Danny said.

Not-Declan surprised him by bouncing to his feet without any apparent effort. He brought his face so close Danny could unravel the toxic mix of Old Spice, old cigarettes and tooth decay.

'Don't make me charge you extra for your smart mouth, you little fucker.' He gave Danny a sharp little slap, a scary reminder of who held the power in the room, then stepped back and gestured to his sidekicks. 'Get them out of my sight before I do something they'll regret.'

They were bundled back into the sacks and out to the cab. For a brief moment, Danny wondered if they were going to end up in the Clyde. Not-Declan probably thought he could behave with impunity. He had their money now and nobody knew where they'd been. The same wave of fear that had engulfed him earlier broke over him again. It combined with the diesel fumes from the cab's dodgy exhaust to provoke a nausea he prayed wouldn't overtake him, trapped as he was inside a sack. If this was what being an investigative reporter involved, maybe he wasn't cut out for it after all?

This time, when they were thrown out of the cab, the ground felt softer. Danny wrestled his way free from the sack to find he was kneeling on wet grass, head down, body convulsing with the shock of fresh air. He raised his head and thought he was hallucinating. An Italianate palazzo rose before him, a frontage that would have been perfectly at home canalside in Venice. He shook his head to clear it, just as Bell said, 'Templetons,' and the tumblers clicked into place in Danny's head. The carpet factory on Glasgow Green, modelled on some Venetian palace or other. He'd only ever seen it from a distance, across the wide expanse of the Green.

Bell was already on his feet, raring to go. 'That was wild,' he said.

'You wouldn't want to get on the wrong side of that guy.' Danny pushed himself off the ground, still feeling wobbly. 'We need to phone the guys, they'll be chewing their fingernails to the knuckle.'

Bell started walking towards the lights of the city centre. 'Soon as we find a phone box, we'll bell them.

284

They can meet us at Central station. Can you believe they stashed it in the same place we settled on?'

'It's not like there's that many safe options. It's basically there or Queen Street station, when you think about it.'

'It feels like it was meant to be, Paul!' Bell's voice thrilled with excitement. To him, it was still nothing more than an adventure.

Not for much longer, Danny thought. He couldn't wait to tear their playhouse down.

★ ★ ★

Allie had been the driver on the tail when the taxi had stopped on a quiet residential street west of Annies-land Cross. Rows of the familiar four-flat blocks that looked like 1930s semis, curtained windows dim with lights. She could just make out the sign for Garscadden train station in the distance. Nothing but her car was stirring. Already in the grip of an adrenaline buzz, hands sweating on the steering wheel, her breath began coming in short gasps. She slowed as she approached the taxi, signalling her intention to overtake. They were clearly waiting for her to pass before they moved their passengers. She risked a quick sideways glance to clock the house number, or some distinguishing feature then stared resolutely ahead as she passed the cab. At the end of the street, she turned left, not a clue where she was.

Five minutes of jinking through side streets brought her on to Dumbarton Road. Relieved to be back on known territory, she decided it would take less time to make straight for the office than to seek out a working phone box and call in. Carlyle was in his office, pacing the floor, tumbler of whisky clamped in his fist. He turned swiftly as she entered, his expression a demand.

'Thirty-Seven Dykeswood Avenue. Since Danny didn't remember going upstairs, I assume the ground-floor flat.'

'Did you see them go in?'

She shook her head. 'They were too canny for that. The cab just sat there while I drove past. It looked like two guys sitting in the back, which fits with what Danny reported about them being chucked on the floor in the back. Willie Suttie was next in line after me, maybe he saw them go in?'

Carlyle gave a grudging smile. She didn't hold the 'grudging' part against him. She had an idea how much pressure a story like this put on a news editor and she had no desire to be in his shoes tonight. 'Good job, Burns. Away down to the library and check the voters' roll. See who's registered at that address.'

The night librarian was working his way through the previous day's papers with a pair of scissors and a date stamp, adding clippings to a pile thicker than a phone book. In the morning, it would be the day shift's job to file them in the appropriate manila envelopes. The photocopier hummed softly at one side, ready for the next story that had to be filed in more than one place because it had multiple reference points. He looked pleased to see her; she suspected any break in the lonely routine of the dark hours would be welcome.

She explained what she needed and he quickly found the relevant volume. Allie thumbed through till she reached the page for Dykeswood Close, Dykeswood Avenue, and Dykeswood Crescent. She ran her

286

finger down the list, stopping at 37: *Desmond O'Loughlin, Mary O'Loughlin, Padraig O'Loughlin.* 'Ya beauty,' she muttered softly, copying the names into her notebook. She sat back and stared out the window where the sodium glow of the city lights diffused the darkness. Somewhere out there, thanks to her, Danny was confronting a different kind of darkness. She hoped he'd make it back to the light. The alternative didn't bear thinking about. Not for him, or for her.

42

As arranged, the four men met just after eleven o'clock under the Highlandman's Umbrella — the railway bridge that carries ten tracks across the Clyde from Glasgow Central station. It had provided a meeting place out of the elements for those living in exile in the city for almost eighty years; so it proved for the four conspirators that night. Danny and Bell found Malloch and Farquhar huddled in the doorway of a pawn shop, wreathed in smoke, coat collars turned up. The three friends clapped each other on the shoulders, then, almost as an afterthought, Malloch did the same to Danny. Excitement radiated from him. He was like a small child waiting for his birthday party to start.

'How did it go? What happened? Are we on? Or what?' Malloch demanded, words tumbling over each other.

Bell laughed and playfully punched his friend's arm. 'Thunderbirds are go, pal!' He pulled the locker key and dangled it in front of their eyes.

'Time to visit the left luggage office,' Danny said.

'Aye, let's go and see what the leprechauns have left us,' Farquhar said, bouncing on the balls of his feet like a boxer.

The quartet made their way up Hope Street to the main entrance and swaggered on to the concourse. There were a surprising number of people around, facing the dregs of an evening out on the last train home to the deserted streets of the suburbs or some sleeping Ayrshire town. A few of the men were in full Highland dress, kilted and sporranned, obvious stragglers from Burns suppers. Anyone whose eye had been caught by the brio of four strangers would have put it down to drink. Or possibly poetry. Terrorism would never have crossed their minds.

Farquhar went ahead into the array of lockers and made a quick circuit. 'Nobody there,' he reported. 'I'll stay here and keep watch,' he added.

They filed in, Bell in the lead. 'Hey, Deke, do you know how many goals Jinky Johnstone scored for Celtic?'

'What?' Bewilderment from Malloch.

'The Wizard of the Wing.' Bell stopped at locker 129 and pointed. 'There's your answer.' He inserted the key and turned it. The door creaked open, Bell stepped back and with a flourish, said, 'Ta-da!'

An anonymous black nylon holdall sat innocuous on the shelf. Nobody would have looked twice at it. Gingerly, Malloch lifted it out and unzipped it. There were four blocks wrapped in grease-stained brown paper. Bell reached in and picked one up, hefting it in his hand. 'About a pound,' he said softly. He unwrapped one end of the paper and they all stared at it.

'Looks like orange plasticine,' Danny said.

'It better not be,' Malloch muttered.

'What about detonators?' Danny asked.

Malloch raked around under the blocks of Semtex and came up with a handful of bundles of thin yellow and orange electric cable with a slender metal cylinder at one end. 'That's a detonator, right enough. You stick the metal bit into the Semtex and send a charge down the wires, and bingo. Big bang.'

Hastily, Bell re-wrapped it and put it back in the bag. 'Fuck,' he breathed. He looked up and grinned. 'This is really happening, boys.'

Danny pulled out his camera. 'I want a photo. You three and the gear.'

Bell recoiled. 'Are you mad? Are you trying to get us all put away?'

'This history in the making, man! We won't show what's inside the bag, just us. It's not like I'm going to pass them round in the pub. It's just for us.'

'He's right,' Malloch exclaimed. 'We cannae be heroes of the revolution without the proof.'

'If you're worried about me selling youse out, Ding-dong, first I'll do you three, then one of you can take one with me in it.'

Bell shook his head. 'It's not that I don't trust you, but we all need to cover our backs. You're going to be the one with the negatives, after all. Why don't we all take turns with you? Three photos, you in all of them?'

'Good idea,' Malloch said.

Danny shrugged. 'Sure. It makes no odds to me.' He turned towards the entrance. 'Roddy, we need you here.'

Farquhar edged back in, his face suspicious. 'I thought I was keeping a lookout?'

'Time for photos,' Malloch said. 'You take the first one, Roddy. Me and Ding-dong and Paul.'

'Who said anything about photos?'

'For the historical record, ya numpty,' Malloch replied. 'Paul, give him the camera.'

Danny broke open the pack of flashes and twisted one block on to the camera. He wound on the film and handed it over. 'You look through the viewfinder and press the button,' he explained.

'I'm not stupid, I've taken pictures before,' Farquhar grumbled. He stepped back and put the Instamatic to his face. The other three huddled together, mugging at the camera.

Banking on the flash temporarily blinding them all, at the last moment, Danny sneakily shifted the open zip down a little, in the hope the camera would catch something of the contents. As soon as the flash went off, he moved out of shot, pulling Farquhar into the line-up and handing the camera to Malloch. Two more flashes and they were done.

Bell zipped up the bag and looked around the locker area. There were plenty of vacant lockers to choose from. 'What about seventy-nine?' he said. 'A year to remember, right?'

Nobody disagreed. He shoved the bag in the locker, put a coin in the slot, turned the key and removed it. He tucked it into the watch pocket of his jeans and grinned. He held out his hand, and at once, they all shook with each other in a confused muddle. 'Now we just need to sit down and plan our campaign.' They strolled back out on to the station concourse. Even in the short time they'd been away, the numbers on the concourse had diminished.

'I can't do tomorrow night,' Malloch said. 'It's my dad's birthday. And Saturday, I've got tickets for the coach for the away game, so I'll be bevvied up. What about Sunday? My flat? High noon?'

Bell nodded. 'Works for me.'

'Me too,' Danny lied.

And Farquhar nodded. 'Fine by me.'

On that note, they separated. Bell and Farquhar shared a taxi since they were heading in the same direction. Malloch waited till Danny was aboard a

291

taxi, giving completely false instructions to the driver, before he set off up Renfield Street to catch a bus. As soon as they cleared the immediate vicinity of the station, Danny told the driver he'd changed his mind. 'Take me to the *Clarion* building.'

'You're kidding? It's hardly worth me starting the engine for that. I've been sitting on the rank for half an hour, and all for next to nothing?'

'I'll make it worth your while,' Danny said wearily. 'Just so long as you give me a receipt. I want something to remember tonight by.'

* * *

Allie hadn't realised how tightly she'd been holding herself until Danny walked into the room and her body physically relaxed. Without a moment's forethought, she gave him a delighted clap of the hands. Judging by the expressions on their faces, most of her colleagues were surprised into joining in the smatter of applause. 'You made it,' Allie exclaimed.

Danny shrugged with an air of bravado. 'Why wouldn't I?' He took the Instamatic from his pocket at tossed it to Willie Suttie. 'Better get that down to the darkroom, Willie. Exclusive pics of a terrorist cell collecting their explosives. Mind, you'll have to smudge me out of the shots, last thing I want is the IRA coming after me.'

He was, she thought, still high on adrenaline. And no wonder. Danny had walked into the lion's den and lived to tell the tale.

'Full memo, Danny,' Carlyle said. 'Every cough and fart. The rest of you — anything new you've got from tonight, get it typed up and passed on to Burns.'

He gave her his widest smile. 'It's going to be a long night, Burns.'

The door burst open and Tony Visocchi stood framed in the doorway, splendid in a kilt of some bright tartan Allie had never seen before and a ghillie shirt, tufts of grey hair sprouting at the neck. The picture editor held up two bulging carrier bags. 'And it needs to get off to a good start.' He dumped the bags on the table. One clinked; the other gave off a rich smell of meat and spice. 'It's Burns Night, Angus.' He winked at Allie. 'In more ways than one.' Two bottles of Glenmorangie appeared as if by magic, and the other bag revealed half a dozen tinfoil containers of haggis pakora. 'I was at a supper at Bashir Singh's restaurant and when he heard I was coming back to the office, he wouldn't let me out the door empty-handed. Wire in, everybody.'

Carlyle threw his hands in the air, but he kept smiling. He knew when he was beaten. Within minutes, there was a party atmosphere that lasted as long as the whisky. Reporters drifted off to their desks to find some words that would give them a toehold in the finished copy. Danny sat staring glumly at a blank copy pad before starting a laborious two-fingered hammering of the keys.

Allie looked around at the detritus of the impromptu celebration and caught her boss's eye. 'Gonnae — ' he began, then saw her expression.

'I'll get the copy boy to clear up,' she said firmly, crossing to the door and calling, 'Copy,' at the top of her voice. Then she rolled a fresh pad into her machine and began.

A plot to terrorise Scotland with a wave of bomb attacks lies in tatters today thanks to a fearless *Daily Clarion* undercover investigation.

A ruthless gang of maverick nationalists conspired with the IRA to bring horror to the streets of Scotland in a bid to force independence to the top of the agenda.

Carlyle loomed over her shoulder. "Force independence to the top of the agenda?' It's not the Guardian you're writing for, Burns. Full point after 'Scotland'. Then, 'Their goal? To free the country from Westminster rule.' Keep it simple. You know how to do this, Burns. Don't lose the plot on me tonight.' He patted her on the shoulder and moved round to see what Danny was writing.

He was spookily right. It wasn't Carlyle's fault that she'd ended up writing tabloid news stories when she'd once dreamed of being on the features desk of the *Guardian* or *The Sunday Times* investigation team. She sometimes feared her grasping at the first opportunity that came along had closed off all other possibilities. 'Once a tabloid hack, always a tabloid hack,' one of her tutors on the training course had said, more than once, in a tone that reflected his own disappointments.

Which made stories like this all the more important. Especially because it proved she was a self-starter. She'd brought this story in herself and made it happen. It showed she didn't depend on whatever crumbs the newsdesk threw her way. If Allie was going to break into the world she aspired to, she'd have to make sure she was impossible to ignore. In a good way, obviously. And this was a very good way.

43

It was a few minutes after three when Allie typed 'ends' on her final piece of copy. Now came the tedious part. Stray pieces of information still buzzed round her head, clamouring for attention like toddlers in a playgroup. She had to drag each of them into the light to check whether they really had any place in her story or whether she could safely leave them to fend for themselves. Some of her colleagues, desperate for a taste of the glory, had pumped up insignificant details with inflated importance, but she couldn't throw them aside without checking whether those scraps had any heft. She was determined not to leave any gaps the lawyers or the nitpicking subs could crowbar open into a chasm of doubt.

She separated the pads into separate piles, yawning. Danny had long since finished his account of the evening and once Carlyle had gone through it with him line by line, he'd sent him home. 'Get some sleep. I need you sharp for the lawyers and probably the polis as well,' he'd said. Carlyle had been next to depart, but he hadn't gone far. There was a sofa in the photographers' room, long and deep and chosen with the specific purpose of providing somewhere the night shift snapper could sleep. 'Wake me when you're done,' he said, yawning so wide Allie could count his fillings.

Allie wasn't ready to endure his inquisition yet. She needed to let the story settle, and she needed different air. A glance out of the window revealed sleet, driven

295

almost horizontal by the wind. Not a night to go for a stroll along the Clyde. That left the vanway under the building that allowed access for the massive trucks that delivered the paper to railheads and wholesalers round the country. It was grey and dismal and smelled of diesel and ink, but it was unquestionably different from a room that reeked of cigarettes and sweat and testosterone.

She went down the stairs rather than taking the lift, nodded at the security man in his booth and found shelter from the wind behind a pallet of newsprint. Allie lit a cigarette and leaned against the wall, trying to let the knots in her shoulders unravel. Now it was over, she could allow herself to admit that she'd been the opposite of gung-ho earlier in the evening. She'd stifled her apprehension that Danny might not return, telling herself the comforting lie that journalists didn't get killed. Well, not very often, and mostly in war zones. She shied away from the uncomfortable conviction that the idiots Danny was with seemed intent on turning Scotland into just that.

The question that kept resurfacing was whether she'd have been willing to put herself in Danny's shoes if that had been possible. Could she have been convincing enough? Could she have held her nerve? In a way, Danny spent most of his life playing a part, hiding the heart of himself from the world. It must almost have been second nature for him to take on another role with the conspirators. Allie lacked that experience. Yes, she'd felt like an outsider at Cambridge, but there was little risk involved in that. They might have mocked her accent and made jokes about Scots being tight-fisted, but nobody would have killed her if they'd found out how little she felt like one of

296

them.

How could she aspire to being an investigative journalist when she still hadn't mastered the art of fitting in? Allie could usually play the chameleon for as long as it took to persuade a story target to talk to her. She was good at getting them on side. In a back-handed compliment, her old boss had once said, 'You do so well because you're the opposite of glamorous. Women don't see you as a threat, and men treat you like a sister.' But that was as far as it went. All these months at the *Clarion* and she was still firmly an outsider. She watched the easy to-and-fro between her colleagues and wondered how they did it. Danny was the only reporter who had become anything like a friend. And it wasn't simply a matter of the all-pervasive misogyny. The other two women reporters were as closed to her as the men. Only Rona had broken the pattern, and she was from a completely different department. Actually, Allie thought with a smile, Rona was from a completely different planet.

Maybe she was misreading them. Maybe they were all riven with the same self-doubt? Maybe they also looked around the newsroom and thought they were inadequate to the task? Then she paused to consider. Donny Park, who'd once promoted himself to prime suspect in a murder inquiry by walking through the crime scene leaving footprints and fingerprints galore; Lance Brown, who spent the night shift phoning random numbers in New York and had once ended up chatting to Kurt Vonnegut; Campbell Macleod who had answered the office medical examiner's query of, 'What do you drink?' with, 'What have you got?' No, these were men who had no doubts at all that they deserved their substantial salaries and inflated expense accounts.

Allie considered. She should compare herself to her colleagues more often. Set alongside them, she had no reason to worry. She needed a new motto. 'More gallus, less feart,' as her grandmother would put it.

She'd show them. And right now, she'd show Angus Carlyle that he'd been right to give her a job.

* * *

Before Danny had left the office, he'd made a phone call. It was late, but the answering service was staffed round the clock. He made his arrangement, then went home in a taxi on the office account. By the time his doorbell rang twenty minutes later, he'd washed off the day before in the shower and poured a couple of whiskies.

While Allie sat at the typewriter sprinkling his rough draft with stardust, Danny was driving out his demons in a far more congenial way. His anxieties exorcised, he happily handed over twenty pounds with a kiss for the young man who had become a regular visitor to his flat. It was a transaction that left both temporarily satisfied. Danny dreamed of an escape to Fleet Street; in London, he might find love as well. But for now, when he considered all the risks, this was the safest sex he could imagine.

* * *

Allie could hear Angus Carlyle snoring the length of the newsroom. She walked into the photographers' den to find him sprawled like a stranded starfish on the sofa. Gingerly, she shook his shoulder. He started awake, spluttering incoherent nonsense. He blinked and focused as he struggled to sit up. 'Burns,' he grunted. 'Are you finished?'

'Copy's on your desk,' she said.

He squinted at his watch. 'Five to four.' He heaved himself upright. 'Good job.' He lumbered through the door and dropped like a stone into his desk chair, grabbing the copy and frowning at it.

Allie sat in the deputy news editor's chair, steeling herself for a barrage of queries. But Carlyle confined himself to marking the copy with his red pencil, changing words and sometimes whole sentences. It seemed his issues were solely with her prose rather than the meat of the story. At last, he looked at her. 'I've made a few notes. You'll need to retype some pages. You've done a not bad job, though. You've strayed into possible contempt in a couple of places, but let's see what the Razor has to say. I'm hoping he'll take the view that the public interest in bringing this conspiracy into the light outweighs the likely contempt of naming your boys. But he's paid to be the doom and gloom merchant.'

She took the proffered pages. 'I'll do that now.'

'And then go home and get a sleep. Back for noon so we can go through the legals. And then we put the polis on standby.'

Allie pulled a face. 'The shit's really going to hit the fan for those boys tonight.'

'No question. But you know what they say. If you can't do the time, don't do the crime. Now bugger off, Burns. I don't want to see your face before noon.'

* * *

299

On the other side of the city, another player in the drama was also awake. Thomas Torrance sat wrapped in his dressing gown chain-smoking and staring out at the night. He'd lain awake, his brain refusing to shut down. Eventually, he'd given up and stopped pretending sleep was going to come.

He'd spent years being careful. His alibi was permanently at the ready; if any of his colleagues were to spot him entering or leaving a gay bar or nightclub, he'd been keeping tabs on a suspect in an ongoing investigation which, by the way, was none of your business. He'd never had to use it, but he felt confident in its power.

He didn't worry about the men he had sex with. They had much more to lose than he did, because his word, the word of the law, would always trump their 'malicious accusations'. Everything was hunky-dory.

And then he'd met Roddy Farquhar. Roddy was different. He was smart and well-informed. He read books and talked about films in a way that delved beneath the surface. They had conversations that went beyond which way they liked it.

Over the past few months, Roddy had wormed his way under Torrance's skin. He'd even let slip what he did for a living. And now Danny fucking Sullivan was casting a vast shadow over their lives. Torrance had thought he might be able to blackmail Sullivan into sabotaging his own story, but by the time he'd realised what was going on, things were too far along. Even if he did somehow get Sullivan to fuck it up, that bitch Burns wouldn't let it go. He'd realised that.

He couldn't sit back and let Roddy be arrested. If he was arrested, he'd be convicted, no question of that. He'd face years in jail. And Torrance knew exactly what those years would be like. Torrance crushed out his cigarette and took another from the pack. He put it between his lips but didn't light it.

The problem was, the very thing that had attracted him to Roddy could be his undoing. Roddy was smart. If he was in Roddy's shoes, sitting in a stinking police interview room with the walls closing in, he knew what he'd do. He'd claim Torrance. He'd say he was acting as a snout for the Special Branch man. That he'd realised his friends were plotting something far beyond what he was willing to contemplate and he'd brought the information to Torrance. Who had persuaded him to continue, to prevent the plot reaching fruition.

It was a good line.

It would break as soon as it was tested. How did Roddy come to know Thomas Torrance? How did he know that Torrance was Special Branch, when the Branch officers were supposed to lie about their role to even their nearest and dearest? When detectives began to dig deep, secrets and lies would be dragged out into the light of day. Roddy would go down, no question. But he'd also take Torrance with him.

And that was one thing Torrance couldn't let happen.

44

The lawyers had had their way with Allie's copy. It had been a long hard road, both sides pushing for what they swore was necessary. For most of the time, the editor had been in the room. It had been the first time Allie had worked alongside him; she'd only ever known him as a distant figure who was the butt of jokes and complaints. But this was newspapers, and everyone in a position of authority was subjected to the same treatment.

Seeing him work close up, she understood why Alexander Garioch had occupied the editor's chair for the past five years. He listened more than he spoke, but when he did speak, it was with authority and incisiveness. He reminded her of the black-and-white line drawing of Dixon Hawke, the Scottish detective, whose stories had occupied a page in the late Saturday edition of the *Evening Telegraph*. After her father had studied the football results and the match reports, he'd tear out the page with the story for Allie to amuse herself with. Hawke was a Scottish pulp version of Sherlock Holmes, but Allie had known no better and had loved the tales. The memory was probably what convinced her that Garioch was on her side.

Allie and Danny were mostly bystanders in the discussion, called on only to clarify details or sequences of events. There were two main stumbling blocks: the source of the money for the explosives, and the issue of interference with a fair trial.

'There's no getting away from the fact that putting

up the money not only makes you agents provocateurs but also providing funds to terrorists. Two sets of terrorists, in fact,' the Razor had protested. 'First to your tartan terrors to buy the explosives, and then by extension to the murdering brutes of the IRA. Arguably, Sullivan and Burns have suborned acts of terrorism.'

'Their actions *prevented* acts of terrorism,' Garioch replied, his bass voice adding gravitas to his words. 'There is no doubt in my mind that had our people refrained from providing the money, those young fools would have found it somewhere else. And without our active involvement at that stage, there's no guarantee that the other three would have included Sullivan in their plans. So nobody would have had any idea what was going on until these idiots either blew themselves up or sent the Scott Monument into orbit. And that, Mr Drummond, is an argument I will defend in a court of law as well as the court of public opinion.'

The Razor threw up his hands in a gesture of frustration. 'I've offered my advice. I can't force you to take it. I'm sure you'll make sure your employees are taken care of if they end up in jail.'

'Stop trying to terrorise my staff, Mr Drummond. That's my job.' Garioch cracked a savage smile. Allie felt less reassured.

'Jeopardising a fair trial is equally serious,' the Razor continued, undaunted. 'The criminal issue only applies to Burns and Sullivan, but the contempt charge can potentially have a huge impact on the paper too. There's precedent for substantial fines both for the individuals and the publisher.'

Garioch steepled his long fingers and considered.

'As I understand it, prosecutions for contempt have centred round the publication of details relating to the accused once the crime has been committed and they've been arrested. Either before or during the trial itself. But we're not interfering with a police investigation or a trial. Nobody's been arrested. At this point, there is no trial to prejudice. There may never be, for all we know.' The Razor scoffed but Garioch was not derailed. 'We're exposing a crime the police knew nothing about. How are we to do that if we don't carry out our journalistic obligations? Publish and be damned is still a decent motto for editors to live by.'

'I'm afraid that's exactly what you will be,' the lawyer muttered. 'On your own head be it, Alexander. Or rather, on the lesser heads of Burns and Sullivan.'

Allie glared at the lawyer. She'd settle for having the editor in her corner any day of the week. The Razor's warnings about the Paragon affair had come to nothing; nobody was accusing Danny of any wrongdoing. Apart from his mother, obviously. She was slowly coming to realise that the lawyer's job was to be ultra-cautious so that when the shit did hit the fan, he'd be well below the splatter zone.

The final copy was signed off just before six, with one exception. 'We need the SNP to give a rousing condemnation of violence,' Carlyle pointed out. 'I'm sure they'll be delighted to cover their arses. Burns, call their press officer and warn them that you'll want to talk to them around nine o'clock so we can get a late quote to drop in at the bottom of the story.'

Garioch stood up and stretched. 'And now I am off to present the police with a vague outline of what to expect when the paper hits the street. They'll be all set to scoop up our villains before breakfast and we'll

304

be the heroes of the hour. Well done, everybody. You too, Mr Drummond. It's good to be kept on my toes.' He swept out, leaving the room somehow diminished.

The Razor gathered his papers together. Then from his waistcoat pocket, he produced a couple of business cards. He handed one each to Danny and Allie. 'When you get arrested, this is the man to call. He's the best criminal brief in the city. Good luck. You're going to need it.'

* * *

Thomas Torrance parked fifty yards from the entrance to Maxton High School. Most of the pupils had already left, but the stragglers and the few staff members who didn't have cars were too committed to keeping the teeming rain out of their eyes to notice his nondescript grey Cortina. He kept the engine running. The last thing he wanted was to miss his target because the windows had steamed up.

He recognised the familiar figure of Roddy Farquhar crossing the playground even though he was hunched against the weather. Torrance eased the car forward level with the gates and leaned across to lower the passenger window a few inches. 'Roddy,' he called. 'Get in.'

Startled, Roddy looked round, checking instinctively for watchers. But in the rain, nobody cared. Hastily he pulled the door open and dived in. White-faced, he said, 'You're not supposed to come here. That's what we agreed.'

Torrance smiled. He hoped it was reassuring but doubted it. 'That's not much of a welcome, Roddy.'

'No risks, remember?'

'I'm sorry. But this is an emergency.'

'What do you mean, an emergency? What's going on? You said everything was under control.'

Torrance put a hand on Roddy's thigh and squeezed gently. 'Your new pal, Paul Reilly? Turns out he's not a fairy godmother after all. He's the big bad wolf, Roddy. He's a reporter for the *Clarion*. And you guys are going to be all over the front page of the paper tomorrow morning.'

Roddy's eyes widened and his nostrils flared as he drew in breath. 'No,' he exhaled in a long sigh. 'How's this happened? You said I'd be safe.'

Torrance put the car in gear and drove off. 'And you would have been if Malloch and Bell had kept their big mouths shut. One of the women at your meeting was a plant. Another *Clarion* hack. She thought the three of you were just a bunch of big mouths, but she was intrigued enough to follow you to the Spaghetti Factory. She overheard your plans.' He tried to keep his anger in check but it spilled out. 'For fuck's sake, Roddy. How could you be so careless?'

'It wasn't me. Like you said, it was Deke and Ding-dong.'

'It doesn't matter who it was, it screwed the whole game. And as if that wasn't bad enough, it turns out this fucking reporter is gay. Did you not recognise him? As soon as I saw him in the newspaper office, I knew where I'd seen him before. He's a regular at Dominoes. Keeps to the shadows, doesn't strut his stuff on the dance floor, but he's one of us all right. So not only is he going to piss all over you in tomorrow's paper, he's got something on me as well.' Torrance drove with a calm assurance at odds with his words.

Roddy's face was screwed up with the effort of

processing so much information. 'But if he tells on you, he's exposing himself too. He's not going to do that. The *Clarion* fucking hates gays.'

'Maybe so. I'll deal with that in my own time. But what matters right now is saving your sorry arse.' He grinned. 'No, I mean, your sweet arse.'

'Fuck's sake, this isn't the time,' Roddy whined. 'How can you save me now?'

'Simple. You're going to disappear.'

Roddy recoiled. 'Are you going to kill me?' It came out as a shriek.

Torrance glanced at him, grinning. 'Christ, Roddy, what kind of films have you been watching? Of course I'm not going to kill you, I'm going to save you.'

The traffic was growing heavier as they neared Roddy's flat. He stared bleakly out of the window. 'How? Are you going to tell them the truth? That when I told you my mates were spewing dangerous nonsense about independence, you told me not to report it? To let it play out? I wanted you to give them a friendly warning, to scare them off the idea. But you said no, wait and see, they could lead me to serious players.' He scoffed. 'It was all about you and your career, not about protecting me.'

'Things got out of hand when that bastard *Clarion* reporter upped the stakes, throwing money around like confetti. Neither of us could have factored that in. But I promise, I've got a plan.'

'Just not the truth.' Roddy's voice was flat.

Torrance shook his head. 'It's too complicated. Everybody from the police to other journalists will start investigating you and that will lead to me and then we're both screwed. Roddy, we're going back to your flat right now and you're going to pack a bag.

307

You're going to walk away from your life tonight and start again.'

'I don't understand. How can I 'start again'? I don't want to walk away from my life. You're my life, Thomas. You said you loved me.'

Torrance's throat tightened. 'I do. And we can be together, in a while. Properly. In England. Where it's not against the law.'

Roddy's eyes were full with tears. 'I don't get it.'

Torrance turned into Roddy's street and pulled up a few doors down from his flat. 'I'll explain inside. Come on.'

'You're making me scared.' His face was piteous.

Torrance wanted to hold him tight and never let him go, but he knew that wasn't an option. Maybe one day, but not now. 'Please, Roddy.'

Inside the neat little flat, Torrance went straight to the bedroom and took down the suitcase that sat on top of the wardrobe. 'You've got to pack, Roddy. You've got to do this. If not for yourself, then for me.' His voice cracked. He sat down on the bed. 'Here's how it's going to be. You're getting on a train tonight. To Manchester. I've booked you in to a B&B near the station for two weeks under my name. I'll sort you out a new ID with a new name — '

'What do you mean? A new ID? How is that even possible?'

Torrance sighed. 'It's a thing we do to set up under-cover operations. We find a kid that died young and basically steal their identity. You'll get a National Insurance number and a birth certificate. You can resit your driving test and get a licence. You can get a passport.'

'And how am I supposed to live? This is crazy, Thomas.'

'I'll sort you out some fake references. You can get a job at a private school, they're a lot less fussy, believe me. We've done this before. We'll get you somewhere nice to live. And I'll come and see you as often as I can. I'll get a transfer to Manchester. They've got a big Irish community, they need all the Branch officers they can get.' His words were tumbling out now. He pulled Roddy into his arms and breathed in his familiar smell. 'It'll be tough at first, but I'm doing this to save you. I'm doing this for us. Please, Roddy. Pack your bag.'

'Why Manchester? Why not London? It's bigger. If I've got to go, why not London?' His words were muffled by Torrance's embrace, but they were clear enough.

'Because every halfwit who goes on the run goes to London, and we're not halfwits. The police will assume that's where you've gone and they'll alert the Met to be on the lookout for you. Manchester won't even occur to them. And because Manchester has a gay community. People don't have to hide themselves down there.'

'What about my family? My mum and dad? My sisters?' He pushed himself free of his lover's embrace.

Torrance gave a dry laugh. 'It'll be just as if you came out to them. You'll be dead to them. You can't contact them, Roddy. I'm sorry, but it's got to be a clean break.'

Roddy burst into tears. 'I can't do this. I'll take what's coming to me. I won't betray you, Thomas.'

Torrance grabbed him again and held him tight. 'I know that,' he said softly. 'But your life would go under a microscope. We'd both sink.'

'If I just disappear, will that not happen anyway?

They'll turn over every stone in my life.'

Torrance stroked his back. 'The difference is that I can control it. If you're still a suspect in this case, I can argue it's a matter for the Branch, and I'm already working on it. You say you want us to be together — I can make that happen. I can protect us both if you go. I can't help either of us if you stay, Roddy.' He willed his lover to capitulate. Once he'd got Roddy to safety, that only left Danny Sullivan as a threat to his future. Fortunately, Torrance had both the means and the training to neutralise that threat.

★ ★ ★

Later that evening, as Allie was making her first call to the SNP's press officer, a train heading south pulled out of Central station. In the buffet car, Roddy Farquhar sat nursing a can of Tennent's lager, his face a mask of misery. In his pocket, he had two hundred pounds and the address of a bed and breakfast hotel. In his head, he had no idea of what his future might hold. A couple of weeks ago, he'd been an insignificant maths teacher with a passionate belief that his country deserved to control its own destiny. Now he was truly a nobody. A nobody whose best friends would be under arrest by morning.

How had it come to this? In his head, the terrible mockery of 10cc's 'The Things We Do For Love' refused to be silenced. He looked at his face reflected in the rain-streaked window and wished he'd never met Thomas Torrance.

45

Allie stood in the gallery overlooking the three-storey-high press hall, waiting for the vast machinery to rumble into action. She still got a kick from watching the process, the stream of paper rolling out from the five-mile-long reels, print a blur as it raced past on its way to be sliced into pages, folded into newspapers and bound into stacks, ready for distribution. Even before the ancient machines that had been printing the *Clarion* for nearly fifty years started up, the air was redolent with the promise of newspapers. Allie loved the familiar combined smell of molten lead and ink. She was fascinated by the ease with which the printers fitted the stereo plates to the rollers, handling fifty-two pounds of lead as if it was nothing more than a carry-out curry. Of course she knew that the printers' union was a tight closed shop, controlling their empire with ruthless corruption, holding the management to ransom in ways that the journalists could only envy. But that didn't stop her feeling the romance of the print.

There was a hum and a groan, then the gradual movement of the row of presses as they got up to speed. The floor beneath her feet thrummed with the energy being expended below. Knowing her story was leading the paper tonight was the best feeling in the world for any journalist; it forced into submission any doubts about how they'd nailed it.

Allie sensed another presence and turned to see Danny slipping in. 'Look at that,' he marvelled. 'Never fails to stir the blood.'

'Has Angus passed on the names and addresses to the polis?'

'Should be all done and dusted now. The head printer was to phone upstairs as soon as he pressed the button.'

They watched in silence for a few minutes. Danny cleared his throat. 'I've to talk to the police in the morning. They want to interview me about what happened.'

'Just you?' Allie couldn't hide her surprise.

'Apparently. Because I was the one actually in the conversations. Angus says if they decide to press charges, they'll likely want to talk to you too, for corroboration of what you overheard in the restaurant. But for now, it's just me.'

A small laugh, without mirth. 'Sent to the sidelines, as usual.'

'Everybody knows it's your story, Allie. First name on the byline. In your shoes, I'd be grateful not to be spending tomorrow morning cooped up with a pair of polis in an interview room.'

Truly, she didn't mind missing out on that. What she minded was being ignored. 'At least you should get some news about who's been arrested.'

'Yeah, I'll let you know as soon as I hear anything.'

She lit a cigarette and stared down at the presses, telling herself not to be so bloody sensitive. 'We should celebrate,' she said brightly.

'The guys are meeting up in the Press Club. I said we'd hook up with them there.'

'Sure. But I meant you and me. We'll be too knackered tomorrow, but what about Sunday?'

Danny brightened visibly. 'I'd like that. We can plan

our next campaign. Tell you what, come over to my place. I'll cook. I do a mean roast chicken dinner. Roast tatties, carrots and peas and gravy, the works. A few glasses of red biddy, we'll be all set.'

'It's a deal. I don't know about the next campaign, but I'm definitely up for Sunday dinner.'

'It's a date. I'll get my pinnie on and have dinner on the table at one. But for now, let's go down the back door and grab a handful of first editions and take ourselves off to the Press Club to show off.'

Allie grinned. 'Some kind of heroes, eh?'

He laughed and did a camp flop of the wrist. 'Aye, but who will be queen?'

'I'll fight you for it.' She pretended to square up to him and he backed off, hands over his face.

'Don't mark my face, bitch,' he giggled.

Arm in arm, they left the building, drunk without a drop of alcohol. This was the life, Allie thought. She was definitely on her way up.

★ ★ ★

Not so Gary Bell. He'd endured almost half an hour of *Christian* on STV but he'd finally cracked. 'I can sing better than this guy,' he'd complained, getting to his feet. 'Plus he dances like he's got itching powder down his pants.'

'He's got lovely eyes,' his mother said.

His father muttered something inaudible. Bell suspected it had something to do with the colour of the singer's skin. It usually was when anyone on the screen was darker than milk-bottle white.

'I'm away up the stairs,' Bell said. 'One of the lads at work lent me this book, *The Day of the Jackal*. Some guy trying to assassinate De Gaulle.'

'Shame he didn't manage it,' his father grumbled.

Bell shut himself in his bedroom and pressed 'play' on his cassette player. Bruce Springsteen's *Darkness on the Edge of Town* sprang into life with the driving beat of 'Badlands'. Bell kicked off his shoes, stretched out on his bed and eased the locker key out of his trouser pocket. He had to keep checking it. He still couldn't believe what they'd done. From a mad idea, they were within touching distance of making something massive happen. Something that might change the course of history.

He chuckled to himself and put the key away. He picked up the book but compared to what was happening in his own life, it felt tame. He wished he'd arranged to meet up with the lads that night. He couldn't wait to see them again. He lay back and closed his eyes, listening to the Boss, and drifted off.

When he woke abruptly, he couldn't make sense of what had woken him. Someone banging on the door, which made no sense because they had a totally obvious doorbell. Shouting from downstairs, his mother's voice raised. Was that the front door crashing against the wall?

Bell was on his feet now, adrenaline pumping. The sound of heavy boots on the thin stair carpet, voices bellowing, 'Police.' Now he knew what a shock wave felt like. Dizzy, on the verge of tears. He looked at the window but didn't even have time to consider escape before the door burst open and two officers crashed in, wearing bulky gear that made them look like extras in a science fiction film.

'Gary Bell?' one shouted.

He nodded. 'Uh huh.' His voice a squeak.

The second policeman moved forward and grabbed him by the shoulders, spinning him round, throwing him on the bed and yanking his arms behind him. Bell squealed, then cried out as he felt the cold metal handcuffs bite into his wrists. The officer bent close to his ear and hissed, 'You're under arrest, you evil little fucker.'

'Gary Bell, I am arresting you on suspicion of conspiracy to cause explosions — '

The rest was lost to him. There was a strange ringing in his ears. He was hauled to his feet, his shoulders screaming in pain. They huckled him downstairs so fast he kept stumbling and falling forward, provoking the officer in front to turn and push him violently in the chest. Now he could hear his mother wailing, see his father gripping the door frame as if his life depended on it. He was aghast, his mouth hanging open, his eyes wide.

Then he was in the street, still in his stocking soles, his feet already wet and freezing. How could he even think about his feet now? Police vehicles clustered in the street, blue lights flashing. Neighbours at their doors. Nosy fucking bastards.

They opened the back doors of a police van and threw him inside. Cold metal floor. Then they slammed the door. To Gary Bell, it sounded like the end of the world.

★ ★ ★

Gone eleven, and the Press Club was as lively as it ever got. Everybody knew by now that the *Clarion* had something to celebrate. A couple of reporters from rival titles had been summoned away from their pints by newsdesks desperate to play catch-up. Allie was on her third vodka and Coke, trying to make them last. It was never a good idea to lose too many inhibitions in a bar full of hacks.

When Angus Carlyle barrelled in, a cheer went up, and not just from his own crew. Journalists always showed grudging respect where it was due. He pushed through the crowd, accepting a large whisky on the way, and came to a halt between Danny and Allie, who shifted to make room for his bulk.

'They've lifted Bell and Malloch, but no sign of Farquhar. My sources tell me it looks like the bird has flown. Is there any way he could have suspected it was a set-up, Danny?'

Danny shook his head, eyes on his pint. Allie couldn't help wondering what had really gone down between Thomas Torrance and Danny. But he was her partner in crime and she had to defend him till circumstances told her otherwise. 'Him doing a runner? It doesn't necessarily mean he knew he was going to be shopped to the polis. I think he got cold feet,' she said. 'He was always kinda lukewarm. And once they had the explosives, he couldn't really turn round and say, 'You're on your own, boys.'' She shrugged. 'After all, he had most to lose, really.' Danny's head lifted and she saw him struggle momentarily. 'I mean, he's a professional. A degree, a good job, more in the way of career prospects than the other two. My impression was that he was the sensible one. The other two? They're hot-heads. Farquhar, not so much.'

Carlyle nodded. 'Makes sense. They got luckier at Dykeswood, though. There was a black taxi parked outside when the polis showed up. They kicked the door in and found your man O'Loughlin in the midle

316

of a game of cards with three other Micks. Sounds like the team that lifted you and Bell, Danny. The polis rolled them up like a hall carpet and they're presently being detained under the Prevention of Terrorism Act.'

Overhearing this, Big Kenny Stone butted in. 'And have they fell down the stairs yet?'

Carlyle guffawed. 'That's not something I'm going to lose sleep over.' He clapped Danny on the shoulder. 'These guys are not going to see the light of day for a very long time once Danny Boy here has stepped into the witness box.' He put down his empty glass and dusted off his hands. 'Job done, boys and girls. Job done.'

46

Saturday drifted past in a pleasantly lazy way. Allie slept late enough to avoid a hangover. A couple of letters had arrived from friends; Marcus from the training scheme, now working as a features subeditor in Birmingham, and Jen, her final year tutorial partner from Cambridge, now close to finishing a masters at Bryn Mawr. She read them over her first cup of coffee then luxuriated in a long slow bath, cracking open the new John Le Carré. *The Honourable Schoolboy* was the sequel to *Tinker, Tailor, Soldier, Spy*, which had fascinated Allie with its glimpses of the secret world of covert intelligence. She'd been looking forward to the paperback for months.

The phone had dragged her resentfully out of the bath a little after two. 'It's me, Danny,' he said. 'The cops just finished with me. For now, apparently. They're not very happy with us doing their job for them.'

Allie scoffed. 'They should be giving us a commendation.'

'What? For making them look stupid? Don't hold your breath. Anyway, I wanted to let you know I'm not behind bars.'

'Have they tracked down Roddy Farquhar?'

'If they have, they've not told me.'

'You don't think that's suspicious? The one person who could point the finger at Torrance is nowhere to be found?'

'Of course it's suspicious.'

'You don't think Torrance has . . . *disappeared* him?'

Danny scoffed. 'What have you been smoking, Allie? I think he's warned him off, not bumped him off. Probably helped him to drop out of sight, but no more than that.'

'All the same . . . Farquhar's the only one who could drop Torrance in the shit, and suddenly he's out of the picture.'

'I'm with you, I don't think there's any doubt that Torrance tipped off Farquhar, but there's nothing we can do about that. If we accuse Torrance, we'd have to unspool to how I knew about their connection. And I can't do that, Allie.'

'I know.' All the same, part of her wanted to find a way to expose the underhand dealing of the Special Branch man. And to show Carlyle that Wee Gordon Beattie's relationship with his contacts sometimes involved him supping a little too heartily with the devil. If she and Danny were running investigations at the *Clarion*, they'd find a different way to the truth. What was the point of uncovering corruption if you were as corrupt as those you were exposing?

Danny interrupted her train of thought. 'You still on for tomorrow?'

'Looking forward to it.'

'I'll away to Presto and get the messages, then. See you tomorrow.'

There was much more she wanted to ask, but it could wait for tomorrow. She picked up her book again and as she returned to the secret world, she realised with a jolt how indiscreet she'd been with Danny. Given what she'd been reading, she couldn't help wondering whether the police had their phones tapped. Had that been the click of a listening device she'd heard, or just the usual crap GPO line? Allie gave a scornful little laugh. Who did she think she was?

Bath over, she dressed and made herself scrambled eggs with a couple of fried potato scones and carried on reading at the kitchen table. She was disturbed again by the phone; her parents had seen the story and in their awkward way wanted to congratulate her. Her mother, of course, was anxious about the people she was mixing with. Her father was more straightforwardly pleased. All told, it was an easier conversation than they usually managed. Maybe they were coming round to the idea of her working for the *Clarion*.

Afterwards, she went through to the living room and put on *Parallel Lines*. She spent the afternoon writing letters to friends because today she had something to shout about. Into every envelope, she folded the relevant pages of the *Clarion*. The reporters she'd trained with in Newcastle would understand what had gone into copper-bottoming a story this intense, and envy her the opportunity to shine. Supersub Marcus would think about how he'd have arranged the material differently. Jen and her other friends from Cambridge days might even be impressed, though she knew that they secretly thought her new employer was decidedly infra dig.

Allie had almost finished the last letter when the phone rang again. Hoping it wasn't the office, she answered with a cautious, 'Yes?'

'Hey, Scoop! It's me, Rona. I know you'll have heard this half a million times already, but you are a wee star. Great job, girl!'

Allie chuckled. 'Takes one to know one.'

'Shut up with the false modesty. I've never ever done stories like this. The nearest I've come to putting my life in danger is giving a fashion designer a luke-warm review. But I tell you, you're not just taking on the bad guys, you're making some serious political enemies too. I don't think those nice lassies you made pals with at the SNP meeting are going to be inviting you to their next hen night.' Rona hooted with laughter.

'Come on, be fair. I made it clear that these bams were nothing to do with the SNP. There's even a quote from their press officer expressing their horror and outrage.'

Another throaty laugh. 'Two pars, right at the end. They'll not be happy with anything less than an intro that went something like, 'SNP leaders denied last night that they had ever heard of the conspiracy to bomb Scotland into independence.' No, Allie, you're well and truly screwed with the Nats.'

'Into every life, a little rain must fall, Rona.'

'Watch out, Allie. When they rule the world, you'll not be getting any of Scotland's oil. Anyway, I'll not keep you, I just wanted to congratulate you.'

'Thanks, I appreciate it. Do you want to do lunch one day next week? I'll be back on the rota on Monday, starting with the day shift.'

A momentary pause, then Rona said, 'What about dinner instead? You know you can never predict what you'll be doing on the day shift.'

She had a point. 'Fair enough. I think my diary's clear, since I'll not be going to any SNP meetings.'

They settled on Wednesday, and Allie went back to her letter-writing. A brisk walk to the pillar box and back to her flat. Some people might consider a Saturday night alone on the sofa with a good book and a box of chocolates to be pretty pitiful. After the week she'd had, Allie thought it was pretty close to paradise.

And besides, it was the first chance she'd had to think about what Danny had told her about Rona's sexuality. She'd encountered lesbians before, but none of them had become close friends. She recognised how quickly she'd warmed to Rona and that she wanted them to be friends. But would the ground between them shift now she'd learned about such an important aspect of Rona's life?

★ ★ ★

When she woke up next morning, the buzz in Allie's blood had stilled. Anticlimax had kicked in, and she didn't have the faintest inkling of the next project that would release her from the tyranny of whatever the newsdesk thought she should be doing. Rona's tip about the pregnant football referee might grant her a day's grace, but it wasn't going to reinforce the marker that the terrorist story had put down.

News of the arrests of Malloch and Bell and of four Irish suspects had made all of the Scottish Sunday papers. Even the *Sunday Thistle* had given it a few paragraphs. There were hints of a terror plot, but the rules governing what could be reported following an arrest meant the stories read as if written in code. When the two men were charged, there would be another trickle of information, but the major coverage wouldn't come till the trial, and that was months away.

Hopefully Danny would raise her spirits. Together they might even come up with a story idea. Surely there must be some thread they could pull to unravel a story that would get them back on the front page?

Allie decided to take a cab over to Danny's. It wasn't that she wanted to drink much. But she was fed up of wrestling the heavy steering of the Morris Minor through icy streets. Sitting in the back of the lumbering taxi, she was grateful not to be peering through a blurred windscreen at the sleet. She hurried from the warmth of the taxi into the welcome shelter of the close.

She rang Danny's doorbell and waited. And waited. She rang again, lips pursed. He must have forgotten some key ingredient and popped out to the shop. Already she could feel the cold from the stone stairs creeping into her feet. This was ridiculous. If she hung about on the landing, she'd be chilled to the bone in no time. Danny wouldn't mind if she let herself in; she'd done it once before, after all.

She pushed the letterbox open and reached inside for the key. There was no welcoming aroma of roasting chicken, but then, the inner door was still closed. She pulled out the key and unlocked the tall wooden door. She stepped into the tiny vestibule and closed the outside door behind her, careful to pull the key back in.

Allie opened the half-glazed door that led into the hall. Definitely no cooking smells. Had he forgotten their arrangement? Had he gone out partying and not come home? When it came down to it, what did she really know about Danny's lifestyle?

The living room door was ajar and she could see the light was on. Not surprising on a grey Glasgow day, but she couldn't imagine Danny going out for the evening and leaving the light on. Was he crashed out on one of his big black sofas after a heavy night? Allie pushed the living room door further open and walked in.

Shock saved her from understanding what she was looking at. Her brain had to unpick it in slow motion. The black-and-white room, that connected to her memory. The black onyx candlestick snagged at the corner of her mind. Out of place, that was the problem.

And the figure sprawled on the black-and-white rug . . . that didn't fit at all. It was even more wrong.

But none of it was as profoundly wrong as the dark red stain that spread in a congealed puddle round the head of the dead body lying in the middle of Danny Sullivan's living room.

324

47

When the police arrived, Allie was sitting on the floor of the hall, knees bent, arms wrapped around her shins. Even though there was still some residual warmth from the central heating's morning cycle, spasms of shivering shook her from stem to stern at unpredictable intervals. Her brain too seemed to stutter from one thought to another. Who had done this? What would Carlyle say? Could the rug be cleaned? Where were Danny's notes? Was the chicken in the fridge? Nothing made any sense.

First on the scene, two uniforms. A bulky middle-aged man with ginger-and-silver hair peeping from his cap and an accent that Allie automatically placed somewhere in the Western Isles; a younger one with almost translucent skin who said nothing and stood chewing his bottom lip. Probably chapped from the cold, Allie thought inconsequentially. She'd got unsteadily to her feet to answer the doorbell and now she didn't know where to stand.

'I'm PC Macleod, and this is PC Campbell,' the older man said. 'Was it you who called 999?'

Allie nodded.

'Can I take your name?'

Campbell took out a small black notebook and started writing.

'Allie Burns. Alison.'

'And do you live here, Alison?' Macleod's voice was surprisingly gentle, she noticed.

'No. I was coming for my dinner. Danny was going

to do a roast chicken.' As if that mattered.

'You told my colleague there was a dead man in the living room. Would that be Danny?'

She nodded. 'It's his flat. Danny Sullivan.'

Campbell made an indeterminate noise. Macleod gave him an inquisitorial look and the younger man spoke. 'Are youse the journalists on the *Clarion*?' Campbell sounded full of doubt. 'The ones that turned over the terrorist Nats?'

'Yes, but that's not what matters. Danny's dead, that's what you should be doing something about.' Allie had raised her voice without thinking.

'I appreciate you've had a shock. But we just need to get one or two things clear in our minds.' Macleod cocked his head towards the living room and Campbell made his way to the door. He turned back and nodded. Another gesture of Macleod's head and Campbell went back out to the landing, pulling the internal door closed behind him. Detached, Allie noted the low rumble of his voice and the crackle of a police radio.

'PC Campbell is letting the control room know we need a specialist team.'

'A murder team,' Allie said. 'I mean, he didn't hit himself over the head with a candlestick, did he?' She felt her voice shake and clamped her mouth shut.

'Was he your boyfriend?'

If it was an attempt to take her mind off the terrible image of Danny lying on the cowskin rug, it failed. All it did was make it worse. 'No,' she said. 'He was my friend. My colleague. Is that too hard to grasp?'

'I'm just trying to get things clear in my mind, Miss Burns. Now, why don't you come through to the kitchen till my colleagues get here?'

She followed him out of the hall and sat down at the kitchen table. There was no sign of any cooking preparations. Had Danny been lying there all night? Had it been quick, or had he lain for minutes or hours, in pain? Drifting in and out of consciousness? Had he known he was dying?

'I'll just leave you here,' Macleod said, edging warily out of the room. She didn't think he was a man who felt comfortable at the prospect of other people's emotions. Allie lit a cigarette, noticing that her fingers were not trembling. She'd never seen a dead body before and episodes of *Shoestring* and *Sutherland's Law* hadn't been much of a preparation for the real thing. She hadn't expected Danny to look so empty, which made her feel stupid.

Allie needed to displace the image of Danny lying dead on the rug. There was a pile of newspapers next to her, and almost without thinking she began flicking through them. Top of the pile was the previous day's *Clarion* with their splash on display. Had that only been yesterday? It felt like ancient history now. How could Danny be dead?

She picked up the paper, then noticed Danny's notebook sitting underneath it. It was the same *Clarion*-issue pad all the reporters used. She had its double in her own bag. Spiral-bound, small enough to slip into a pocket, lined pages with a margin so the interviewer could mark the significant quotes as they went along. Technically, she knew, it was the property of the paper. Anything Danny had noted down belonged to the *Clarion*. She wondered whether he had transcribed all his notes. She ought to take it back to the office to make sure, she thought. It was her story as much as his.

Besides, the police wouldn't be able to make head nor tail of it. Allie was pretty sure that anyone who worked with the police or the courts would use the traditional Pitman's shorthand. Accurate and formal, it took time and skill to master. But for her generation of reporters, it had been replaced by Teeline, a much simpler system based on stripping down the forms of letters and interpreting signs according to where they appeared in relation to the lines on the page. But where a Pitman's note could be read by anyone familiar with its forms, Teeline was idiosyncratic. No two people's outlines were the same. Allie often found she couldn't even interpret her own note if she'd left it more than a couple of weeks. For someone expert in Pitman's it might as well be written in Ancient Greek. The best chance of anyone making sense of Danny's notes was not simply that they used Teeline — they'd also have to know what the notes were about.

Without any further debate, Allie slipped Danny's notebook into her bag. It wasn't as if she was withholding evidence from the police. If there was a clue to the identity of his killer in what he'd written, she was their best hope of finding it. She'd examine his notes and if she found anything she didn't already know, she'd pass it on to the detectives.

Then the enormity of what she'd seen hit her again and an overwhelming wave of nausea hit her. She barely made it to the sink, and she was still retching when she heard footsteps and voices in the hall. She rinsed her mouth from the tap and was spitting the water back into the sink when a middle-aged man with a bald head and the face of an unsuccessful prize fighter appeared in the doorway. 'I'm Detective Chief Inspector Buchan. You're the lassie who found the body, I take it?' He had the kind of Glasgow accent that made the most innocuous remark sound like a threat.

'Yes, that's me.' Allie heard the wobble in her voice.

'And you arrived when, exactly?' She told him, and he nodded. 'We're going to need to take a statement from you. Are you happy to do that here, or would you prefer to do it back at the division?'

The thought of sitting in Danny's kitchen surrounded by things he'd chosen while the police picked over the circumstances of his death made her shudder. 'Anywhere but here,' she said.

The witness interview had swiftly turned into something unexpected. The room was cramped and stank of male sweat and stale cigarettes and the two officers sitting opposite her seemed intent on browbeating her into some sort of admission. Detective Sergeant Hardie and Detective Constable Groom had the flat cynical eyes of men who had seen every sort of lie. They both had a cultivated air of disbelief that occasionally tilted over into incredulity and Allie didn't know how to counter it.

'Look, I've told you. Danny invited me round for a roast chicken dinner. To celebrate our story. I turned up as we'd arranged, and I found him lying on the living room floor.' She swallowed hard. 'Dead. I called 999, and the rest you know.'

Hardie raised his eyebrows. 'So you've said. But here's the thing, Alison. When it comes to murder, we are the boys with the know-how. And one thing we know for sure is that everybody in a murder case lies. Sometimes innocent wee white lies, but sometimes big fat guilty ones. Now, which kind is it with you, my darling?'

'I'm not your darling and I'm not lying,' Allie said, her jaw tight. Anger had moved her grief to the back burner.

Groom leaned forward. 'Here's something else we know. Often the last person to see a victim alive is the same person who calls in to say they've discovered a body. So when did you really arrive at Danny's flat? Because it seems to me that if you were planning a proper celebration, you'd have done that on Saturday night. I mean, that's when folk round here party.'

'Remind us what you were doing on Saturday night.' Hardie again. It was relentless.

'It doesn't matter how many times you ask me that. The answer'll be the same because it's the truth. I wrote some letters to friends. I heated up some soup for my tea then I lay on the settee with a box of chocolates and the new John Le Carré novel. I never left the house.'

'But you can't produce any witnesses to back you up. Nobody phoned. Nobody popped in. Nobody can prove you're telling the truth. What's to say you weren't round at Danny Sullivan's flat, having a wee celebration?'

Allie rolled her eyes as Groom picked up once more. 'We understand how these things go, Alison. Misunderstandings occur. Things get out of hand. Men do that. We push for more than you lassies are willing to give. We don't take no for an answer. And the next thing you know, you grab the first thing that comes to hand, and wallop. Now things have really got out of hand.'

'You guys are living on Fantasy Island,' Allie said wearily. 'Danny was not my boyfriend. We were colleagues and friends, that's all. I wasn't at his flat last

330

night, and I sure as hell didn't kill him.'

'OK, you're saying Danny wasn't your boyfriend.' Hardie's tone had developed a steely edge. 'Maybe that was the problem. He wanted to be your boyfriend but you weren't coming across. And maybe a few drinks had been taken and he was taking advantage. He wouldn't be the first, would he? I mean, you'd know all about that, being a reporter and all.'

'None of this is true.' A mix of anger and panic was building inside her. Nothing she said was having any effect on their lurid fantasies. Her head was pounding and images of Danny lifeless on the rug kept flashing across her vision.

'Did he try to rape you, Alison?' Groom said gently. 'I know it's a hard thing to say. But it's not your fault.'

The dam finally burst. 'Why will you not listen to me?' Allie exploded. 'How many times? Danny wasn't interested in me. Danny was gay.' As soon as the words left her mouth, she felt a wave of shame. Her revelation might have got her off the hook, but what had she done to Danny?

331

48

The light on the answering machine was flashing when Allie finally got home. They'd kept her for another two hours after she'd blurted out her betrayal of Danny. She'd refused to answer another question but still they kept at her. 'Was it you made the pass at him, then? And you couldn't take the knock-back? Or were you just disgusted when you found out the truth?' On and on, more variations than she would have believed possible. She'd sat with her arms folded across her chest, her jaw set in a stubborn line that her mother would have recognised. Mrs Burns would have told Hardie and Groom they were wasting their time. 'Sooner expect Falkland Hill to grow legs and walk round to Largo Law for its tea than expect our Alison to change her mind once it's made up,' her mother had been wont to sigh since childhood.

Eventually they'd conceded defeat, though Allie realised it was probably a temporary relief. It had been dark by the time they'd told her she could go. She was too angry or too proud or too something she couldn't name to ask if she could call a taxi. She regretted that within a hundred yards of the police station. Her feet were wet and drips were slithering down her hair between her coat collar and her neck. Rescue came in the shape of a bus looming out of the snowy dark. She didn't care where it was going, it had to be better than tramping the streets of the South Side.

Head full of what had happened to Danny, Allie rode the bus across the river and into the city centre, abandoning it near the taxi rank at Central station. Ten minutes later, shoes and coat starting to steam in the fug of the taxi, she'd reached home. She gave the answering machine a hard stare and decided it could wait for her to warm up. She had a quick shower, put on a clean pair of flannelette pyjamas and the thick towelling dressing gown she'd stolen from a posh Highland hotel she'd been sent to on a job, and finally pressed play.

It was Carlyle. No surprises there, then. 'Christ, but that's shocking news, Burns. Hellish for you. I hope you're OK. They tell me you're at the cop shop, so call me as soon as you get back. I'm at home.'

She was going to have to tell him the secret she'd spilled to the police. It was nobody's business and it shouldn't change how anybody thought of Danny, but now the leaky sieve that was Strathclyde Police knew, it would only be a matter of time before it was common gossip in the Press Club. 'You and your big mouth,' she muttered. She couldn't do this cold.

Allie poured herself a stiff whisky and took a gulp. She felt the heat of the spirit all the way down her gullet, and remembered she hadn't eaten since breakfast. And she'd lost that in Danny's kitchen. Thinking better of the rest of her drink, Allie put the glass to one side and called Carlyle. When he answered, she didn't know where to start. 'It's me,' she said.

'Dear Christ, Burns, this is a hell of a thing. I can't take it in. Danny, dead? Murdered? You must be in a bad way, walking in on that.'

'It was horrible, boss. And then the polis? Acting like I was a suspect?'

'You're kidding? They thought you had it in you to batter Danny to death? What kind of idiots are they?'

333

'The kind that hate to admit they haven't got a clue.'

'We've got the bare bones from the police. And you're right, they don't seem to have anything to go on. No witnesses, no prints on the murder weapon. That doesn't leave me with a lot of options for tomorrow's front page.' He let his words hang in the air between them.

Allie's mouth had dried on her. 'I can't,' she croaked.

'I think you can, Allie.' Carlyle spoke more gently than she'd believed possible. And he'd used her first name. 'I think you're one of the ones that has ink in their veins. And I believe there's nobody Danny would rather write your story. And it is your story, Allie.'

Tears pricked at her eyes. 'I betrayed him.'

'What do you mean, 'betrayed him'? There was nothing you could have done to save him.'

'No, not that. The police . . . They kept on and on at me, accusing me of being there last night, suggesting Danny might have . . . might have tried to rape me. I held out for as long as I could, boss.' Even to her, she sounded piteous.

'Are you saying . . . ' Carlyle's voice tailed off, incredulous.

'No, no,' Allie exclaimed. 'No, of course not. I told them even if I had been there, they couldn't have been more wrong about Danny because he was gay. He confided in me because he thought he could trust me, and I let him down. And now those bastards . . . they act like he's worth less because of it.' She paused. 'I'm only telling you because they'll already be spreading it round their contacts.'

'I never knew,' Carlyle said softly. 'He didn't act gay.'

'Whatever that means,' Allie said, a savage note

334

creeping in. 'He was more friendly to me than anybody in the whole bloody newsroom. He was passionate about his work, he never sneered at the people who read the *Clarion*. He was kind and smart and that's how he deserves to be remembered. Not because he fancied men.'

'You'll get no argument from me on that score. And that's why I need you to write tomorrow's splash. Because that's what you'll tell the world. Whatever comes afterwards? Hell mend them. You get your truth out there first.'

This was the robust Carlyle she was accustomed to and Allie gave her conditioned response. 'OK, boss. But I don't know what to say. How to pitch it.'

She heard the hiss of a flame and the crackle of burning tobacco. 'An 'I' piece. Write it from the heart, Burns. Straight from the heart. You were there. You know what you saw. You know what it felt like. Fourteen pars by eight o'clock. I'm going into the office to see this one to bed.'

A clatter in her ear as he replaced the handset. Time to honour her dead.

Allie set herself up in front of her portable, whisky to one side, ashtray to the other and stared at the blank sheet of paper. 'Daniel Sullivan, *Daily Clarion* investigative reporter . . . ' Fuck them all, she was going to give him the title he deserved, even if it gave Wee Gordon Beattie a coronary.

. . . was found brutally murdered in his Glasgow flat yesterday.
    I was the one who found him. Danny had invited me round for my Sunday dinner to celebrate the Tartan Terror front-page story

that we collaborated on last week. He'd promised me roast chicken with all the trimmings.

But when I arrived at his Pollokshields
flat, there was no reply. I assumed he'd gone
to the shop for some forgotten ingredient. It
was freezing on the landing and I knew where
he kept his spare key, so I let myself in.

The flat was quiet and I couldn't smell
anything cooking. That puzzled me. Danny
wasn't the sort of person to forget an
arrangement, especially not a celebration.

I went through to the living room, and
everything in my life changed. Danny lay
sprawled on his black-and-white cowskin rug,
a pool of dark congealed blood around his
head.

I'd never seen a dead person before, but
I knew right away that my friend was dead. I
know now that there's no mistaking that. It
wasn't the blood or the silence that told me.
It was the complete absence of Danny.

Now Danny is part of the machine of justice
that rumbles into action when one person ends
another's life with deliberate violence.

If the subs didn't cut that on the grounds of variance
from tabloidese, the night lawyer would, for prejudg-
ing whether this was murder or culpable homicide.

Danny grew up in Edinburgh and attended St
Augustine's High. He often spoke with great
affection of his parents, Marie and Eddie,
his brother Joseph and his close extended
family.

336

He began his career in journalism as an editorial assistant on the *Edinburgh Evening News* but his ambition and talent soon won him a place as a junior reporter. A series of high-profile news stories brought him to the attention of the *Daily Clarion* where he was employed as a reporter for the past three years.

Danny was a popular member of the news team here. He had a nose for a good story and once he was on its trail, nothing would stand in his way. But he was also a great team player, happy to work collaboratively to ensure the difficult stories were told.

I learned so much from working alongside him. He was always kind, never arrogant, invariably generous, imaginative and inventive. Among the important stories he worked on recently were the Paragon Insurance tax fraud exposé and the Tartan Terror revelations that rocked the nation yesterday.

Strathclyde Police believe the crime occurred on Saturday evening. There is no sign of a break-in at the flat.

Detectives are working on several lines of inquiry ...

As if, she thought bitterly.

... and we urge any readers who may have information relating to the murder of Danny

Sullivan either to contact them or to call
our newsdesk in confidence on 041 681 3333.
   This was a savage attack on a brave journalist whose only crime was to seek out truth
and report it fairly. But for me, it is far
worse than that. For Danny Sullivan was my
friend. And now he is dead.

Allie read through her copy. It was a long way from
what she wanted to write, but that would take time to
craft. Time she didn't have. And Danny would have
understood that.

She went through to the phone and dialled the
copytaker's number. 'This is Alison Burns,' she said.
'I've got urgent copy for the personal attention of
Angus Carlyle.'

A phlegmy chuckle. 'My, we're awfu' grand tonight,
Miss Burns,' came the arch reply.

'It's about Danny.'

'Oh, Christ, I'm sorry. You and him were pals, right?
He was an awfu' nice lad, for a Catholic.'

Allie rolled her eyes. 'Are you ready? Angus is waiting for this.' And she was off, the machine-gun rattle
of typewriter keys the counterpoint to her words.
Still, after so long, she was surprised by the speed
of the copytaker. Almost before she realised, the end
was upon her.

'For Danny Sullivan was my friend. Full point. And
now he is dead. Full point. Ends.'

49

Carlyle had called Allie after her copy had dropped. 'Not a bad job,' he said. In the reluctant lexicon of Scottish praise, that amounted to laurels. 'I've trimmed and tweaked it a wee bit, but you'll get the splash again. This is becoming a habit.'

'I could do without this one.'

'We all could. Listen, I'm taking you off the rota again but we're having a meeting in the morning at eleven to talk about where we go with the story next. I want you there.'

'Sure. Has anybody spoken to the family?'

'Maureen Jarvie from the Edinburgh office went round.' He let out a sigh. 'Rather her than me. A death knock's hard enough at the best of times, but when you're dealing with somebody you know . . . I gather it was pretty grim. But she's got some good quotes for a sidebar to your piece.'

Allie could only imagine the grief drowning the Sullivans. The one thing worse than losing a beloved son must be to know that things were wrong between you at the end. And Joseph, the man responsible for the rift? It would be so much worse for him, knowing how that wedge had been driven between Danny and his parents. 'And they can't even plan the funeral till the police release the body,' she said.

'They'll have a wake, at least. As will we, Burns. As will we.'

She'd barely put the phone down when it rang again. This time, it was her mother. 'Alison, we were just watching the news, and we saw about a journalist getting murdered in Glasgow. Your dad says it was that Danny laddie that you've been working with, but that can't be right?'

'It was Danny, Mum.' She didn't want to admit to finding him; she knew where that would lead. But it would be in the paper in the morning and that would be worse. So she gave in and put up with an inquisition into every detail of the day. God, but she was weary of reliving the worst day of her life.

'Was it one of those terrorists you were writing about?' her mother demanded.

'I don't think so. They have very particular ways of punishing people and this doesn't fit.' Allie forced herself to sound casual in a bid to allay her mother's anxieties. She had no idea whether the IRA had taken Danny's life. It was true that the method of murder wasn't their typical approach but with their Active Service Unit in the cells, who knew what options had been open to them?

The attempt hadn't succeeded. 'I'm worried for you, Alison. You did the same stories as him, what if they come after you next?'

'Mum, it might not be anything to do with his work. Nobody has any idea why it happened.'

'It said the police are following leads.'

Allie scoffed. 'Trust me, Mum, the police haven't got the first idea what's behind this. But honestly, there's no reason to think I'm at risk. Now, I'm away now to get my tea —'

'You've not had your tea yet? It's nearly half past eight. You need to be looking after yourself, Alison.'

Allie closed her eyes and tried to keep her sigh inaudible. 'I'll give you a ring later in the week, Mum.

But don't worry about me. I'm not in any danger. I'm just very sad, that's all.' As she put the phone down, Allie realised that was nothing less than the truth. Sadness wasn't something she felt often but tonight, it was almost overwhelming.

She was halfway to the kitchen when the doorbell rang. A flash of panic pierced her momentarily. She was expecting no one. Was that what had happened to Danny? A ring on the bell, a familiar face, an open welcome, an invitation to murder? Allie tiptoed across the hall and opened the inside door with infinite care. She had a chain for the big outside double door and now she slid it into place with all the care of a safe-cracker turning the tumblers. Only then did she crack open the lock and peer into the narrow gap.

Allie gasped with the laughter of nervous release. 'Jeez, Rona, you nearly gave me a heart attack.'

Rona Dunsyre shrugged. 'That's no way to greet your pals.'

Allie fussed with the chain and let Rona in. 'What are you doing here? I wasn't expecting you. How do you know where I live?' All in a flash flood.

Rona followed her inside and gave the hallway a critical appraisal. 'Still a work in progress, then?'

'It's rented. I'm not wasting money on it. But I don't understand why you're here.'

'Danny. I thought you could maybe do with company. A shoulder to cry on. Or maybe just a wee voddy for the body?' Rona raised the carrier bag that she'd been clutching. It clinked with promise.

'All of the above,' Allie sighed. 'Come through.'

She led the way into the living room. Rona shrugged out of her voluminous olive-green coat and let it slump to the floor beside the chair that had last been occupied by Danny. Her outfit was more subdued than Allie had grown accustomed to — jeans tucked into knee-length boots with a slouch in the leather, a loose grey mohair sweater with a flattering cowl neck, her only jewellery a pair of earrings shaped into gold ingots. The trademark splash of colour came from a multicoloured tie-dye scarf knotted round her shoulders. She considered the chair, then said. 'If you need a hug, I suppose it makes more sense for us to coorie down on the couch.' She eyed the tubular chrome construction. 'Not that it's exactly designed for snuggling.'

Allie felt her sadness shift a little. There was something about Rona that always made her smile. 'I'll get glasses.'

By the time she returned, Rona had pulled the coffee table closer and emptied her carrier bag. A bottle of Smirnoff Blue Label. Half a dozen cans of Coke. A large bag of dry-roasted peanuts, tipped into a clean ashtray. 'I'm just making myself at home,' Rona said, cracking the seal on the vodka bottle cap.

'I'm glad you're here.' Allie sat down beside her and proffered two highball glasses with a single lump of ice in each. Rona poured generous measures and added enough Coke to produce the colour of weak tea.

They chinked glasses, and Rona said, 'Here's to Danny.'

'To Danny. I loved working with him.'

'What was it about him that made it special?' She rolled her eyes. 'God, listen to me. Ever the bloody feature writer.'

Allie took a swig of her drink. 'He didn't patronise me or treat me like a secretary. He always listened to

342

what I had to say, and he didn't mind admitting when I had a better suggestion than him. And he didn't try to pretend it had been his idea.' She reached for her cigarettes and lit up. 'But I let him down, Rona. I so let him down.'

'What do you mean?'

'He trusted me with his biggest secret. And I blurted it out to the polis.' A sigh of smoke. 'I told them he was gay.'

Rona put her arm round Allie's shoulders and squeezed gently. 'You can't hurt him now, doll.'

'I can hurt the other people in his life. And I can hurt his reputation.' She squeezed her eyes shut. 'I couldn't help it. They just kept on and on at me with their vile, stupid insinuations.'

'Tell me about it.'

So Allie did. In more detail than she'd explained to Carlyle. With her boss, to have said too much about her emotional response would have felt like giving him a hostage to fortune. With Rona, she had the freedom to explain how frightened and angry and out of control she'd felt. With her, Allie could be honest about what felt like a disastrous failing without the fear of being judged.

'You had to tell them,' Rona said. 'Otherwise you'd probably still be there. It sounds like they've got nobody else to browbeat. It's not a betrayal, Allie. Wherever Danny is, he's beyond any hurt you could deliver. And anybody that thinks less of Danny because he was gay . . . ' She shook her head, contempt on her face. 'They're not worth bothering about.' She half-turned and gave Allie a measured look. 'Let it go. Stop beating yourself up. If you don't let it go, it'll turn into self-pity and that's just ugly. Plus it's no help to you or to Danny. You hear me?'

Rona's brisk good sense gave Allie a brief shock before she recognised its validity. She leaned into her friend. 'You're right. What matters now is finding out what happened. What I keep coming back to, Rona: who could have done this? Why would anybody kill Danny?'

'I'm no detective, but I've read enough crime novels to know the motive's either personal or professional. Plus, Strathclyde Police are nothing like Wexford or Morse or Dalgliesh. Mostly, they couldn't detect their way out of a paper bag with a map and a torch. We need the likes of Miss Marple or Philip Marlowe here.'

Allie gave an incredulous laugh. 'What? I need to take up knitting?'

'No, you need to use your little grey cells, you daftie. You know Danny better than anybody in that office. He trusted you with who he really was. And you know the story *behind* the stories you've been working on these last few weeks. There must be a whole bunch of people the pair of you have pissed off royally.'

Allie felt a shudder in her chest. 'If our stories pissed anybody off enough to kill Danny, then maybe I'm next.'

Rona's hand flew to her mouth. 'Oh, fuck. Allie, me and my big mouth. I didn't mean to freak you out.'

'It's not like I hadn't thought of it myself. I've been trying to put it out of my mind. After all, Danny was the lead name on the Paragon story, and he had the starring role in the Tartan Terrorists one. He did the undercover, so as far as the IRA were concerned, he was the face of our investigation.'

'Exactly.' Rona patted her knee. 'But you don't kill a journalist after the fact, do you? You kill them to shut them up.' She paused. 'The IRA do like a punishment beating, though. A warning to anybody else that's thinking about betraying them.'

'They have trademarks, though. That's how people know it's a warning. They kneecap people or execute them. This isn't their style. Even if they were reacting on the spur of the moment, they'd want to leave people in no doubt, wouldn't they? *Pour encourager les autres*.'

Even Rona had no answer to that. The two women sat in glum silence for long enough to finish their drinks and pour fresh ones, just as strong as the first.

'Do you know much about Danny's personal life?' Rona asked, grabbing a handful of peanuts.

'Next to nothing. I know he went to bars and clubs, but he said he was careful about who he connected with. When I asked him whether he had anybody he could talk to, he said he had an 'arrangement'. I don't know what that means?'

Rona shrugged. 'I don't know either. Honestly, I think gay men are from a different planet to lesbians. That whole picking up strangers in bars, and worse? I just don't get it. I don't have arrangements, I have relationships. And I'm guessing Danny didn't have one of those?'

'Not that he admitted to me. But there was something.' Allie gave Rona a sideways look. 'Between the two of us, right?'

Rona hugged her again. 'Just the two of us, doll.'

'You know Gordon Beattie, the crime corr?'

'Wee Gordon? Wee in stature and wee in talent. Don't tell me he's secretly Gay Gordon?' Rona guffawed.

'No. God, no. But he's got a Special Branch contact, Thomas Torrance. And he brought him into the office to consult on the Tartan Terrorists story. Danny just about had a heart attack when he saw Torrance. He turned the colour of putty. When I asked him about it, it turned out he recognised Torrance from one of the clubs in town.'

'That's interesting, but surely not any kind of threat? Face it, doll, if Danny pointed the finger at Torrance, he was exposing himself at the same time.'

'I know, but get this. The guy Torrance was with — and I mean with, as in he was snogging him — it turns out this guy was Roddy Farquhar, one of the Tartan Terror crew. When we discussed it, Danny reckoned it was just casual between them. But it's a helluva coincidence that Farquhar did a runner just before the paper hit the streets.'

'So, what? You think they were an item? And Farquhar told Torrance what his pals were up to?'

'It makes sense, doesn't it? And rather than arrest them before things got out of hand, Torrance let them run to see where they were going. Then when Wee Gordon Beattie brought him into the tent he learned what Danny and I had found out. Torrance must have warned Farquhar to get out before the police came for him.'

'Oh my God,' Rona breathed. 'So Torrance had a very good reason for shutting Danny up. He could still have totally fucked him up.'

All at once, the unshed tears that Allie had managed to hold at bay burst through her defences. In a matter of moments, she was shaking and sobbing, gulping for air and howling like a child. Rona wrapped her arms around her and held her tight. Allie clung to her, clutching handfuls of her sweater, letting her grief flood through her. Danny was dead, and there was no solace.

50

Allie woke to darkness, a faint throb of pain at her temples. The evening came back in fragments. Her tempest of tears. More vodka, more swapping stories. More vodka. Then a blank. She turned on to her back and yelped when she collided with another body. Rona? Rona was in bed with her? What had happened in the gap between the end of memory and the beginning of morning?

An indeterminate grunt, a shift of weight on the mattress and Rona said, 'It's like the Black Hole of Calcutta in here.'

Nervous about what she'd find, Allie turned on the bedside lamp. Rona lay next to her, but on top of the duvet. She'd brought the one from the spare room through to cover her. Allie felt her panic subside. Nothing untoward had happened.

Rona recognised the relief. 'Your reputation's unblemished, doll. I'm not into necrophilia.'

Allie felt the blush rising up her throat. 'I wasn't casting you as a predatory lesbian, I was casting me as a stupid drunk. You know how it goes — 'ah love you, you're ma best pal.''

Rona yawned and stretched. 'You just needed a cuddle, Allie. It's not a criminal offence.' She released her mane of hair from the topknot she'd tied it into before sleeping and it tumbled on to her shoulders in what looked like a carefully calculated disarray. Allie envied the ease with which she slipped back into the day. Rona reached across and gave her a quick hug. 'I need to get moving. I can't turn up at work looking this normal.' She slipped out of bed and pulled on jeans and sweater. Allie turned away, awkwardly realising she'd noticed how good Rona looked in underwear. What was going on in her head?

'Thanks,' Allie said. 'It really helped, having you here.'

Rona shrugged. 'When I heard the news, I thought about how I'd feel, in your shoes. Then it was a no-brainer.'

'I can see how you get the punters to talk to you. One thing you didn't answer — how did you know my address?'

'I asked Jock. The editorial driver. Those guys know everything, did you not realise that? Who's having an affair and who with, who can't stay out of the casino, what everybody's favourite carry-out is. We have no secrets from the drivers. Well, almost none.' She winked. 'I'll probably see you later. I'll let myself out.'

* * *

The atmosphere in the office was subdued. Nobody was shouting down a phone, nobody was arguing about their assignments. Allie was aware of the eyes following her the length of the editorial floor. Everyone from the copy boys to the chief sub knew she'd been the one to find Danny Sullivan's body; everyone, she knew, would have their own take on the circumstances.

'You OK?' the newsdesk secretary asked as she approached.

'Getting there.' Allie took off her coat and hung it up. 'Where are we meeting?'

'Angus's office.'

To get there, she had to pass the rows of reporters' desks. They all looked up as she passed, mostly murmuring embarrassed condolences. None of them knew how to react when one of their own became the story. They'd all faked sympathy so many times, they were uncertain how to deliver it for real, Allie thought. She'd be the same herself.

The Razor and Wee Gordon Beattie were already sitting round Carlyle's desk. It was clear none of them knew what to say to her either. 'That was a good piece this morning,' the Razor said. 'Carefully done.'

Typical lawyer's praise, Allie thought. 'To be honest, that wasn't what I was thinking about.'

'It's a shame about the boy,' Beattie said. He didn't even attempt sincerity. Then he muttered so quietly that only she would hear, 'But that's what happens when you send a boy to do a man's job.'

Allie's shocked disbelief silenced her momentarily. Before she could recover herself, Carlyle cleared his throat. He looked five years older than he had the week before, his eyes like oysters nestled in bags of wrinkled skin. 'Gordon brings tidings,' he said. 'Not quite comfort and joy, but heading in the right direction. And it's thanks to the lead you gave the polis yesterday, Burns. Gordon, pick up the story.'

'Aye, well, once they realised Sullivan was queer, they took a good look at the wee address book he kept in the drawer under the phone. Most of the numbers were obvious — family, colleagues, friends. But there was one that was different. It just said, 'B: messages.' So they rang the number and it turns out it was an answering service that takes messages for what they call 'rent boys'.' He twinkled a lewd look at Allie.

'Male prostitutes,' he added, smug.

'I'm familiar with the term,' Allie said, brusque.

'It turns out Sullivan — '

'Danny,' Allie interrupted. 'His name was Danny.'

Beattie raised his eyebrows. 'It turns out he had a favourite among the answering service's rent boys. B for Barry. Barry Curran, to give him his Sunday name. The polis put a bit of pressure on them — you help us, we won't arrest the lot of you for soliciting and gross indecency, that kind of thing — and lo and behold, Curran was booked in for a session with Danny on Saturday night. So they've arrested the wee shirt-lifter,' he concluded triumphantly.

'And that's it?' Allie said, struggling to keep calm in the face of Beattie's poison. 'He's a rent boy so he's automatically a murderer?'

'He was there, Burns,' Carlyle said, the voice of reason.

'What's the motive supposed to be?'

Beattie leaned forward, leering again. 'Looks like it was a lover's tiff gone wrong. Or else Curran was trying on the blackmail. Or maybe the sex turned nasty. Case solved, by the looks of it.'

'Danny was fully dressed,' Allie said. 'He didn't look as if he was preparing for an evening of wild sex. What time was this Barry there?'

'His booking was for seven o'clock. The police surgeon estimates the time of death between eight o'clock and midnight. We'll maybe get something different from the post-mortem, but it'll not be radically different.'

Allie shook her head. 'If Danny was a regular client of this Barry, why now?'

Beattie shrugged. 'His name's been all over the

350

paper this last couple of weeks. Maybe Curran only just realised his punter was worth blackmailing.' He shook his head in fake sorrow. 'Just as well for our reputation you didn't make Sullivan head of investigations, eh, Angus?'

'Curran wouldn't have recognised him from the paper. That makes no sense,' Allie butted in. 'Danny didn't have a picture byline. He had a thing about that. He wanted to be an investigative journalist. He knew he'd be blown for undercover jobs like the one we just did if his face was all over the story. Unless you're a columnist, most people pay no attention to bylines. We're the only ones that notice. It's just our vanity that bylines appeal to.'

'She's got a point,' the Razor said. 'I'd say the police might be struggling with this one. Unless they actually find his prints on the murder weapon, or Danny's blood on his shoes or his clothes, it's going to be a stretch.'

'I need to do some digging into this wee toerag's background,' Beattie said. 'See what form he's got. I bet he's got a record.'

The relish Beattie made his pronouncement with enraged Allie yet further. Barry Curran had a target on his back. She could imagine only too well the kind of life he'd led — poverty, violence, bullying, shame. And because he'd been forced to make money with the one thing that had any market value, he was automatically in the frame. 'He's not the only one with a motive for murder,' she said mutinously.

'What do you mean, Burns?' Carlyle gave her a measured look.

'I can think of at least one other person who had good reason to silence Danny.' She had the avid attention of the three men now. 'Someone who has a lot

351

more to lose than some rent boy.'

'Are you going to share that with us?' Carlyle said after a long pause.

'I wasn't planning on it, not without more to back me up. But if I'm right, I'd be stupid to keep my mouth shut because he's as much a potential threat to me as he was to Danny. So I'll tell you, boss. But only in private.'

'Are you saying you don't trust me?' Beattie glared at her. 'I'm the bloody crime correspondent here, not you. You're just a wee lassie who's only been in the door five minutes.'

She said nothing. The Razor gathered his papers and stood up. 'There are some things better said without a lawyer present.' He gave her a wry smile and a one-fingered tip of an invisible hat. 'Come on, Gordon, don't be an arse.'

The pair filed out, Beattie grumbling under his breath every step of the way. Carlyle watched them go, then said, 'An arse. That's Wee Gordon's natural state. Just ignore him. So tell me — who's this mysterious suspect you've got?'

Allie took a deep breath and hoped Carlyle would take her seriously. 'Thomas Torrance. Of the Special Branch.'

51

Carlyle didn't laugh, which was a relief. He gave her a long level stare, then said, 'Let's hear it.'

Allie ran through the story again — Danny's reaction, his explanation, Roddy Farquhar's vanishing act. 'So although we've published the initial story now, Torrance must realise we'll be looking for follow-ups. With Farquhar on the run, it'd be hard to resist the idea of running a story outing his relationship with a Special Branch officer.'

'You think Torrance would be confident that getting Danny out of the way would protect him? That he'd believe Danny would have kept his secret?'

Allie sighed. 'I know that might be hard for you to credit, but I think it's certainly possible. I don't know anything about their world from personal experience, obviously. But gay men know the risks they're taking. Sex between men's still illegal here. You get outed, you don't just suffer a stigma, you can go to jail. Lose your job. Lose your home. The habit of secrecy, it's ingrained. Torrance would assume that, by exposing him, Danny would be exposing himself. So yes, I'd say Torrance could feel pretty sure Danny wouldn't have given him away.'

'So why get rid of him, if Torrance could rely on Danny keeping his mouth shut?'

Allie paused, marshalling her argument. Finally she said, 'It's that old saying, isn't it? Two can keep a secret if one of them is dead.'

Carlyle picked up a pen and fiddled with it. 'It's a

big jump from a proverb to a murder.'

'His first reaction might have been to rely on mutually assured destruction. But brooding about it . . . Remember, Torrance is Gordon Beattie's source. You know Gordon. He's incapable of shutting up about all the stories he's broken in the past. How he's wormed his way to the truth. Torrance knows what a scoop means to a journalist. We'll go to any lengths for a revelation we're passionate about. And Torrance must know the story behind the Paragon story. He must know Danny had already betrayed his own brother. Even though Danny did all he could to protect Joseph, his brother's still out of a job. Probably out of prospects too. Knowing that, would you — *could you* — trust Danny to cover your back?'

'Aye, but you've already said — outing Torrance would out Danny himself.'

Allie shook her head. 'Not necessarily. Danny was smart. He spent his life hiding. He could have covered his back. All he had to do was say that he'd discovered what was going on between Torrance and Farquhar in the course of our investigation, that he followed Farquhar to a gay club where he witnessed the two of them snogging. Or more. And I don't think Torrance has any hard evidence of Danny's sexuality. Danny told me he was always careful. Barry Curran's place in his life speaks to that care, boss. Danny was freaked out at the thought of Torrance revealing his secret to the world, but if he'd had time to think about it, he might have realised he didn't have much to fear.'

Carlyle sighed and clicked the end of the pen half a dozen times. 'It's plausible, Burns. But it's no more than that. You've not got a shred of evidence. Nothing that places Torrance anywhere near Danny's flat on Saturday night. Nothing but hearsay about any of this. Torrance could argue that Danny was just making up malicious lies to discredit Wee Gordon's source, to make himself look like the main man on the investigative side of things. You can't even begin to stand it up.'

Allie had an idea how she might do that. But she wasn't going to run it past Carlyle and risk ridicule or failure. 'You think I don't know that? But the polis aren't even looking anywhere else now they've got Barry What's-his-name in the frame. Boss, give me two days off the rota. Two days and a pic man.'

'What do you want a pic man for?'

She found a cheeky smile from somewhere. 'Taking pictures?'

Carlyle sighed. 'Let me think about it. Away down to the canteen for an hour.'

* * *

Two hours later, Allie was folded on to a makeshift bench in the back of a van that claimed to belong to Plumb-It Services. In reality, Plumb-It Services consisted of a magnetised plastic board stuck to the side of a Hillman Imp van. It held no plumbing supplies, just a low bench, a tin of biscuits and a cardboard box with half a dozen cans of Irn Bru. It also held the van's owner, Bobby Gibson. One of the reasons Bobby G was Allie's favourite photographer was the van, evidence of his dedication to getting the snap that counted. It was elderly, shabby and inconspicuous, the sort of tradesman's white van that nobody would give a second look. But the back windows were one-way glass, meaning Bobby could stake out his targets without being seen.

They were parked at the mouth of Douglas Lane, the rear of the van facing Strathclyde Police HQ. Two cameras on tripods pointed at the entrance to the building. When Carlyle had given Allie the go-ahead, she'd asked him where Torrance was based, knowing that if he was unaware himself, he'd soon find out. But he'd told her immediately that Torrance worked out of the Pitt Street HQ. So now she was playing the waiting game with Bobby G.

'Do you think he'll come out for his dinner?' Bobby asked, not for the first time.

'We don't even know for sure if he's in today.'

'You could phone and see.'

'How? If I go off to find a phone box, he could do a naked Highland Fling on the front steps and you wouldn't know it was him.'

Bobby chuckled. 'Ever since we did that nudist beach story, you're obsessed with people running about in the scud.'

Time crawled by. By two o'clock, they both agreed Torrance wasn't taking a lunch break. Allie tried to teach Bobby to play 'I'm not Napoleon', a game she'd learned on long car trips back to Scotland with a couple of fellow Cambridge students. 'I don't know anything about anything,' Bobby had protested after Allie's first attempt left him in the dust.

'I probably shouldn't have gone with Virginia Woolf,' she conceded.

'The trouble with you, Burns, is you want to win all the time.'

'The trouble with me is that I don't think that's a problem.'

Three hours trickled past and they were losing the light. 'I can't get a decent shot in this,' Bobby complained. 'The length of exposure I need, unless your man stands like a statue, all I'll get is a blur.'

'I know. But I need you to see him. That way, I don't have to stick to you like a limpet all day tomorrow. You can sit and scratch your balls in peace.'

Another half hour, then the door opened and three men came out together, talking and laughing. 'That's him,' Allie exclaimed. 'The man in the middle. That's Torrance.'

Instinctively Bobby's finger hit the button and the motor drive fired off a bunch of photographs. 'Pointless,' he muttered. 'Do you want me to follow him?'

'Is it worth it?'

'At least it'll give me an idea which direction he'll be coming from in the morning.' As he spoke, he pushed the partition between the rear compartment and the seats out of the way and climbed out, throwing the keys back to Allie. 'Take it back to the office car park, I'll catch you there later.' And he was gone, walking briskly after the trio.

She watched them to the corner, where they stopped. A few words exchanged, then Torrance headed right while the other two went left, towards the city centre. She clambered into the driving seat and set her course for the office, passing both Bobby G and Torrance on the way.

She didn't have long to wait for Bobby to return. 'He picked a car up from the parking area under the Kingston Bridge,' he reported. 'So tomorrow, I can set up with a better chance of catching him face on. Meet me in the office car park at half past seven.' Seeing her expression, he grinned. 'He left early. He might be an early bird.'

Allie was home in time to actually cook a proper meal for once. The only problem was that she couldn't remember the last time she'd gone shopping. The fridge was almost bare, save for some elderly potatoes and three onions that were sprouting green shoots. There was however a tin of corned beef in the cupboard, which meant she had all she needed for stovies. You could never go wrong with a plate of stovies, in Allie's opinion.

As it cooked, she poured herself a beer and wished Danny was there to bounce her ideas off. She'd lost count of the number of times in the past couple of days she'd caught herself on the edge of asking Danny his opinion.

But if it was bad for her, how much worse must it be for his family? Danny had been so determined to prove to his parents that he was doing good in the world but his killer had robbed him of any chance of reconciliation.

On the spur of the moment, Allie called the newsdesk. 'Have we got a number for Danny Sullivan's parents?' she asked the secretary.

'Sure. I don't usually give out numbers, but seeing as it's you, Allie . . . ' The sound of her flicking through her Rolodex. Then she read out the number. 'How are you doing yourself?'

'Just about holding together. Thanks, you're a pal.'

Allie took a deep breath and dialled. The voice that answered was deep and male and exhausted. 'Who is this?' he said.

'Mr Sullivan? My name's Allie Burns. We've not met, but I worked side by side with Danny these past few weeks. I'm the one — '

'You're the one that found him.' His voice was flat and cold.

'I can't tell you how sad and sorry I am about Danny.'

A long pause. Allie willed herself not to gabble.

'We still can't take it in. But thanks for phoning.'

She sensed he was about to put the phone down. But she still had important things to say. 'Don't go, Mr Sullivan. I wanted to tell you how much Danny loved you all. You were at the heart of everything he did.'

A bitter little laugh. 'Tell that to his brother. It's hard to get by the last thing Danny did to this family.'

'Mr Sullivan, he did everything he could to keep Joseph in the clear. But Danny had too much integrity to turn a blind eye to crime and corruption. He couldn't ignore something that was staring him in the face. It tore him apart, Mr Sullivan. It tore him apart.'

'Good. Because that's what it did to us. And now we've lost him and we have no idea why.'

Allie felt herself tearing up. 'This story we did last week — Danny kept telling me he hoped it would show you and his mum that he was doing good work. Important work. That he was doing the right thing. He was desperate to make you proud of him, Mr Sullivan. Desperate.' She heard another voice in the background. Higher pitched, questioning in tone, words indistinct. 'He wanted your forgiveness. He wanted you to understand why — '

'I can't do this, lassie.' His voice cracked. 'Talk to his mother.'

The scuffling of a handset handover, the muffling of an exchange, then the thin voice of Marie Sullivan filled her ear. 'Eddie says you're the one who found my Danny?'

'That's right. I'd gone round for my dinner, we were supposed to be celebrating — '

'Were you his girlfriend?' his mother interrupted.

Christ, not this again. 'No, it wasn't like that. We were friends. We worked together. I really liked Danny but not in that way. I respected him. I admired him. I looked up to him.'

'Aye, well, a couple of weeks ago I'd have said the same thing. Then you and him, between you, you did for Joseph.'

'Danny tried to protect Joseph, he really did. He nearly ditched the whole story, but he couldn't bring himself to turn a blind eye to Paragon, breaking the law, ripping off all of us who pay our taxes. Danny had such strong principles, Mrs Sullivan. You brought him up to be honest, to tell the truth. And he loved you for it.'

A stifled sob. 'Aye, and it killed him.'

'We don't know why Danny was killed, Mrs Sullivan. But one thing I do know is that he hated falling out with you. He was desperate to find a way back into your good graces. That's why he was so determined to chase stories that really mattered. And I was proud to help him. Because I know how much his family meant to him.'

'He's away now, and that's all that matters to me. And it was thanks to the likes of you encouraging him that he fell out with us in the first place. So if you don't mind, I'm going to hang up now.' And she did. So much for trying to ease their pain, Allie thought bitterly. She'd have been better off leaving well alone.

An intense smell from the kitchen alerted her to

an imminent danger to her dinner. Automatically, she dished up a steaming plate of stovies, then realised her appetite had vanished. She scraped the food back into the pan, feeling inadequate and stupid. Was there anything she could do to make things better for the Sullivans? Would finding reasons for what had happened give them any ease? She sat staring into space, then at length it occurred to her that she still hadn't looked at Danny's notebook. She fetched it from her bag and turned to the last page of notes. It was dated '27/1' in the top right-hand corner. Saturday's date. Was this something to do with their story?

In the margin, where reporters left asterisks or hashmarks to identify an interviewee, there were two short horizontal dashes near the top of the space between the lines — marks that indicated two Ts. Who else but Thomas Torrance?

Allie frowned at the Teeline script on the page. Danny's outlines seemed particularly clear and crisp. She flicked back a couple of pages and saw that his normal shorthand was much scrappier. Had he deliberately made this note more legible, as an insurance policy, a final act of revenge if anything were to happen to him?

She scribbled down her interpretation of the symbols: *TT cld. Sd 2 kp m ns ot / ls. Sd hd B kpng i on m. Sd 2 frgt RF*. Familiar with the contractions the system used, Allie translated it as, 'Thomas Torrance called. Said to keep my nose out or else. Said he'd be keeping an eye on me. Said to forget RF.' Who could only be Roddy Farquhar.

It was a note that left more questions than answers. At times like this, Allie missed her flatmates in Newcastle. With them, she could have thrashed it out over the dinner table with a couple of beers. Among them, they'd work out the permutations and agree on the most reasonable option.

She eyed the phone. The only person she had anything like that connection with here was Rona. But she was reluctant to impose on a friendship so new. The last thing she wanted was for Rona to think she was needy and desperate.

On the other hand, there had been nothing feigned about Rona's interest when Allie had related the events of Sunday to her. And she was a journalist too. How could she not be interested? Putting her reservations aside, she headed for the phone and dialled Rona's number before she could think twice.

It took her so long to answer that Allie was on the point of hanging up. Rona sounded out of breath when she answered with her number. 'It's Marple here. I deduce you just got in,' Allie said.

'Some of us have to work for a living. How are you doing?'

Allie brought her up to speed, finishing with her transliteration of Danny's note. 'But here's what isn't clear to me. When Danny says, 'Thomas Torrance called,' does he mean a phone call, or that he called round in person?'

'You could take it either way, but I think if Torrance had been there in person, Danny would have expressed himself differently. Do you not think he'd have said something like, 'Torrance came round'?'

'Maybe. But even if it was only a phone call, that doesn't mean Torrance didn't follow up with a visit in person. Danny's response might have worried him enough to provoke him into action.'

Rona made an indeterminate noise in the back of

her throat. 'It's weak,' she said. 'You're going to need a lot more than that before you point the finger at somebody who could make your life hell. Guys like Torrance, they've got a long reach. Every petty misdemeanour, you'll have the polis on your back. Drive a mile over the speed limit, they'll be on your tail. Take one drink over the limit and drive home, you'll be busted. And that's before we even get to the drugs they'll find in your car when they pull you over. These arseholes stick together, doll.'

'I know. That's why I've got Bobby G on the stakeout.'

'How is a picture going to help you, though? Are you going door to door down Danny's street? Because I'd bet you a pound to a gold clock everybody was tucked up round the telly on Saturday night. It was snowing like buggery, remember?'

'I've got something better than that. I've got a secret weapon.'

Rona gave a dark chuckle. 'Why am I not surprised? I suspect you've got a whole bloody arsenal of them. So what's your secret weapon?'

'A man called Jimmy.'

52

Tuesday was taking a long time to wake up. A low mass of cloud squatted over the city, threatening rain but not quite following through. What the morning did deliver to Allie and Bobby G was Thomas Torrance, swaggering down Pitt Street without an apparent care in the world. Captured full face on both cameras, in colour and in black-and-white. They were back in the office before nine, Bobby making straight for the darkrooms on the floor below the news and picture desks. Allie headed for the canteen, keen to avoid the questions of her colleagues. Armed with a scrambled egg roll and a mug of coffee, she made for the furthest corner and hid behind the broadsheet spread of the *Scotsman*. She'd have to show her face soon enough; Bobby had promised her prints in forty minutes.

She found him in the photographers' room, sprawled on the sofa, a cardboard-backed envelope next to him. 'Here's your snaps.' He passed it to her.

Allie took a look. Half a dozen shots, a mixture of black-and-white and colour. Two had caught Torrance in mid-stride, the others were close-ups. Nobody who'd encountered him could fail to recognise him. 'Perfect. Thanks, Bobby.'

'No bother, I like a challenge.'

On her way out, Gordon Beattie called her over. 'A wee bit of news for you,' he said. 'Looks like the rent boy must have had an accomplice.'

'Why do you say that?'

'According to my impeccable sources, they found a

partial thumbprint on the candlestick.' He paused for effect. 'And it doesn't match Curran.'

'And you assume he had an accomplice, rather than it was nothing to do with him.'

Beattie chuckled. 'You've got a lot to learn, darling. He was there. His kind, they're no strangers to violence and crime. He'll have let one of his wee pals in, maybe to see what he could rob while Curran was distracting Danny.'

'You've got a nasty mind, Gordon.' Allie paused, as if struck by a thought. 'Have they got your prints on file, by the way?'

His eyes narrowed. 'Fuck do you mean by that?'

She shrugged. 'Just curious. Last time we were all together, you were pretty upset at the thought of Danny running an investigations team.'

'You're a cheeky wee bitch, you know that, Burns?'

'I've been called worse.' She turned to go.

'By the way, did you see the notice about Danny's wake?' There was a malicious smile on his face now.

The words caught her by surprise, bringing a stab of grief. 'No. When is it?'

'Friday night, at the Press Club. There'll be a good turn-out.'

Disgusted at this hypocrisy, she gave a curt nod. 'Thanks for pointing it out.' Even though it was the last place she'd want to be, she'd show her face. She walked back down the newsroom, oblivious to the activity around her. She'd almost made it to the lifts when she heard a familiar voice. She turned to see Rona waving to her.

'I need a minute,' Rona said.

Allie managed a smile. 'Sure.'

'Come into my office, there's nobody else in yet.'

Allie followed her into the tiny cubicle that barely had room for the three desks of the trio who worked on the women's pages. The walls frothed with glamour shots, pages torn out of magazines and advertising posters for make-up. The cluttered desks were littered with samples of everything from vitamins to face-packs. Rona pointed her to one of the chairs. Allie couldn't read her expression. She seemed uncharacteristically nervous. 'What is it?'

'This is really awkward,' Rona said.

'Hey, I'm a hack, I've heard it all.'

'The guy that the polis have arrested for Danny's murder? The one you think maybe didn't do it?'

'What about him?'

'What if I was to tell you he's got an alibi?'

Allie stared, incredulous. 'What do you mean?'

Rona wasn't meeting her eyes. 'I've got a good friend. He's an advocate, a QC. And he's gay. He's totally closeted. I only know because I had an affair with one of the other advocates in his stable, and they're each other's beards.' Seeing Allie's bewildered look, Rona clarified. 'They pretend to be an item. They go to dinners and public functions together. They even had me fooled to begin with — it was only when Margery came on to me that I realised what was what. So, this friend of mine, he came to see me late on last night. And he reckons he's this rent boy's alibi.'

'I don't understand. How can he be his alibi?'

'You said he was with Danny at seven? Well, he was with my friend on the other side of town at half past eight. In Hyndland. My friend says he was just the same as he always is. Nothing unusual in his behaviour. No blood on him or his clothes.'

Allie turned it over in her head. The timing was

tight. Even if he'd killed Danny as soon as he'd walked in, she didn't see how Barry could have made it back to his bedsit in the East End, washed and changed and made it to Hyndland by half past eight. 'Will he come forward?'

'Talk to the police?' Rona scoffed. 'No way. That'd be the end of his career. The police are lousy at keeping secrets, you know that.'

'So why did he come to you, if he's so determined to keep his secrets safe?'

Rona lit a cigarette to buy a few moments. 'He trusts me. He knows I'd never give him up. He thought we might be able to run a story without naming him.'

Allie groaned. 'That would be a nightmare. An anonymous tip-off? That's worthless.'

Rona tapped her cigarette nervously above the ashtray. 'I told him he could trust you, Allie. What if you were to interview him and write the story, leaving his name out of it? Just say 'a top lawyer' or something?'

'The polis would jump all over us.'

'Can you not refuse to reveal your sources?'

'There's no legal protection for that. They could arrest me for obstructing a police investigation.'

'Even if you're doing the opposite of obstructing it?'

Allie gave a mirthless laugh. 'That's not how it goes, Rona.'

'The paper would make you look heroic.'

'I'd still be in a police cell.'

'Will you at least talk to him? Maybe there's a way of using his evidence that gets this lad off the hook without exposing my friend?' Rona's pleading was hard to resist. Somehow, she looked both vulnerable and determined.

Allie sighed. 'All right, all right. Obviously we can't meet anywhere public.' She sighed. 'I've got something to do, but it can wait a wee while. Can you get him to come to my flat in the next hour or so?'

Rona was already reaching for the phone. 'If he's not in court . . . '

★ ★ ★

Allie scooped up the post from her doormat and carried it through to the kitchen. A glance at the clock told her that Rona and William Morrison would be with her in ten minutes. She took off her coat, put on the kettle and flicked through the letters. A phone bill, an envelope with the familiar hand of a Cambridge friend, and a third with a Glasgow postmark and a second-class stamp. She recognised the handwriting at once and it made the hair on the back of her neck prickle.

She ripped the envelope open and pulled out a folded sheet of paper and a second envelope. She paused for a moment, spooked by what felt like a communication from beyond the grave. But curiosity overcame her qualms and she opened out the paper.

Danny's letter was short and to the point:

Allie, I'm about to go off and buy armaments from the IRA and I'm scared I'll maybe not make it out alive. So I thought I'd better write a will, just in case. I know I can trust you to do the right thing if anything happens to me, so here it is. Hopefully we can laugh about this once the dust has settled. Your friend, Danny.

Grief struck again, closing her throat, but she forced herself to stay calm. Rona and Morrison would be here any minute and she needed to make the right impression on the lawyer. But she couldn't resist ripping open the envelope that contained Danny's handwritten will. It didn't take long to read. He'd left everything to his brother Joseph. He'd had his neighbours across the landing witness it, making it all perfectly legal.

The move shocked Allie. If she'd had to guess, she'd have gone for his parents as his beneficiaries. It wouldn't be an insignificant inheritance — Danny's mortgage company would have made him take out insurance to cover his loan on the flat, they all did that. And the *Clarion* had a generous death-in-service benefit too. What had made Danny choose to leave it to his brother?

The last time they'd spoken, as far as she knew, Joseph had been viciously angry. All she could think was that Danny had been riven with guilt at causing so much pain. Being forced to confront the outcome of their Paragon story had obviously left him with a need to atone. In the heat of the moment, he'd tried to make himself feel better by making Joseph his beneficiary. Allie suspected he'd never really believed the will would come into play, and that the passage of time would have blunted the sharpness of his remorse. But here it was, and here it would stand.

Her thoughts were interrupted by the arrival of her visitors. William Morrison looked like an advert for high-class male tailoring — camel coat with brown velveteen collar, charcoal three-piece suit with the faintest hint of a pinstripe, paisley silk scarf with matching tie and a shirt so dazzling it made Allie blink. It took her a moment to register his face, so perfect was his outfit. 'Well-kempt' was the adjective that sprang to mind. Neatly barbered hair with an artful single lock falling over his forehead, well-groomed eyebrows and a clean shave. But curiously, nothing memorable about his face other than a mouth whose line made it look as if he were on the verge of a smile.

He fixed Allie with a calculating look as Rona introduced them. He took off his soft tan leather gloves and offered his hand. Allie shook it and led them into the living room. 'I appreciate this is difficult for you,' she said, gesturing that they should sit.

'You have no idea,' he said. 'And I want you to be in no doubt that I will deny this conversation took place if you dare to reveal my name.' His accent spoke of Edinburgh privilege. Private school and all that went with it.

'Always good to establish a relationship of trust,' Allie snapped back.

'The only reason I have to trust you is that Rona vouches for you. And second-hand trust is always a risk.'

'But you're here.'

He gave a delicate, one-shouldered shrug. 'I've dedicated my adult life to the law. I can't sit on my hands and let a miscarriage of justice happen.' He twisted his mouth in a strange, wry expression. 'I've known Barry for a couple of years now. So in effect, I've trusted him. Not simply because we have a transactional relationship but because he's an honest, decent lad. I know that may sound strange, considering how he earns his money. But he's never threatened me, never stolen from me. He spent most of his childhood in care and he doesn't think he has any other

370

means of earning a living. I have tried to point him towards other possibilities, but I suspect they have small appeal while he still possesses his looks. So I'm basing my actions here today not only on the facts of the circumstances but also on my knowledge of his character.'

It was, Allie thought, a masterpiece of self-delusion. He wasn't the first lawyer she'd met with a saviour complex. 'If you want to save him, it would be a lot more straightforward if we could put a name to your story.'

'That's not possible.' His face was blank; there was no chink in the armour.

'I'll protect your identity,' Allie said. 'But I have to warn you that my news editor may decide he can't risk running the story on that basis. It's too easy to throw the accusation of fabrication at us. So I need to make a contemporaneous note of this conversation.'

Morrison nodded. 'I understand. And you promise you won't be tempted to renege on our agreement for the sake of saving your story?'

Allie hid her dislike of his self-interest behind a smile. 'Not even for the sake of saving Barry Curran.'

He turned to Rona. 'I really hope I can trust her, Rona. Because if I go down, there will be others who fall alongside me.' The delivery was smooth but Allie heard the threat.

'You can trust her, William.' Rona's reply was brusque.

'You had a booking with Barry Curran on Saturday evening?' Allie was fed up with pussyfooting around.

'Yes. I see him a couple of times a month. Sometimes more often. I like to unwind after a hard week in court. And of course, I can't just hang around in gay bars.' There was a drip of contempt in his tone.

'So how does it work?'

'I call the answering service and Barry calls me back. We make an appointment and he arrives at the agreed time. He showers, we have sex, we have a couple of drinks, he leaves.' Chin up, delivery crisp.

'And this is what happened on Saturday?'

Morrison nodded. 'Everything as usual.'

'Why does he shower first?'

Morrison's eyebrows rose. 'I'm not foolish enough to think I'm his only client. But before you leap to conclusions, he had no blood on any part of his body. Nor on his clothes. There was no sign that he'd been doing anything other than his . . . his job. Nor did he exhibit any signs of stress or upset. His football team had won their cup tie that afternoon and he was in a good mood as a result.'

'Did you know he'd been with Danny Sullivan before you?'

'No. We never discussed his other clients. That was one of the reasons I felt able trust him. He didn't gossip, or attempt to impress.'

'You live in Hyndland. Yes?'

Morrison nodded.

'Do you know where Barry lives?'

'Not precisely, no. He once mentioned Easterhouse, because some junior royal had paid a visit. He was quite scathing about them.'

'What time did he arrive on Saturday?'

'He was booked in for half past eight. He actually arrived a few minutes early. Before you ask, not in a taxi. His feet were wet because he'd walked from the bus stop on Dumbarton Road. He stuffed his shoes with newspaper and put them on the radiator to dry.

And I saw no trace of blood on them.'

'I wouldn't have expected you to. There were no footprints in the pool of blood around Danny's head.'

The bald statement brought Morrison up short. Chin tucked, his head moved back. 'I'm sorry for your loss.'

Allie pursed her lips. She didn't care if he was Rona's friend, she knew she was never going to warm to William Morrison, QC. 'Is there anything else you can tell me that might help in exonerating Barry?'

Two frown lines appeared between his brows. He appeared to consider the question. 'I can't think of anything other than the timings,' he said at last. 'I do hope this helps. He doesn't deserve this.'

Allie stood. 'Thanks for talking to me. If I need any more details, Rona knows where to reach you, I take it?'

On the way out, Rona hung back. She put a hand on Allie's arm and leaned in to kiss her cheek. 'I know he can be a bit of an arse,' she said softly. 'But he did want to help.'

Allie gave her a one-armed hug. 'Thanks. I'll call you later, OK?'

Rona smiled. 'Whatever it is you're up to, take care.'

53

Allie pulled on to the vacant lot next to Danny's flat. As usual, Jimmy materialised by her window as if by some sixth sense. 'How do you do that?' she asked, opening her car door.

He shrugged. 'I just keep an eye out. It's not like I'm busy. Hey, I was sorry to hear about your man Danny.'

'Thanks.' She got out and handed Jimmy a five-pound note.

'I'll get change,' he said.

'No, don't.'

'How not?' He seemed put out.

'Call it a consultation fee.' Allie smiled. 'You were here on Saturday night, right?'

'Where else would I be? Even if the pub would let me in for a heat, it's cheaper to get a carry-out and stay in the car.'

'So you were keeping an eye on things?'

'Aye. Slim pickings though, especially after it got dark.'

'Did you see anybody going into Danny's close?'

Jimmy considered for a moment. 'Is this what I'm consulting about?' Then a suspicious frown. 'Are you a polis?' He sounded surprised.

'No, I'm a journalist. Like Danny. Remember? We worked together. So, did you see anybody?'

He nodded. 'I tried to tell one of the polis that was going door to door but he wasn't interested. Said I was just a piss-head waste of space.'

'Sounds like he was the waste of space. Tell me what you saw.'

Jimmy considered. Allie forced herself not to fill the gap with more words. At last, he spoke. 'During the day, there was the usual comings and goings. Weans out playing, wifies out getting their messages. Men nipping to the bookies or the pub. Once it gets dark, though, it's like a ghost town. I saw her from the top floor tottering out the door the back of six, looked like she was off to the bingo. Then nothing till Danny's wee poofie pal around about seven.'

'"Danny's wee poofie pal"?'

Jimmy shrugged. 'He looks like a wee poof. The way he minces. That bum-freezer jacket with the fake sheepskin collar turned up. He usually shows up every week or two, stays for about three quarters of an hour then buggers off again. I mean, he doesn't look like somebody Danny would be pals with in the regular way of things, see what I'm saying? Though mind you, come to think of it, I thought I saw him on Friday night as well.'

'What? The night before Danny died?'

Jimmy nodded. 'Maybe Danny had something to celebrate, eh? Two nights on the trot?'

'He'd had quite a week. He probably needed to unwind a bit. So on Saturday, this guy turned up about seven. When did he leave?'

'Must've been about quarter to eight.'

'How did he seem?'

Jimmy hooted. 'Cold! He came out the close and hoicked his collar right up. He was skittering down the street like he was trying to get some heat in his skinny wee bones.'

'Did he look upset?'

'Naw, just cold. Hands in his pockets, which if you ask me is bloody stupid when there's ice and snow on the ground.'

'What about later on? Did you see anybody else?'

Jimmy gave her a sideways. 'Her on the ground floor, her fancy man turned up the back of eight. He had a big carry-out, they were clearly all set to make a night of it. Then there was one other gadgie.'

'What time was that?'

'About nine, I reckon.'

'Did he stay long?'

Jimmy shrugged. 'Must have been about half an hour.'

'How do you know he was visiting Danny?'

Jimmy tutted. 'Because I've seen him before. He's been here a few times since I've been living here.'

'When did you . . . move in?'

'A year past December. Just before Christmas.' Jimmy's sigh seemed to come from the depths of his boots. 'I cannae blame the wife. I'd lost my job, I was drinking our savings away and behaving like an arse. Her father gave me what for one night, and I lost the plot and slapped him about. That was the last straw for her and she put me out.'

'That's a hard time to be on the street.'

Jimmy spread his hands. 'I got what I deserved.'

Allie let the conversation rest for a moment. 'So you'd seen this guy over the last year?'

'Aye. He parked his car here. Always mumped and moaned about paying, but he coughed up in the end. Though on Saturday night, he never parked here. He left the car on the street, down around number five's close mouth. Tight wee bastard.'

'How did you know it was Danny he was visiting,

though?'

Not a moment's hesitation. 'The second or third time I saw him, he didn't have the car. He was walking down the street with Danny.'

'Did they seem like pals?'

Jimmy leered. 'Not like you're getting at.'

'I'm not getting at anything,' Allie protested, though in truth she had wondered.

'They knew each other, that was obvious. But it never crossed my mind that he was Danny's boyfriend. He looked like a ladies' man, if you get my drift. His motor, that was for pulling the birds. A bright red sports car.' He gave a derisive snort. 'A poser's passion wagon.'

'What did he look like? Can you describe him?'

'He looked like anybody. Average height, slim built. Dressed quite smart but nothing fancy. Brown hair, looked a bit like him off *The Krypton Factor*.'

'Gordon Burns?'

'Is that his name? Well, he looks a bit like him. Long face, kind of smiley.'

Nothing like Thomas Torrance, she thought. 'What about the car? Do you know what kind it was?'

Jimmy shook his head. 'Sporty. Has funny headlights that kind of pop up and down.'

Allie, who knew almost nothing about cars, was none the wiser.

'One thing, though . . . ' Jimmy frowned. 'It's just coming back to me. He sometimes had folders sitting on his passenger seat.' He scratched his beard. 'Paradise? Parade?'

Allie's brain was shocked into action. 'Paragon?'

Jimmy cackled. 'You read my mind, lassie. Paragon, that was it.'

'You're a star, Jimmy.' That his brother appeared to have been in Danny's flat on Saturday night was an uncomfortable discovery. Allie hated the idea, but she couldn't ignore it. Still, she had to try one more roll of the dice. 'And you're sure you didn't see anybody else? This is really important, Jimmy.'

He looked away and sidled a couple of steps away from her. 'I've told you what I saw,' he said.

Allie recognised evasion. Her voice slipped into the register she used for small children. 'Are you scared, Jimmy? Has somebody threatened you?'

She saw the flare of panic in his eyes. 'He never— I mean, no, nobody threatened me, honest, they never.'

Allie reached out and patted his arm. 'Or did they maybe pay you a consultation fee, like I did? In exchange for you forgetting they'd been here?'

He frowned, anxious. 'Nothing happened.'

'I think you're not telling me the whole story, Jimmy. Danny was good to you, wasn't he?'

Reluctantly, Jimmy conceded with a nod. 'Aye. He used to bring me a curry sometimes when he was getting a carry-out for himself.' A half-smile. 'And he gave me these for Christmas.' He held out his hands, displaying a pair of filthy woollen gloves.

'Would you not like to do something in return?'

'How? He's dead.' Jimmy shrugged. 'He's not gonnae know.'

'Something's bothering you, Jimmy. I've only known you a wee while, but even so, I can see you've got something on your mind. You're right, you can't make Danny feel better now. But you can still make yourself feel better. By doing something he'd want you to do.'

He pulled away from her touch and fumbled a crumpled pack of cigarettes out of a pocket. He half-turned away to light up, the sudden blurt of the match's flame revealing uncertainty. He inhaled sharply. 'You're like the rest of them, you want something for yourself.'

Allie shook her head. 'I want justice for Danny. Somebody caved his head in, Jimmy. I can't sleep at night for thinking about what that must have been like for him. You know what it is to be scared, Jimmy. Imagine how it was for Danny.' His only response was to smoke as if the cigarette was a transfusion of security. 'Do you think whoever did that to him deserves to get away with it? I don't.'

He reached the filter in his cigarette and tossed it in disgust. 'I saw a man hanging about in the close mouth opposite Danny's,' he gabbled. 'He was in the shadows. At first I thought he was just a shadow. But then he keeked out to look up at the tenement. Could have been Danny's flat.'

'Did you recognise him?'

'I couldn't get a good look at him. But when the gadgie with the flash motor came back out of the close, the other guy started to cross the street. I'd only just taken the parking fee for him at number ten, so I was standing near the pavement and he saw me clocking him.' He took a shuddering breath. 'He headed straight for me and grabbed me right here.' He gripped the lapels of his coat, near his throat.

'He goes, 'What the fuck are you looking at?' And I says, 'No' nothing.' And he goes, 'Damn right. You saw nothing. And see if you ever say different? That'll be your last words.' He was fucking terrifying. Then he let me go. He took two fivers out of his wallet and said, 'Away and get pished and forget tonight ever happened.'' Jimmy was shivering, and Allie figured it was nothing to do with the cold.

'That would have freaked anybody out, Jimmy. I'm honoured that you trusted me with it.' She took a step closer and put a hand on his upper arm. 'Thank you.' Pause. 'Did you see where he went?'

'He pushed me away and I just legged it back to my car. But I looked back, and I saw him going round the corner towards Danny's close. I cooried down behind my steering wheel, but I kept an eye out. He was back on the street inside ten minutes, hoofing it down the pavement, heading for the main drag.' He let out a long breath. 'I've not seen him since.'

'Jimmy, I want you to take a look at a couple of photographs. To see if you maybe recognise him? Is that OK?'

His face crumpled, as if he were on the edge of weeping. But no tears came. 'It's going to get me into bother.'

'You'd be helping.'

He shook his head, but said, 'What're are the chances anyway?' A nervous laugh that turned into a cough.

Allie pulled from her bag the envelope Bobby G had given her. She extracted the best image of Thomas Torrance, a black-and-white shot that captured him full face. Wordlessly, she held it out to Jimmy.

He recoiled physically, refusing to touch it. 'How did you know it was him?' he shouted. 'Is he a pal of yours, or what?'

'He's no friend of mine. Thank you, Jimmy. You've done great. I just need to check one more thing with you, then I'll leave you in peace. I'll be right back.' Allie didn't even bother locking her car. She hustled across the slushy ground and into Danny's close, taking the stairs two at a time. Heart racing, she arrived

380

outside his door. Would the cops have removed the key on the string or would it still be in place? She'd told them about it, after all. On the other hand, it wasn't evidence.

Muttering a prayer to the god she didn't believe in, Allie slid her fingers through the letterbox and groped for the string. At first, she couldn't feel it but when she slid her hand to one end, her fingertip brushed the coarse nub of the knot. She struggled to grasp the string, realising it was snagged round something on the inside. She feared it had been tied but at last she worked it loose and pulled the key through.

Sweating now, she let herself in. Hopefully the neighbours hadn't heard her. She wasn't planning to be there long, but she'd still prefer the police to be unaware of her visit. Allie headed for the kitchen. She knew that was where she'd find what she was looking for.

There on the wall above the table in the bed recess was a family photograph. Danny, his parents and his brother Joseph. The man most likely to have a flash car with Paragon folders on the passenger seat. Allie reached up and lifted it from the hook. She was about to put it in her bag when she heard a sound that turned her guts to water.

The front door she'd carefully locked behind her was opening.

54

Allie froze momentarily, then fear galvanised her into action. She had never moved faster. She stuffed the framed photo into her bag and pulled off her scarf. She'd barely completed the move when a man appeared in the kitchen doorway. 'Who the hell are you?' he demanded. 'And what are you doing here?'

'My name's Allie Burns. I worked with Danny. I'm the one who found him.' She didn't have to ask who he was. She recognised Joseph Sullivan from the photo she'd hidden in her bag moments before. Her breath was fast and shallow; all her instincts told her she had no reason to trust him.

'Right.' He dragged the word out. 'You're the one who helped him shaft me. I'm his brother, in case you didn't know. And you're trespassing. This is my flat now. So I'll ask you again. What the hell are you doing here, Allie Burns? I could call the police on you, you know that?' His tone was light but he was standing too close to her. She felt an undeniable air of menace.

She forced a smile and waved her scarf at him. 'I realised this morning when I went looking for my scarf. I knew I had it on Sunday, and it dawned on me that with the shock, and everything . . . I figured I must have left it here. So I thought I'd come and get it.'

'You broke into a crime scene for a scarf?'

She couldn't blame him for his incredulity. Nothing for it but to play the ditsy wee woman. 'I know, it's mental, right? But it's my absolute favourite. I know it doesn't look much, but my granny knitted it for me, and she died last year. It's almost like it's my lucky charm.'

His lip curled. 'It wasn't very lucky for Danny, was it?'

She looked down. 'I'm so sorry about Danny. He was a great guy.'

'Not from where I'm standing. The pair of you, you cost me everything I've worked for. Thanks to you, I've lost my job, my reputation. I could still go to jail — did you think about that when you were writing your smartarse story?'

'Danny did everything he could to keep you out of it. But he couldn't ignore the fact that the people you worked with were a bunch of crooks.'

'Unlike the people you work with,' he sneered. 'You tell lies, you sneak about with fucking terrorists, you don't give a fuck what damage you leave behind you. You and Danny, you broke our mother's heart, did you know that?'

Fuck ditsy. Allie's dander was up now. 'In all fairness, I think it was you that did that, Joseph. When you became the errand boy for a bunch of crooks.'

He moved even closer. 'Get the fuck out of my flat.'

'*Your* flat? You keep saying that, but Danny's not even in his grave.' She knew it was his flat. But how did he know? She was the one with the will, not him.

'Not that it's any business of yours, but he phoned me on Friday to beg me to speak to our mum, to get her to forgive him. He dangled the bait that he was leaving this place to me. Compensation for what the pair of you did to me. That, and his death-in-service benefit from the paper. Enough to move abroad and start again, that's what he said.'

383

'But why would you expect to inherit that any time soon? It's not like Danny had terminal cancer.'

He shrugged. 'I wasn't looking for it. I thought it was a pretty empty gesture. But that was what he said. He was desperate to get back into Mum's good books. Besides, the kind of people you and him have been turning over, it could only be a matter of time.'

'What? You expected him to die soon?'

He scoffed unconvincingly. 'What are you suggesting?' Now, a little laugh. 'What the fuck has any of this got to do with you anyway, Allie Burns? Did you have the hots for my baby brother?'

Was there nobody who could imagine a man and a woman just being pals? 'He was my colleague and my friend. Seeing him lying dead next door was the worst thing that's ever happened to me.'

For a moment, his expression seemed to grow softer. But not his words. 'Get on your way, before I lose patience and call the cops.'

Allie held up her hands, palms facing him. 'OK, OK, I'm going, soon as you get out of my road?'

He stepped to one side. 'You better not have been lying to me.' Then, as if it had just dawned on him, 'You better not have stolen anything.' He snatched at her bag, but Allie saw the move coming.

'You lay one finger on me, and I'll be the one calling the polis. How dare you accuse me of robbing the dead? Your brother was my friend.' As she spoke she backed away. 'You think I want to be here? The last time I was here, I came face to face with the murdered body of my friend. I'm not the grave robber here. You're the one who can't wait to get your hands on Danny's things.'

She made it to the front door and pulled it open. At

384

the last minute, she turned back and said, 'Good luck finding the will, by the way.'

★ ★ ★

Allie stood in the lee of the stairs, trembling. She was determined to be in command of herself when she returned to Jimmy. In spite of Joseph's behaviour, she was struggling to believe he could have killed Danny. They'd grown up cheek by jowl in a close-knit, loving family. Joseph was an insurance clerk, not a gangster. On the other hand, she'd met men like him before, men who felt entitled to grab whatever they wanted from the world. Nevertheless, it didn't seem likely that he'd attack his brother so brutally.

Thomas Torrance, on the other hand . . . A man familiar with a world where violence was so often the proffered answer. Why had Torrance visited Danny, if not to silence him? He had no legitimate reason for being there, and he'd been so determined to stay under the radar that he'd put the fear of God into a homeless derelict that no police officer would ever take seriously.

Once she'd calmed down, she returned to Jimmy's fiefdom. Sitting a few yards away from her car was the sports car he'd described — a bright red Triumph TR7, its wedge-shaped bonnet unmistakable, the square metal cut-outs covering the lowered headlamps. There was no sign of Jimmy.

She picked her way across to where his car hunkered down on its wheel rims. He was sitting in the passenger seat, a can of Tartan Special on the dashboard in front of him. At her approach, he wound down his window. 'Did you see your man?'

385

'I did. I just about jumped out my skin.' She pulled the photograph out of her bag. 'Just to confirm. You saw this man on Saturday night?'

A finger ingrained with dirt tapped Joseph's face. 'That's him. Same guy you just saw, right?'

'Right. And he went in after Danny's wee pal and before the guy that threatened you?' Jimmy nodded. 'And they're the only people you saw going into the close, apart from the folk that live there?'

'Uh huh. Well, not counting her on the ground floor's fancy man. Have I earned my consultancy fee?'

Allie managed a sad smile. 'You have, Jimmy. And if the polis come and ask you about it, mind you tell them what you've told me, OK? Even if they are arseholes.'

He rolled his eyes. 'If you say so.'

Allie walked away in a state of conflict. She had not one but two candidates for the killing of Danny. She also knew the testimony of a homeless jakie wouldn't cut much ice with the police. She needed more.

First, she tried the close opposite Danny's. Eight flats, five with somebody home. Two housewives, one night-shift worker, a retired couple and a teenage daughter. None of them had noticed anyone hanging around their close around nine o'clock on Saturday night. But then, as the pensioner wife said, 'If we'd noticed anything like that, we'd have told the polis when they chapped our door on Sunday. It's not every day we get a murder in the street.'

She'd come back later and hope for better luck.

Jimmy had told her Joseph's car had been parked down the street, outside number five. Maybe the occupants of the ground-floor flats had spotted it. It looked striking; it probably sounded throaty enough to draw someone to the window. It was worth a try.

It took ten minutes for Allie to find out that the residents of both flats had been too engrossed in the TV to have noticed anything short of a bomb going off in the street. She sheltered in the close mouth and lit a cigarette, debating whether to go back to the office to try to convince Carlyle that she had something.

A pair of kids came storming out of the close opposite, skidding along the slippery packed snow at the edge of the gutter. It was hard to tell their gender, wrapped up as they were against the weather, but when they reached the gap where the cars were parked, they stopped and nudged each other. Judging by their apparent fascination with Joseph Sullivan's car, she guessed they were boys. It was Glasgow, after all. Girls seldom showed much interest in cars before puberty.

'I wonder,' she muttered, tossing her half-smoked cigarette into the gutter. They barely glanced at her when she came alongside. 'Nice motor, eh?' she said.

'It's a belter,' the taller of the two said. 'Triumph TR7. My dad says it's the car of the future.'

'Have you seen it before, then?'

They both nodded enthusiastically. 'It was parked across the street from us on Saturday night,' the little one said. 'I wanted to go and look at it close up, but Dad said it was past my bedtime.'

'Your dad saw it too?'

'Aye, that's how he said about it being the car of the future,' the first boy said impatiently.

'Is your dad in?' She tried to make the question sound casual.

'Aye. He's on earlies this week, he's at his dinner.'

'You think you could take me to meet him? I'd like to talk to him about the car of the future.'

55

Angus Carlyle's expression gave nothing away. Allie had caught him on his way out the door and persuaded him that what she had to say wouldn't wait. He'd led the way, grumbling, to the quiet corner of the canteen that she was beginning to feel was her home from home. He sat down heavily, hands on his knees, overcoat spread out on either side of him marking his substantial territory.

There was no denying her apprehension. She'd gone out on a limb on a story she suspected they wouldn't be able to print, thanks to the laws that caged them. And along the way, she'd stumbled over something she hadn't expected but which could be equally problematic. Each was a story that had to be told, first to her boss and then ultimately to the police. If she played her cards right, she might not even have to mention the existence of the alibi William Morrison had provided. That would secure her a valuable contact for the future. It would please Rona too. And for some reason she didn't want to examine, Allie wanted to please Rona.

Step by step, she outlined what she'd learned about the visits to Danny Sullivan's flat on Saturday night. Carlyle's eyebrows rose momentarily. 'Christ, the place was going like a fair!' His face returned to its impassivity. 'Let me get this straight, Burns. After the lad Curran had left, brother Joseph showed up, stayed for half an hour then went away? And then Torrance put the frighteners on Jimmy the jakie before he disappeared into Danny's close? You're sure about all this?'

'I know it all sounds unlikely, but honestly, boss, Jimmy seemed very clear about it. I know he's living on the streets, and he obviously takes a drink, but he's a damn sight more coherent than half the newsroom in the Printer's Pie on a Friday night.'

Carlyle almost cracked a smile. 'You're setting the bar kinda low, Burns.'

'I've got a wee bit of corroboration, though. Stuart Paul, the man who lives on the ground floor at number four, is adamant that Joseph Sullivan's TR7 was on the street after nine. He remembers specifically because when his wee boys pointed the car out to him, he realised it was past their bedtime. And on a Saturday, that's nine o'clock. So it's hard to make a case for Barry Curran murdering Danny. I can't conceive of any reason why his brother would discover Danny's murdered body, not call the polis, then hang around for half an hour before he left. Can you?'

Carlyle reflected for a long moment. 'No,' he said eventually. 'Which is not to say that Joseph Sullivan might not be able to come up with a plausible explanation. Like, he was afraid he'd get the blame, with him being his brother's beneficiary. According to the will you've got tucked into that handbag of yours.'

'He's desperate to find that will,' Allie said.

'That's not a crime. If he wants to start a new life in another country, he might have a sense of urgency in case the polis change their minds about charging him over the Paragon case. And maybe that's what he was doing for half an hour — searching for the will?' he said, spreading his hands in a gesture of sweet reason.

'He'd have to be a cold-hearted bastard to be so

389

unmoved by the sight of his brother lying dead on the floor. Even if they'd fell out.'

'Agreed. Still, there are a fair few cold-hearted bastards out there. But the key problem you've got is a complete lack of evidence against Joseph. And then there's the problem of Thomas Torrance inconveniently turning up on Danny's doorstep. What was he doing there? And why would he kill Danny?' He held his hands out, cupped, as if weighing two options. 'On the other hand, if he found Danny dead, why would he not report it?'

'We've got Danny's shorthand note of a threat from Torrance.'

Carlyle sighed. 'We've got your interpretation of Danny's note, which isn't quite the same thing.'

'Danny had the power to destroy Torrance's career. Not just the revelation that he's gay, but also that he was in a relationship with one of the Tartan Terrorists, the one who conveniently joined the missing list before the polis knocked on his door. That's pretty compelling,' Allie argued.

'All we've actually got is hearsay. Danny's not here to tell us what he saw, what he knew. Again, it comes down to your version of events.' His mouth twisted in a wry smile. 'And we both know there's at least one person in this office who will pour a torrent of cold water on any attempt to discredit Torrance.'

Allie groaned. 'Wee Gordon Beattie. He'll do anything to defend his source.'

'Especially after I floated the notion of an investigations department separate from his crime corr fiefdom.' Again, the wry smile. 'You make convincing arguments, but even you can't choose between the pair of them. Brother Joseph or Thomas Torrance.

Who's it to be?'

Allie had one card left to play. 'We could let the evidence decide. Wee Gordon told me they found a partial print on the candlestick. He said it doesn't match Barry Curran's prints. I was wondering whether the Edinburgh police would have taken Joseph's fingerprints when they were investigating him over Paragon? If it's not Joseph's, we could maybe persuade the polis to check Torrance? Could we ask them?'

At that, Carlyle laughed, deep and long. 'No, Burns. Well, theoretically, yes. But they'd tell us to take a flying fuck at a bag of nails. But they would tell Detective Chief Inspector Davie Buchan.' He glanced at his watch. 'This time of the evening, he'll be drinking with his team.' He sighed from the bottom of his belly and got to his feet. 'Come on, we need to go and buy drink for the polis.'

* * *

The bar was little more than a hole in the wall in one of the back lanes near Blythswood Square. As far as Allie could tell, the clientele consisted solely of plainclothes police officers and huddles of women who looked like they'd come in out of the cold between clients. 'Nice,' she muttered at Carlyle's back as they made their way to the compact horseshoe bar. She was aware that every eye in the place had swivelled to take her in.

'Makes a change,' he said. He turned back to the barman. 'I'll take a large Grouse.' He raised an eyebrow at Allie.

'Vodka and Coke.'

'Make that a large one too. And send one through

to Davie Buchan. Tell him Mr Carlyle would like a word.' He cocked his head towards the far corner. Allie hadn't noticed, but a door was tucked in there. The barman poured a generous measure of Glenfiddich, lifted the hatch in his counter and disappeared through the door.

When he returned he served their drinks, took Carlyle's money and said, 'You've to go through.'

Allie heard a cackle of laughter at her back as they opened the door and entered a cosy parlour filled with cigar smoke and whisky fumes. Buchan occupied a leather club chair behind a small table topped with beaten copper. To one side, Detective Sergeant Hardie, glowering at her; to the other, a woman who bore no resemblance to any kind of police officer Allie had ever seen.

Buchan nodded to Carlyle. 'Long time no see, Angus.'

'A word, if you please, Davie.' A winning smile. 'In private, if you don't mind?'

Buchan considered, then said, 'Bugger off, you two. This is grown-ups' business.'

Hardie looked like he wanted to argue the toss, but the woman scuttled out as if she'd been prodded with a sharp stick, and the junior detective followed slowly.

Buchan gestured for them to sit. 'It's Miss Burns, isn't it? Have you come to confess?' His voice was playful and his battered face creased into a smile.

'We've come to present you with a gift-wrapped case, Davie. You must know by now that Barry Curran had nothing to do with my boy Danny's murder. We know it's not his print on the murder weapon. And I bet if push came to shove, he'd give up at least one of his other clients as an alibi. He's only holding back because he knows he didn't do it and he's banking on you coming round to the same opinion.'

Allie tried not to show how startled she was at Carlyle's words. Did he know about Morrison? Or was he just making an educated guess?

Buchan shook his head, beaming at Carlyle. 'If you're sniffing after a story, you should know better. We've got the boy in custody because we know if we put him in front of a jury, we'll get a result.'

'Wouldn't you rather get a result with the guilty party?'

'What makes you think you know better than me and my boys?'

Carlyle turned to Allie. 'Tell Detective Chief Inspector Buchan what you told me. Spare no details, he's in no hurry as long as the bar's open.'

Buchan chuckled. 'The bar's always open for me here. All right, lassie. Let's hear what you've concocted since you spoke to my lads on Sunday.'

Like Carlyle, he listened in silence. But the cheerfulness gradually left his face, replaced by a stony gaze that fixed Allie in her seat. This was not a man it would be easy to lie to, she thought, glad she was bringing him truth.

When she reached the end of her story, he sat staring at her. Then he lifted his glass and emptied it in one. 'You've got some nerve, going after a Special Branch officer. You have the will?' he demanded, holding out his hand.

Carlyle nodded, and Allie handed it over. Buchan glanced through it and tucked it in his inside jacket pocket. 'Evidence,' he said. 'I'll need a formal statement from you. First thing in the morning at Stewart Street.' He shook his head. 'Your homeless guy should have told our officers on Sunday.'

Allie held his stare. 'They didn't want to listen,' she said. 'Homeless, smelly, drink issues, beggar.'

A tight smile that didn't come near his eyes. 'Not witness box material.'

'No, but he led me to Stuart Paul, who is. And you've got the fingerprint evidence. That should settle it.'

Buchan shrugged. 'You know you can't write this, right? A word of this appears in the *Clarion* and I'll have the pair of you behind bars for interfering with the course of justice. The courts love to slap you lot down for contempt.'

'We understand that,' Carlyle said. 'But once you do your job and the case is over, we'll be telling our side of the story.' He rose to his feet. 'We've done you a favour here, Davie. Once you've checked out that print against the suspects your boys never even noticed, you'll owe me a large drink.' He moved towards the door and Allie scrambled to follow him.

Buchan stood up. 'On your way out, Angus, tell that useless fucker Hardie to get his arse back in here, would you?'

* * *

'He didn't seem very happy,' Allie said as they walked down to Bath Street in search of taxis.

'Nobody likes to be told how to do their job. But he'll pick up the ball and run with it. I've known Davie Buchan since he was on the beat and I was a junior reporter in Clydebank. He's straight, and there are plenty of polis in this city who are anything but. As you may have noticed.' Carlyle stepped off the

394

pavement and let rip a piercing whistle. A cab swerved to the kerb and he waved her into it. 'I'll see you tomorrow after you're done at Stewart Street. You need to get both versions of this story written while it's all still fresh in your head. Then it'll be ready to roll when one of those treacherous wee shites goes down.'

The closing of the door cut off whatever Allie might have been going to say. 'Where to?' the driver asked.

She was about to give her address when an alternative came to her. Rona Dunsyre wasn't the only one who could winkle information out of the office drivers.

★ ★ ★

Allie wasn't sure what she'd expected Rona's home to be like, but it wasn't this. Tucked away in a mews behind a row of grand early Victorian villas on the busy artery of Great Western Road was a cluster of converted coach houses. Rona's was furthest from the mews entrance and sat slightly apart from the rest. A frosted glass panel ran across the top of what had originally been the double doors of the carriage house, giving light without ceding privacy. Next was a single door with a heavy brass knocker in the shape of a horseshoe. Allie knocked and waited.

A light snapped on behind the frosted glass, and seconds later, Rona opened the door. 'Woo hoo!' she hooted, her face revealing amazement then delight. 'This is a nice surprise.'

'I'm not interrupting?'

Rona drew her in, an arm around her shoulder. 'No, I was just contemplating half a dozen eggs and some smoked salmon and wondering whether I could be bothered. I'd much rather open a bottle of wine and a bag of crisps.'

The room was a revelation. It occupied the whole ground floor but its most striking element was a bright mural that covered an entire wall. Chairs and sofas were all arranged to take it in, but Allie only had eyes for the painting. It was a complex composition of buildings and people, some of them familiar, others unknown to her. The juxtapositions were surreal, the colours eye-popping. 'Good God,' she gasped. 'That's amazing.'

'Isn't it?' Rona stood, hands on hips, gazing at it. 'I am one of the luckiest people in Glasgow. Have you come across Alasdair Gray? He's an astonishing artist, he lives near here. He's also allegedly writing a novel, but who knows when that'll happen or what his imagination will make of the world. He painted this for me.'

'It's . . . I don't have the words.'

'They say art should speak for itself. In Alasdair's case, it shouts.'

'It's beautiful.'

'I know. And I get to live with it.' Rona swung round to face her. 'I wasn't expecting to see you tonight. Can you stick around for that bottle of wine and bag of crisps? Or is this a flying visit?'

'I'd love a drink.'

'That's what I hoped you'd say. Take your coat off, make yourself at home.'

Allie wondered whether she was imagining a seductive tone in Rona's voice and suddenly felt both shy and embarrassed. 'I have got news, though,' she added hastily, dropping her coat on the nearest chair.

'Come upstairs to the kitchen and tell me while I sort out the wine.'

Allie followed her upstairs into a compact galley kitchen with a single window that looked out on someone else's garden, barely visible in the dark. 'This is great. Did you do the conversion?'

'Thankfully, it had already been done.' Rona pulled a bottle of wine from a countertop rack.

'I'd never considered living somewhere like this. But I do think it's lovely.'

Rona grinned. 'That's what people say when they really think, 'Where the hell would I put all my crap?' The answer to that is, my dad's garage. And I'm with you, I think it's lovely. I've never regretted buying it for a minute.' She pulled the cork. 'Grab a couple of bags of crisps from that cupboard behind your right shoulder and then you can tell me your news.' She poured a couple of glasses and as soon as they'd clinked them, eyes meeting, they both took fortifying slugs of Bulgarian red.

'We've got two of them in our sights and I don't know yet which one it is,' Allie began. Then for the third time, she told the story of her day. But because it was Rona, and because deep down she wanted to impress, she larded it with detail and cliff-edge moments. Her narrative provoked gratifying exclamations of surprise and delight, and that simply made her try harder. Even as she did so, some part of her acknowledged the story was dramatic enough without being buffed to a sheen. As she reached the climax, Rona refuelled their glasses; without noticing, they were motoring through the cabernet.

Allie, lips stained red, took a deep breath. 'But the most important thing, from your perspective, is this.' Pause for effect. 'Because Joseph and that snake Torrance both turned up after Barry Curran had already

397

left, and because neither of them raised the alarm, it's hard to see Curran as the killer. I'm sure that partial print will be shown to belong to Joseph Sullivan or Thomas Torrance. And that will lead them straight to the dock in the High Court. Go to jail, do not pass go.' Final pause. 'I didn't have to mention William Morrison's alibi evidence.'

To Allie's surprise, Rona's eyes had filled with tears. 'I can't believe you did that. You understood. And you did that for a stranger.'

Allie shook her head. 'Not for William, Rona. Like you said, the man's an arse. No, I did it for you.'

Rona put down her glass and threw her arms around Allie. Taken by surprise, she managed to get her own glass on the countertop without dousing them both in wine. Hesitantly, she returned the hug. Her senses flipped into overdrive. All she could smell was Rona's hair, the remains of the day's perfume, the sweet breath of fresh wine. All she could see was intensified; brighter, sharper, richer in tone. She heard the blood rushing in her ears, felt the tickle of hair on her ear, the brush of dry lips on her cheek and the warm solidity of Rona's body in her arms. Her anxiety and apprehension disappeared, replaced by anticipation. Allie fought momentarily against the sense it made inside her, then gave in.

Time passed and she had no idea how much. Then she murmured, 'It's been a strange year. It's like I started to find my feet and then the ground shifted.' Rona gently stroked her back. 'I found a friend in Danny, and then I lost him in the worst possible way. And now there's you.'

Rona drew back slightly and smiled. 'There's still a lot of year to come, Allie.'

Aftermath

2 March 1979

YES BUT NO FOR DEVO

By Our Political Correspondents

Scots woke this morning to the news that although they voted for a Scottish parliament, not enough voters had taken part to force Westminster to pay attention. Because the bar was set at 40 per cent of the available electorate, Scotland will not have a direct say in its own affairs.

The high threshold came about thanks to an amendment put forward by George Cunningham, a Scot who represents a London seat.

'Those who did not vote were therefore effectively counted as a No vote,' an SNP spokesman said last night. 'If you applied those rules in a General Election, hardly a single MP would be elected.'

Ignored

'The wishes of 1,230,937 Scots have been completely disregarded.

Jim Callaghan's government should hang their heads in shame.'

A senior Scottish Labour MP said, 'I understand why people might feel aggrieved but it's not as if an overwhelming majority voted for it.' Fifty-one point six per cent of votes were cast for the devolved parliament, with 48.4 per cent against.

But a leading Yes campaigner has complained that the electoral registers are so out of date and inaccurate that in many parts of the country, achieving a 40 per cent vote would be next to impossible. 'The government tried to appease the Scots by making it look as if we could have a say in our own future. But they were determined to keep their hands on Scotland's oil.

'Scotland said yes last night, but Callaghan's corrupt government will keep saying no.'

ARREST IN TARTAN TERROR PLOT

By Alison Burns

A third Glasgow man has been arrested in connection with a horrifying plot to set off terrorist bombs in Scotland.

Roderick Farquhar fled the city hours before police pounced on the extreme nationalist plotters who had already bought explosives from the IRA.

But police were tipped off that Farquhar was still in touch with a contact in Glasgow. Detective Chief Inspector David Buchan revealed that his officers had put that contact under surveillance.

'Our undercover officers followed him to Manchester, where they witnessed him meeting Farquhar. With the assistance of officers from Greater Manchester Police, Farquhar was taken into custody.'

'We are not looking for anyone else in relation to this conspiracy,' he added.

The suspect's two accomplices have already been charged with conspiracy to cause explosions and will appear at the High Court later this year.

GOODBYE JIM HELLO MAGGIE

By Our Political Correspondents

Margaret Thatcher is celebrating becoming Britain's first woman prime minister. In a decisive victory, her triumphant Tories trounced Jim Callaghan's Labour government.

Not all votes have been counted, but although Scotland still has an overwhelming Labour majority, the Tories are likely to command a majority of over 40 in the House of Commons.

It was a catastrophic night for the SNP, whose support for bringing down Callaghan's government cost them dear. Their vote collapsed and they lost nine seats, leaving them with only two MPs.

A senior Labour Party figure told us, 'It's clear that the voters who deserted the SNP in droves have migrated straight to the Conservatives. If anyone doubted that the Nats are just Tartan Tories, this result should put them right.' (Cont p2)

HOW *CLARION* EXPOSED KILLER BROTHER

Evil man who murdered reporter found guilty thanks to us

Exclusive by Alison Burns

Last night Joseph Sullivan began a life sentence for the murder of his brother, *Clarion* reporter Daniel Sullivan.

This was the final page of a chapter that began when I discovered Danny's brutally murdered corpse in a pool of blood in his living room.

I'd come to have Sunday dinner with Danny, 27, at his flat in Fraoch Street in the Pollokshields area of Glasgow. But when I arrived, he'd clearly been dead for some time.

Horror

It was a devastating discovery.

Our first story together was a happy accident. We were both travelling back to Glasgow after New Year with our families when our train was stuck in the blizzard and a woman went into labour.

We went on to complete two major investigations that produced headlines for the *Clarion*. Both have led to a series of arrests and convictions for crime ranging from tax fraud to conspiracy to cause explosions.

But when the police arrived at Danny's flat that day, they weren't interested in anyone we might have crossed. Because I had discovered his body and because I didn't have an alibi, I became their prime suspect.

Accusations

During a long interview, they persistently accused me of having killed my friend when fighting him off during a sexual attack. They bullied and threatened me so much I betrayed Danny's biggest secret – that he was gay.

But that wasn't enough to clear me. Next they accused me of attacking him because he'd rejected my sexual advances. They badgered me for hours before finally giving up when their colleagues found a better suspect – a young man who had regularly visited Danny at his flat.

Even though there was no evidence against him except that he'd been in the flat for a short time on the night of Danny's death, they arrested him.

It was only when I started to dig deeper that the truth emerged. First, I heard that police had found a fingerprint that didn't match the suspect.

Fraud

Then when I spoke to neighbours, I discovered Joseph Sullivan's distinctive car had been seen in the street later that evening.

The final piece of the puzzle came from a former Special Branch detective who had visited the murder flat that fatal night. His explosive testimony – given anonymously to protect his identity – revealed that he'd arrived to interview Danny shortly after Joseph had left and found him dead.

He admitted he should have reported it to Strathclyde Police but claimed that would have compromised an ongoing operation.

It was evidence that damned Joseph Sullivan. But why would a man kill his brother?

The answer lies in the first investigation we conducted together.

Danny told me his adopted brother had let slip a careless remark about tax-dodging schemes run by the insurance company he worked for. Danny enlisted my help. We were shocked to discover Joseph was a key player in the scheme, but because he was Danny's brother, we did what we could to keep his name out of the headlines.

When police swooped on the insurance company, Joseph was able to lie convincingly about his role because we'd suppressed his involvement. But his bosses knew better and he was sacked from his job as a clerk.

Guilty

He blamed Danny for what had happened and turned their parents against him. Danny was heartbroken when his mother refused to have anything to do with him.

Danny had done nothing wrong but he felt guilty. Because he was about to take on the Tartan Terrorists undercover assignment that he feared might cost his life, he not only made a will leaving everything to his brother, he also told Joseph what he'd done.

As the prosecution outlined at the trial (*Full report, p5–6*) Joseph didn't want to wait for the money – around £20,000. He wanted to go abroad and start a new life. So he went to see his brother and demand an upfront payment.

I know Danny would have offered what he had to hand, which would have been no more than a few hundred pounds. That wasn't enough for Joseph. He needed Danny to be dead. In the row that followed, he grabbed a heavy onyx candlestick and smashed it into his brother's head.

He thought he'd wiped it clean of prints, but he'd missed the thumbprint that convicted him.

If not for the investigation mounted by the *Clarion*, an innocent man might be in jail and a guilty man enjoying the proceeds of his vile act. Now Joseph Sullivan's conviction means he cannot benefit from Danny's will.

Danny Sullivan loved his job and he loved the *Clarion*. We're proud to have been at the heart of bringing him justice.

Acknowledgements

Like Allie Burns, I was a journalist living and working in Glasgow in 1979. Working on *1979* has been a potent reminder of how much we forget . . .

Writing a novel set in the past always demands more research to get under the skin of another period, even if it's still very much within living memory. For me, the quickest route to grasping the issues that concerned people and had an impact on their daily lives is to look at the newspapers of the times. I couldn't have written *1979* without access to the archives of the *Daily Record* and the *Glasgow Herald* (as it was then). That was hugely complicated by the COVID restrictions we all lived under between March 2020 and March 2021, when I finished writing *1979*. I want to thank the team at the National Library of Scotland who went out of their way to smooth my path to what limited archive access was available during that period. Everyone I encountered was friendly, helpful and careful. Your attitude made this book more authentic than it would otherwise have been.

That legend of Scottish journalism, Ruth Wishart, was Women's Editor of the *Daily Record* when I joined in 1977. I owe her for a hilarious and insightful trip down memory lane and its disreputable back alleys, and for taking the time to read my first draft for accuracy and authenticity. Thanks too for the salmon and the breathtaking views . . .

Many of the details were provided or corroborated by other people's expertise. In no particular order, my gratitude to Tommy Hughes (@TommyQH) for advice about Scottish banknotes; to Ruth Reed, Head of Archives & Art, NatWest Group for detailed descriptions and images of Scottish banknotes; to the Diageo archive staff for vodka notes; to the ever-stalwart source of so much of my forensic information, Professor Niamh Nic Daeid of the Leverhulme Research Centre for Forensic Science at the University of Dundee; to Christine Hamilton, for her recollections of the Citizens' Theatre; to Paul Lyons, the fount of all knowledge relating to Glasgow Central station.

Reading other people's work is also a powerful tool for understanding other times, other lives. Ruth Rendell, Reginald Hill, P.D. James, Ernest Tidyman, John Le Carré, Norman Mailer, Penelope Fitzgerald and Colin Dexter all transported me into very different heads from my own and reminded me of the seismic social changes of the last five decades. Among the non-fiction books I found helpful were:

Dominic Sandbrook: *Seasons in the Sun*
Ian Cobain: *Anatomy of a Killing*
Peter Taylor: *The Provos: IRA and Sinn Fein*
Peter Taylor: *Brits: The War Against the IRA*
Ed Moloney: *Voices from the Grave: Two Men's War in Ireland*
Alwyn W. Turner: *Crisis? What Crisis?*
Julie Welch: *The Fleet Street Girls*
Thomas Grant: *Court Number One: The Old Bailey Trials that Defined Modern Britain*
William Leslie Webb (ed) *Bedside* Guardian: No. 28
Stuart Maconie: *Hope and Glory*

Thanks too to my support team at Little, Brown and at Grove Atlantic. You've all been amazing in this strange and often frightening year. This book would not be in the hands of readers without the tireless and imaginative work of Lucy Malagoni, Laura Sherlock, David Shelley, Amy Hundley, Anne O'Brien, Sean Garrehy, Cath Burke, Thalia Proctor, Kimberley Nyamhondera, Tilda McDonald, Brionee Fenlon, Gemma Shelley and Cal Kenny.

Thanks too to everyone at DHA who works with my books, particularly Jane Gregory, Stephanie Glencross, Camille Burns and Georgina Ruffhead. You've managed to keep the wheels turning in spite of everything.

And the booksellers...! Booksellers have been heroic over the last year. Innovative in how they engage with customers, whether via click and collect or events across many different platforms; supportive of readers and writers alike; but most of all, feeding our imaginations with a million different worlds.

This has been a year like no other. I was in lockdown with my partner Jo for much of it. We never ran out of conversation, we were never bored, we never failed to challenge each other or explore a vast and sometimes bizarre range of topics, or to laugh at ourselves. (We binged a lot of box sets too...) Not a day went by that I wasn't conscious of how lucky I am. And that millions of others were far less fortunate than us. Kudos to Jo for keeping me sane and keeping me going when writing felt impossible in the teeth of what was going on around us.

Onwards, my friends.

My *1979* Top 40

In no particular order, this is the forty- track rotation I listened to when I was researching, prepping and writing *1979*. They were all released in the late 1970s, though not all in 1979 itself. But then, like Allie, we all listen to tunes from our past . . .

I hope it gets you in the mood for reading!

'Picture This' — Blondie
'Lovely Day' — Bill Withers
'Automatic Lover' — Dee D. Jackson
'Brass in Pocket' — The Pretenders
'It's a Heartache' — Bonnie Tyler
'Wild West Hero' — Electric Light Orchestra
'Because the Night' — Patti Smith
'Into the Valley' — The Skids
'YMCA' — Village People
'Like Clockwork' — Boomtown Rats
'Stayin' Alive' — Bee Gees
'Uptown Top Ranking' — Althea & Donna
'No More Heroes' — The Stranglers
'Take a Chance on Me' — Abba
'Werewolves of London' — Warren Zevon
'Psycho Killer' — Talking Heads
'Kiss You All Over' — Exile
'Top of the Pops' — Rezillos
'Heroes' — David Bowie
'Don't Hang Up' — 10cc
'English Civil War' — The Clash
'2-4-6-8 Motorway' — Tom Robinson Band

'Rebel Rebel' — David Bowie
'Glad to be Gay' — Tom Robinson Band
'Heaven Can Wait' — Meatloaf
'It's Different for Girls' — Joe Jackson
'The Man With the Child in His Eyes' — Kate Bush
'Go Your Own Way' — Fleetwood Mac
'Sex and Drugs and Rock 'n' Roll' — Ian Dury
'David Watts' — The Jam
'Until the Night' — Billy Joel
'Rikki, Don't Lose That Number' — Steely Dan
'Watching the Detectives' — Elvis Costello
'(I Am Always Touched by Your) Presence, Dear' —
   Blondie
'I Will Survive' — Gloria Gaynor
'Goodbye Girl' — Squeeze
'Make Me Smile (Come up and See Me)' — Steve
   Harley
'Girls Talk' — Dave Edmunds
'I Fought the Law' — The Clash
'Life in a Day' — Simple Minds